Beautiful Corpse

As a newspaper reporter, Christi Daugherty began covering murders at the age of twenty-two. She worked as a journalist for years in cities including Savannah, Baton Rouge, and New Orleans. Now a novelist, she lives in the south of England. Find out more and win signed books by visiting her website: www.ChristiDaugherty.com.

🐦 @CJ_Daugherty

f /CJAuthor

Also by Christi Daugherty

The Echo Killing

A
Beautiful
Corpse

CHRISTI DAUGHERTY

HarperCollins*Publishers*

HarperCollins*Publishers* Ltd
1 London Bridge Street,
London SE1 9GF

www.harpercollins.co.uk

First published by HarperCollins*Publishers* 2019
1

A catalogue record for this book is available from the British Library

ISBN: 978-0-00-823882-7 (PB b-format)

Set in Sabon LT Std by Palimpsest Book Production Limited,
Falkirk, Stirlingshire

Printed and bound in the UK by CPI Group (UK) Ltd, Croydon, CR0 4YY

MIX
Paper from
responsible sources
FSC
www.fsc.org
FSC C007454

For all the women whose murders end up on page six

Chapter One

'Eight ball in the corner pocket.'

Leaning over the edge of the pool table, Harper McClain stared across the long expanse of empty green felt. The cue in her hands was smooth and cool. She'd had four of Bonnie's super-strength margaritas tonight, but her grip was steady.

There was a delicate, transient point somewhere between too much alcohol and too little where her pool skills absolutely peaked. This was it.

Exhaling slowly, she took the shot. The cue ball flew straight and true, slamming into the eight, sending it rolling to the pocket. There was never any question – it hit the polished wood edge of the table only lightly, and dropped like a stone.

'*Yes*.' Harper raised her fist. 'Three in a row.'

But the cue ball was still rolling.

Lowering her hand, Harper leaned against the table.

'No, no, no,' she pleaded.

As she watched in dismay, the scuffed white cue ball headed after the eight like a faithful hound.

'Come on, cue ball,' Bonnie cajoled from the other side of the table. 'Mama needs a new pair of shoes.'

Reaching the pocket lip, the ball trembled for an instant as if making up its mind and then, with a decisive clunk, disappeared into the table's insides, taking the game with it.

'At last.' Bonnie raised her cue above her head. 'Victory is mine.'

Harper glared. 'Have you been waiting all night to say that?'

'Oh my God, yes.' Bonnie was unrepentant.

It was very late. Aside from the two of them, the Library Bar was empty. Naomi, who had worked the late shift with Bonnie, had finished wiping down the bar an hour ago and gone home.

All the lights were on in the rambling bar, illuminating the battered books on the shelves that still covered the old walls from the days when it had actually been a library. It could easily hold sixty people but, with just the two of them, the place was comfortable – even cozy, in its way, with Tom Waits growling from the jukebox about love gone wrong.

Despite the hour, Harper was in no hurry to leave. It wasn't far to walk. But all she had at home was a cat, a bottle of whiskey and a lot of bad memories. And she'd spent enough time with them lately.

'Rematch?' She glanced at Bonnie, hopefully. 'Winner takes all?'

Propping her cue against a sign that read: 'Books + Beer = LIFE', Bonnie walked around the table. The blue streaks in her long blond hair caught the light when she held out her hand.

'Loser pays,' she said, adding, 'Also, I'm all out of change.'

'I thought bartenders always had change,' Harper complained, pulling the last coins from her pocket.

'Bartenders are smart enough to put their money away before they start playing pool with you,' Bonnie replied.

There was a break in the music as the jukebox switched songs. In the sudden silence, the shrill ring of Harper's phone made them both jump.

Grabbing the device off the table next to her, Harper glanced at the screen.

'Hang on,' she said, hitting the answer button. 'It's Miles.'

Miles Jackson was the crime photographer at the *Savannah Daily News*. He wouldn't call at this hour without a good reason.

'What's up?' Harper said, by way of hello.

'Get yourself downtown. We've got ourselves a murder on River Street,' he announced.

'You're kidding me.' Harper dropped her cue on the pool table. 'Are you at the scene?'

'I'm pulling up now. Looks like every cop in the city is here.'

Miles had her on speaker phone – in the background she could hear the rumble of his engine and the insistent crackle of his police scanners. The sound sent a charge through Harper.

'On my way.' She hung up without saying goodbye.

Bonnie looked at her enquiringly.

'Got to go,' Harper told her, grabbing her bag. 'Someone just got murdered on River Street.'

Bonnie's jaw dropped. 'River Street? Holy crap.'

'I know.' Harper pulled out her notebook and police scanner and headed across the room, mentally calculating how long it would take her to get there. 'If it's a tourist, the mayor will absolutely lose her shit.'

River Street was the epicenter of the city's tourism district – and the safest place in town. Until now.

Bonnie ran after her.

'Give me a second to lock up,' she said. 'I'll come with you.'

Harper turned to look at her. 'You're coming to a crime scene?'

3

The music had started up again.

'You've had four margaritas,' Bonnie reminded her. 'I made them strong. You'll be over the limit. I've only had two beers tonight.'

Behind the bar, she opened a concealed wall panel and flipped some switches – in an instant, the music fell silent. A second later, the lights went off one by one, until only the red glow of the exit sign remained.

Grabbing her keys, Bonnie ran to join Harper, the heels of her cowboy boots clicking against the concrete floor in the sudden quiet, short skirt swirling around her thighs.

Harper still wasn't convinced this was a great idea.

'You know there'll be dead people there, right?'

Shrugging, Bonnie unlocked the front door and pulled it open. Steamy southern night air poured in.

'I'm a grown-up. I can take it.'

She glanced over her shoulder with a look Harper had known better than to argue with since they were both six years old.

'Let's go.'

River Street was a narrow, cobblestone lane running between the old wharves and warehouses that had once serviced tall ships, sailing for Europe, and the wide, dark water of the Savannah River.

The most photographed street in the city, it would be packed in a few hours with workers, tourists, and tour buses, but it was virtually empty now.

Most bars had closed at two a.m. and the heatwave currently underway sent everyone who might ordinarily have lingered by the river scurrying for air-conditioning.

Bonnie swung her pink pickup, with 'Mavis' painted on the tailgate in bright yellow, into a parking spot and killed the engine.

They could see flashing blue lights a short distance away at the water's edge.

The sight made Harper's heart race. It was nearly three in the morning. At this hour, the local TV channels might not have anyone on call. This could be her story exclusively.

'Come on,' she told Bonnie, throwing the door open and jumping out.

When her feet hit the curb, the bullet wound in her shoulder throbbed a sharp warning. She winced, pressing her hand against the scar.

It had been over a year since she'd been shot. It was rare for the wound to twinge. It usually only acted up when the weather changed.

'You'll be a walking barometer now,' her surgeon had remarked jovially at one of her checkups. 'Always be able to tell when rain is coming.'

'That's not the superpower I was hoping for,' she'd responded.

Secretly, she was glad the pain was still there. The wound – which she'd sustained while exposing her mentor, former Chief Detective Robert Smith, for murder – served as a reminder to be careful whom she trusted.

Bonnie missed her pained expression – her eyes were on the police cars.

'Damn. It really is right in the middle of everything. That's just a couple of blocks from Spanky's.'

Spanky's Bar was a popular tourist joint. If the murder had happened a few hours earlier, hundreds of people could have been caught up in it.

Harper had already noticed the proximity. She needed to get down there.

'Let's go.'

Half-running, they hurried down a steep cobbled lane toward the river. It had rained earlier, and Harper's shoes struggled to find traction on the slick, rounded stones.

It was darker down by the water. The breeze off the river cut a cool path through the humidity.

Harper usually avoided River Street altogether. It was mostly tourist traps and, until now, she couldn't think of one interesting crime that had ever happened here.

Ahead, crime tape had been strung from light pole to light pole, blocking the narrow street. Flashing emergency lights lit up the jaunty flags outside the locked bars and shuttered shops.

Harper scanned the scene – the road was packed with police cars but she could see no trucks bearing the hallmarks of the local TV news stations.

Bless Miles for staying up all night listening to his scanner.

About thirty yards beyond the tape, a cluster of uniformed cops and plain-clothed detectives had gathered. They were all looking down at something Harper couldn't see from here.

'Look, there's Miles.' Bonnie pointed across the street.

The photographer stood alone at the edge of the crime tape. Hearing her voice, he turned and beckoned them over.

As always, he looked dapper in slacks and a button-down shirt. It was as if he'd been waiting for this crime to happen.

'Well, well, well,' he said, as they walked up. 'Is it two-for-one night? I didn't bring my coupon.'

'Hi, Miles.' Bonnie beamed at him. 'Fancy running into you at a murder scene.'

'The night is full of surprises,' he agreed.

'What'd we miss?' Harper gestured to the crowd of cops. 'Any ID on the victim? Is it a tourist?'

'Nobody's saying anything,' he said. 'The tape was up when

I got here. They've kept it quiet on the radio – there's no chatter. I almost missed it myself. I heard some chit-chat about the coroner that let me know something was up, otherwise I'd still be home.'

'You called Baxter yet?' she asked.

He shook his head.

'Don't have enough to tell her.'

Bonnie listened to all of this, but said nothing. Her fine eyebrows were drawn together as she watched the police. They were shining flashlights on something lying on the cobblestones.

In the eight years Harper had worked at the newspaper, this was the first time she could remember Bonnie being at a crime scene. It felt strange. This wasn't Bonnie's world. She was an artist – bartending paid for the paint. Murder wasn't her business.

It was Harper's.

She'd been a crime reporter since she'd dropped out of college to take up an internship at the *Savannah Daily News* when she was twenty years old. Ever since then she'd spent her nights investigating the city's worst crimes. Murder no longer turned her stomach as it had early on.

When she looked at a body now, all she saw was the words she'd need to describe it.

In the distance, the crowd of officers shifted. Squinting, Harper saw a small woman in a dark suit, crouching low.

'Daltrey's lead detective?' She glanced over at Miles.

'Looks like it.' Raising his camera, he took a speculative shot, pausing to check the image on the screen.

It wasn't terrible news. Daltrey wasn't the easiest detective to work with, but she wasn't the worst, either.

Anyway, none of them were very easy to work with anymore.

A rumble broke the stillness, and they all turned to see a white van with the word FORENSICS UNIT on the side rolling up to the crime tape, its tires stuttering on the cobbles.

Its cold, bright headlights swung across the cluster of investigators, lighting up the scene like a film set.

They all saw the body in the same instant. The young woman lay sprawled on her back on the uneven cobbles. She wore a dark T-shirt with a knee-length skirt.

Harper couldn't make out her face from where she stood but one thing was certain – this was no gang-banger crime.

Lifting his camera, Miles fired off a rapid series of shots.

Harper stood on her toes to get a better look. Something about the woman was familiar.

Beside her, Bonnie made a stifled shocked sound.

'Don't look at the body,' Harper said.

But Bonnie didn't look away. Instead, she leaned against the crime tape, pushing hard enough to make it bow.

One of the uniforms pointed his flashlight at her disapprovingly.

'Hey, you – get back.'

Harper turned to ask her what the hell she was doing. The last thing she needed was for Bonnie to piss off the cops. Things were bad enough with them already.

But the complaint died on her lips.

All the color had left Bonnie's face.

'Oh my God, Harper,' she said, staring at the body in the street. 'I think that's Naomi.'

Chapter Two

Before Harper could tell her she was wrong – she *had* to be wrong, it didn't make sense and they couldn't see the body properly from here – the uniformed cop beat her to it.

'Did you say you know the victim?' He raised his flashlight, shining it on Bonnie's face.

Her pupils shrank to pinpricks in the harsh light.

'I think . . . maybe.' Her voice was unsteady. 'Her shirt – does it look like mine?'

The cop shined the light on her black T-shirt. Across the front, it read: 'THE LIBRARY: FROM BEER TO ETERNITY'.

He was young. They always put the young ones on the late shift. He hadn't yet learned to hide his thoughts. Harper could see the truth in his face.

She squinted at the body in the distance.

Was that really Naomi? It couldn't be, could it?

She'd only been working at the bar a few months, but Harper knew enough about her to know she was an unlikely victim. Bookish and a bit shy, she eschewed the short skirts that Bonnie preferred. Amid the crowds of art students that favored the bar, with their brightly colored hair and eclectic clothing, she'd seemed quite conservative. In that way, she stood out. That, and the fact that she was gorgeous – high cheekbones, cat-shaped eyes, a perfect figure.

She never seemed to try to be noticed, but everyone noticed Naomi.

Who killed a girl like that?

'Stay right here,' the cop ordered, swinging his flashlight to take in all three of them. 'None of you moves.'

Turning, he ran across to the official cluster.

A moment later, the detective Harper had noticed earlier broke loose from the group at the foot of the stairs and walked toward them with the uniformed cop.

She was dark-skinned, about forty years old, no taller than five foot four. She wore a simple navy suit with a white blouse. Her hair was short and no-nonsense straight. She ducked under the crime tape with the ease of an athlete.

'Which one of you thinks you know the victim?'

Detective Julie Daltrey's tone was crisp and official. Her eyes skated across Harper's face without a flicker of acknowledgement that she'd known her for years. That they used to gossip and joke at crime scenes like this one.

Hesitantly, Bonnie raised her hand. 'Me.'

Harper watched as Daltrey took in Bonnie's blue-streaked ponytail, her miniskirt, and black work T-shirt.

'Your name, please?'

'Bonnie Larson,' she said, after a fractional pause.

Daltrey wrote this down in a small notepad.

'Who do you think that is?' Daltrey gestured with the notepad to the body on the ground.

Bonnie's throat worked. Her hands clenched at her sides.

'I . . . I thought . . . I mean, I think it's Naomi.' Her voice dropped to a whisper. 'Naomi Scott.'

Daltrey had been a cop a long time. Her expression gave nothing away as she wrote something else and then raised her eyes to meet Bonnie's again.

'What can you tell me about Naomi Scott?'

Bonnie blinked. 'I don't . . .'

'Anything you know,' the detective encouraged her. 'Who she is, where she works, how old she is.'

'She works with me at The Library,' Bonnie said, uncertainly. 'We're both bartenders. She's at school during the day. Law school.'

Daltrey made a note.

'Please,' Bonnie said, her voice faltering, 'tell me it isn't her.'

The detective paused, as if deciding what to say. When she spoke, though, she delivered the news quick and she didn't sugarcoat it.

'I'm sorry to inform you that identification found on the victim indicates that it is Naomi Scott.'

'Oh my God.' Bonnie reeled back, taking the news like a blow. Her blue eyes filled with tears.

'She can't be dead,' she pleaded, looking from the detective to Harper. 'She was at work tonight. She was *fine*. She's only twenty-four. What happened?'

Daltrey focused on Harper.

'This is off the record, you got me?'

Harper nodded, although she was taking mental notes of everything that was said.

Daltrey turned back to Bonnie.

'She was shot.' Her tone was almost gentle. 'Is there anything you can tell me about her that might explain who would do this? Did she tell you she was scared of anyone? Did she have any problems you can think of? Drugs?'

But Bonnie was numb now. In a kind of shock.

She shook her head. 'I don't know. I don't think so.'

Tears spilled over, running down her cheeks. 'I have to tell her dad.'

'We'll take care of that,' Daltrey said quickly.

She turned back to Harper. 'Did you know the victim, too?'

'Only a little. I saw her at the bar tonight. Her shift ended about an hour ago. She said she was going home.'

'She live on River Street?' Daltrey asked.

Harper shook her head. 'I don't think so.'

The detective snapped her notebook shut and checked her watch. 'OK. I need both of you to come down to the station and give me a statement.'

Harper's heart sank.

'Could we come later?' she asked. 'I've got to get my story in first. And there's not much I can tell you . . .'

'I don't care about your story.' Daltrey cut her off. 'This is *homicide*, McClain. Either you get to the station under your own power immediately or I will have you both taken there under mine. Am I clear?'

There was no point in arguing.

'We'll go straight to the station,' Harper agreed glumly.

'I'll meet you there,' Daltrey said.

She ducked under the crime tape and headed back to the body.

When she was gone, Harper turned to Miles.

'You heard all that?'

He nodded, concern in his eyes. 'You want me to call Baxter?'

Harper let out a long breath. The last thing she wanted was

for him to call the city editor and wake her up to tell her Harper wasn't at the scene of a murder in the center of the tourist zone because it turned out she'd been talking to the victim an hour ago.

But that was exactly what he had to do.

'Yeah.' She rubbed her forehead. The tequila she'd drunk earlier was transforming into a nice little headache.

'She's not going to like this,' he warned her. 'She finds out you left, she's going to be pissed.'

But Harper was already leading Bonnie away. She threw her answer back to him over her shoulder.

'What's new?'

When they walked into the lobby of the Savannah police station ten minutes later, the air-conditioning streamed an arctic breeze across Harper's skin, sending a chill down her back.

The night desk officer, Dwayne Josephs, glanced from Bonnie to Harper and back again.

'Something wrong, Harper?' As he took in Bonnie's red face and swollen eyes, he rose from his chair. 'Is Bonnie hurt?'

Harper had known Dwayne since she was twelve. He'd been one of the cops who took her under his wing after her mother was murdered.

These days, he was one of only a handful of cops she still considered her friends.

The rest had shut her out. They believed she'd betrayed the force by exposing Smith's crime.

She'd had a solid year of shrugs and turned backs. Of phone calls that began with her giving her name and ended a second later with the click of a phone being put down. Of getting pulled over for minor traffic offenses she knew she hadn't committed.

13

So she was grateful every time Dwayne greeted her kindly.

'She's not hurt,' Harper assured him. 'You heard what happened on River Street?'

'The shooting?'

She nodded. 'She knows the victim. Daltrey asked us to come give statements.'

His expression grew somber. 'I'm truly sorry to hear that.'

While Harper led Bonnie to a hard plastic chair, Dwayne disappeared behind his desk, reappearing a second later with a paper cup.

'Here's some water,' he told Bonnie. 'I'm sure you could use it.'

She accepted it numbly. 'Thank you, Dwayne.'

'Detective Daltrey won't be too long,' he said, squeezing her arm.

He was wrong about that, though.

Harper and Bonnie waited for more than half an hour in the arctic lobby.

Periodically, the buzz of Harper's phone broke the silence as Miles sent her cryptic messages from the scene.

> Cop source tells me purse untouched but phone missing.

Reading this, Harper's brow furrowed. *Surely no one had murdered Naomi over a phone?*

She texted a quick reply:

> What about wallet/money?

She stared at her phone, waiting impatiently for his response.

It killed her not to be out there with him. There was so much she could be doing right now, instead of sitting here.

When her phone buzzed again, though, it wasn't with the answer she expected.

> Told Baxter you knew the vic – she's thrilled. Wants
> you in the office by nine.

Harper shoved her phone back in her pocket with more force than necessary.

When a police car pulled up out front, she craned her neck to see if it was Daltrey. Instead, a pair of uniformed officers got out, leading a handcuffed suspect to the back for processing.

By the time Daltrey finally walked through the bulletproof glass door, they were half-asleep. Bonnie had curled up in the plastic chair, her head resting on Harper's shoulder.

It was nearly four in the morning. The night had begun to feel endless.

'Sorry you had to wait,' the detective told them crisply. 'Come with me.'

They stood up slowly, muscles aching from the hard seats.

Bonnie's eyes were puffy; her skin blotchy from crying. She was so out of place in this official world, with her turquoise hair and cowboy boots, it made Harper's heart hurt.

At his desk, Dwayne pressed a button, unlocking the security door with a jarring buzz.

The long back corridor was lined with offices – this was where the real work of the police department got done. During the day it would be teeming with detectives, 911 operators and uniformed cops. At this hour, it was shadowy and still.

'This way.'

Daltrey's voice echoed as she guided them to the right. They walked past several doors before reaching the room she wanted.

Flipping on the light, she set her bag down next to a metal folding chair.

'Have a seat, ladies,' she told them with a brief twist of a smile.

The room was small and windowless, holding only a scarred wooden table and four chairs. A narrow sliver of mirror glittered coldly on one wall.

Daltrey waited as they settled into place across from her. In the harsh fluorescent light, Harper could see the long night was showing on her as well. There were shadows under her eyes, and the humidity had left a sheen on her skin.

'This won't take long,' she said, pulling a notebook and a ballpoint from her bag. 'I'd like you each to tell me in your own words about tonight. Your impressions of the victim.'

Harper knew she wouldn't have much to say. All she knew was that three hours ago, Naomi had been alive – small and absorbed in her work, her heart-shaped face serious as she scrubbed The Library's bar with a towel, her motions fast and angry. She'd barely looked at Harper when she sat down, and Harper hadn't paid any attention to her. She was focused on her own problems. And on the margarita on the rocks Bonnie was setting in front of her.

Daltrey motioned at Bonnie. 'You first, Miss Larson. I understand you knew her best.'

Bonnie glanced uncertainly at her.

'I don't know what to say . . .'

'Anything you noticed could be helpful,' Daltrey coaxed. 'Start with the basics. How did she seem tonight? Happy? Unhappy? Frightened? Or did anything strange happen on her shift?'

Knotting her fingers on the tabletop, Bonnie thought it over.

'Well,' she said cautiously, 'she seemed fine most of the night. Like, normal.'

Daltrey cocked her head.

'You said "Most of the night". What did you mean by that?'

'She got a call on her cell just before one o'clock,' Bonnie explained. 'After that she seemed . . . I don't know. Anxious, maybe? Upset. She asked if she could go early. We weren't busy, so I told her she could. She cleaned her station and headed out right after Harper arrived.'

Daltrey made quick notes. 'She didn't say why?'

Bonnie shook her head. 'I assumed it was something to do with her boyfriend or her dad.' She paused before explaining, 'She and her dad are really close. Sometimes he picks her up after work.'

Daltrey's eyes sharpened. 'Do you know her father's name?'

'Jerrod Scott.'

'He pick her up tonight?'

'I don't know,' Bonnie admitted. 'I was working the bar alone by then. If he did, he didn't come inside.'

'But you say she seemed anxious,' Daltrey said. 'What made you think that?'

Bonnie paused.

'Earlier in the night she'd been joking about things, kind of chilled. But after that call . . . It's hard to explain. She seemed tense. Distracted. Like she'd gotten bad news.'

Unexpectedly, her eyes filled with tears. 'If I'd known she was in trouble, I'd have done something. Tried to help.'

Daltrey made notes while Bonnie pulled herself together.

She had a good technique, Harper thought, approvingly. *Brisk but not unfeeling.*

When Bonnie had recovered, the detective resumed the interview.

'I'm sorry to ask so many questions. I know it's been a long night. But I am grateful for your help, Miss Larson.'

Bonnie gave a tremulous nod.

'Now . . .' The detective referred to her notes. 'You mentioned a boyfriend. Did you see him tonight?'

Bonnie shook her head. 'I don't think he was at the bar. If he came to get her, he'd usually come in for a drink and wait for her to finish.' She paused. 'I think they've been taking a break lately, anyway.'

Harper noticed the interest flare in Daltrey's eyes.

'What's the boyfriend's name?'

'Wilson,' Bonnie said. 'Wilson Shepherd.'

She offered it willingly, thinking she was helping. Harper had a feeling she wouldn't have been so eager if she knew why the detective wanted it.

Daltrey made her spell it. When she'd finished, she said, 'Remind me again – what time did Naomi leave last night?'

'Just after one,' Bonnie said. 'I'm not sure of the exact time . . .'

'I can answer that,' Harper cut in.

Daltrey shot her a steely glance.

'Oh yes?' she said. 'And why is that?'

'I happened to look at the clock above the bar when she walked out,' Harper said. 'I noticed it was one thirty, and I thought that was early for her to go. It isn't normal for Bonnie to be left alone to close up.'

'There are always supposed to be two workers in the bar,' Bonnie explained, before Daltrey could ask. 'For security. But since Harper was there, I figured it was fine.'

After noting this down, Daltrey said, 'If you're right, she left the bar on College Row at one thirty, and was shot to death thirty minutes later on River Street. Do either of you have any idea what she might have been doing down there?'

Her eyes welling, Bonnie shook her head, mutely.

'No idea,' Harper said.

'Meeting the boyfriend?' Daltrey suggested.

'Her boyfriend lives in Garden City.' Bonnie wiped a tear away with the side of her hand. 'Naomi lives on 32nd Street. Those are both miles from downtown.'

Daltrey's phone buzzed. She picked it up to look at the screen.

'All right. That's it for now, ladies.' Pushing back her chair, she stood abruptly. 'Leave your numbers with Dwayne, he'll give you mine. Let me know if you think of anything you haven't mentioned tonight. I'll be in touch if I have more questions.'

She directed them toward the lobby. Dazed, Bonnie headed down the hall, but Harper hung back with Daltrey, who was turning out the lights in the interview room.

'Was Naomi robbed? If she wasn't, what happened to her phone? We know she had it before she left the bar.'

Daltrey fixed her with a cool look. 'I don't know why you're still talking, McClain. I don't give tips to turncoats.'

Harper flinched.

No matter how many times it happened, she never got used to it. The detectives who'd invited her to their parties, drunk beer with her, showed her pictures of their kids, now treated her like a criminal.

'I'm only trying to help,' she said, stiffly, and left the room.

She didn't wait to hear Daltrey's response. It was always the same with all of them these days.

Traitor.

Chapter Three

Five hours later, Harper walked into the newspaper's offices, clutching a large black coffee and blinking in the sunlight flooding through the tall windows.

After leaving the police station, she'd grabbed a few hours' rest in Bonnie's insanely pink spare room. She'd crept out early to go home for a shower and change of clothes before heading to work, and she felt like she hadn't slept at all.

The newsroom was busy and loud, with twelve writers and editors all typing and talking at once.

With its rabbit warren of corridors and narrow staircases, the sprawling, century-old building was designed to be a boarding house rather than a newspaper but, despite its worn edges, there was something undeniably grand about the place. This was most true of the newsroom, with its sturdy white columns and tall windows overlooking the river.

The reporters' desks were set in rows, overlooked by three editors' desks at the far end of the room and, beyond them, the glassed-in office of the paper's managing editor, Paul Dells.

Harper's desk was midway down the row closest to the windows. She'd had this prime position since the last round of layoffs removed many of the paper's senior writers two years ago, and left the newsroom half empty.

As soon as she set her coffee down, DJ Gonzales spun his chair around to face her. His wavy dark hair was even more unruly than usual.

'What are you doing here this early?' he asked accusingly. 'I thought you burned in daylight.'

'I'm not a vampire, DJ,' she told him, dropping into her seat. 'I work nights. We've had this conversation.'

She switched on her computer with a move so automatic she couldn't remember doing it two seconds later and took a sip of coffee.

'Christ, I'm tired,' she said, rubbing her eyes.

DJ rolled closer. 'Were you up all night on this murder everyone's talking about?'

Harper waved her coffee in affirmation.

He didn't try to disguise his envy. DJ worked the education beat. He found Harper's work endlessly glamorous.

'Sounds like a juicy one. It was all over the TV this morning. You're going to own tomorrow's front page.' His tone was wistful. 'I can't believe some chick got capped right in the middle of River Street.'

'I can't believe people still say "capped",' she replied.

'Is it out of fashion?' DJ sounded surprised. 'I thought it was cutting edge.'

'*Harper.*'

At the sound of Emma Baxter's sharp bark from the front of the room, DJ spun his chair back toward his desk with pinpoint precision, and ducked behind his computer screen as if it were a shield.

The city editor strode across the room, her blunt-cut dark hair swinging against the shoulders of her navy blazer. Dells was right behind her.

'Crap,' Harper whispered.

The managing editor usually didn't get involved in the crime beat. But this one must be big enough to attract his attention.

'What've you got on River Street?' Baxter asked as she neared Harper's desk. 'Why does Miles say you know the victim?'

Out of the corner of her eye, Harper saw DJ's head bob up.

'I don't really know her. I just happened to be in the bar where she works last night,' Harper explained, glancing at Dells.

'Perfect,' Baxter snapped. 'Do me a first-person, emotional account – "A Brush With Death". It can run alongside your main piece on the shooting.'

Dells stepped forward. As always, he was impeccably dressed, in a dark-blue suit with a crisp white shirt that looked like it cost more than her car, and a pale blue silk tie. His dark hair was neatly styled.

'What do we know so far?' he asked. 'The TV stations haven't got much.'

'The dead woman is Naomi Scott – a second-year law student.' Harper flipped open her notebook. 'Seemed to be your basic all-American girl. Left work at one thirty, died of two gunshot wounds. Found with her purse but not her phone. Cops aren't saying if it was robbery. Nobody knows what the hell she was doing down by the river.'

'Do we know who her family is?' Dells asked. 'Are they locals?'

'I think so,' Harper said. 'Her father's Jerrod Scott, I'm trying to track him down now.'

Baxter peered at the half-empty notebook. 'Is that all you've got?'

'Come on.' A defensive note entered Harper's voice: 'I was in the police station half the night.'

'We're holding most of the front page for this,' Dells told her. 'The TV stations are going to be all over it.'

'I'll start making calls,' Harper said.

'Good.' Baxter's tone was brisk. 'I want to know who this girl was. If she was so perfect, how'd she end up dead in the street at two in the morning? Call the mayor's office. Ask her what she's going to do about people getting shot in the middle of the damned tourist district.'

Dells headed back to his office. Baxter followed, turning so fast her jacket flew off one bony shoulder.

Her last words floated behind her like a cluster bomb: 'Do it fast. We need something for the website, *now*.'

When they were gone, DJ swung around to look at Harper, brown eyes wide behind smudged, wire-framed glasses.

'Dude. You drank in her bar and then she died?'

Harper nodded.

He looked impressed. 'Tell me something – do you ever think you might be cursed?'

Shooting him a withering glance, Harper logged in to her computer.

'I'm busy, DJ.'

'I'm only saying it's worth a thought,' he said, spinning back toward his own desk.

It was a bad joke but, as Harper hurriedly checked out the stories about the shooting on the local TV station websites, she found herself thinking about it, nonetheless. After all, Naomi wasn't the first murder victim in her life.

The first murder victim had been her mother.

Harper had discovered her body on the kitchen floor when

she was twelve years old. That still unsolved homicide set off a chain of events that led to her close relationship with the police.

It had also led to everything that happened last year, when Lieutenant Smith was convicted of a murder that had mirrored her mother's killing in every way.

Breaking that story – and becoming part of it when she was shot by Smith – had raised Harper's profile; ensuring her position at the newspaper, even in these shaky financial times.

Still, Baxter wasn't one to stand on history. She needed a steady stream of juicy crime stories to anchor the front page. Even without police cooperation, Harper could provide that. She had her ways. She knew the system better than anyone.

As long as she could keep the headlines coming, her job was safe. She hoped.

Picking up the phone, Harper dialed the mayor's office number. It rang five times before an assistant answered.

'Thank you for calling Mayor Cantrelle's office, how can I help you?'

'This is Harper McClain at the *Daily News*. I'd like to ask the mayor some questions about the shooting on River Street last night.'

'She's in a meeting.' The assistant's tone indicated she wasn't the first to call. 'I'll ask her to get back to you.'

'Make it quick, would you? We're in a rush.'

'As I said,' the assistant sounded unmoved, 'she's in a meeting.'

While she waited for the mayor to call her back, Harper opened an internet search engine and typed: 'Naomi Scott'.

A flood of false returns filled her screen. A blogger with 40,000 Twitter followers dominated, along with a Chicago attorney.

When she added 'Savannah' to the search, though, she found what she was looking for.

It was a social networking site for students at the Savannah

State College. The picture on Naomi's page was arresting. Her shoulder-length black hair hung loose in waves. Her unblemished skin, high cheekbones and huge, cinnamon eyes gave her an ethereal beauty.

Harper stared at the familiar face for a moment.

'What did you get yourself into?' she murmured.

The short bio beneath the image said: 'Young, free, and ambitious. Ready to change the world.'

It listed her area of study as criminal law. The only other information was a phone number and a student email address.

Leaving the landline open for the mayor's call, Harper picked up her cell and dialed Naomi's number.

It went straight to voicemail.

'Hi. This is Naomi. Leave a message.'

Hearing the dead woman's familiar voice was chilling.

Harper hung up and then immediately dialed another number. This one she knew by heart. As it rang, she stared at the picture of the vibrant young woman with her challenging eyes.

The ringing stopped abruptly. 'Savannah Police Public Information.'

The voice was male and breathless – as if he'd snatched up the phone while running in search of a fire extinguisher. She could hear other voices in the background and people typing – the sounds of a busy office.

'This is Harper McClain,' she said. 'I'm looking for whatever you've got on the Naomi Scott murder from last night.'

'You and everybody else,' he said. 'What do you want to know?'

'The basics. Got any suspects?'

'Nothing I can tell you on that.'

'You looking for the boyfriend?' she tried, already knowing the answer but also suspecting he wouldn't verify it on the record.

He snorted a laugh. 'Is this some sort of hoax? Or do you have any real questions?'

Harper tried a new angle. 'Could you verify that her wallet was found in her bag?'

She heard him typing something.

'That's affirmative,' he said.

'Money in the wallet?' she asked, propping the phone under her chin as she made notes.

'Affirmative.'

In that case, it definitely wasn't a robbery. Miles's source had been right.

'But her phone was MIA?' she pushed it.

'That is what it says on my screen,' he said, adding, 'Right now we don't know if she lost it, left it at home, or got shot for it.'

Harper knew she hadn't left it at home. Bonnie had seen Naomi take a call less than an hour before she left work.

'Any witnesses?'

There was a pause, and she heard him clicking keys on his computer.

'Negative,' he said, after a second. 'No witnesses have come forward. The body was found by two members of the public, walking home from a party at the Hyatt hotel.'

'Can you give me their names?' she asked.

'Oh sure,' his tone was sarcastic. 'And would you like perfume on your birthday, or do you prefer flowers?'

'Please?' Harper begged. 'Just one name?'

He made an exasperated sound. 'You know I can't tell you that, McClain.'

Through the line, she could hear another phone ringing.

'Is that everything?' His voice was impatient. 'I'm a popular man today.'

'I guess that's it –'

26

Before she'd even finished the sentence, the phone went dead in her hand.

Well, at least, thanks to Bonnie, she had the father's name. And the internet had given her his phone number.

She dialed the number and waited as it rang and rang. After eight rings, she hung up.

If she couldn't reach family, she'd need to find someone else. But she had enough for the website now.

Turning to her computer, she quickly wrote up a short, sparse news story about the shooting.

Murder on River Street

By Harper McClain

The city was shaken in the early hours of this morning by news of a murder at the very heart of the city's tourism district.

The victim was Naomi Scott, 24, a law student who also worked as a bartender at the Library Bar on College Row. Police say she was shot twice, at around two o'clock Wednesday morning.

No motive has been determined at this time, although robbery is unlikely.

As this story was being written, detectives were still looking into the details of the crime.

The body was discovered minutes after the murder by two members of the public. Police say no witnesses to the crime have come forward.

Calls for comment to Mayor Melinda Cantrelle's office were not immediately returned.

She'd just sent the story across to Baxter when her phone rang.

'McClain,' she said, throwing her empty coffee cup in the bin.

'Now look, Harper, my office will be issuing a statement at ten thirty. Don't you dare write that I'm not replying, or that I'm trying to dodge this murder case.'

Mayor Melinda Cantrelle had a distinctive voice – rich and resonant, made for television. In fact, twenty years ago, she'd started her career anchoring the morning news on a local station. That experience gave her an air of cultivated calm most of the time, and she had a made-for-TV smile. But today she was talking fast, her words short and clipped.

Harper fired a quick message to Baxter: 'Hold the story. Mayor on phone.' And then leaned back in her chair, propping a notebook on her knee.

'Of course not, Mayor Cantrelle,' she said sweetly. 'But the first story will go up on the website any minute now and I can't have our readers think I didn't try to reach you.'

'Oh come on, Harper . . .' The mayor did not sound happy.

'Can't you give me something small?' Harper cajoled. 'What does this murder mean for tourism? And will you be sending more police downtown? Anything like that would be enough to get that "no comment" out of my story.'

There was a long pause, during which Harper suspected the mayor was fighting to control her temper. She'd taken over the city leadership a year earlier, and Harper almost liked her – she had a blunt approach that, if nothing else, gave the appearance of honesty. At forty-five, she was younger than the gray-haired men who normally served as mayor, and she was still new enough at her job to pick up the phone at times like these.

'The police have informed me they are searching for a suspect,' the mayor said smoothly. 'We believe this to be a family incident. It would be inappropriate for me to comment further while the investigation is underway. But we intend to get to the bottom of this, I can promise you that. I consider it my number one job to keep visitors and residents here safe.'

Harper wrote as she talked, pen skidding across her notepad.

'A family incident? Can you be more specific?' she asked, not looking up from the page. 'You're not saying her father had something to do with it, are you?'

'This is off the record.' The mayor lowered her voice. 'But I'm told the detectives are looking for her boyfriend. They think this was a personal thing.'

Someone spoke in the background, and the sound suddenly became muffled. When Cantrelle returned she sounded rushed.

'Look, I'm afraid I have to go. We'll be issuing a full statement in an hour. Cathy will email it over. Call her if you need anything else.'

When she'd hung up, Harper read over her notes.

As she'd suspected when Daltrey questioned them last night, they thought it was the boyfriend.

She flipped through her notepad until she found his name: Wilson Shepherd.

It wasn't a surprise. The vast majority of murdered women are killed by someone close to them – husband, boyfriend, friend. No more than one in ten murdered women are killed by someone they don't know.

Harper had long thought women were afraid of the wrong thing. Women are scared of the hooded teen at a gas station, or the unknown man walking down the dark street late at night.

They should be afraid of their husbands.

When you get right down to it, if you're a woman, being killed by someone you love is the most ordinary murder of all.

This was bad news. The paper hardly covered domestic violence.

'There's nothing there,' Baxter had said, more than once. 'No one wants to read about that stuff.'

She wasn't wrong.

A random murder is a threat to everyone. It's lawlessness in the streets.

But if a woman's ex-boyfriend shoots her? Well. She should have made better choices.

If Naomi Scott was killed by Wilson Shepherd it would move the story to page six within a couple of days.

Harper kept trying to remember if she'd met Naomi's boyfriend. Her mind summoned an image of a serious, chubby-cheeked guy, neatly dressed, sitting quietly at one end of the bar.

Otherwise, she knew nothing about him.

Before she'd gone to sleep last night, she'd asked Bonnie what she knew about him. All she'd said was that they met at school. She'd been so worn out Harper hadn't wanted to push it.

She'd still be asleep now. But later today, she could see if she remembered more.

For now, she searched his name in the newspaper database and came up empty.

Staring at the empty screen, she tapped her fingers against the desk. She'd done all she could in the office. It was time to go hunting.

After typing up a quick update with the mayor's statement and sending it through to the editor, she grabbed her scanner and stood up.

DJ glanced at her enquiringly.

'I'm heading out,' she said, stuffing a fresh notebook in her pocket. 'If Baxter comes looking for me, tell her I'm off to find a killer.'

Chapter Four

When she stepped out of the newspaper office, the sun was fierce. Humidity hung so thick it left a white haze in the air, giving the gold dome of the City Hall an oddly electric shimmer in the distance.

August was always brutal, but this year it seemed even worse than usual. It had been over a hundred degrees every day for two weeks. The heat was relentless.

Harper shoved her auburn hair back, twisting it into a knot at the base of her neck as she surveyed the traffic backed up on Bay Street. She'd planned to get in her car and drive straight to The Library to try to find out more about Naomi and Wilson Shepherd, but it would take half an hour to get anywhere right now.

Instead, she walked toward the scene of the crime.

Already sweating, she threaded her way through stalled traffic, breathing in the acrid scent of exhaust and hot pavement. Whatever the mayor's worries, news of the murder clearly hadn't reached the city's visitors yet. Tourists circulated in brightly colored crowds of T-shirts, baggy shorts and baseball caps, guidebooks shoved under arms.

As she headed down an uneven cobblestone ramp towards River Street, Harper was struck by the audacity of the murderer. All around her were people. Walking, strolling, driving. A Savannah Police car was stuck in traffic twenty feet away.

Even at two in the morning, this area would not have been empty. The Hyatt hotel stood nearby, overlooking the river. Hotels, restaurants, and apartment buildings surrounded her on all sides.

People were close the whole time.

Most murders take place in the shadows. They're shameful acts hidden from prying eyes.

This hadn't been a normal murder. This location made it a kind of public execution.

Down by the river, a breeze cooled her skin. The exhaust faded away, to be replaced by the smell of muddy water, and the cloying scent of burned sugar from the praline shops.

It was already busy. Kids ran through the riverfront plaza, oblivious to what had happened here a few hours ago. In the distance, a paddle-wheel riverboat, painted candy-cane red and white, sat waiting for passengers. A busker played the banjo, a battered top hat shading him from the sun as he jangled out a version of 'Summertime'.

This was why the mayor was panicking. Why Harper and Baxter had both come to work seven hours early today.

The death of Naomi Scott threatened all of this.

Savannah lived or died by its tourist trade. A murder on this street put poison in the well.

Hurrying her pace, Harper walked down the narrow street, searching for the spot. It was hard to square the dark street from the night before with this bright, busy scene. It took a few minutes to find what she was searching for.

In the end, it was the ragged white remnants of crime tape that guided her, fluttering from the base of the lampposts.

From there, the crime scene was easy to find. Discarded latex gloves lay at the curb, along with other medical detritus, overlooked in the hasty clean-up in the dark.

The cobbles were damp – someone had hosed them down, trying to wash the evidence away. But blood stains everything it touches.

The darker stones showed clearly where the body had fallen.

She turned a full circle, oblivious to the tourists jostling her as they passed.

It didn't make sense. Why had Naomi left The Library in the middle of the night and come here? Was she meeting her boyfriend, as the police suspected, only to be shot dead? And if so, why here of all places?

This was a crazy place for a murder.

Half an hour later, Harper parked the Camaro in a shady spot on a narrow lane on the other side of downtown.

Tucked away not far from the Savannah College of Art and Design, College Row was quiet and dingy during the day, littered with empty beer cans and cigarette butts. The short alley served no purpose except to hold two bars and a small clothes shop, known for its quirky T-shirts.

The lights were off in the Library Bar when she walked up. Its sign – an open book with a martini glass perched on it – was unlit.

When she tried the door, Harper found it locked.

'Hello?' she called, knocking on the door. 'Is anyone in there?'

No response. She knocked again, raising her voice.

'Hello?'

This time, something inside stirred. She heard footsteps shuffling across the room.

After a minute, the door opened a crack.

A rumpled, lived-in face peered out at her.

Harper barely recognized Jim 'Fitz' Fitzgerald, the bar's jovial owner. Normally, he was a natty dresser, with a penchant for tweed jackets, turned-up cuffs and crisp, white shirts. Today, he wore a flannel shirt and wrinkled slacks, his thick, graying hair waved wildly.

'We're closed right now,' he told her, and began to shut the door.

Harper moved quickly, angling her body so it would have been rude – if not impossible – to close the door on her.

'Hi, Fitz,' she said. 'I don't know if you'll remember me, but I'm a friend of Bonnie's. Harper McClain, from the newspaper?'

For a moment he didn't react, but then recognition dawned.

'You're that police reporter,' he said. 'The one who got shot.'

Even from here, she could smell the medicinal tang of vodka on his breath.

'That's me,' she said. 'Look, I hate to bother you at a time like this, but I need to ask you a few questions about Naomi Scott.'

'Oh, lord. I don't know.' He peered at her blearily. 'Would you want to print this?'

'I need someone who knows her to talk to me about the kind of person she was,' she said, avoiding his question. 'I only met her a few times, but I know she was a smart, kind person. I need someone to tell me who she was so people who never met her can understand.'

He studied her with red-rimmed eyes. 'I don't know if her family would want me to talk.'

'You'd be doing them a favor,' she told him. And this, at least, was the truth. 'They know how wonderful their daughter was but talking to me will be hard for them right now.'

He hesitated, leaning hard against the door, one hand still poised to push it shut.

'I'd really appreciate your help.' Harper held his gaze steadily.

Finally, he took a step back.

'I guess you better come in. We're letting the air out.'

Harper followed, closing the door behind her.

Inside it was dim and cool. It smelled faintly of disinfectant and beer.

Fitz shuffled to the bar and climbed unsteadily onto a stool in front of a tall glass filled with ice and clear liquid.

Harper perched on the stool next to his.

'I can't understand it.' He turned to her, his face haunted beneath that tangle of hair. 'She was right here last night.' He pointed across the bar to the empty space in front of the bottles. 'She was fine. Now, they say she's dead.'

Ice rattled as he lifted the glass and took a long, shaky drink.

It was ten thirty in the morning. If he was already drunk, Harper couldn't imagine what he'd be like a few hours later.

She needed him to talk quickly before he passed out.

'What can you tell me about Naomi?' she asked. 'What was she really like?'

'Oh, everyone who knew her will tell you she was a great kid.' He stared into his glass. 'And it's true. Hard worker. Smart as hell. Always smiling. People came in here just to see her smile, I swear. And ambitious as hell. I thought she'd be president someday.' He looked at her helplessly. 'Who would do this to her? Can you tell me that much at least?'

He seemed genuinely grief-stricken.

To an extent, this fit with what Harper knew of him. She didn't encounter Fitz often – he didn't tend to hang around on the late shift, and she rarely arrived at the bar before one in the morning. But Bonnie always described him affectionately.

'Fitz is everyone's dad,' she'd told Harper once. 'He worries about me more than my own father does.'

Still, Naomi had only worked at the bar a few months. Harper was a little surprised at the intensity of his reaction.

'Were you close to Naomi?' she asked. 'Did you know her family well?'

'I met her dad a few times when he came to pick her up.' He reached for his glass. 'Can't say I know him particularly well. But he's a good man.' He took a long drink, the ice rattling in his glass, before adding, morosely, 'This'll kill him.'

'I know the police are on this,' she told him. 'They want to get this guy.'

'They *better* get him.'

Reaching across the counter he swiped up a bottle from the other side and poured himself an unhealthy measure.

'Can you tell me anything else about her?' she asked.

He waved his glass.

'Her mom passed a few years ago. Her dad's a cab driver.' He'd begun to slur his words. 'She was an only child – she and her father were very close.'

He slapped his hand hard on the bar. 'Dammit. This doesn't make sense. I keep thinking someone will come in here and tell me it was a mistake. For a minute, that's what I thought you were here for.'

'What about her boyfriend?' Harper asked. 'Wilson Shepherd, isn't that his name?'

'Wilson?' His gaze sharpened. 'What about him?'

'How long had they been together?'

'A year maybe?' He rubbed his face, his hand rasping across his unshaven jaw. 'Poor old Wilson.'

'The police think he did it,' she told him, watching for his reaction.

'What?' His head jerked up, eyes wide in a drunken pantomime of shock. 'You can't be serious.'

'They're looking for him now.'

'Then they're nuts.' He was angry. 'No way. They were crazy in love. He wouldn't hurt Naomi.'

But the first hint of uncertainty had entered his voice. They both knew crazy in love people hurt each other all the time.

'Did they ever fight?' Harper asked. 'Fall out over anything?'

'Hell, I don't know.' He held up his hands. 'I'm not the one she'd talk to about that. But she seemed happy with him. Except –'

He paused, thinking.

'Except what?' Harper pressed him.

But he wouldn't be hurried. He gripped the glass tight, and rattled it, lost in his thoughts.

'It's probably nothing, but I've been going over it all in my head – trying to think of anything – something I should have noticed,' he said, peering at her. 'Only thing I can think of was something that happened a couple weeks ago. Struck me as strange. Seemed like nothing at the time, but now . . .'

'What happened?' she asked.

'It was a busy night. A Saturday. Naomi was helping Bonnie at the bar. Everything was fine, and then out of nowhere she came over to me and said she had to go *right now*. I wouldn't have noticed, but she seemed real upset.'

Harper's brow creased. 'Did she tell you what happened?'

'Sort of. We were packed. It was midnight. I mean, where could she have to go at midnight? I asked if she could at least stay half an hour. And she begged me – literally begged me. "Let me go, Fitz. I have to." In the end, I gave in. Couldn't stand to see her so upset. She was shaking. It was like she was scared or something. She ran out the door like the devil was on her tail. Didn't even stop to take her apron off.'

'Did you ever find out what she was scared of?' she asked.

The lines in his craggy face deepened.

'She was off the next three days. By the time she came back to work, I had other things on my mind.' He looked at her. 'You know how it is. You lose track.'

'But after that she was fine?'

He made a vague gesture. 'She seemed fine. Maybe a little more distracted than usual. But I figured it was school keeping her busy.'

Harper thought it over. 'Are you saying that you think she was scared of Wilson?'

He glowered at her.

'I'm saying I don't know what happened but she was scared.' He reached for his glass again. 'Ah, hell. Why'm I yelling at you? It's my own damn fault. If I'd thought to ask what was going on – why she was so scared that night – what was going on in her life . . . If I'd paid more attention . . .

'She might still be alive.'

39

Chapter Five

After talking with Fitz, Harper went back to the newsroom to update her article and work the phones. The story moved quickly. At noon, the police formally identified Wilson Shepherd as a suspect on the run.

At a hastily convened press conference that afternoon, the police chief described him as 'armed and dangerous'. In a message delivered directly to the news cameras, the chief asked Wilson to turn himself in.

'Do it for your family,' the chief said seriously. 'Nobody else needs to get hurt.'

With the TV stations all in overdrive, several false reports came in of sightings around the city, but by eight o'clock that night, when things finally quieted down, his location remained unknown.

It was still four hours until the paper's final deadline, but Harper had done all she could for now. She'd worked eleven hours straight on precious little sleep, and the exhaustion was taking its toll.

She stretched the tight knots in her shoulders and looked around blearily. The newsroom had emptied without her even noticing. Through the tall windows, the last rays of the sun were fading to rose and gold as she glanced at her watch, her brow creasing.

She'd been so busy there'd been no time even to check in on Bonnie.

She grabbed her phone.

Bonnie answered on the first ring.

'Harper! You sneaked out while I was asleep, like a bad date.'

'Hey.' Harper fought a yawn. 'You needed your sleep.'

'If I'd been conscious I would have thanked you for looking out for me,' Bonnie said. 'I'm sorry I lost it when you were working.'

'Don't apologize. It was a shock seeing her there.'

'I still can't believe it.' Bonnie sounded somber.

Harper hated to give her more bad news – but she had to know.

'Have you been following the case? Do you know what's happening?'

'I heard about Wilson, if that's what you mean.' Bonnie let out a long breath. 'It doesn't make sense, Harper. He's such a nice guy.'

Harper made a dismissive gesture. 'Nice guys kill, too.'

That came out more sharply than she'd intended.

'I'm sorry,' she said, instantly contrite. 'It's been a long day.'

'I'll bet it has,' Bonnie said. 'Listen, Fitz has closed the bar for a couple of days. So, I'm around if you need me.'

'I spoke to him today,' Harper told her. 'He was incredibly drunk.'

'Yeah . . .' Bonnie sighed. 'He sounded sloshed when he called.

I don't blame him. Wouldn't mind being drunk myself right now. I just wish I understood what the hell Naomi was doing down on River Street. When she left the bar, she said she was going home. I've been thinking about it all day. The way she left in a big hurry. Like she was late for something. What could she be late for in the middle of the night?'

This sounded strikingly similar to the story Fitz had told her about another night when Naomi left early, in a rush.

Harper straightened. 'Did she say anything to you when she left? Was she meeting Wilson Shepherd?'

'All she said was she needed to go right away; something had come up. She was really urgent about it.' She paused. 'The only thing was, thinking back, it seems to me that . . . I don't know. Something didn't feel right.'

'What do you mean?' Harper picked up a pen.

'Maybe I'm adding this to my memories because I know what happened later,' Bonnie cautioned, 'but she seemed jittery. Like, she was trying to be normal but she was nervous. Almost like she was scared of something.'

Her words mirrored Fitz's, precisely.

'You know, Fitz told me a similar story earlier today. The same thing – Naomi leaving on a busy night, without warning. Being scared. He said it happened a few weeks ago. Do you remember that?'

'No.' Bonnie sounded surprised. 'I must not have worked that night. He didn't mention it to me.'

'He said he more or less forgot about it after that night. But something was going on in Naomi's life. Someone scared her. And they scared her enough that she kept it to herself.'

Harper paused, the pen hovering above a blank sheet of paper.

'Did she ever tell you she was afraid of Wilson? Did they fight?'

'She never said anything like that,' Bonnie said. 'I always thought they were happy. But, like I said last night to that detective, Wilson hasn't been around much lately. I thought they were taking a break because school and work were so busy.'

Harper considered this. 'Maybe Wilson didn't want to take a break.'

'You think he was mad enough about a break to kill the girl he loved?' Bonnie was skeptical.

'Wouldn't be the first time it happened.'

'I just don't see it,' Bonnie said. 'He's not the type.'

'They're all the type.'

'God, Harper. You're so cynical,' Bonnie chided. 'This is why you don't have a boyfriend.'

'This is why I'm still alive,' Harper replied without missing a beat.

As she spoke, she wrote one word in her notebook and underlined it: *Motive*.

'The thing is, if it wasn't Wilson, who was it?' she asked. 'There's no way she was caught up in drugs or gangs, is there?'

Bonnie gave a husky laugh. 'Oh, hell no, Harper. Naomi was a Girl Scout. I could hardly get a beer down her.'

Dropping the pen, Harper rubbed her forehead.

It just didn't make sense. Girl Scouts did not go to River Street at two in the morning to get themselves shot.

It was becoming clearer that Naomi had secrets. She'd kept them well. And somehow it had gotten her killed.

'Look,' Harper said, 'if you think of anything else, let me know.'

'I will,' Bonnie promised, adding as an afterthought, 'Oh, God, I almost forgot to mention. I went to see Naomi's dad. He wants to talk to you.'

43

Harper nearly dropped the phone.

'You met her *father*? I've been trying to reach him all day.'

'Yeah, I went to his house to give him my condolences. I couldn't reach him on the phone,' Bonnie said. 'His address was in our records at the bar – Naomi still had her pay slips sent there. He told me he turned his phone off because it won't stop ringing.'

Harper didn't know whether to laugh or cry. She'd called Jerrod Scott at least five times today without success. And Bonnie had just walked right in.

'What'd he say?' She couldn't keep the eagerness out of her voice.

'Yeah. He's real upset about Wilson,' Bonnie said. 'Says there's no way it was him, but the cops won't listen. I told him he should talk to you. I gave him your number. I hope that was okay.'

Harper could have kissed her.

She'd dropped the hottest interview in town right in her lap.

When she hung up the phone, Harper climbed to her feet.

It had been twelve hours since the last time she ate anything more substantial than a candy bar. Her stomach felt hollow.

Shoving her scanner and phone into her bag, she headed across the empty newsroom.

Baxter was at her desk, typing furiously, her face creased with concentration. Dells had finally gone home a couple of hours ago.

'I'm going to grab some food,' Harper announced. 'It's gone quiet.'

'Could you keep your phone on, for a change?' Baxter's tone was peevish. 'I will personally fire you if I can't reach you.'

'You sweet talker,' Harper said, heading out the door.

There was no point in arguing. They both knew Harper would keep everything turned on tonight.

The guard glanced at her without interest as she pushed the button that unlocked the double glass doors and stepped into the dark street.

Outside, the muggy evening air hit her like a warm, soft fist. Even this late, it wasn't cool. Night merely took the edge off the heat.

The streets were quiet at last. The air carried the faint syncopation of music from one of the River Street bars, which were filled at this hour with people whose nights involved something other than murder.

Harper had parked her ageing red Camaro in front of the newspaper building, and the engine started with a pleasing rumble. The car had nearly a hundred and thirty thousand miles on the meter but Harper kept it in mint condition.

She loved only a few things in this world and her car was one of them.

As she drove, she kept the window down, hoping the fresh air would revive her. The scanner propped in a holder on the dash buzzed and crackled with a constant stream of information. Her mind sorted through the noise for anything about Wilson Shepherd.

After years of listening to it non-stop, the codes used by the police were second nature to her.

'Unit 498.' A voice said.

The dispatcher replied after a second. 'Unit 498, go ahead.'

'Unit 498, I'm at the Code 5 on Veterans.'

Code 5 – car accident, Harper translated to herself.

'Everybody's pretty shook up,' the cop said, in a deep southern drawl. 'Better send a Code 10 to check them out.'

Code 10 was an ambulance, and Harper honed in on his voice for a minute. But he never came back to ask for backup.

She was hungry and tired, and she wasn't about to go out to a wreck where everyone was shaken up. She needed more than that.

'Death and destruction,' she murmured to herself, as she pulled the car into the parking lot at Eddie's 24-Hour Diner. 'I don't get out of bed for less.'

When she walked in the door, a bell jangled merrily but nobody could hear it above the Everly Brothers blasting from the stereo.

Eddie's was a retro diner, with vinyl and chrome booths, and waitresses with perky ponytails wearing high-collared blouses and tight jeans.

Harper signaled to one, who bounded up to her, dark hair swishing.

'Can I get you a table?'

Her bright eyes skimmed Harper's face, and took on a sympathetic glint. It occurred to Harper that she must look like hell. Her hair hadn't been brushed since she left the house this morning.

The waitress was young – her scarlet lipstick annoyingly perfect. She had no idea yet how hard a day could be.

'I need food to go,' Harper told her. 'A turkey sandwich, no mayo, and fries. And the biggest coffee you've got, as black as you can make it.'

'You got it.' Pulling a pen from behind her ear, the girl scribbled the order down.

'Take a seat,' she chirped. 'I'll get it out to you in a jiffy.'

When she'd disappeared into the kitchen, Harper sat on a padded bench by the door.

The restaurant was mostly empty. The music played loudly for no one.

The bench wasn't that comfortable but, at this stage, she could have slept in the middle of the highway in rush hour. She leaned back against the wall, her eyelids drooping. Even her hands seemed to have weight.

Feeling herself drifting, she jerked upright.

Busy. She needed to stay busy.

Pulling her scanner out of her bag, she plugged her earbuds in, turning it loud enough to hear it over the music.

The usual chatter filled her head and she forced herself to listen. She was half-asleep when a female voice said, 'Unit 364.'

'Unit 364 go ahead,' came the crisp voice of the dispatcher.

'Signal 25 in the 34000 block of Abercorn Street. I've got a white Ford pickup, stand by for the license.'

Signal 25, Harper thought, distantly, her eyes drifting shut. *Traffic stop.*

Other voices came and went. Then, without warning, the female officer's voice returned, breathless and high-pitched, words pouring out.

'I need backup on Abercorn Street. Send them fast. I've got the River Street shooting suspect in a white Toyota pickup truck. He's got a gun.'

Chapter Six

Harper jumped to her feet.

'Copy, Unit 364,' the dispatcher replied, in the same flat tone she'd used earlier to acknowledge another officer's refueling break.

The waitress was walking back now, a bag in her hand, that perfect, symmetrical smile already in place.

The dispatcher put out the call. 'All available units to the 34000 block of Abercorn to assist Unit 364 with a fugitive arrest. Be aware: Suspect is wanted for homicide. Suspect is armed and dangerous. All units Code 30.'

Code 30: blue lights and sirens.

The dispatcher was so calm, only someone who listened to this radio every day of her life could hear the tension in her voice.

Pulling her keys from her pocket, Harper turned for the door.

The waitress stepped smoothly in her path, blocking her.

'I'm sorry, I have to go,' Harper said, trying to push past.

'It's already made.' The waitress – her smile disappearing – pressed her back against the door handle so Harper couldn't reach it. 'You have to pay or I've got to call the cops. Eddie's got rules.'

Harper had underestimated her. There was more to the perky girl than a smile.

She didn't have time to argue. Frantically, she dug in her pocket, pulling out a disordered pile of bills. She shoved them in the woman's neatly manicured hands without counting them.

'If it isn't enough, call the *Daily News*, ask for Harper,' she told her. 'But not for another hour. I've got to go.'

'What do you want me to do with the food?' The waitress still clutched the bag.

'Keep it,' Harper said.

As an afterthought, though, she grabbed the cup.

'I'll take the coffee.'

The waitress stepped aside. Harper ran through the door and jumped into the car, pulling out her phone.

Miles answered on the first ring.

'I'm on my way to Abercorn,' he said. She could hear his police scanners in the background. 'You?'

'Leaving now.' She started the car. 'I'll call Baxter. See you there.'

As the phone speed-dialed Baxter's direct line, she backed out into the road.

'Emma Baxter,' the editor answered.

Harper hated to admit it but there was something comforting about the way Baxter could always be reached when the shit hit the fan.

'Traffic cops just pulled over Wilson Shepherd on Abercorn.' Harper raised her voice to be heard above the scanner and the engine. 'Sounds like he's putting up a fight. Miles and I are en route.'

'I'll tell the copy desk,' Baxter told her. 'We'll hold the front page. Don't do anything stupid, McClain.'

'Never,' Harper said, hanging up.

Dropping the phone, she pulled out onto the parkway so fast her tires squealed.

She wasn't tired anymore. Adrenaline raced into her system faster than caffeine possibly could.

A story like this was as good as eight hours' sleep. Better even. No drug ever invented could match it.

Every cop in the city was going to the same place she was. There was no one to pull her over. The speed limit was forty-five but she hit a hundred and stayed there until she saw flashing blue lights ahead. Then she tagged along behind them.

Abercorn carved a curving path across the edge of the city before pouring into the flat, coastal countryside. At the speed she was going it only took minutes before the crowded city streets outside the Camaro's windows dissolved into lush green suburbs, scarred by strip malls and big box stores.

The police standoff was easy to locate. A dozen patrol cars blocked the road, lights flashing.

Harper slammed the car into park and jumped out, running through the haphazardly parked vehicles.

Miles had positioned himself behind an empty squad car.

'Have they got him?' Harper asked, breathless.

'They do.' Miles squinted through the viewfinder. 'He just doesn't know it yet.'

With his Canon balanced on the roof, he was focused on a crowd gathered around a pickup truck in the distance. The patrol car that had pulled it over earlier was parked behind it, blue lights still swirling.

The doors of both vehicles gaped open.

In the flickering blue lights, Wilson Shepherd stood facing a line of police officers. He was sweating and panicked.

A silver, semi-automatic handgun glittered as he aimed it at the cops, all of whom were pointing their guns at him.

Everyone was yelling.

'Drop your weapon! Put down the gun! Drop it! Drop it now!' Wilson ignored their commands.

'I didn't do it!' he screamed back. 'I didn't kill Naomi – do you hear me? Does anyone hear me?'

'Drop your goddamn weapon! No one will hear you until you *drop that weapon*!'

Miles tilted the camera to look at the images on the display, a frown creasing his forehead.

'I need to get closer.'

He looked around, his face tense. They both knew time was everything right now.

'There.' Harper pointed to an empty space to the left of the pickup – protected by two trees, but with what looked like a clear view.

Miles nodded, tucking his camera under his arm. 'Let's go.'

Ducking low, the two of them threaded between the parked patrol cars. None of the police noticed them. Everyone was too focused on the scene unfolding.

Leaning against the tree to steady himself, Miles raised the Canon.

'That's better,' he breathed.

They were so close, Harper could see the panic in Shepherd's wide, frightened eyes as he swung the gun wildly.

It was impossible to square this Wilson Shepherd with the one she'd seen sitting at The Library, waiting for Naomi and nursing a beer.

He looked ten years older. His clothes were stained and disheveled. He appeared deranged, waving that gun at the police, tears and sweat streaming down his round cheeks; snot running from his nose.

'No, no, *no*,' he kept screaming hoarsely. 'It wasn't me. Why won't you *listen*?'

The cops weren't in any mood to do what he wanted. They were concentrating on that gun. Shouting constant commands in a kind of hyperactive, almost hypnotic wall of sound.

Harper wondered how long their patience would last.

Not long, as it turned out.

A shadow moved, low and slow, in the darkness to the left of the pickup's front tire.

She touched Miles lightly on the arm, pointing.

Turning the camera, he zoomed in.

Glancing up at her, he whispered, 'SWAT team.'

They both crouched low.

It happened quickly.

Two shadowy figures leaped onto Shepherd's back with machine-perfect timing, knocking the gun loose, and sending him sprawling.

Harper was close enough to hear the sickening slap of his face hitting the pavement.

A uniformed officer kicked the gun away. Then the others descended on him.

With four adrenaline-fueled cops on top of him twisting his hands behind his back, Shepherd was done.

Through it all, though, he repeated the same words over and over like a mantra. Sobbing them into the ground.

'I didn't do it. I didn't do it.'

Miles jumped to his feet. 'Let's get closer.'

But the two of them had taken only a few steps from the sheltering trees when a cop, large and sweaty, wired from the excitement of the arrest, moved in on them.

'Get back,' he ordered.

Harper didn't like the look of him. Cops get itchy whenever they've had to pull their weapons.

This one's hand was dangerously close to his holster.

She and Miles took an automatic step back into the glow of the headlights.

To her surprise, the cop's demeanor changed abruptly.

'Oh, hey, Miles,' he said. 'I didn't recognize you in the dark. How's it going?'

'I'm great, Bob,' Miles said, keeping his hands clearly in view nonetheless. 'Trying to get the front-page picture for tomorrow's paper.'

'You go ahead.' Bob waved him on. 'Try to stay out of their way.'

'I'll keep my distance,' Miles promised.

'Be sure and get my good side,' Bob joked, turning sideways.

Laughing politely, Miles moved past him toward the crowd of cops who were now lifting Shepherd to his feet.

When Harper started to follow, though, Bob's pleasant demeanor evaporated.

'I didn't say *you* could get closer.' The warmth left his voice. 'Traitors stay at the edge. In fact . . .' He pointed behind the row of parked patrol cars. 'Why don't you go over there?'

'Come on,' Harper pleaded. 'I won't get in the way. Can't you give me a break?'

Bob's face hardened.

'I don't have to do a thing for you,' he said. 'And right now, you're trespassing on a crime scene and failing to obey an officer.

Actually, you got some ID? I'm writing you up for disorderly conduct.'

'*What?*' Harper couldn't believe it. The cops always harassed her these days, but they didn't go this far.

She squared up to him. 'You can't do that. I'm a member of the press. I have a right to be here. This is a public highway.'

His face reddened. He reached behind him to where his handcuffs hung from his utility belt.

'That's it. Turn around.'

Before she realized what he was planning, he grabbed her by the shoulder, spinning her around and shoving her roughly against the nearest car.

Harper struggled, but he was twice her size. She never had a chance. Her face was pressed hard against the glass.

'Goddamn it,' she said, her voice muffled. 'Let me go, you dickhead.'

Suddenly, another voice spoke over her.

'What's going on, Bob? Caught yourself another suspect?'

This voice was cool and steady. It was saying all the right things, but with an underlay of threat that indicated the speaker didn't like Bob very much.

With her face still pressed against the car, Harper couldn't see anything.

But she knew that voice.

'Well, Detective.' Bob sounded defensive. 'This reporter's trespassing on the crime scene and refusing to obey orders. I'm arresting her for disorderly conduct.'

'You are fully within your rights to do that, Bob,' the other voice said. 'She's a handful, all right. But I gotta say the chief won't like it. Her publisher will give him a hard time. They could sue the force for illegal arrest.'

'She ignored an order.' Bob sounded less confident now.

'I hear you, but if you ask me, it's not worth the hassle,' the voice said. 'Tell you what. Why don't you let her go. I'll keep an eye on her. If she causes any trouble, I'll take her in myself. Save you the paperwork. We got a deal?'

Harper twisted her neck, trying to see what was happening, but Bob's meaty hand still held her head against the patrol car.

'I guess so.' Bob gave in reluctantly. 'You want me to cuff her?'

'No,' the detective said, a hint of ice in his voice now. 'I think I can handle her.'

'If you say so.'

Slowly, Bob relinquished his hold on Harper's head and hands.

Freed, she spun around, and looked straight into the calm blue eyes of Detective Luke Walker.

Chapter Seven

'Thanks, Bob,' Luke said, his eyes still on Harper. 'You can get back to work now.'

Seeing that his game was over, Bob trundled away with slow reluctance.

Pinioned in Luke's gaze, Harper was so flustered she couldn't think of anything to say.

It had been nearly a year since the two of them last spoke. And more than a year since the last time they slept together.

'What an idiot,' she managed to sputter, finally.

'I think it's fair to say nobody's ever accused Bob Kowalski of being smart,' Luke agreed.

He looked annoyingly good.

His hair was cropped short, and his chiseled jaw clean-shaven. Only the suit was wrong. She'd rarely seen him in anything but jeans before.

And he'd just seen her nearly arrested.

All she could think of to do, was to fume.

'Well, he's gone too far,' she said. 'He had no right to do that. I'm filing a complaint this time. This has got to stop.'

Luke didn't reply. Instead, he studied her, a faint smile on his face.

'What?' she asked, touching her face self-consciously.

'Nothing,' he said. 'Seeing you like this – so pissed off. I just thought . . . Some things never change.'

Harper didn't know how to reply to that.

It wasn't supposed to be like this. They were supposed to meet when her makeup and hair were perfect, and she was wearing a carefully chosen outfit. They'd go out for coffee and he'd be sorry he dumped her.

That was how she'd imagined this moment for the last year.

In Harper's dream meeting, they talked easily. Forgave each other for the sins of the past. And agreed to try again.

But then, nothing about their relationship had ever been dreamlike.

Their brief, passionate affair had started when she was investigating a murder and ended when she broke into the records room at police headquarters. Luke only found out about it after she got caught.

Tainted by his connection to her, he'd felt betrayed.

He'd walked away and, as far as she could tell, never looked back.

It had been easy not to run into each other, even by accident. He worked the late shift. She was going home when he clocked on. So, what was he doing here now?

'I thought you were still on the graveyard shift,' she said.

'I'm moving to evenings,' he said. 'Bit of a promotion.'

Their eyes met and held. The moment felt weighted down with all their history. Harper wondered if he regretted it all as much as she did.

But there was no way she'd ever ask.

Luke cleared his throat.

'This case is something else,' he said, turning to look at where Shepherd was now being bundled into the back of a police car. 'Did someone tell me you knew the victim?'

'Only a little,' she said. 'The dead girl worked with my friend Bonnie at the Library Bar.'

'Oh yeah. I'd forgotten you had a friend who worked there,' he said. 'You ever meet this guy?'

He pointed at Wilson, who was now in the car and still pleading his innocence through the glass.

Harper shrugged. 'A couple of times. I sure didn't know he had any of this in him. He always seemed like a nice guy.'

'He doesn't seem so nice now.' Luke's tone was dry.

He glanced at his watch. 'Well, I better get a move on. My part in this little drama's about to kick off.'

Harper's eyebrows winged up. 'You're interviewing Shepherd? Isn't this Daltrey's case?'

'I'm partnering with her on it,' he told her, pulling his keys from his pocket.

Harper kept her expression neutral but her mind was racing. If Luke took on this case, they'd see each other all the time.

'Well, for what it's worth, Bonnie swears he doesn't have it in him,' she said.

'We'll see.' He gave her that slow, serious smile she remembered so well. 'It was good running into you, Harper.'

'Right back at you,' she said, like it was no big deal. 'Good luck with the new shift.'

He hesitated for a second, as if there was something else he wanted to tell her.

But then, lifting one hand in silent farewell, he turned and walked away with that easy, long-legged stride she knew she would always be able to pick out of a crowd of thousands.

It was one in the morning before Harper finally finished work and headed home.

Almost twenty-four hours had passed since she first heard about the body on River Street. Her head felt light from exhaustion. She gripped the wheel hard, eyes fixed on the blurring road.

All the way, she kept going over that meeting with Luke. Thinking of the things she should have said.

When she parked in her normal spot on East Jones Street, the raised, two-story Victorian house looked still and safe.

A young lawyer had moved in to the upstairs apartment a few months ago, replacing the group of art students who had previously occupied it. The lawyer worked a lot and kept reasonable hours. No more late-night parties that left the entire house smelling of pot smoke and incense. No more strange music permeating the ceiling at all hours.

To her own surprise, Harper missed the kids. The house was almost too quiet these days.

Her keys jangled as she fitted one after another into the three, high-security locks on the solid front door.

As the door opened, the burglar alarm gave a series of shrill, warning beeps, and she punched in the four-digit code that silenced it.

She'd had the alarm fitted after her apartment was broken into last year.

There hadn't been another incident but she was hyper-aware that the person who'd done it hadn't been identified. And she didn't know what he wanted or why he'd targeted her.

She crossed the entrance hall to the living room and flipped on the lights.

Hardwood floors gleamed. There wasn't much furniture – two dark gray sofas facing each other across a low coffee table. All of it hospital clean.

The place looked a bit like a furniture showroom, in part because everything still had a sheen of newness.

Almost all her previous furniture had been damaged in the break-in. After her insurance paid out, she'd replaced the lot. Doing it that way made sense but it gave her the occasional disconcerting sense that someone else lived here. And that this was their stuff.

From the kitchen, a small shadow darted toward her.

A sleek, gray tabby rubbed itself against her ankle.

'Hey, Zuzu,' Harper said, bending down to stroke her soft fur. 'Did you chase away any burglars today?'

Purring, the cat led her to the kitchen.

She pulled a can from the half-empty cupboard, found a spoon in the dish drainer from that morning and put some tuna into her dish.

As the cat ate, she pulled a bottle of Jameson's whiskey from the cupboard and poured a double shot into a water glass.

It had been a long time since she let herself think about Luke.

She'd underestimated how much it would hurt to see him, and not be anything special to him. Just a woman he used to know.

Their conversation had been so normal. They used to have conversations like that all the time. Until they ruined it.

She swallowed the whiskey neat and poured herself another.

One drink wouldn't be enough. Not if she was going to think about this stuff. There wasn't enough whiskey in the world.

The night Lieutenant Smith was arrested, Luke had been the one to come to her aid. After Smith shot her, it had been Luke who'd knelt over her body, trying to stop the bleeding.

She could remember every detail of that night. The fear in his voice. His hands trying to hold back the fountain of blood.

After that, though, he'd avoided her for weeks.

Finally, one day, he'd called her.

'I'm sorry for disappearing on you,' he'd said, far too casually. 'We need to talk.'

He'd chosen a neutral spot – a bar neither of them frequented regularly. When she walked in and saw him sitting there, a bottle of beer untouched on the table in front of him she'd felt helpless with longing.

She could tell from the moment she sat down next to him that it was over. There were things she had to say though.

'I wanted to thank you,' she'd said, 'for saving my life.'

He'd looked uncomfortable. 'You don't need to thank me. I was doing my job.'

'Like hell you were,' she'd said. 'You risked your life for me. At least let me say thank you.'

Their eyes met and she felt the connection between them like a blast of furnace heat.

A muscle in his jaw fluttered – the only sign that he felt it, too.

'I would have been there sooner, but I couldn't get to my phone,' he'd said, after a long silence. 'I got your message too late.'

She wouldn't let him downplay his role. 'You were there when it mattered. I'm only sorry I had to drag you into it. I know it was the last thing you wanted.'

At that, his face hardened. 'You getting hurt was the last thing I wanted. It didn't have to happen. You're just so damned stubborn . . .'

Stopping himself, he'd reached for his beer, taking a quick swig.

'Luke, I hope you can understand why I did what I did,' Harper pleaded, lowering her voice to a whisper. 'I truly believed I could solve my mother's murder if I solved that case. I only wish there was some way I could make it up to you for everything I did that hurt you.'

She leaned forward, begging him to understand. Surely anyone who knew her history would see why it meant so much to her. Who wouldn't push the limits to solve their own mother's murder?

He'd looked up from his beer then, studying her with those enigmatic eyes – dark blue, like a midnight sky.

'I know you do.' His flat tone shattered her hopes. 'But that's not how things work. Trust doesn't come back because you want it to. Some things you break can't be fixed.'

They'd talked for a while after that, and then parted, knowing it was over.

They'd barely spoken again. Until tonight.

Raising the glass to her lips in a swift, economical movement, she downed the second whiskey, waiting as it traced a line of fire down her throat to her heart.

Some of the tension in her body released. She let out a long, shuddering breath.

He'd be working her shift from now on.

Maybe that wasn't so bad.

Maybe they'd find a way to forgive each other.

But in her heart she knew that was only another dream.

Chapter Eight

The next day, Harper arrived at the newspaper at noon with no story to write.

There'd been a time when she could have called Detective Daltrey and teased a few snippets of information out of her, but those days were over.

After her conversation with Bonnie, she'd hoped Naomi Scott's father might get in touch but, so far, her phone hadn't rung. She'd tried his home number several times, but her calls went straight to voicemail.

She couldn't blame him – his only daughter had died the day before. But still.

Dropping her bag next to her desk, she switched on her computer and turned her scanner on low, right as DJ walked into the room from the back hallway.

'Not you again,' he said cheerily.

Harper ignored this.

'Is Baxter around? Please say no.'

'OK. No,' he replied, before adding with an apologetic wince,

'But she is. She's in Dells's office right now. Why? What did you do?'

'Nothing, and that's the problem.' Harper reached for her coffee. 'I haven't got anything new on River Street. My source didn't come through.'

'Oh, you're screwed then,' DJ assured her. 'Because she's been telling everyone the update will be live at one o'clock. Says you've got an exclusive with the dad.'

This was worse than she'd thought.

'She's going to kill me,' Harper said. 'The dad stood me up.'

'Ah, bummer.' Giving her a sympathetic glance, DJ turned back to his desk. 'RIP, Harper. It was a great career while it lasted.'

Harper logged into the system and began searching local websites to see if any other news outlets had something she'd missed. Anything she could substitute instead of the father. But nobody seemed to have anything new. All news on the Scott case had stopped when Wilson Shepherd was arrested last night.

One article on a television website said Shepherd had a history of drug dealing, back in Atlanta. Harper made a note to look into that. It didn't seem to fit the clean-cut, law student he'd always appeared to be.

But that was it. Just a line, buried in the middle of the article about his arrest.

The desk phone began ringing insistently but, absorbed in her research, Harper took her time before finally snatching it from its cradle.

'McClain,' she snapped.

'Miss McClain, this is Gary at the front desk. There's a man down here who says he needs to talk to you.' He sounded irritated. Gary hated visitors. 'His name's not on the visitors' list.

Now, you know the rules about updating the list with any expected guests. It's a security issue, Miss McClain. I keep telling you –'

Harper let her head drop back hard against her chair.

'I'm not expecting a visitor, Gary,' she said, cutting him off impatiently. 'Who is it?'

'Says his name's Jerrod Scott. Should I send him away?'

Harper stood up so abruptly she knocked over her coffee, sending dark liquid flowing across her desk toward her scanner.

'Don't send him away for God's sake.' Her voice rose. 'Send him right up.'

'Fine,' Gary sniffed. 'But he should be on the list.'

Swearing under her breath, Harper set the phone down and threw a copy of yesterday's paper on the spill.

Grabbing a clean notepad and pen from a drawer, she ran across the room, reaching the newsroom door just as a tall, thin man with dark skin and neatly cropped, graying hair walked in.

'Mr Scott?' Harper said.

He nodded, looking around the newsroom warily.

'I'm here to see Harper McClain.' His voice was deep, with a strong Savannah accent that gave her last name three syllables.

'I'm Harper.' She held out her hand. 'I'm very sorry for your loss, Mr Scott.'

His fingers were long and sturdy, and his grip on her hand was so powerful it almost hurt. Up close she could see that his brown eyes were rimmed with red – from exhaustion and grief, she guessed.

'Miss McClain. Your friend Bonnie told me I could trust you.' His eyes searched her face with unexpected intensity. 'Can I trust you?'

'You can,' she promised him, hoping it was true.

Conscious of the reporters watching this exchange curiously, she gestured for him to follow.

'Come over here. Let's talk.'

She led him to a quiet back corner of the newsroom.

Something about Scott – a kind of exhausted energy in his manner – told her she should get straight to the point.

'I suppose you know about Wilson Shepherd's arrest?' Harper said.

His eyes rose to meet hers. 'It was all over the front of the newspaper today. If I wanted to miss it I'd have to go blind.'

'Bonnie told me you don't think he killed your daughter,' she said. 'You still feel that way?'

He didn't hesitate.

'I am one hundred percent positive Wilson didn't lay a finger on Naomi.' His voice was firm. 'That's why I'm here. You have to do something about this situation.'

Harper thought of the Wilson she'd seen last night – waving a gun and screaming at the police.

'I watched him get arrested last night,' she told him. 'He didn't look very innocent to me.'

'I don't know about that.' Scott fixed her with a stern look. 'I know how he was when we got the news about Naomi. He didn't sleep. He didn't eat. Grief . . .' He paused – his eyes reddening. 'Grief can break your mind as well as your heart.'

Harper knew this better than anyone. But what she'd seen last night had seemed beyond grief. Still, she didn't want to argue with a man who'd just lost his daughter.

She studied his tired face. Deep lines were scored into his forehead. More radiated out from the corners of his mouth.

'I hear you,' she said.

Scott must have seen her doubt.

'I know what you think, Miss McClain,' he told her. 'You think I'm a sad old man, who doesn't know what's going on right in front of him. But I'm telling you, the police arrested the wrong person. And while they're so focused on Wilson, the real killer is walking free.'

'Tell me why you believe he couldn't do it.' She reached for her notebook. 'Do you know where he was that night? If you know someone who can vouch for where he was at the time of the shooting that would really help.'

He shook his head.

'I don't know where Wilson was when my girl was shot. What I know is, that boy would let a spider crawl across him before he'd hurt it. He's got no killer in him, Miss McClain. And he *loved* my daughter.'

His voice broke and he pressed his fingers against his forehead.

'Mr Scott.' Harper softened her voice. 'He had a gun when the police pulled him over. If it's the weapon used in the murder, they're going to charge him.'

He shook his head stubbornly.

'You have to believe me. It was someone else. I know my Naomi was scared of someone. A man from school. She wouldn't tell me what happened, or why she didn't like him, but something about him made her afraid.' He jutted his finger at her. 'Find him. Find that man. Ask him your questions.'

Harper had hoped he'd have something concrete for her about Shepherd or Naomi – but random theories about unknown men the dead woman might have been anxious about . . . That wasn't what she was looking for.

She tried to guide him back to what she needed.

'First, tell me about Naomi and Wilson,' she urged. 'How did they meet? What brought them together?' Seeing a rebellious look in his eyes she added quickly, 'This will help me understand why you think Wilson couldn't hurt her. I need to know more about them.'

'Well.' He rested his hands on his legs. 'They met at college. And Naomi knew right away that he was special. She made her mind up fast about things, even when she was little. She decided she wanted to become a lawyer when she was ten. Watched some TV show and said, "That's what I want to do, Daddy. I want to help people."'

He smiled at the memory.

'Being a lawyer – that was a big dream in our family. Maybe you know, but I drive a cab. My father, he lived outside Vidalia. Worked the land. Our family has always been working people. People who use their hands. Naomi wanted something different.'

He drew a breath, hands clenching convulsively.

'She made straight As all her life, always top of her class. When the time came, she wanted to go away to college. Got a scholarship to UGA, over in Athens. But we couldn't afford to send her. Housing's too much over there. So she went to Savannah State, instead.'

His voice trailed off.

'And that was where she met Wilson?'

He nodded slowly.

'She worked part-time as a tutor for kids who were the first in their family to go to college. Some of them had a hard time fitting in, so the school had people like Naomi to guide them.'

He glanced at her.

'Wilson – he got in trouble when he was a teenager. Got messed up with a gang back in Atlanta. Got caught dealing drugs. For a while, he was on the wrong path. By the time she met him, he'd cleaned himself up. Made up his mind to walk a true road.

Came to Savannah to get away from that life. Wasn't going to look back.'

His brow lowered as he tried to explain. 'Kids like Wilson, they usually don't find their way. He did, though. When Naomi met him, she knew he was intelligent. His grades were good – she helped him stay focused. In the end, she talked him into applying to law school at the same time she did.'

He gave a faint, wistful smile. 'Tell you one thing, once that girl set her mind to something, nobody had a chance. Wilson knew better than to argue. They both got in, like she knew they would. Around then, that's when they decided they were in love. After that, you couldn't get a cigarette paper between them. They were always together.'

'Did they fight?' Harper suggested. 'Get mad at each other about things?'

'Every couple argues,' he said. 'But they never had a fight like you're talking about. He never raised a hand against her. She'd never put up with that. Neither would I.'

'Are you sure?' Harper's tone was skeptical. 'We don't tell our dads everything about our relationships.'

His held her gaze steadily.

'Miss McClain, my wife died of breast cancer when Naomi was ten years old. She and me, we've always been close. We had to be. Closer than most fathers and daughters. The first time she got her period? She came to me. I took her to the drug store, got the things she needed. She got her first boyfriend? She talked to me about him. I made sure she knew the facts of life. When she met Wilson, she told me, "Daddy, I think I'm going to marry this man. His heart's big enough for me."'

His voice trembled, and he paused for a moment. When he looked up again, his face was shadowed.

'If he ever hurt her, she'd have told me.'

So much about Naomi's story sounded familiar. Harper knew what it was like to grow up without a mother. Only in her case, it hadn't made her closer to her father. Quite the opposite, in fact.

Her father had been a suspect in her mother's murder in the early days of the investigation. He was cleared of suspicion by the young paralegal in whose bed he'd been lingering while someone stabbed his wife to death in their kitchen.

Harper had never forgiven him.

She wondered what it was like to be so close to your father that you would confide everything to him. And she simply wasn't convinced Naomi had been so open with her dad. It was clear that she had secrets.

'Wilson often went to The Library to meet Naomi when she worked late,' she said. 'But in the last few weeks he hadn't been there. Were they having some trouble?'

Scott's brow lowered. 'Who told you he wasn't there?'

'Bonnie,' Harper said.

'I don't know about that.' He rubbed a hand on his jaw. 'She was so busy. Working and studying. But I'm sure they were fine.'

'She didn't say anything to you?'

He shook his head. 'No. And if it was bad, I think she would have told me something.'

But, for the first time, he sounded uncertain.

There it was. Naomi's secrets. Kept even from him.

'Mr Scott,' Harper leaned forward, 'isn't it possible they had a fight and Naomi didn't tell you because she didn't want to upset you? And someone like Wilson, with his background, maybe his temper snapped –'

He didn't let her finish. 'Ms McClain, I know what you're thinking but if you keep looking at Wilson you'll be looking at the wrong man, just like the police are.' His voice trembled with frustration. 'You need to find the other man. The one who scared her.'

Harper sighed.

'Fine. Tell me about the man.'

He hesitated. 'Now, you're going to think I'm a liar because I told you she told me everything. But with this man, all she said was she wanted him out of her life. Told me he wasn't a good person and that if I ever saw him I should walk away without even talking to him.'

This was exactly what Harper had feared. He wanted the murderer not to be Shepherd, so he was looking for anyone else to blame. Even some random guy his daughter didn't like.

'Do you have a name?' she asked, trying not to sound as doubtful as she felt. 'If you give it to me, I'll see what I can find out.'

'His name is Peyton Anderson,' Scott told her. 'His family's big in this town. Maybe you heard of them . . .'

But Harper was no longer listening – she stared at him in stunned disbelief.

'Do you mean Peyton Anderson as in the son of the *district attorney*?' she asked, cutting him off.

'That's him.' Scott nodded. '*He's* the one Naomi was scared of.'

Harper couldn't think of anything to say.

Randall Anderson had been District Attorney for twelve years before stepping down a year ago to join a private practice.

His family was part of the city's old guard – with a patrician legacy and a palatial mansion near Forsyth Park. The Andersons were everywhere in Savannah – they were part of every major organization that ran the city.

The idea that his son could have somehow threatened Naomi Scott seemed bizarre.

'You don't know what happened between them?' she asked, after a long pause.

He shook his head. 'All I know is they were in law school together, they sometimes studied together in her first year. Then, something happened – he did something, I think – and after that she tried to avoid him. I know she complained to the school.'

Harper kept nodding politely but she could see exactly what was happening here. Scott was grasping at straws. He wanted the facts to change. He wanted Wilson to be the good boyfriend who loved his daughter. And he wanted a man he'd never met to be the killer.

Neither she, nor the police, could give him that.

'Well,' she said, closing her notebook, 'I think I've got all I need. There's plenty here for me to work with.' She stood up. 'I can't thank you enough for coming in to talk to me about all this.'

He unfolded his long legs, and stood, a disappointed look in his eyes.

'You think Wilson did it,' he said sadly. 'You're going to tell people they have the right man.'

She opened her mouth to argue, but he shook his head.

'It's fine. The police didn't believe me either.' He pushed the chair carefully back into place. 'I guess no one wants to believe.'

Not without evidence they don't, Harper thought. But she couldn't say that to him. He looked so defeated.

'Tell you what,' she said. 'I'll dig around a little. See what I can find out. Just in case there's anything there.'

Scott accepted this with quiet dignity.

'Thing is, Miss McClain, whether you believe me or not, I know Wilson didn't do this. And I intend to fight to see justice done. For my daughter's sake.'

Chapter Nine

The conversation with Jerrod Scott stayed with Harper, but it didn't change her mind. Wilson Shepherd was almost certainly the killer of Naomi Scott. Everything pointed to him.

Still, his mention of Peyton Anderson was intriguing.

The blue-collar daughter of a taxi driver falling into and out of friendship with the scion of one of the wealthiest and most influential families in Savannah and then ending up dead?

Maybe there was more than friendship between Naomi and Peyton. After all, she was a beautiful, intelligent girl. What if Wilson found out Naomi and Peyton were an item and he was driven mad with jealousy?

That would be one hell of a story.

But when she wrote the article about Jerrod Scott, she included no mention of Anderson. And she didn't mention anything about it to Baxter. Too early.

She'd nose around a little first – see what she could find out.

With this in mind, she drove to police headquarters that

afternoon, intent on speaking with Detective Daltrey, and finding out if Shepherd had begun to talk.

They'd held him for the better part of a day now. Plenty of time to get something out of him.

She reached the station at shift-change. The evening crew was heading out to get in their patrol cars. The day shift was going home.

The lobby was unusually crowded.

Harper made her way through the throng towards the front desk to ask Dwayne if Daltrey was in. She was halfway there when Daltrey stepped in front of her, heading the other way.

The detective wore her usual work outfit of dark pants with a matching jacket and a high-necked white blouse. Her short dark hair was combed back, giving her an androgynous edge.

'Detective, do you have a minute?' Harper said.

As the crowd jostled past them, Daltrey assessed her coolly.

'God, McClain,' she said. 'Don't you ever sleep?'

'Not very often,' Harper responded. 'Look, I wanted to ask you something about the Naomi Scott case.'

Daltrey's face closed.

'Public Information Office is on the second floor.' She strode away, pushing open the glass door and heading out into the August heat.

When Harper hurried after her, Daltrey shot her an irritated glance.

'I heard Kowalski put you in a headlock last night because you wouldn't leave the crime scene. You're not learning much, are you?'

'Kowalski is an asshat,' Harper said.

Daltrey snorted a laugh. 'For once we agree.'

Taking this as an opening, Harper launched into her questions.

'How are things going with Wilson Shepherd? Is he talking?'

'No comment,' Daltrey said.

'Was the gun he had last night the murder weapon?'

'No comment.'

'Have you charged him yet?'

'No comment.'

Daltrey seemed to be enjoying this. But Harper refused to give up.

'I had a long talk with Jerrod Scott today,' she said. 'He told me Naomi was friends with Peyton Anderson. Did you know about that?'

Daltrey stopped so abruptly Harper nearly ran into her.

'What are you doing, McClain? Are you getting involved in my case? You should know better by now than to meddle.'

'I'm only telling you what Jerrod Scott said.' Harper's voice was even. 'That's not getting involved. That's me doing my job.'

Daltrey took a step closer, pushing into Harper's space. She was small in stature but no less intimidating for it.

'Well, I'm not going to defend my case to you. And I'm not giving you any juicy tidbits for your rag. Those days are over. They ended the day you testified against Smith.' Daltrey moved so close, Harper could see the faint smear of mascara against her left eyelid, smell the mint on her breath. 'You can't come to me expecting help. And something else: If you come harassing your ex-boyfriend for bits of information I will see to it that he's busted back to the night shift. Am I clear?'

The reference to Luke sent anger flaring in Harper's chest. Daltrey was out of line dragging him into this and she must have known it.

But arguing with her would only make things worse.

'Fine.' She held up her hands, stepping back. 'I won't ask you any more questions. I get the picture. No help for the traitor. You have a great day, Detective.'

She didn't hide her sarcasm.

'Get out of my face, McClain,' Daltrey said. 'I have work to do.'

'Yeah, whatever,' Harper muttered, turning away.

The tall brick rectangle of the old police building towered over her. Its even rows of arched windows gazed down at her dispassionately as she trudged back along the steamy street to the front entrance.

But when she reached it, she didn't go inside. Instead, she turned and walked back to the sidewalk again, pacing in the summer heat as she thought things through.

She barely noticed the long green branches of the ancient oaks overhead, or the tour bus crawling by a few feet away. She was too angry.

Normally, she'd brush off Daltrey's attitude and get on with her job. But after last night, she felt like this had all gone too far.

She hadn't told Baxter about Kowalski, yet. She'd been too busy last night, and distracted by running into Luke. She'd wanted to give the incident time to settle before making her next move. But she knew she couldn't let it pass.

The tension with the police was ratcheting up. If something didn't change, she could find herself in the position of not being able to do her job. Or worse. Idiots like Kowalski were dangerous. If the brass gave every patrol officer carte blanche to punish her, she could get hurt.

If she filed a complaint, though, it would start an almighty war between the police and the newspaper. Manhandling a reporter doing her job at a crime scene on a public street was grounds for one hell of a lawsuit.

There was no question that would give her satisfaction. But it would make headlines. She really didn't want to be the news story again.

Instead, she had a different idea. And the more she thought about it, the more she liked it.

It was entirely possible Bob Kowalski and Detective Daltrey had given her the ammunition she needed to put a stop to this.

When she walked back into the police lobby a few minutes later, things had quieted down. Dwayne was at the front desk, eyes on the pile of paperwork in front of him. He was so caught up in his work she was all the way to the desk before he noticed her.

'Hi, Harper,' he said, distracted. 'Man, things have been crazy today.'

Without waiting for her to ask, he slid the day's police reports across to her.

After the heat outside, the air-conditioning felt Siberian. The sweat on her back didn't so much dry as freeze. Harper shivered as she looked through the paperwork absently – a dozen burglaries, car break-ins, domestics – the usual thing. She didn't write anything down.

There was only one news story today unless someone else died – and that was Wilson Shepherd.

Glancing over her shoulder to make sure no one was listening, Harper whispered, 'Dwayne.'

His head jerked up.

'Is there any word on Shepherd? Is he talking?'

He looked around furtively before leaning toward her.

'He's talking,' he said quietly. 'He's just not saying what they want to hear. All he says is it wasn't him. Keeps saying it over and over.'

No wonder Daltrey was in such a foul mood. She must have been hoping for a full confession after they brought Shepherd in. Without that, they'd need evidence of guilt before they could charge him and, from the looks of things, they didn't have it.

Closing the folder, she pushed it back across to him.

'Is the lieutenant in?' she asked.

It had been a long time since she'd asked to talk to Blazer about anything – she saw the surprise register on Dwayne's face.

'He is . . .' His voice trailed off, doubtfully.

'I'd like to speak with him,' Harper said.

Dwayne didn't move. 'He's in a bad mood today.'

She didn't take the hint. 'When is he not?'

'If that's what you want . . .'

Still looking doubtful, Dwayne picked up the phone and pushed a few buttons.

'Lieutenant? Harper McClain is here. She'd like to talk to you about that River Street case.'

A long pause followed then, and Harper could hear the faint rumble of Blazer complaining. Dwayne's expression didn't change as he listened patiently.

When Blazer finally stopped, he said, 'Great, then. Should I send her back?'

Blazer barked a one-syllable command. Dwayne slid the phone onto the receiver and looked up at her, worry visible in his eyes.

'He says come on through.'

Harper rested a hand on his desk. 'Thank you.'

'You may not say that after you talk to him.'

Harper crossed the room to the security door leading into the police offices. Dwayne pressed a button on his desk, and the door unlocked with a loud buzz.

She pulled it open and walked through.

When she and Bonnie had been here two nights ago, it had been silent and dark. Now it was teeming with police. Harper joined the flow heading down the long corridor.

Blazer worked out of an office that she still thought of as Smith's, at the end of the hallway. Smith's name had been removed from the door more than a year ago, but Blazer's didn't look right to her, painted on the wood in funereal black.

Without giving herself time to think it over, she raised her fist and knocked with as much confidence as she could muster.

'Enter,' a voice ordered gruffly.

Lieutenant Larry Blazer sat at his desk in front of a laptop. He wore a charcoal-gray suit. When he looked up at her, his pale-blue tie perfectly matched his cold eyes.

Even she had to admit he was a handsome man – lean and athletic, with a lush head of hair going silver in an artful way. But he wasn't her type. At all.

The feeling, she knew, was mutual.

'This better be important, McClain,' he grumbled, gesturing at the chairs in front of his desk.

As she crossed the room and sat where he indicated, Harper's eyes were drawn to all the things he'd changed. Smith's ostentatious mahogany desk had been replaced with a modern table made of some light, Scandinavian wood. Gone were the photos of Smith with local dignitaries and the golf ball paperweight. The desktop was empty save for the sleek silver laptop and a few files.

The only thing on the wall was a poster-sized street-map of Savannah, dotted with about forty crimson pins.

A quick glance at the streets marked told Harper it was a map of murders.

'I'm sorry to bother you,' she said, turning her attention back to Blazer. 'I think we need to talk.'

'Talk about what, exactly?' His tone was chilly.

Harper braced herself. If he was going to throw her out, it would happen in the next sixty seconds.

She cleared her throat. 'Lieutenant, it's been over a year since Smith was arrested and I'm still being punished by your department. The constant harassment is making it impossible for me to do my job. It needs to stop.'

Blazer shot her an incredulous look.

'Did you really come to my office to complain that my hard-working officers are being mean to you?'

'This isn't about being mean,' she said evenly. 'It's about unprofessional behavior by public servants toward a member of the press. Last night, one of your officers assaulted me at a crime scene.'

Any remnants of humor left Blazer's face.

'That's a serious allegation. You better be able to back that up.'

'It happened during the arrest of Wilson Shepherd,' Harper said. 'Numerous officers were present and witnessed the incident. Bob Kowalski shoved me against a patrol car and said he was going to arrest me for disorderly conduct because I didn't move quickly enough when he asked me to leave the scene.'

Blazer made a dismissive gesture. 'Is that all? Perhaps you should have moved. My officers need to work unimpeded. That situation was dangerous. It's Kowalski's job to keep you safe.'

Swallowing her indignation, Harper kept her tone cool.

'Come on, Lieutenant. Last night the only thing threatening my safety was Bob Kowalski. He went too far. He manhandled me. And I think he did it because you encourage that kind of behavior.' Seeing his face darken, she raised one hand. 'Please hear me out.

I'm not here to hurl allegations. I'm here to ask you to stop this. You wanted to punish me?' She held up her hands. 'Congratulations. I've been punished. You succeeded. I got the message. Now I need you to call them off. Before someone gets hurt.'

Blazer leaned forward, a thin smile twisting his lips.

'Aren't you up to the job, anymore, McClain? Maybe you should consider another beat if this one is too hard for you.'

This time, Harper couldn't control her temper. She'd kept this all bottled up for too long.

'Too *hard* for me?' Her voice rose. 'One of your detectives shot me in the shoulder, Lieutenant. And I kept coming to work. Every single night I go out on the same streets as your officers, only I do it without a vest or a gun. And they humiliate me. They ignore my questions and they ridicule me. They tell sources not to speak to me. I have to get my photographer to ask questions for me because your officers are so unprofessional and childish. Too *hard*?'

She stood up, gripping her notebook with such force it bent. She hadn't known until this moment how furious she really was. How painful this had been.

How much it had hurt.

'I am not asking for special treatment. I'm asking for basic respect and professionalism. For God's sake, Lieutenant. One of your detectives murdered a woman, but *I'm* the one being punished for exposing what you should have found.'

The Lieutenant tried to interject, but she refused to let him talk over her.

'If this is the way you want to play this, be very careful,' she said. 'Because I am not going anywhere. And if you want war, you should know my editors would love me to demolish your department. Nobody could do that better than me. Your case resolution rates are shit. Your incident response times are worse. Murder rates are up and you *know it*.' She pointed an accusing finger at the map behind his desk. 'Things have gotten worse since Smith left and I could be asking you about that. If we're going to talk about who's up to the job they're in, we could start with you. Instead, I'm giving you the chance to fix this.'

Finally running out of fury, she drew a breath. 'You should thank me.'

Blazer held up his hands.

'All right, McClain. Jesus. I get your point. Now, please. Sit down. Let's talk this through.'

Harper stayed where she was. She was breathing heavily; her face still hot with anger. She'd held all of that in for so long, now that it had finally been said she felt unfinished.

'Look,' Blazer said, 'you've been around here long enough to understand the rules. You go after one of ours, we all go after you. That's the deal. You knew that going in. Didn't you?'

All the ridicule was gone from his tone. It was the first time she could remember him speaking to her like an equal.

Some of her fury ebbed away.

'Yes, but . . .'

He held up one hand.

'But nothing, McClain. You can't play by the rules you know are there and then ask for those rules to be changed when it suits you. The system is what it is. Cops don't forgive easily. You have always known that. They look after their own.'

Hardly aware she was doing it, Harper lowered herself onto the chair.

'This wasn't a small crime, Lieutenant. Smith wasn't pocketing the petty cash. He wasn't shaking down the corner kids or messing with the hookers,' she said. 'He murdered someone. And then he shot me. What did your officers expect me to do?'

Her voice quivered, and she paused to steady herself. But, to her own surprise, she found herself telling him the truth.

'I loved him like a father,' she said. 'What he did broke my heart.'

She didn't know why she was telling him this. It just came out.

Blazer went very still. And then he said something she never would have expected.

'He broke mine, too.'

Harper was stunned. She'd known Blazer and Smith were close friends, but it had never occurred to her that he would feel the same pain she did. The same betrayal.

But now she could see the hurt on his face.

Raking his fingers through his hair, Blazer gave a small sigh.

'Look, McClain, it's possible my guys have gone too far. As you say, it's been a year. And we all have jobs to do. I can't have this sort of thing interfering with their work.' He picked up a pen off his desk and wrote something on a notepad open in front of him. 'I'll have a word with them. Ask them to ease up.'

Harper couldn't believe it. Whatever she'd expected, it hadn't included him agreeing with her.

'Thank you, Lieutenant,' she said fervently.

'Don't get too excited,' he cautioned. 'Some of my guys will still believe they can't trust you. If you want that to change, you're going to have to find a way to earn their trust again. I can't help with that. But I can stop the harassment.' His lips curled up. 'And I'll have a word with Kowalski.'

'That will help,' she told him. 'I appreciate it.'

Her gratitude seemed to irritate him.

'Are we done here?' he asked, his usual brusque tone returning.

'There's one more thing.' Harper opened her crumpled notebook and pulled out a pen. 'What can you tell me about Peyton Anderson?'

Blazer rocked back in his chair.

'Oh perfect. Let me guess. You've been talking to Jerrod Scott.'

She nodded. 'He's very upset about the arrest of Wilson Shepherd. Says there's no way he could have done it. Tells me the police won't listen.'

'Well, he's wrong about that,' he said. 'There are about a dozen ways Shepherd could have done it.'

He ran a hand across his jaw.

'Off the record?' he said.

She nodded, putting the pen down.

'Shepherd has no alibi. The night Scott was murdered, he says he was home studying. No one can swear to his whereabouts. We suspect Scott and Shepherd had a fight. Maybe she was cheating on him, maybe she was breaking up with him – we don't know. Way I see it – he sits home fuming all night, then, when he knew she'd be getting off work, he gets her to meet him downtown and does the job.'

There was a ruthless logic to the theory. It was exactly what Harper would have thought if she were a cop.

'Has his gun been tested to see if it's the murder weapon?' she asked.

He hesitated for too long. If the guns had matched he'd have told her immediately.

'It's the wrong gun?' She was unable to keep the surprise out of her voice. 'But what does that mean?'

'It means nothing, McClain,' he said firmly. 'He's a smart young man. He had the good sense to shoot her with an illegal gun and get rid of it. That doesn't make him innocent.'

'What about Anderson, though?' she asked. 'Could he be the other guy in that relationship?'

'For Christ's sake, McClain. Do you actually *look* for trouble?' Blazer stood abruptly. 'If you drag Peyton Anderson into this his father will eat you alive. If you want something to do, find out more about Wilson Shepherd. He's the killer. He's the one you should be interested in. Look into his background. You might find some things there that interest you. He had quite an arrest record. Ask Detective Daltrey about it.'

He pointed at the door.

'Now, I've got to get back to work. I'd like to go home sometime tonight.'

Seeing that she wasn't going to get anything else from him, Harper stood.

'Thank you, Lieutenant,' she said.

Before she made it to the door, though, Blazer stopped her.

'Take my advice, McClain.' His expression was serious. 'For once in your life, stop stirring up trouble. Shepherd is going down for this.'

Chapter Ten

Later that night, as she drove home from work, Harper was still elated about her conversation with Blazer.

Maybe things really could get back to normal now. Or something like it.

On autopilot, she made her way through the dark city streets, her thoughts a tangle of Naomi Scott, Larry Blazer, and Luke. She parked in her usual spot under the long, shading branches of an oak tree, locked the car and walked up the steps.

When she opened her front door, she did it thoughtlessly – punching the code in for the alarm system without thinking. Flipping on the lights.

Her mind was so focused on the story and her own decisions, it took her a moment to notice something was wrong.

She froze in the entrance hall, trying to place it.

There was a faint smell of cigarette smoke in the air – that shouldn't be there. And why was the hall light off?

Turning on that light and setting the alarm were as much a part of her daily routine as getting dressed. She was as likely to walk out the front door naked as she was to forget to do one of those things.

So, who turned it off?

The hairs on the back of her neck rose.

Slowly, she stepped backward, and re-checked the alarm. It was on standby, just as it should be. If someone had broken in, it would have triggered. Right?

She reached back and felt for the baseball bat she kept next to the front door. Her fingers knocked against the cool, smooth wood of the handle, and she hefted it, feeling the reassuring weight in her hands.

Moving soundlessly, she walked into the dark living room.

Never letting go of the bat, she flipped on the lights with her elbow and jumped into the room, crouching low, ready to swing.

It was empty. Everything was as it should be – two sofas, facing each other across an empty coffee table. Books on the shelves. Her mother's paintings reassuringly bright on the walls.

No sign of a break-in. No threats scrawled in dripping paint.

And yet, something wasn't right. She could *feel* it.

Still clutching the bat, Harper half-ran to the kitchen. In the bright overhead light it was clean and empty. The sturdy back door was closed and triple-locked. Her coffee cup from this morning sat upside down in the dish drainer where she'd left it.

Some of the tension left her body. Nonetheless, she carefully searched the rest of the apartment, before finally propping the bat in a corner and leaning against the kitchen counter, her eyes searching the room for an explanation.

There was no sign of Zuzu. That wasn't unusual – there was a cat door in the kitchen, and she often went prowling at night.

But Harper would have felt better if she were here.

She went through the motions of getting the cat's food out of the cupboard; filling her dish and leaving it on the floor in the usual place, her mind going through everything she'd done before leaving that morning. Trying to reason it through.

Perhaps she really had forgotten to leave the light on. There was a first time for everything. Maybe the smoke had come through from next door.

She'd been paranoid ever since the break-in. Jumping at shadows. This wasn't the first time she'd had the odd sense that someone had been in her apartment when logic dictated that no one could have been.

Telling herself the apartment was fine – that she was safe – she switched on her scanner, and poured herself a drink. Settling on the sofa with the baseball bat at her elbow, she sat in the glow of the lamplight, listening to the crackle and hum of the city's bad news.

Thefts, robberies, traffic stops . . .

The reassuring litany of routine police work swirled through her apartment until finally she drifted off to sleep.

An hour later, she woke as a heavy weight settled on her hip.

Groggy, she reached out and touched soft, warm fur.

'There you are,' Harper whispered, sinking back into the sofa cushions.

Zuzu's purr drowned out the scanner.

And Harper allowed herself to rest.

She was awoken early the next morning by a car honking outside her house. In her half-conscious state she thought it was her phone, and scrambled to grab it, knocking into the baseball bat, which fell over and hit the coffee table with a thud.

After that, she couldn't get back to sleep. She kept thinking about her suspicion the night before. And wondering if she was losing her mind.

It was Friday. Two days had passed since Naomi Scott was murdered and she'd been working non-stop. Maybe she was just worn out.

Still. She wanted to be certain.

She was pouring her first cup of coffee when she heard her upstairs neighbor's heels clicking on the side stairs.

Harper ran to her front door, flinging it open as the woman was passing.

About thirty years old, Mia Flores was small, with shoulder-length, dark hair and tawny skin. She glanced up in surprise as Harper hurled herself out onto the small front porch, shoeless, a coffee mug with 'FBI' on the side clutched forgotten in one hand.

'Hello?' Looking her up and down, Mia let the word hang there, as a question and a comment.

Harper both admired and feared her ability to do that.

'Hey, I'm sorry to bother you,' Harper said. 'A weird thing happened last night and I wonder if you've seen anyone suspicious hanging around my place in the last day or so?'

'Suspicious?' Mia's brow creased.

Her makeup was perfect – her dark eyes outlined with the right eye pencil. Her navy-blue jacket and short skirt suited her curvy figure.

Harper tugged at the hem of the faded Savannah Music Festival T-shirt she'd thrown on when she got out of the shower.

'Yes,' she said. 'It could be someone hanging around outside the house, or walking by too often. Anything at all.'

Mia looked concerned.

'Did someone try to break into your place again?' she asked. 'Because you should call the police.'

'I don't think so,' Harper said. 'Not yet, anyway. I'm just trying to keep an eye on things.'

Mia's expression made it clear that this hadn't made her feel any better.

'I haven't seen anyone,' she said, after a brief pause. 'But I've been busy at work, lately. I'm not sure I would have noticed.' She glanced at her watch. 'Look, I've got to go. But I've got your number. If I see anyone hanging around – you want me to call you?'

'Yes,' Harper said gratefully. 'I'd appreciate it.'

Mia began walking toward the sidewalk again. But at the last second she turned back, almost reluctantly.

'Look . . . Is everything all right?' she asked.

'It's fine.' By then, though, Harper had thought of something else. 'One more thing – do you smoke?'

Mia looked bewildered.

'No. I have asthma. Cigarettes are not my friends. Why?'

'I thought I smelled smoke last night. Must have been my imagination.' Fully aware that she must seem odd right now, if not actually unhinged, Harper forced a smile and said lightly, 'Anyway, you need to get to work. And I need to get some actual clothes on.'

'Sure . . .' With one last baffled glance, Mia headed down the sidewalk to her blue Mazda.

It occurred to Harper that normally she and Mia had a good system. Mia was gone all day, while Harper was home. Harper was out most of the night, while Mia was home.

Only lately, while working on the Naomi Scott case, she'd been out during the day more. The building was empty more of the time.

Back inside, Harper grabbed her phone up from the coffee table, walking across the polished oak floor to the kitchen.

Her landlord's voice, with its thick Louisiana accent, answered. 'Billy Dupre, here.'

'Hi, Billy. It's Harper.'

'What are you doing up so early?' he asked cheerfully. 'You sick? Somethin' wrong?'

'I'm not sick.' Putting the phone on speaker, Harper set it on the counter and poured more coffee into her mug. 'I'm working on a story.'

'Is it that River Street woman?' He grew more serious. 'Saw your piece in the paper this morning. Looks like the police are thinkin' that boyfriend did it.'

'Well,' she said, 'the jury is still out on that. But that isn't why I called. I need to ask you a favor.'

'Sure,' Billy said. 'What do you need?'

'Could you keep an eye on the apartment for me when I'm at work for the next couple of weeks? Maybe swing by now and then. Make sure it all looks all right.'

'What happened?' A new alertness entered his voice. 'You had a problem?'

Billy was shorter than Harper, and bandy-legged, perpetually in faded jeans and an old LSU baseball cap. He'd grown up dirt poor, and his upbringing had left him with a deep and abiding loyalty to those he cared about. Ever since the break-in last year, he'd been concerned about her safety. Harper knew that he took that intrusion personally.

'Something happened yesterday,' she told him. 'I have this strange feeling someone might have gotten in.'

'How'd they do that?' he asked. 'Window broken?'

'No,' she said. 'Nothing was damaged.'

91

'Anything missing?'

'Not as far as I can tell,' she admitted.

There was a pause. She could almost see him scratching his head.

'That's a funny break-in, *chère*. Nothing broken? Nothing taken? What about the alarm?'

'The alarm wasn't triggered.' She searched for a way to explain it that would make sense. 'Look, I know it sounds crazy. But something isn't right, Billy. I got the feeling someone had been in here. Things had been moved. It's probably all in my head but I want to be really careful for a while, just in case.'

'You give that code to anyone?' he asked. 'Some boyfriend?'

'No,' she said. 'No one has that code except me and Bonnie.'

'Then how'd they get in?' He sounded as confused as she felt. 'That don't make no sense.'

'I know it doesn't,' she admitted. 'Maybe someone guessed it.'

Harper's code was her mother's birthday, and the idea that anyone could have guessed that was so unlikely even she didn't believe it.

In fact, explaining it to her landlord made the whole thing seem ridiculous. Why would someone break in and not take anything? Who breaks into a house and just turns off a light?

'Actually – never mind. I'm sure it's nothing,' she said. 'But I got a weird feeling when I came home last night. I've been working too hard. It's probably all in my head.'

There was a brief silence as her landlord absorbed this change of heart.

'Tell you what,' Billy said. 'I'll swing by when you're at work – make sure nobody's hanging around, looking for trouble. I see anybody, I'll let you know.'

'Thanks, Billy,' she said gratefully. 'I'd appreciate that.'

In the background, his lawnmower started up with a roar. He shouted above it.

'But you change that alarm code, you hear? Just in case.'

Chapter Eleven

In the end, that day was so busy Harper had little time to worry about the apartment. After hanging up the phone with Billy, she was getting dressed when Miles called her cell phone.

'There's a ten-car pile-up on I-95,' he told her, cheerfully. 'Bring your dancing shoes.'

Still shoving her arms into her top, she grabbed her notebook and keys and dashed out the door so quickly she almost forgot her promise to reset the alarm code.

Swearing under her breath, she went through the steps, punching the buttons hard as she reset it to Bonnie's birthdate.

As she ran down the front steps into the steamy morning air she hoped to hell she'd remember she'd done it when she came home that night.

When she arrived on the accident scene twenty minutes later, the interstate was closed. She didn't know the highway patrol officers at all, and she had to argue her way past the one guarding the access lane.

When he got tired of looking at her press pass and listening to her complaints, he waved her on with a bored twitch of his wrist.

'Try to stay out of the way,' he grumbled, as she put the gearshift into drive.

Beyond him, I-95 was uncannily silent on the southbound side.

'Where's the wreck?' she asked.

He gestured into the hazy distance.

'Head that way. You can't miss it.'

Once she drove past him, she had the entirety of one of the nation's major arteries all to herself. Five empty lanes surrounded her. It was ghostly, and far too quiet.

She found herself driving below the speed limit – something about the emptiness made her hackles rise. Freeways are made to be busy. This was a wasteland.

She knew she was getting close to the wreck when she saw abandoned cars in the distance. Some had been left with their doors open. Beyond them, perhaps a hundred yards ahead, blue lights swirled, and a small crowd had gathered.

Three TV news trucks had already arrived, their satellite dishes raised to the sky.

She parked the Camaro behind them, and struck out on foot.

The drivers of the abandoned cars were clustered at the edge of the scene. Their faces wore the dazed, worried looks of people whose lives had intersected dramatically with that day's news.

Beyond them, blackened pieces of an unidentifiable vehicle smoldered; scattered across the interstate as if hurled there by a giant, angry child. Ambulances were parked everywhere, emergency lights spinning silently.

Harper slipped past the crowd and followed the bits of car before finding the rest of the accident, cars tangled together into a confusing, still-smoldering mass, surrounded by police and ambulances beneath the huge, late-summer sun.

Miles was right in the middle of it, standing next to Josh Leonard, the reporter from Channel 5 News. He was pointing at something next to the tangled mass.

Only when Harper reached them did she see the beer can. There was another lying nearby. And more in the distance.

'At this hour?' she said. 'It's not even eleven o'clock.'

Miles's face was somber.

'Three dead,' he told her quietly. 'Six injured. Cops think one of the drivers was drunk.'

Josh didn't make any of his usual jokes.

'It's a bloodbath,' he told her. 'They think it was a bachelor party.'

'Oh, man.' Harper pulled her phone from her pocket. 'I'll let the paper know. Where are they taking the injured?'

'I'm not sure.' Miles pointed at an ambulance nearby. 'Ask Toby.'

Looking over where he indicated, she saw paramedic Toby Jennings, his white-blond hair rumpled, his face serious as he connected an IV tube to a bag suspended above a bloodied man on a stretcher.

Harper made her way toward him.

As the stretcher was loaded onto one of the ambulances, Toby raked his fingers through his hair, and looked around for more to do.

'Hey, Toby,' Harper called, waving.

Glancing up, he gave a distracted half-smile, and lifted his hand.

'Hey,' he said, as she approached. 'You got a ticket to this show as well? I thought this place was supposed to be exclusive.'

'The bouncer knows me,' she said.

He gave her a quick hug.

Hugging was new for them. Ever since he'd been the paramedic on call the night she was shot he'd 'taken a new interest in your survival', as he liked to put it.

'How's it going?' Harper asked.

'Oh, you know . . .' He looked back as he spoke, assessing the remaining two victims, who were both surrounded by other paramedics. 'Another day, another disaster. Keeps the bills paid.'

Harper lowered her voice. 'Is it true one of the drivers had been drinking?'

His condemning nod said everything.

'They were driving back from Jacksonville after an all-night stag party,' he said. 'I'm told the groom was in a different car, that didn't wreck, which makes him one lucky son of a bitch, because nobody walked out of this in good shape.'

Harper shook her head. 'When will people learn?'

'Never, is what I'm thinking,' Toby said. He gestured at her shoulder. 'What about you? Still predicting the weather with that thing?'

Harper's hand rose toward her scar. 'It's good. Only hurts when I tell a lie.'

He grinned. 'Well that's going to be a nightmare for you at the paper. I mean, all you journalists do is make things up, or so I'm told.'

She kicked him lightly, and he grabbed his shin.

'Toby!' The voice came from one of the ambulances. 'Load up.'

Toby gave her an apologetic smile. 'Duty calls.'

'Oh hey,' she said, as he headed to join the others. 'Where are you taking them?'

'Savannah Memorial.' He jumped into the back of the nearest ambulance and turned to face her. 'Come over! We've got cake.'

By the time she'd gathered enough information from the scene, and then driven to the hospital and back to the newsroom to write up her story, it was afternoon and she hadn't had a chance even to think about the Scott case.

She had just hit 'send' on her piece when DJ spun his chair around and rolled himself closer to her desk.

'How do you always know when I'm finishing something?' she asked him suspiciously.

'Intuition.' He tapped his forehead. 'I saw you guys caught yourselves a live one. Baxter said it was a slaughterhouse out there.'

'Yeah,' she said. 'If you were thinking of driving down to Florida this afternoon, I'd put it off until tomorrow.'

'I'll bear that in mind . . .'

'Harper.' Emma Baxter stormed across the newsroom towards them.

DJ flinched.

'Why does she *do* that?' he whispered, returning hurriedly to his own desk.

'I got the pictures from the crash scene,' Baxter said. 'Our front page is ninety percent death thanks to you.'

'Any time,' Harper said.

'What's the latest on Wilson Shepherd? They charge him yet?'

Harper shook her head. 'All the press flack will say is, "No comment at this time".'

Baxter glared. 'What the hell is taking so long?'

'Good question.'

Remembering what Blazer had let slip last night, Harper leaned forward.

'I heard a rumor the gun he had on him when they arrested him wasn't the murder weapon. If they had other forensic evidence connecting him to the crime, they'd have charged him this morning. But they didn't do that, either.'

Baxter held her gaze as the pieces fell into place.

'Shit,' she said. 'They've got the wrong guy.'

Harper held up a cautioning hand.

'Maybe. Or maybe they messed up the evidence collection. Or maybe it's something else.'

Baxter tapped a short, blunt fingernail against the edge of Harper's desk, thinking it through.

'They've already held him more than twenty-four hours, so they must have applied for an extension, but if they haven't got evidence, they'll have to let him go soon,' she mused. 'Then we go back to the possibility that this was a random murder.'

'That's true. But the only person who thinks Shepherd's innocent is Naomi's dad,' Harper reminded her.

'Oh yeah?' Baxter said. 'What's his theory, then?'

With no new information, Harper had kept Jerrod's theories to herself until now. But if Wilson wasn't the shooter, she decided it was time to share.

'He says Naomi had a thing with some other guy at law school. Said she acted like she was scared of him. But you're not going to like who it is.'

Baxter's brows drew together.

'What do you mean I'm not going to like it? Who is it?'

'He says it's Randall Anderson's son, Peyton.'

Baxter gave her a look of fierce disbelief. 'You've got to be kidding.'

'Look, I know what you're thinking. But I'm wondering if Anderson wasn't involved in some way,' Harper said. 'Maybe Naomi cheated on Shepherd with Anderson, and Shepherd wanted revenge. Or maybe Anderson liked her and she didn't like him back and it all got ugly.'

'Oh terrific,' the editor groused. 'I'll hand in my notice now before Anderson sues us and shuts us down completely.'

'I'll do this quietly,' Harper promised. 'But I think I have to make some calls.'

As she spoke, Harper's cell phone began to ring.

Baxter talked over it.

'I'll talk to Dells, but bear this in mind, McClain. Randall Anderson loves a lawsuit. If you piss him off, I can't save you,' she said. 'No one can.'

She stormed back to her desk as Harper picked up her phone. Bonnie's name was on the screen.

'Hey, Bonnie,' she said absently, eyes fixed on Baxter's receding figure. The editor had walked past her own desk and was now knocking on Dells's office door.

'Harper. Can you talk?'

Bonnie sounded serious – her voice was low, as if she didn't want to be overheard.

'Always,' Harper said. 'What's wrong?'

'Fitz asked all the staff to come to The Library for a meeting,' Bonnie whispered. 'I'm there now. He says there's going to be a wake at the bar, tonight, for Naomi. I thought you'd want to come.'

'Absolutely. What time?'

'Eight o'clock,' Bonnie said.

Harper heard raised voices in the background. It sounded ugly.

'Is something wrong?' she asked. 'What's going on over there?'

'The police are here, talking to Fitz. They're asking him a lot of questions and he's losing it.' Bonnie's voice grew so low she had to struggle to hear her.

'Harper, it's so weird. It's almost like they think he had something to do with the murder.'

Chapter Twelve

That night at eight, Harper and DJ sat in a dark corner of The Library, waiting for the wake to start.

When he'd heard where she was going, DJ had insisted on accompanying her, even though his shift at the paper was over.

'You need two sets of eyes at these things,' he'd said. 'Plus, there'll be beer.'

Outside, Miles was positioned in a discreet spot, taking pictures of people as they entered.

A poster-sized photograph of Naomi Scott beamed at them from the bar. It was a beautiful picture – the sun had tipped her dark hair with bronze, and the straps of her floaty white dress contrasted strikingly with the warm brown of her skin. A smile lit up her face.

A face to kill for, Harper thought, as she scanned the growing crowd.

A cluster of TV reporters were gathered inside the door – their makeup and buoyant hair seemed out of place in a dive bar that tended to be populated by art students.

Anyway, the bar had banned all cameras – so they could only watch. Harper could sense their frustration all the way across the room.

Behind the bar, half hidden by the picture of Naomi, Bonnie and Fitz were pouring drinks. Bonnie had pulled her blue-streaked blond hair back, and she wore a simple black shift dress. Her normally sunny expression was serious.

Fitz had combed his shaggy hair and put on a natty dark suit. He looked like himself again, except that his face was puffy and sagging, broken veins prominent on his cheeks.

Shielded by the crowd, she studied him curiously.

In her call, Bonnie told her that, when the police arrived, the staff watched as they took Fitz into one of the back rooms at the bar for questioning.

A few minutes later the yelling started. Most of it done by Fitz.

Bonnie overheard enough to know that they'd asked him where he was the night of the murder. When he said he'd been home alone, one of them had suggested he might want to get a lawyer.

'They asked him to go to the station with them. Fitz lost it,' Bonnie said. 'Told them to get the hell out of his bar and come back when they had a warrant. After that, he started drinking and ranting about how the police didn't know what they were doing. But, if you ask me, he looked scared.'

Despite this, the police had remained silent about their investigation into Wilson Shepherd. They hadn't charged him or said a word about where the case was headed.

Harper had spent the rest of the afternoon trying to get someone to tell her what was going on. But everyone involved was tight-lipped.

Turning in her chair, she searched the crowd. Most were around Naomi's age – their earnest young faces sober and stunned.

'Who are you looking for?' DJ asked, sipping his beer.

'I'm checking out who's here,' she said. 'I don't see Naomi's father.'

As she scanned the room, her gaze rested on a table near the door, where Luke sat with Detective Daltrey and Lieutenant Blazer. Daltrey seemed to be having an animated but hushed conversation with Blazer. Harper couldn't make out what they were saying, but Daltrey said something angrily and then Blazer cut her off with a quick sweep of his hand, which Harper interpreted as meaning 'Not here'.

Luke, his eyes fixed on his glass, was staying out of it.

'Who are those guys?' DJ asked, following her gaze. 'They look like cops.'

'That's because they are cops,' Harper replied. 'Detectives, to be precise.'

'That is so cool.' Pushing his glasses back into place, he peered at them. 'It's a shame they look so normal. I always hope they'll look more like actors. Instead of just . . . people.'

The place was filling quickly – guests stood at the bar and crowded in the doorway.

The bar was lit by flickering candles – they'd been placed on every table and on the bookshelves that lined the walls. The combination of crowds and candles overwhelmed the air-conditioning – the bar felt hot and airless.

As she turned back, Harper's gaze lighted on a man leaning with his back against the bar. Something about him was familiar. He was young, and more formally dressed than most of the crowd in dark slacks and a blazer, a tie knotted at his throat. He had dark blond hair with a prep-school cut.

It came to her in a rush.

It was Peyton Anderson.

'What's he doing here?' she murmured.

'Who?' DJ asked, following her gaze.

Harper only half heard the question.

'Stay here,' she told him, getting to her feet. 'Keep an eye out.'

'For what?'

'Anything.'

Harper strolled to the bar, positioning herself next to Anderson. She pretended to wait for Bonnie to notice her.

She saw Anderson turn his wrist and glance at an expensive-looking watch.

'Guess they're running late,' she said, catching his eye.

He started, as if he hadn't expected to be addressed.

His eyes skated across her face. She knew what he'd see – someone only a few years older than Naomi had been, neatly dressed in dark clothes. Before coming in, she'd brushed the tangles out of her auburn hair and fixed her makeup.

'It's normal, I suppose,' he said politely. 'No one can blame them for losing track of time. Under the circumstances.'

He had the smooth, patrician accent of the Savannah upper class. It poured honey over each sentence and gave even single-syllable words a complexity and length they didn't ordinarily have.

Abandoning the pretense of waiting for a drink, Harper turned to face him.

'Were you a friend of Naomi's?' She kept her voice appropriately hushed and sympathetic.

'We went to law school together,' he said. He looked at her as if trying to place her. 'Did you know her from school?'

'No. I knew her through The Library,' she explained. 'My friend is a bartender here.'

'Ah, Bonnie,' he said, glancing over to where Bonnie was pouring wine into glasses. His eyes lingered on her figure. 'Naomi liked her.'

'I didn't know Naomi well,' Harper said, drawing his attention back to her. 'But she seemed so talented and full of life. It's hard to believe this could happen.'

'It's simply awful,' he said, shaking his head. 'I worry about our city. The crime is out of control.'

Interrupting himself, he held out his hand. 'I'm sorry, I should introduce myself. I'm Peyton Anderson. I didn't catch your name.'

Harper hesitated. She hadn't thought he'd ask who she was. She couldn't give a fake name – too many people here knew her. There wasn't time to come up with a plan for avoiding the question.

'I'm Harper.' She shook his hand. His fingers were cool and smooth.

He had a good grip, but he held her hand too long.

'Harper. What an unusual name.' He studied her with flattering interest, as if she were the only person in the room. 'It sounds familiar. Are you sure we haven't met?'

'I'm positive.' Politely extricating her hand from his, she changed the subject. 'So . . . Were you and Naomi close?'

There was a brief but noticeable pause before he replied.

'If I'm honest, we were more than friends, at times. We went out before she met her current boyfriend.' He leaned closer, confidingly. 'I suppose you've read that he's been arrested?'

'Yes, I heard,' she said. 'Do you know the boyfriend? Oh, now, what's his name?' She pretended to think. 'Wilson Shepherd, right?'

'Yeah, we've met.' His tone cooled. 'I never thought he was capable of something like this. It's frightening if you think about it. He seemed like a nice guy. Not all that bright, maybe. But not a killer.' He turned to look at the picture of Naomi propped up at the center of the bar, eyes lingering on her face. 'I can't believe he'd hurt her. She was so beautiful.'

This wasn't what Harper had expected. The way Jerrod had described Peyton's relationship with his daughter, it would seem that he should be at least somewhat uncomfortable at her wake, but he didn't give any indication of that. Instead, he appeared confident and relaxed.

She wasn't sure what to make of him, and she didn't have time to think it through. There was a commotion as people packed in the bar's doorway moved aside, and a moment later Jerrod Scott entered the bar, accompanied by a protective cluster of family and friends.

Across the room, Harper saw Daltrey and Blazer watching Scott attentively. Luke, though, wasn't looking at him. He was looking at her and Anderson.

Their eyes met across the room. His expression was inscrutable. He could have been thinking anything. Or nothing.

Then Daltrey said something to him and he turned away to listen.

She had to force herself to keep her attention on Anderson.

'I feel so sorry for her father,' he was saying. 'I know they were close.'

Harper thought of what Naomi had told her dad – that he wasn't to speak to Peyton under any circumstances. And wondered what the hell all of this meant.

But Jerrod was almost to the front of the room now, and there was no time to pursue it further.

'Looks like things are about to start,' Peyton said, turning to her with those penetrating eyes that seemed to see more than she would have liked. 'I'm going to take a seat. It was a pleasure talking to you, Harper. I'm sure we'll meet again.'

The service was emotional. Jerrod and some of Naomi's friends spoke about her beauty and lost potential. A preacher led everyone in prayers for her and the city: 'Which on days like today can seem to be losing its soul.' A choir from Naomi's church sang her favorite songs. People cried.

As soon as it ended, Harper was out of her seat, fighting through the crowd. She needed to talk to Jerrod Scott and find out if he'd spoken to Shepherd. But she couldn't immediately find him.

When she did locate him, he was near the door, talking to Blazer, their heads close together.

She dropped back to the bar, waiting for them to finish. The next time she looked, though, she couldn't see either of them.

With a sigh of irritation, she started her search again. The small, packed bar wasn't getting any less crowded. Most people were staying, keeping Fitz and Bonnie busy mixing drinks.

Finding a spot near the bar with a good view of the room, Harper waited for people to leave. It was only ten o'clock. She still had time before her midnight deadline.

Along with Jerrod, she needed to talk with Fitz. If the police were looking at him for Naomi's murder, she had to find out why. And there was no way the cops were going to tell her.

The crowd parted and she spotted Luke and Detective Daltrey standing at the edge of the room, observing the crowd, much as she was.

Harper noticed Fitz glance at them from time to time and then look away quickly, his lip curling, as if he wanted them gone.

DJ strode up to her, holding a full glass of beer.

'I love wakes,' he announced. 'The booze is half-price and they say there's going to be food later.'

'Why don't you go see if you can get some quotes first?' Harper suggested, tilting her head to where the choir had clustered near the jukebox. 'Start with them. Find out if Naomi was in the choir. Were any of them her friends?'

Most of the singers were young women and she saw DJ's face brighten.

'You got it.' He hustled over to them obediently.

While he ingratiated himself with the singers, Harper made her way to the bar, waving to catch Bonnie's eye.

'Well, that was depressing,' Bonnie said, as she mixed a vodka and soda.

She forced a light tone, but Harper didn't miss the fact that her mascara was smeared and her nose was red.

'Yes, it was,' Harper said, glancing down the bar at The Library's owner. His face was set in deep, sad lines as he measured wine into glasses. His hands were unsteady.

'How's Fitz?' she asked quietly.

Bonnie glanced at her boss before answering.

'Not great,' she said. 'He's hardly spoken since the cops left today. He drank all the way through the ceremony.'

'Did you find out any more about why the police came for him?' Harper asked. 'Did Naomi complain about him?'

Motioning for her to wait, Bonnie handed a drink to a man further down the bar. When she returned to Harper she leaned close.

'Not Naomi,' she said. 'Someone else.'

'Someone else complained?' For some reason, Harper hadn't expected this. 'Who?'

'Two years ago.' Bonnie glanced back at her boss to make sure he couldn't overhear. 'We had a bartender – beautiful girl. She only lasted a few months. Fitz had a thing for her. She didn't like being alone with him. After she quit, he went to her house drunk, late at night, pounding on her door. She called the cops.'

Harper didn't know what to make of this new information. It didn't sound like Fitz. He was an amiable, laidback guy. He seemed to get along with everyone.

'Did you believe her?'

Bonnie hesitated before replying.

'His wife had left him.' She held up her hands, as if that statement explained everything.

'Oh for God's sake,' Harper said. 'What is wrong with men?'

'Amen to that, sister.'

'I need to have a word with him,' Harper said. 'Just in case he'll tell me anything about what's going on. Do you think now's a bad time?'

Bonnie's shrug was eloquent. 'I don't think there's ever going to be a good time for that conversation.'

'I'll make it fast.'

Harper waited for a lull at the bar, then headed over to where the owner was now stacking glasses.

'Hi, Fitz,' she said. 'Beautiful ceremony.'

His eyes on the crowd, he barely glanced at her. Hands mechanically cleaning the already clean bar.

'It was,' he said.

'Bonnie told me the cops were hassling you today. What's that about?'

He blinked at her blearily. It was obvious that he was drunk. His eyes were unfocused.

'They've already got somebody and now they want to blame

me, too.' Bewildered, he turned to the photo of Naomi still resting on the bar. 'I treated her like a daughter. The way I treat all my girls.' He gestured at Bonnie, who was absorbing herself in cleaning the bar. 'I wouldn't ever hurt her. You believe me, don't you?'

'Of course I do,' Harper assured him. 'But why? Why are they targeting you? Did something happen between you and Naomi?'

He held up his hands, a cleaning rag flopping from one.

'They said they wanted to check everything out. Be sure. But they already have someone in jail for it. Why'd they think I'd hurt her? I don't understand. I never hurt anyone, Harper. Never hurt anyone.'

He was too drunk and morose for her to question further – even about the case Bonnie had mentioned. She needed to catch him sober.

'OK, Fitz,' she said, stepping back. 'You hang in there.'

She left him shaking his head and mumbling to himself.

The room was getting louder. Harper got the feeling some were there for the wake and others were regular drinkers who'd stumbled in.

Across the room, DJ was chatting with the choir, who'd surrounded him like birds around a feeder.

Harper was scanning the crowd for Jerrod or Blazer when her phone vibrated in her pocket.

It was Miles.

'Hey,' she said, lifting it to her ear. 'What's up?'

'I just pulled up at the police station,' he said. 'Get down here. They're letting Wilson Shepherd go.'

Chapter Thirteen

Clutching her phone in her hand, Harper raced across the barroom to where Daltrey and Luke had been standing minutes ago. But they were no longer there.

She stood on her toes, trying to see above the crowd, but there were too many people. Grabbing a chair, she climbed on top of it, surveying the room.

All the detectives were gone.

Hopping down, she pushed her way through the crowds to DJ, who was regaling the choir with reporting stories.

She grabbed his arm without warning.

'Here's my assistant,' he announced.

'We need to go,' she urged, her voice tight.

'She's so demanding,' DJ told the choir, waving goodbye as Harper pulled him across the bar by his sleeve.

'What's going on?' he asked as they rushed out into the dark street. 'It better be good – I think I was about to get a date with five cute Christian girls.'

'The cops are letting Wilson Shepherd go,' she explained

without slowing her pace. 'That means they don't have enough evidence to charge him. The whole case is up in the air and there's two hours until deadline.'

'Day-um,' he said. 'Where are we going now?'

'I need to find the detectives. They just left.'

She stopped outside the door, looking up and down the short lane. But it was empty.

This must have been what Blazer was telling Jerrod Scott when she saw them. The two of them had probably left then. The other detectives, though, had only just gone, because she'd seen them minutes ago.

'They must have gone to the station,' she said.

She ran to the Camaro, which she'd parked a block down from the bar, glancing back to see DJ hurrying after her.

'I have to go find them,' she said. 'Do you want to come with me or stay with your choir girls?'

'Are you kidding?' He opened the passenger door. 'This is the most exciting thing that's happened to me since I lost my virginity.'

'Well, buckle up.' Harper gunned the engine and slammed it into gear, pulling out from the curb with her tires squealing.

Grinning broadly, DJ clutched the handle above the door. He had to raise his voice to be heard above the roar of the engine.

'This is *exactly* what I thought your beat was like.'

They tore across the city taking every shortcut Harper knew, pulling up in front of police headquarters eight minutes later with a screech of brakes. Leaving the car in a well-indicated fire zone, Harper jumped out and ran to where Miles stood by the front door, his camera in one hand.

'Has he come out?' Harper asked. 'I got here as fast as I could.'

'Not yet,' Miles told her.

'Hi, Miles.' DJ walked up to join them.

'DJ.' Miles gave him a bemused look. 'Nice to have you join our merry crew.'

'I'm only here because badges turn me on,' DJ explained.

'Have Daltrey or Walker come in?' Harper asked. 'I lost them at the bar.'

'No, but Lieutenant Blazer came through here fifteen minutes ago, looking like he was ready to kill someone with his bare hands.' Miles paused, looking through the glass door into the station. 'Hold on. We've got action.'

Stepping to one side, he raised his camera.

On the other side of the thick, smudged glass, Harper could see a small crowd gathering. Wilson Shepherd was in the middle. A cluster of police officers moved around him, going through the official steps of release.

A black Ford pulled into the lot and stopped behind Harper's Camaro.

Looking over her shoulder, Harper saw Luke and Detective Daltrey get out of the car. They'd just begun to walk toward her when the station's doors swung open and Shepherd stepped out, flanked on either side by uniformed officers.

The last few days seemed to have diminished him. He looked small and exhausted.

As Miles moved in to get his shot, Shepherd stared at him blankly.

Harper stepped into his eyeline. 'Wilson.'

His head swung towards her. The skin on his round face looked gray, and he had several days' growth of whiskers.

'Wilson, did you hurt Naomi?' she called. 'Are you the killer?'

His face crumpling, Shepherd turned as if to run back inside the station, but the two cops grabbed him.

'This way,' one of them said, pulling him to the left.

Until then, Harper hadn't noticed the taxi parked on Habersham Street, behind the shielding branches of an oleander bush.

With the two officers half-helping half-dragging him, Shepherd stumbled to the car. Harper, Miles, and DJ followed.

'I swear I didn't hurt anyone,' Shepherd said, in belated response to Harper's question. 'I swear.'

Before he could say more, the cops maneuvered him into the back seat and shut the door behind him. The taxi sped away right as a Channel 5 van tore into the parking lot.

'Too late,' DJ noted with pleasure.

Leaving him with Miles, Harper walked over to where Luke and Daltrey stood beside their car.

She kept her focus on Daltrey.

'Why are you letting Wilson Shepherd go?'

'We have no comment at this time,' Daltrey said.

'Is he on bail?' Harper persisted. 'Or has he been released due to lack of evidence? Did you arrest the wrong man?'

Daltrey fixed her with a hard stare. Luke avoided her gaze.

Harper held up her hands. 'Come on, guys. I've spent twenty-four hours assuring the taxpayers of Savannah that the killer was in custody. Now you let him go. Give me something here. Are you still sure he's your guy?'

'McClain, I know you're doing your job but I need you to tread lightly right now,' Daltrey warned her.

'What does that mean, exactly?' Harper was exasperated. 'I can't not report that Shepherd's been released. And when I tell my editor this, she's going to want to know why.'

Daltrey stepped toward her; she was shorter than Harper but when she was angry she seemed much taller.

'You were at that service, McClain. You saw how destroyed that girl's father is. I want to solve this case. I intend to do justice by Naomi Scott.' Her eyes flashed. 'I need you to stay out of my way.'

Harper bit back a harsh reply.

Forcing a measured tone, she said, 'That is what I want, too.'

She looked at Luke, whose lips were pressed in a tight line. 'But you have to give me something to work with here. And Channel 5 is heading this way, so they're going to ask the same question. Do you still think Shepherd's the killer? Tell me what you think, and I can take it from there.'

Turning to Daltrey, Luke said, 'I think you should talk to her.'

Daltrey glared at him, but he held his ground.

'You know I'm right.'

After a long, icy pause, Daltrey turned back to Harper.

'On the record: Shepherd has been released without charge while the investigation continues.' She paused for a long, tense moment before continuing in a quiet voice: 'Off the record: We haven't got the physical evidence we need to charge him with the killing. But I still believe he's our guy. We're going to take it slow and steady and bring him back in.'

At his van, Channel 5 reporter Josh Leonard was draping microphone cable across his shoulder, and tucking a camera under his arm. He kept glancing at them urgently.

'What about Jim Fitzgerald, though?' Harper asked. 'I understand you questioned him today.'

Luke and Daltrey exchanged an incredulous look.

'How the hell do you know about that?' Luke asked. 'We haven't even written up our report yet.'

'It's my job,' Harper said.

'Unbelievable.' Daltrey leaned back against the car, her arms folded. 'Look, McClain, we're going through the criminal history of everyone close to the victim. Fitzgerald's name came up because of allegations filed against him two years ago. And all of that is one hundred percent off the record.'

'You don't really think Fitz would do it, do you?'

Neither of them responded but the look Daltrey gave her said she thought anything was possible.

Leonard slammed the Channel 5 van door and began running toward them, laden with equipment. He looked uncharacteristically flustered.

Harper thought about her conversation with Peyton Anderson at the bar. His odd, flirtatious intensity.

'What about the Anderson kid?' she asked. 'Did you look into him? Jerrod Scott said Naomi had a problem with him.'

'And that's my cue.' Daltrey lifted herself off the car and headed for the station. After a second's hesitation, Luke followed.

'What?' Harper stood behind them. 'You won't even talk about it?'

Josh was only a few feet away now.

'You want to take on the Anderson family? Knock yourself out,' Daltrey told her without breaking stride. 'I don't need that kind of heat. I know who my killer is.'

Josh skidded to a stop in front of Harper. Despite his rush, his blow-dried hair was perfect.

'Dammit,' he said, looking at the detectives' receding backs. 'What'd I miss?'

'Not much.' Harper patted him on the shoulder and turned back to her car. 'It's been a quiet night.'

Chapter Fourteen

The next day Harper woke at noon and her first thought was about Wilson Shepherd.

She kept thinking about how he'd looked. Jail takes life out of almost everyone. But some people get it worse than others. It's hard to tell the difference between a guilty man, racked by conscience, and an innocent man, destroyed by being falsely accused. Wilson could have been either.

One thing was certain, she needed to talk to him. And she knew who could reach him.

As soon as she'd showered and made the coffee, she called Jerrod Scott.

He answered on the first ring.

'Miss McClain.' His deep, steady voice was somehow comforting. 'I was thinking I might hear from you.'

'I guess you know they let Wilson Shepherd go,' Harper said.

'I do.' Scott didn't sound unhappy. 'I think it's the first right thing the police have done since Naomi died.'

'You still don't think he did it?' Harper asked.

She was in her kitchen, sitting on a wooden chair, bare feet resting on the chair across from her, laptop open in front of her.

'I do not believe for an instant that Wilson is the man the police are looking for.' Scott spoke with quiet dignity. 'I talked with him last night, and he is a broken man, Miss McClain. The police must leave him alone and find the true murderer.'

Harper was surprised he'd already talked to Shepherd. But then a hazy fact she'd known and forgotten swam into view.

Scott drove a cab for a living.

She thought of the taxi, hidden behind the oleander bush.

'Mr Scott,' she said, 'was it you who picked up Wilson Shepherd at the police station last night?'

'He didn't have anyone else willing to help,' Scott told her. 'Naomi wouldn't want me to abandon him in his time of need.'

Harper was speechless. Scott had left his own daughter's wake and gone to pick up the man the police believed had killed her to drive him home.

His absolute faith in Wilson's innocence was extraordinary. In her entire career, she couldn't remember another case like this one.

But statistics told her, whatever Jerrod believed, his daughter's boyfriend was still the most likely suspect. And if she could talk to him she'd have the scoop of the year.

'Mr Scott, I want to help Wilson if I can,' she said. 'Is there any way you could put me in touch with him? I'd like to hear his side of the story.'

There was a long silence.

'I don't know,' he said finally. 'I'll talk to Wilson, see what he thinks. It's not up to me, Miss McClain. He's got to make up his own mind.'

'I understand,' Harper said. 'But time is very important. If I can help him, I'll need to talk to him soon. Please let him know that.'

When they'd hung up, Harper walked across the kitchen to pour herself a cup of coffee.

She looked out the tall windows into the back garden. It was another brutally sunny day.

The back garden needed tending – the grass was getting high. She should let Billy know.

Her neighbor's bougainvillea poured flowers over the fence in a vivid magenta cascade.

She was staring at the yard and thinking about Wilson when something shifted in the shadows.

Leaning forward, Harper squinted, shielding her eyes from the bright sun. She could have sworn she saw someone standing very still at the corner of the house next door.

It didn't look like Mrs Watson, the old lady who lived there with her little dog. This person looked much taller and thinner. A man, she thought. But she couldn't quite make out his features from here – he was at the very fringe of her sight line.

Before she could get a good look, her phone began to ring.

Instinctively, she glanced at it.

When she looked back, the shadow had gone.

Her phone rang insistently. She ran across the kitchen to grab it, pushing the answer button without looking at the screen.

'McClain,' she said, hurrying back to the window.

'Harper.' Luke's familiar voice stopped her in her tracks. He hadn't called in so long.

She forgot all about the shadow.

'Luke?' She hated how hopeful she sounded. 'What's up?'

'Can we meet? I need to talk to you about Wilson Shepherd.'

*

It was after midnight when Harper drove to The Library that night.

She and Luke had agreed to meet after work – both their shifts ended at the same time.

After hanging up the phone, Harper had torn through her closet looking for something to wear. Finally, in a panic, she called Bonnie for advice. What *do* you wear to meet your ex-boyfriend – the one you never got over – to talk about a murder you're both investigating?

In the end, they'd chosen a sleeveless black top that made the most of her figure and her fair coloring. Instead of running out of the office when her work was done, she'd gone to the ladies room and taken time, brushing the frizz out of her auburn hair, and (for once) paying attention to her makeup.

It must have worked because Junior, the bar's amiable, 300-pound bouncer, nearly popped his uneven teeth when he saw her.

'Marry me, Harper McClain,' he pleaded. 'I know I can make you happy.'

'I'm married to my job, Junior,' she told him breezily.

'Someday you'll see what a catch I am,' he said.

Ignoring that, Harper gestured at the mostly empty bar behind him. 'How's it going?'

'Well, let's just say it's a good thing you're here.' His amiable face grew serious. 'It's too quiet.'

'Things are that bad?' she asked, surprised.

'Terrible.' As she headed inside, he lowered himself onto the stool propped against the doorjamb. 'This keeps up, they won't need me, anymore.'

In the bar, Johnny Cash was singing from the jukebox and nobody was dancing.

Harper glanced around in dismay. It was Saturday night – the place should be packed. Most of the tables were empty.

Bonnie waved at her from behind the bar.

'You look *devastating*,' she said, as she walked up. 'I knew I was right about that outfit.'

Without asking what she wanted, she slid a bottle of cold Becks across the bar.

Catching it, Harper gestured at the mostly empty bar.

'Where is everyone?'

Bonnie's smile faded.

'I guess nobody wants to hang out at the death bar. Who would think art students could be so picky?'

Turning, Harper scanned the thin crowd of bearded hipsters, aspiring musicians, and artists for any sign of Luke.

'Is he here?' Bonnie asked, guessing what she was doing. 'I've been keeping an eye out but nobody I've seen looks like a hot detective.'

'No.'

Harper tried to look like she wasn't worried, even though her insides were spinning.

'He'll get here.'

'This is so *romantic*,' Bonnie sighed.

'It's work,' Harper reminded her. 'He only wants to talk about a case.'

'Sure he does.'

Bonnie didn't sound convinced. Leaning her elbows on the scarred wood of the bar, she looked at her sympathetically.

'How're you doing? Are you ready for this?'

'Honestly, it's not a big deal,' Harper insisted. 'We're only going to talk. It's not like I want to get back together with him. I just need his help.'

'I know, babe.' Bonnie's expression said she didn't believe a word.

'I'm serious . . .' Harper began, but Bonnie was looking at something over her shoulder.

'Don't look now' – she tilted her chin at the door – 'a super-hot cowboy just walked into my bar, and we don't get many of those in here.'

Harper turned to see Luke striding across the concrete floor. In jeans, boots, and a white, button-down shirt, he was as out of place in the arty bar as a cocktail at a prayer breakfast.

Her heart stuttered.

When he reached her his face was carefully blank.

'I can't believe this place,' he murmured quietly, by way of hello. 'I've never felt more like a cop.'

'I like it,' she insisted. 'I'm very into books.'

He shot her an amused look.

Bonnie watched them with undisguised fascination. If Harper didn't introduce them soon, she'd explode.

'Luke, this is my friend Bonnie. Bonnie, this is Luke Walker.'

Luke held out his hand politely. 'I think we met the other day.'

Beaming at him, Bonnie reached across the bar.

'I've heard so much about you,' she said. 'I didn't realize you were Harper's Luke.'

His smile didn't flicker.

'Can I get you a drink?' Bonnie gestured at the bottles behind her.

Luke glanced at Harper's beer.

'I'll have one of those,' he said, pulling his wallet from his back pocket.

'You got it.' Bonnie pulled two from the fridge.

'Oh, by the way,' she said, setting the bottle on the counter and reaching for the opener, 'If you two want to talk privately, there's no one in the Poetry room.'

Luke's eyebrows rose a little higher.

'The Poetry room?' he said as Harper led him across the bar a few minutes later.

'There are three side rooms,' she explained, pointing out the arched doorways that edged the main bar. 'Poetry, Prose, and Pool.'

Exuding quiet condemnation, Luke followed her into a narrow room dimly lit by a few battered lamps.

The walls were black. Phrases of poetry were painted in white on them – the words surrounded them.

The lights were dim in here. It was, as Bonnie knew perfectly, also known as the make-out room.

Three fake-leather sofas had been arranged around a low table. Harper dropped onto one and stretched out, propping her feet on the coffee table as she took a swig of beer.

Luke's gaze slipped across her legs, clad in snug-fitting black leggings.

'You look good, Harper,' he said.

It took all she had to keep her expression steady.

'Thanks,' she said. 'You, too.'

It was true. His deep blue eyes were clear. The summer sun had given his straight brown hair a golden sheen. The shadows that had underscored his eyes during the days when he worked undercover had gone.

Sitting on the sofa across from her, he set his beer on the sticky table.

Harper watched his every move hungrily. She'd dreamed of this moment so many times. Now that it was happening, she didn't know what to say.

'How's work?' she asked. 'You and Blazer tried to kill each other yet?'

The lieutenant and Luke had a long, contentious history. Luke had once left the detective squad solely to get away from him.

'Not yet,' he said dryly. 'Blazer seems to be trying to put the past behind him. With Smith gone, he wants to be a real boss.' He gave a slight shrug. 'We're grown-ups after all, apparently.'

He hadn't shaved. A faint shadow of whiskers dusted his jaw. Harper knew how they would feel against her skin, and now she had to get that memory out of her head as quickly as possible.

'You said you wanted to talk about Wilson Shepherd?'

'Yeah.' He studied her face. 'You don't think he did it, do you?'

'I wouldn't say I don't think he did it,' she said, after a beat. 'But I doubt it.'

'Me too.' He leaned forward, resting his hands between his knees. 'I wasn't sure at the start. He sure as hell looked guilty the night we took him in. There were rumors of problems in that relationship. It all made sense. I thought it was a done deal.'

'But then?'

'Then the gun didn't match. And the motive was fishy.' He turned his hands over. 'He doesn't fit the type at all. Looks to me like, yeah, he and the victim were having a tough time. Maybe taking a breather. He wasn't happy about it. But they weren't fighting like that. There's no evidence he ever threatened her, as far as we can tell. Basically, my warning lights started flashing. It doesn't feel right.'

'Breakups are strong motives all on their own,' she reminded him. 'Nice-guy killers are a thing.'

'I know that. But if it was him, he planned it in pure isolation.

Telling no one. Sending her no emails or threatening texts. Fooling her father completely.'

'Not likely,' Harper agreed. 'But not impossible, if he's smart.'

'Yeah.' He sighed. 'He's smart. But I'm not feeling it.'

He tilted the bottle over in his hands, examining the label as if it held the answers he sought.

It had been a long time since he was this candid with her about a case. Something was definitely bothering him.

'What does Daltrey think?'

'She thinks it's usually the boyfriend, why should this one be different?' He glanced up at her. 'But she knows it's not right. She's a good detective. She can feel this, too.'

In the other room, Johnny Cash segued to Nine Inch Nails. But the volume was muffled in here.

'OK.' She straightened. 'Let's do this. If it's not Shepherd, who do we have? Fitz?'

When she said The Library owner's name, she lowered her voice. She knew he wasn't in tonight – Bonnie had assured her he wouldn't be – but it felt wrong talking about him in his own bar.

Luke looked doubtful.

'Maybe,' he said. 'That case a few years ago was a young woman very much like Naomi, and his behavior was worrying. She was scared of him.'

'He wasn't ever charged,' Harper pointed out.

'She dropped the charges,' he told her. 'But she got an injunction.'

'He never violated it?' Harper guessed.

Luke shook his head.

'Bonnie said his wife left him that year, and he was drinking too much,' she pointed out. 'Could have been an aberration.'

'He still drinks too much, far as I can tell,' Luke said, lifting his own beer.

'But murder?' Harper didn't disguise her doubt. 'Naomi never said a word about Fitz bothering her. Bonnie never saw anything. And, I mean . . .' She gestured back at the bar. 'You've seen Bonnie. She's sex on a plate. Fitz never messes with her.'

'I hear you,' he said, clearly unconvinced. 'But that could just mean he doesn't go for blondes.'

'But it's *unlikely*,' she said, repeating the word he'd used earlier about Shepherd. 'And anyway. You've got no evidence.'

He smiled, conceding the point and tilted his empty bottle at her.

'Your round.'

Taking his bottle, Harper grabbed her wallet and walked from the room, conscious he was watching her.

This whole night was confusing. Was this his way of saying he forgave her? Or was he really worried about the case?

He was impossible to read. His time spent working undercover had made him permanently enigmatic.

When she approached the bar, Bonnie hurried over to her.

'How's it going?' she hissed, as if Luke might hear them from the other room.

'Fine,' Harper said. 'Weird as hell. But fine.'

She handed the empty bottles to Bonnie, who got two more out of the refrigerator without asking.

'Weird how?' Bonnie asked, popping the tops.

'Weird in that he's acting like everything's normal.' Harper glanced over her shoulder. 'And nothing's been normal for a long time.'

She gave Bonnie a ten-dollar bill and leaned against the bar.

'It's confusing.'

'Well, I say go with it.' Bonnie opened the register, busying herself with the money. 'Maybe he's finally seeing what he lost.'

'Maybe.' All of Harper's doubts were in that word.

'Anyway, I've got to say he's the cutest cop I've ever seen.' Bonnie handed her the change.

'Me too.' Harper gave her a melancholy smile. 'But I broke him last year and I don't know how to fix him.'

'He looks fine to me,' Bonnie called, as she walked away.

When Harper walked back into the Poetry room, Luke was looking at his phone. Hearing her approach, he closed the screen and shoved it into his pocket, taking the beer she held out to him.

'Thanks,' he said.

'Now,' Harper said, sitting back down. 'Let's talk about Peyton Anderson.'

Luke looked amused. 'You really want to go there?'

'Yes I do.'

'You're actually going to push this theory that Randall Anderson's favorite boy shot a bartender to death on River Street?' he scoffed. 'You know how crazy that sounds, right?'

'It's only crazy if you don't look closely.' Setting her beer down, she warmed to her theory. 'One.' She raised her index finger. 'They knew each other. They became friends at law school. Two. They fell out, no one knows over what. And, three. She was very angry at him and reported him to her law school, according to her father.'

'That's a motive for him to unfriend her on Facebook. Not kill her,' he said.

It galled her that he had a point.

'Well, if we both think it isn't Wilson, and I've got no evidence that it's Anderson, and you've got no evidence it was Fitz – where are we?'

He gave a bemused chuckle.

'I have no idea.' He took a drink, his smile fading. 'Honestly? I can't help feeling we're missing something. Something she didn't even tell her father. Something important. And I don't know what the hell it is.'

Their eyes met.

'Damn,' Luke said, out of nowhere. 'I've missed this.'

Harper's heart seemed to stop.

'Me too,' she said.

His phone buzzed insistently, shattering the moment.

'Excuse me.' He gave her an apologetic look as he pulled it from his pocket. 'I need to check this.'

She waved her bottle. 'Check away.'

He bent over his phone, his face serious. After typing a quick response to whatever the message was, he put it away and picked up his beer, taking a long drink.

'I'm sorry – I've got to go,' he said, after a second. 'I promised someone I'd meet them, and I'm late.'

'Oh, of course. I understand.' She tried not to show her disappointment.

'Tell you what,' he told her. 'I'll take another look at the Anderson kid. See if I can find anything. We gave him a basic look, but his alibi was rock solid and he's got no priors. We know he had some sort of thing with the victim, but it didn't work when we put it all together.'

'Let me know what you find?' she said, adding, 'Off the record, obviously.'

'Obviously.' He rose from the sofa. 'Walk me out?'

They headed into the main bar. Harper avoided looking at Bonnie.

'I'm sorry about this,' Luke said. 'I wouldn't go at all except it turns out I promised, and then forgot I promised.' He shot her a smile. 'You know how I am when I'm working.'

She waved that way. 'Don't apologize. I get it.'

Harper waited until they were out in the muggy night air to speak again. For a change, there wasn't a crowd of smokers clustered around the door. The street was empty.

Luke stopped by a dark-blue sports car.

Harper wasn't sure how to say goodbye. Were they friends again now? Colleagues?

'It's been nice talking with you,' she said, after a second. 'It's been a long time.'

'Too long,' he said.

She couldn't read his eyes in the shadows, but she felt something in the air between them. A kind of electricity.

'I wish we had longer,' he said. 'There are some things I wanted to say to you . . .'

In Harper's pocket, her phone began to buzz and his voice trailed off.

'Jesus,' she said, not reaching for it. 'What is going on tonight?'

Luke smiled, his teeth a flash of white in the dark.

'We'll talk another time,' he said. 'You better take that.'

He unlocked his car, and opened the door. In the pale-blue light that poured out his eyes glittered.

She thought he seemed as reluctant to leave as she was. Finally, he turned away.

'Well, I better hit the road.' He climbed into the front seat. 'See you.'

'See you,' she replied.

Her phone vibrated angrily as he started the engine. Turning away, she pulled it from her pocket and glanced at the screen.

It was Mia, her upstairs neighbor.

Frowning, she pushed the answer button.

'This is Harper.'

'Harper? It's Mia.' Her neighbor sounded strange – her voice was too loud, and there was a loud persistent siren in the background.

'Your burglar alarm's going off. You better come home.'

Chapter Fifteen

Five minutes later, Harper pulled up on East Jones Street and slammed on the brakes.

Even before she opened the car door she could hear the alarm – a high-pitched, panicked wail that grew deafening as she ran to the house.

Her eyes scanned the building for signs of damage but the narrow Victorian building looked just as she'd left it. The front door was closed, the windows were sealed tight.

Her phone buzzed again – the alarm company had called twice but she had nothing to tell them, yet.

She was so focused on the house, it wasn't until she drew near that she saw a shape in the darkness at the side.

Someone was standing on the side steps.

She froze, mid-step, her heart pounding.

'Harper?' Mia's voice sounded faint beneath the shriek of the alarm. 'It's me.'

Her upstairs neighbor was wrapped in a white bathrobe that fluttered around her ankles as she ran to join her.

'Christ,' Harper said. 'For a second there, I thought you were the burglar.'

When she got close, Mia grabbed her arm. Her oval face looked pale in the darkness.

She was tiny – barely five feet tall – Harper had to look down at her.

'I called the cops,' Mia told her, leaning close to be heard above the noise. 'They're on their way.'

'Did you see anyone?' Harper asked, raising her voice.

Mia shook her head.

'I thought I heard footsteps running away right after the alarm went off. I looked out the window but it's so dark out here. That was when I called you.' She gave her a puzzled look. 'The thing I can't figure out is, how did you know someone would try to break in?'

Harper didn't have time to think of a response because flickering blue lights had appeared at the end of the street. Seconds later, a police cruiser rounded the corner moving slowly and with purpose. The spotlight mounted to the driver's door sent a wash of white light into the shadows, exposing every house and driveway until it found the two of them, enveloping them in a blinding glare.

The women shielded their eyes.

'You the folks who called this in?'

The gruff, official voice emerging from the dark depths of the car sounded familiar.

'Riley?' Harper took a step forward, squinting into the light. 'Is that you?'

'Oh. Hey, Harper.' Riley flipped a switch and the spotlight turned off. 'I forgot this was where you lived.'

'Yeah, that's my alarm,' she said, still raising her voice to be heard above the din. 'I haven't been inside, yet.'

Stopping the car at the curb, he climbed out with a jangle of gear and keys. Picking up his Maglite from the passenger seat, he closed the door, leaving the blue lights on, and strolled toward them.

Mia watched him with unbridled interest.

Patrol officer Eric Riley was about thirty years old, tall and muscular, with a graceful, long stride. Like the two of them, he lived in the historic downtown, making him rare among the cops, most of whom preferred suburban life.

He was unusual in more ways than that – he did yoga, practiced meditation, was vegetarian. In general, he was everything cops usually ridiculed. But somehow he got away with it. He was known for his laid-back attitude and notorious parties.

'Hello,' he said, suddenly noticing Mia. 'Do you live here, too?'

'I . . . I'm Mia Flores,' she said, stumbling over her words. 'I live upstairs.'

Belatedly, she gestured at the house behind them. Even in the dark, Harper could see her cheeks flaming. All of her usual poise had abandoned her.

'Mia called this in,' Harper explained, stepping in to rescue her before she said something idiotic. 'I was out when the alarm went off. Mia thought she heard footsteps running away.'

As she spoke, Riley switched on his flashlight and swung it over the house, stopping at the door and each window.

'Did you check the backyard?' he asked, directing the beam down the side path that led to Mia's door.

'No . . . I mean . . .' Mia stammered cutely. 'I came out that way. That's my door down there.'

Riley looked at her. 'Did you lock up when you came out?'

She drew in a breath.

'No,' she said, stepping toward him. 'You don't think . . .?

But I've been out here the whole time. I would have seen, wouldn't I?'

She looked beautifully frightened, Harper thought. Small and fragile, with those big, brown eyes.

Riley seemed to be more interested in her than the potential crime.

It was like the worst Tinder hookup in the world.

'Maybe you should check the back?' Harper suggested, raising her voice more than she needed to be heard above the shrieking alarm.

Riley straightened.

'Stay here,' he told them. 'I'm going to do a quick search.'

Pressing the button on his shoulder, he gave his call number and a series of codes. Standing in the dark, Harper translated the code numbers in her head automatically.

Officer on foot. Entering residence. Possible burglary. No backup required at this time.

The dispatcher's reply buzzed from the radio at his hip. 'Copy that.'

The two women watched as he made his way down the side of the house, flashlight bobbing in the dark. After a brief search of their backyard, he disappeared inside Mia's place.

'He is so *cute*,' Mia said. 'How do you two know each other?'

Harper didn't have time for this right now.

'We don't date,' she said shortly. 'I know him from work.'

Her tone was more dismissive than she'd intended. Mia recoiled.

'Of course,' she said hastily, 'I wasn't suggesting anything.'

In her robe, caught in the flickering blue lights, she looked fragile.

Harper could have kicked herself. After all, Mia had kept her word – she'd called her the second anything went wrong.

'Look,' she said, 'Riley's a good guy. And he's single. So, if you're interested, I'd go for it.'

Mia gave her a grateful look.

'Thanks.'

At the side of the house, Riley's flashlight lit up the path from Mia's apartment. They both fell silent.

'I've searched the top floor and the backyard,' he called above the alarm's noise. 'It's all clear. No fresh footprints in the mud.' He swung the light at Harper. 'Y'all really need to cut that grass, by the way.'

'I'll talk to the landlord,' she said. This whole night was starting to give her a headache. The shrill shriek of the alarm was like a knife to her brain.

'I'm heading to your apartment now, Harper,' he told her. 'Could you let me in and turn that damn alarm off?'

She followed him up the front steps to her door. The noise was even louder here.

Leaning over, he examined the doorframe before turning the knob to test the lock.

'Locked,' he shouted, stepping aside for her to unlock it.

When she'd done it, he motioned for her to stay where she was.

Pushing the door open with the butt of his flashlight, he stepped inside.

Too impatient to wait, Harper followed.

The entrance hall light was on, as she'd left it. Her baseball bat still leaned in its corner, next to the door.

With his back to the wall, Riley moved cautiously into the living room.

The alarm was a constant shrill call to panic that drowned out all other sounds. She waited for what seemed like forever before he strode back into view, lowering the flashlight.

136

'All clear,' he shouted. 'God, that thing is annoying. Would you turn it off?'

She dashed to the alarm box and punched in Bonnie's birthdate.

The quiet that followed was so sudden and complete it was like falling into a deep well of nothing.

'No sign of a break-in?' Harper's voice sounded far too loud above the ringing in her ears.

'Nothing at all,' he said. 'Was that your cat I saw in the garden? The gray one?'

Harper nodded.

'Could have been the cat set it off.' He leaned against the wall, flashlight loose in one hand. 'Or a palmetto bug. Some of those things are as big as robbers. Honestly, though, I doubt it was a bug. Your kitchen is insanely clean.'

'I don't like mess.'

'I can see that.'

Riley pressed the call button on his microphone. 'Unit 396. Residence is clear. Alarm disabled. No further action.'

'Unit 396 copy,' the dispatcher replied.

'So,' Riley said casually. 'We all got a talk from the lieutenant the other day. Said everyone needed to lay off you.' His gave her an encouraging look. 'I think things might get better now.'

'I hope so,' she said. 'I'm doing my best to get back to normal.'

'Good.' He swung the long flashlight in one hand like a baton. 'My parties aren't the same without you and Toby getting drunk in the kitchen and arguing with everyone about politics or books or whatever.'

Harper's lips curved. 'I hear you.'

Riley looked through the doorway to where Mia stood alone in the front yard, the robe tight across her waist.

'Harper, your neighbor's hella hot.'

'Well, coincidentally, she told me she thought you were, too.' Harper nudged him with her foot. 'She's also sane, single, and gainfully employed. And I'm going to be inside for a minute talking to my alarm company if you want to make your move.'

Grinning, he stepped past her and headed for the steps. His parting words floated back up to her.

'Nice to see you, Harper.'

When he was gone, Harper walked into the living room and flipped on the lights. Through the open door, she could hear the murmur of Riley and Mia's voices as she sank onto the sofa and pulled out her phone. The alarm company had called her seven times.

With a sigh, she hit the call-back button.

Given the hour, the call was answered quickly.

'This is Gerald, how can I help you?'

'My alarm went off tonight, but there doesn't seem to be a break-in.'

'Have you called the police?' Gerald sounded concerned.

'I have. They've been here and checked the place – there's no sign of intrusion.' Harper fought back a yawn. Now that the crisis was over, she felt drained. 'Could you tell me what set off the alarm? Maybe someone tried the door?'

'Let me check for you.'

She could hear the sound of typing. Leaning back against the soft back of the sofa, she closed her eyes. As she waited, her mind kept replaying the conversation with Luke. The strong vibe between them, especially when they'd said goodbye.

Had she misread that? Was it all wishful thinking?

Surely it couldn't be? In those last moments by the car, it was as if he couldn't tear his eyes away from her.

Was it possible he'd forgiven her?

'Miss McClain?' Gerald's Midwestern voice returned to the line.

'I'm here,' she said.

'I've identified the problem,' he said, cheerfully. 'Looks like you punched in the wrong code at twelve thirty-six tonight?'

Harper shook her head without lifting it from the sofa back.

'No,' she said. 'I was out.'

'Perhaps a family member or roommate was home?'

'No,' Harper said. 'I live alone.'

'Well, that doesn't make any sense. According to my system, we had two failed attempts at that time.'

Harper opened her eyes.

Slowly she sat up, her hand tightening on the phone.

'Are you certain about that?' she asked.

'Positive,' he said. 'At twelve thirty-six Eastern Time tonight someone punched in the wrong code at your address twice, setting off the alarm.'

Harper went cold.

At twelve thirty-six, she'd been in The Library, talking to Luke.

Who had been in her house?

Chapter Sixteen

That night, for the second time in a week, Harper slept with the baseball bat next to her.

After talking to the alarm company, she'd gone down to tell Riley what she'd learned.

He'd been worried enough to stop flirting with Mia and recommend she get her locks changed.

'You give your keys to anyone?' he asked. 'A friend? A guy?'

She shook her head. 'Nobody has keys except the landlord and my best friend, and before you even suggest it, there's no way it's either of them.'

'Well, change those locks tomorrow,' he told her. 'I can add you to the patrol rotation for the night shift – they'll swing by to keep an eye on things.'

'That's so scary, Harper.' Mia looked at her, wide-eyed. 'Who could it be?'

'I had a break-in last year,' she said, glancing at Riley.

'I remember that.' His brow furrowed. 'They never caught the guy?'

She shook her head.

'Well, at least the alarm worked,' he said, and she could hear how hard he was trying to spin this positively. 'But if I were you, I'd want a CCTV camera on my front porch.'

When Riley had gone and Mia was up in her own apartment, Harper paced the floor.

She kept thinking of the smell of cigarette smoke the other day – the overwhelming sense that someone had been in her apartment.

She'd changed the alarm code after that. That was two days ago.

She hadn't told Riley about it because she didn't have any proof – there'd been no sign of a break-in.

Because he had keys.

Except that it didn't make sense. She had a limited number of sets of keys.

One set to Billy in case of emergencies, a set to Bonnie in case she needed her to be able to get in. That was it.

She kept a spare set in the kitchen, and she'd seen those keys this morning, right where they always were, next to the coffee cups.

Still. In order to punch in the wrong code, someone first had to unlock her door and walk into her apartment.

And that someone might have had the right code once, before she changed it.

The thought made her skin crawl.

She called the locksmith's emergency number before going to bed.

When she got up the next morning, the red-and-white Rocky Locks van was waiting outside the door.

It was Sunday. But Rocky, the owner, was an ex-con with a heart of gold, and he'd known Harper for years.

He had the look of an old rocker. His short, graying hair had been tufted into spikes; tattoos covered his arms from his wrist to his neckline. Tall and buffed, he'd have been an intimidating figure to pass on a dark street at night, but he grinned when she opened the door.

'What the hell, Harper,' he said. 'You haven't had another break-in, have you?'

He had a thick Georgia accent and a hoarse voice – as if he'd been choked at some point and never fully recovered. Which could well have been the case, under the circumstances.

When Harper told him what had happened the night before he didn't waste any time.

Kneeling, he examined the door closely, thick muscles bulging as he lowered himself all the way to the ground and peered underneath it.

When he'd finished, he climbed back to his feet and dusted off the knees of his faded jeans.

'If he got in, someone gave him a key. Ain't nobody tampered with these locks, or I'd know.'

This confirmed what she'd begun to suspect herself.

'I haven't given anyone the key,' she told him. 'If he has the key, he stole it.'

'Happens all the time.' At ten in the morning, it was already hot, and he wiped the back of his hand across his damp forehead. 'You say you think he got in here before and took nothin'?'

'I've got no proof, but I know he did. I know when someone's been in my house.'

'Instincts.' He nodded. 'Better than a college degree, you ask me.'

He began pulling tools out of a large plastic case and laying them down neatly on the porch at his feet.

'Then you changed the alarm code, and a few days later, he

punches in the old code and *shazam*.' He waved a hammer. 'He finds out you're onto him.'

Harper leaned back against the metal rail on the front step. 'That's my theory.'

'So he had your key, and he had your alarm code. And you didn't give those to nobody.' Rocky squinted up at her, the sunlight gleaming on the flat bridge of his nose. 'Whoever broke in? That ain't no burglar.'

'How do you figure?'

'First off, what the hell kind of burglar breaks in and takes nothing? I go to all the trouble of getting in your house? I'm takin' somethin'. You got a computer, aintcha? And a TV? Got some electronics, probably a bit of jewelry. That's cash money right there. How come he didn't take nothing?' His expression was skeptical. 'Someone breaks into a house and takes nothing? That's an ex-husband.'

She made a face. 'You know I've never been married, Rocky.'

'Only because you keep sayin' no to me.'

He grinned but she wasn't finding any of this funny. Seeing her dark expression, his own smile faded.

'It could be an ex-boyfriend, an ex-lover,' he said, turning serious again. 'Or it could be someone who wants something from you.' Picking up an electric screwdriver, he switched it on, nodding with satisfaction as it whirred smoothly, the narrow blade a blur. 'Maybe it's someone who has a thing for you and wants to watch you up close and personal. Either way, this is the worst kind.'

Leaning forward, he began removing the screws holding the locks in place.

'Because ain't nothin' you can do about no stalker.'

*

After Rocky left, having installed new high-security locks on the front and back doors, Harper moved around the apartment with caution.

She did everything just as normal – she fed the cat, listened to the scanner, made herself lunch. The whole time she was trying to figure out who could have gotten a set of her keys.

Whoever it was would have had free access to her home, her laptop, her belongings – her whole life.

Something told her they'd been in her apartment more than once. The more she thought about it, the more it seemed to her she'd felt uncomfortably aware that something wasn't right for a long time. She'd written it off as a natural reaction to the break-in last year.

And then there was *that* break-in to consider. What if it was the same person?

The person who'd told her to run.

Maybe she should have listened.

As she thought it through, she kept peering out the kitchen window, looking at the place in the shadows where she thought she'd seen a man standing yesterday, watching her building.

There was no one there.

Finally, she made herself stop. This wasn't healthy. She needed to do something proactive.

After pouring herself a cup of coffee, she sat down at the kitchen table and called Bonnie.

'Harpelicious!' Bonnie sounded giddy. 'You and that gorgeous hunk of man cop ran out of here so fast last night, please tell me he only just left your apartment.'

'I wish,' Harper said.

When she told her about the break-in, all the humor left Bonnie's voice.

'Oh hell, what is going on, Harper? This is crazy. Do you want to come stay with me for a few days?'

It was tempting. But Harper couldn't run away from this. She needed to be systematic about it. She had to understand how it had happened. And who was doing this.

And she needed to protect her home.

'Thanks. But I'm all right,' she said. 'I was wondering – do you still have my keys?'

'Of course I do,' Bonnie said. 'If I'd lost them I'd have told you.'

'I believe you, but do me a favor – could you check and make sure? I hate to ask. But somehow this bastard got my keys and only you and Billy have copies.'

Bonnie didn't take offense. 'Hang on. I'll go check right now.'

Harper heard the click of Bonnie's boots as she walked down the wooden stairs to her ground floor, crossing her small living room. Then the jangle of metal as she searched through the bowl where she kept her spare keys.

'They're right here,' she said, after a second. 'Right where I left them.'

That settled that. Harper knew the keys wouldn't have come from Billy – he kept all his keys in a makeshift safe in his house, which was guarded by a pack of Rottweilers. The man took security seriously.

Maybe Rocky was wrong. Maybe this guy could've gotten in some other way.

'Thanks, Bonnie,' she said. 'I need to get you a new set. I had them changed today.'

'Listen, Harper,' Bonnie said, 'I don't like the sound of any of this.'

'I don't like it either,' Harper said. 'And I intend to put a stop to it.'

Harper barely left the house the rest of Sunday. If someone was going to try to break in, for a change they'd find her home.

She spent the day drinking coffee, going through her notes on the Scott case, looking for anything she might have missed. After going through everything painstakingly, Wilson Shepherd still seemed the most likely suspect. But she understood Luke's frustration – there was nothing in there that looked like proof.

After a restless night, by Monday she needed a break from the case.

She wasn't expected at work – Sundays and Mondays were her nights off. She didn't wake up until noon – her nocturnal schedule was permanently fixed by this stage. She spent the day cleaning the apartment, listening to her scanner and trying not to think about Naomi Scott.

At four o'clock she started thinking about dinner, but her refrigerator was empty of everything except dried-out cheese and a bottle of wine.

After double checking the back door locks, she headed out for supplies.

Before she left, though, she changed the alarm code again. Rocky had suggested she should change it every few days from now on.

'You don't know how this guy is getting this stuff,' he'd said. 'Or who he is. You keep switching it up, keep him off balance. Make it harder for him.'

Certain she wouldn't remember another new code, she scrawled the four numbers she'd chosen at random on the inside of her wrist before grabbing her scanner and walking outside into the full heat of the midday summer sun.

The street was quiet at this hour – most people were at work. A warm breeze blew the oak trees' branches, sending the Spanish moss swaying in a slow, sultry dance.

Her elderly neighbor, Mrs Watson, was walking her rotund pug and talking a blue streak to the animal as if he understood every word.

'Another damn hot day. Seems like the Lord has it in for us this summer. Now, don't you go peeing in those flowers, Cooper. Those daisies are far too pretty to piss in. Oh, look, Cooper – there's young Harper.'

She lifted a hand and waved.

'Hi, Ms Watson,' Harper said, walking down the front steps toward the Camaro. 'Is Cooper still preferring the prettiest places to pee?'

The older woman, who wore pale-blue pedal-pushers with a pair of startling pink plastic sandals, tilted her gray head down at the dog, which was now rolling in a patch of pink petunias, and making a disturbing snorting noise.

'Oh, that fat little bastard,' she said lovingly. 'He's never gonna change.'

The dog was still rolling in the flowers as Harper crossed the street to her car.

She opened the door, and stood back as a molten flood of heat poured out.

When it was cool enough not to burn her skin, she slid inside and put the key in the ignition.

That was when she saw the folder sitting on the passenger seat.

It was an ordinary, unmarked manila folder, thick with papers. There was nothing unusual about it. Except she hadn't left anything in the car.

Her brow furrowing, Harper reached to pick it up. The paper was hot from the sun.

Cautiously, she opened it.

Inside, she found what looked like an official document, stamped and dated six months earlier.

The first line read:

Superior Court of Chatham County, State of Georgia.
Naomi Willow Scott (Plaintiff) v. Peyton Titus Anderson.
Civil action. Verified emergency injunction for Restraining Order . . .

Harper's jaw dropped.

Heedless of the sweat running down her back, she scanned the rest of the documents in the folder rapidly. Along with the injunction filed by Naomi, there were two documents that appeared to be injunctions filed by different women against Anderson at different times.

Her mouth half open in disbelief, Harper skim-read the documents, turning page after page, words flying up at her: 'Abuse'. 'Intimidation'. 'Harassment'. 'Intrusion'. 'Invasion'. 'Trespassing'. 'Fear'.

When she'd seen enough, she leaned back in the car seat and stared at the street ahead without seeing it.

If these papers were everything they seemed, Peyton Anderson had a history of stalking women. The police knew about it, because the women had filed charges.

One of them had ended up dead.

The file was a goldmine. Who the hell put it in her car?

Harper started the engine to turn on the air-conditioning but didn't put the car in gear. Instead, she pulled out her phone and found Baxter's cell phone number.

It was the editor's day off, too, and her phone rang five times before she answered.

'This better be good, McClain.'

Harper smiled.

'Someone just left a front-page story in my car.'

Chapter Seventeen

'What the hell does that mean?' Baxter asked.

Talking fast, Harper explained about the documents, describing them as best she could.

She read from the most loaded line in Naomi's injunction: 'Defendant threatened to kill plaintive if plaintive continued to date current boyfriend. Defendant said plaintive belonged to defendant. Plaintive fears for her life.'

Baxter let out an audible breath.

'And you're telling me some guardian angel left that in your *car*?'

'Yeah and the weird thing is the car was locked,' Harper said. 'How'd they get it in a locked car?'

Baxter dismissed this concern. 'You probably only thought you locked it. And you don't have any idea who might have put it there? A source?'

'Not a clue,' Harper said. 'What do we do now?'

'Start by authenticating them. Someone could be screwing us over,' the editor said. 'What do you think? Are they real? Or is this some kind of twisted joke?'

Harper lifted up the top document.

'It's a photocopy,' she said, holding it up to the light. 'It's got the official stamp, dated in the right place.' She flipped to the last page. 'I recognize the name of the judge who signed it. It looks real. But I'm not an expert on court papers.'

Putting the document down, she said, 'I'd need somebody official to verify it before I'd trust it.'

Baxter thought for a second, tapping one nail against the phone. 'You got plans today?'

'I need food,' Harper said. 'But otherwise, no.'

'Eat later,' Baxter ordered. 'Go straight to the police station. Show those documents to someone high ranking. Your usual cop buddies aren't going to be enough this time.'

'You're thinking Blazer?' Harper guessed.

'Yeah, it better be him. If we go to anyone too low on the totem pole we leave our asses hanging out. And I want us to have pants pulled up on this one, Harper.'

There was no humor in her voice at all. 'Randall Anderson is on the newspaper's board of directors. He's a close friend of everyone in this town who matters. And he won't hesitate to use that against us.'

Harper put the car in gear.

'Meet me at the newspaper when you're through,' Baxter said. 'I have a feeling this story's going to need some time. Lawyers will have to look at it. Don't tell anyone aside from Blazer what you've got. And for God's sake, keep those papers safe.'

'On it.'

Harper ended the call, dropping the phone on the seat, and made a U-turn, heading for the police station.

So much for her day off.

*

When Harper walked into the lobby at police headquarters a few minutes later, Darlene Wilson did a double take.

'What are you doing here on a Monday? You forget how to take a day off?' She leaned her elbows on the front desk. 'Tell you what, on my day off you won't find me anywhere near this building. You better believe it.'

'Something came up and I need to talk to Lieutenant Blazer,' Harper said. 'Is he in?'

Darlene's eyebrows shot up.

'Yes he is. You really want to see him?'

'Yes,' Harper said. 'If he's not too busy.'

Darlene gave her a look. 'That man is *always* busy. Let me check with him.'

She pushed some buttons on her phone, tilting her fingers so her long nails, which had been painted with red, white, and blue stripes, didn't touch anything. Holding the receiver to her ear, she hummed tunelessly as she waited.

'Oh, hello, Lieutenant.' She put the emphasis on the first syllable of his title, giving the word a jaunty tone. 'I've got Harper McClain from the newspaper here, asking if you've got a minute for a quick question.'

She flashed Harper a supportive smile that faded as he responded.

'I'll ask her.' She put her hand over the mouthpiece. 'The lieutenant wants to know what you need him for.'

God, he was such a pain in the ass. He did this every single time.

Harper said, 'Tell him I've got some documents related to the Scott case. I think he'll want the chance to comment.'

Apparently, Blazer heard this, because he didn't wait for Darlene to transmit the message. Harper could hear his barked command.

A second later, Darlene set the phone down and flashed her a mischievous smile.

'He says you can go right back.'

'Thanks, Darlene.' Harper headed for the security door. When she reached it, Darlene pressed the buzzer.

'Have a nice conversation,' she sang after her.

This was why Harper worked nights. Everyone was so perky during the day.

She made her way down the crowded corridor, conscious of the weight of the documents she carried in her bag.

This was big. Those papers changed everything.

How could the police have kept this quiet? If Peyton Anderson stalked Naomi, he had to be suspect number one. Why hadn't Luke mentioned it the other night?

Her excitement was tempered by the strange way she'd received them. Why would anyone choose to give them to her like this? It would be so easy to drop them at the newspaper office and run away.

And Baxter was wrong – she knew the car had been locked. She'd heard the locks release before she opened the door.

The only logical answer was that it was a cop or a lawyer – someone who knew about Peyton's history and wanted to expose it.

The only problem was, nobody she knew fit that description. In fact, the one person she could think of was Luke.

At their meeting, she'd told him about her suspicions. He'd said he'd look into it.

If he'd gone straight to the office the next morning, he could have obtained copies of the documents.

If he didn't want her to know they'd come from him, *maybe* he would have dropped them off to her anonymously.

Perhaps this was his new system to avoid putting them both in a tricky position.

But even she wasn't sure she believed this.

Lieutenant Blazer's door was ajar – she could hear a low hum of voices inside. After a brief hesitation, she tapped on the frosted glass.

'Enter,' a voice commanded from within.

When she walked in, the lieutenant was sitting at his desk, and Detective Daltrey was sitting in one of the chairs across from him. Both watched her with cool caution.

'Sit down, McClain.' Blazer sounded irritable. 'Since you insist on discussing the Scott case, I've asked Detective Daltrey to join us.'

Harper did as she was told.

'And make it quick.' Blazer dropped a pen onto his clean desktop. 'We're busy.'

Whatever rapprochement she and Blazer had reached the other day, it clearly didn't mean they were friends now.

Harper got straight to the point.

'I've come into possession of a number of legal documents involving Peyton Anderson,' she said. 'These are restraining orders, filed in state district court over the last twelve months. One was filed by Naomi Scott.'

The two detectives exchanged a loaded look. Harper kept talking.

'The allegations these documents contain are explosive. I want to know if the detectives investigating Scott's death are aware of these documents. And whether they impact the case.'

For a second, neither detective moved. She could see them deciding what to say.

Daltrey spoke first.

'We are aware of the documents filed by Naomi Scott.' Her voice was even.

'Are you also aware of previous injunctions filed by two other women?' Harper pressed her. 'Their names are Cameron Johnson and Angela Martinez. They made very similar allegations of intimidation, threats of violence, and stalking.'

'We do our jobs, McClain,' Blazer snapped. 'Of course we're aware.'

There was the confirmation Harper needed that the documents were real. She kept her expression steady, hoping he wouldn't realize what a gift he'd given her. She hadn't once said this meeting was off the record, and neither had they.

'Detectives, the charges contained in those documents seem to make Peyton Anderson a person of interest in this case,' she said. 'And yet, as far as I'm aware, you're not investigating him. Does this have to do with his family's influence? After all, his father was the district attorney.'

Blazer's eyes were chips of ice.

'Mr Anderson is not above suspicion because of his father,' he said. 'He's not a suspect because he has an alibi.'

'What alibi?' Harper pulled out her notebook.

'We are not at liberty to reveal that,' Blazer said.

Harper made a show of writing that down. She wanted him to imagine the 'no comment' in the newspaper.

'His history of intimidation and threats toward Naomi would seem to make him a prime suspect,' she said. 'Six months ago he said he'd kill Naomi if she ever dared to date another man. She dated Wilson Shepherd. And then someone murdered her. And your answer to this is, "Trust us, it wasn't him?"'

'McClain –' Blazer began, but Daltrey talked over him.

'I'll tell you something off the record,' she said. 'I agree with you, on one thing at least. If there were any way he could have done it, Peyton Anderson would be my lead suspect right now.'

Blazer shot her a narrow look. She kept her eyes on Harper.

'The problem is, there isn't any way he could have killed her. His whereabouts at the time of the murder have been verified by numerous people,' she continued steadily. 'And that's why we focused on Wilson Shepherd. Shepherd's alibi is weak as hell. He says he was home alone. Friends tell us the two of them were potentially breaking up. We have to look at him.'

Stopping, she let out a long breath, and for the first time Harper could see how frustrated she was. Her body was held tight, every muscle taut.

'You can see our situation,' Daltrey continued. 'If we thought for one second Anderson might have had the opportunity to kill our victim, we would be on him. But he couldn't be in two places at once. His alibi is rock solid. He can't be the killer.'

'What's his alibi?'

Blazer spoke before Daltrey could. 'We're not at liberty to share that.'

Harper didn't want to accept this. The wording of Naomi's injunction was striking. She kept her focus on Daltrey.

'Detective, have you read those restraining orders? Personally read them?'

Daltrey's lips tightened. She gave a curt nod.

'Then you know what Naomi Scott was dealing with.' Harper leaned toward her. 'She was afraid of him. Her fear is on every single page. He turned up inside her home. He threatened her. She told her father everything and she didn't tell him this. She was protecting him.'

'I know that.' Daltrey's voice was clipped. 'But Anderson

didn't do it, McClain. Somebody else killed Naomi Scott. And now you've got to step back and let us find him.'

'If it wasn't him, then who?' Harper didn't hide her frustration. 'Don't tell me you still like Wilson Shepherd for this. Because I don't see it.'

'Oh sure.' Blazer threw up his hands. 'Now I'm going to take investigative advice from a reporter. You want to look at our case files? Flip through our forensic evidence? I know you like going through our records, please help yourself.'

He shoved the papers on his desk toward her.

Harper didn't reach for them. 'Come on, Lieutenant.'

'No, *you* come on.' His face hardened. 'This is an active murder investigation. We have been very patient with you. But if you seriously consider writing about Peyton Anderson as a suspect we are failing to investigate, it won't only be his father gunning for you. You'll hear from our attorney, as well.'

He pointed at her. 'You have no idea what we're doing behind the scenes. And that's the way it's going to stay. For once. Now, we have to get back to work.'

But Harper wasn't ready to give up.

'Just tell me this.' She fixed Blazer with a challenging look. 'On the record. You aren't giving Anderson a pass because his father was district attorney, are you?'

Blazer flung out his arm, pointing at the door.

'Get out, McClain,' he said. 'We've given you enough time. We have work to do.'

Chapter Eighteen

After leaving the police station, Harper made her way through rush-hour traffic back to the newspaper's Bay Street office going over the interview in her mind. What had Blazer meant when he said 'You have no idea what we're doing behind the scenes'? Did that mean they had another suspect? Was it Fitz? She could kick herself for not asking. What if they had something solid on the bar owner?

Or was Blazer trying to throw her off the scent?

Harper pulled into an open space outside the newspaper's front door and killed the engine.

Ominous gray clouds billowed overhead, turning the river steel gray. A warm breeze blew strands of hair into her face as she got out of the car.

It was going to storm before the day was over, and it looked like it might be a bad one.

Walking into the paper's small, utilitarian entrance hall, she waved at the guard, who grunted something in response as she hurried up the stairs, her bag thumping against her hip.

'I know it's my day off,' she said to DJ, who looked up as she threw herself into her chair. 'I have reasons for wasting my life in this room.'

'It's me, isn't it?' DJ spun his chair toward her, stretching out his arms. 'You can't bear to be away from this hunk of manly love for five minutes. It's so sweet.'

'Good God.' Harper set down her bag by her desk, scanning the room for the editor's trademark dark helmet of hair. 'Is Baxter in yet?'

He pointed to the far end of the newsroom. 'She's in a meeting with Dells. Nobody looks very happy about it.'

'Damn.' Harper craned her neck to try to see into the glass office. 'I need her.'

'Well, maybe give her a second. Everyone with an editor's desk is in a seriously bad mood today.' Glancing around to make sure they wouldn't be overheard, he lowered his voice. 'Rumor has it more layoffs are coming.'

Harper's heart sank.

'You're kidding. They lay off any more of us, the paper's going to shrink to a pamphlet.'

DJ's expression was somber.

'I think it's going to be me this time. I've got to tell you, if I were laying people off, I'd get rid of the education reporter. Nobody reads my stuff anyway.'

'No way, DJ,' Harper said. 'Parents would revolt if they couldn't read about their little darlings' schools in the paper. You're safe.'

In truth, they both knew no one was safe. In the last round, the paper had laid off all the photographers, including Miles, who was now a freelancer. Nobody had thought that could happen.

The memory made Harper's stomach churn. She'd seen enough talented people pack their things into cardboard boxes and leave in tears. She didn't need to go through that lottery again.

'Dammit.' She sat down heavily. 'I hate this.'

'There's Baxter,' DJ said, pointing.

Harper turned as the door to Dells's office swung open and the city editor walked out, her short dark bob swinging around a narrow face set in tight, worried lines.

Grabbing the folder of court documents, she hurried over to meet her.

'Good,' Baxter said, as she approached. 'What'd the cops say?'

Harper searched her face for any clues as to what had happened in that meeting. But Baxter knew better than to give that sort of information away for free.

She turned her attention to the case at hand.

'They say Peyton Anderson has a rock-solid alibi and it can't be him,' Harper told her. 'They say if we run an article that implies they're failing to investigate him because of who his father is they'll come down on us like a ton of lawyers.'

Baxter didn't seem surprised.

'What's so rock solid about his alibi?'

'They won't tell me.'

Baxter snorted a laugh.

'Typical.' She held out a hand. 'Let me see those documents.'

She quickly flicked through them, scanning the information. Her fingertip paused over Anderson's name.

'And you still don't know how these got in your car?'

'I think it might have been a detective source,' Harper said.

'You *think*.'

Baxter made thinking sound worse than homicide.

'The Anderson kid is a piece of work.' She waved the file.

'This is damning stuff – whether he's our killer or not, it's news-worthy. And it's public record, regardless of how you came by it.'

'Blazer will blow a gasket,' she warned her.

Baxter made a dismissive sound.

'Last time I checked, we don't work for the Savannah PD.' She scrawled a note to herself on a pad on a desktop cluttered with paper. 'Still, it'll be a shitstorm. Dells will have to read the article before we print. He knows the Anderson family. He'll want to give them a heads-up.' Dropping the pen, she looked at her. 'Track down the Anderson kid and get a comment. We need him to have a chance to say it's all lies, those ladies were out to get me, or whatever his excuse is going to be. While you're at it – call Jerrod Scott. See if he knew Anderson was threatening his daughter. And we need an official comment from the police on the record, even if that comment is "No comment". Are we clear?'

'Crystal.' Harper took the papers back from her.

'Harper.' Baxter's expression grew serious. 'We need to be right about this. Take your time. We won't run it tomorrow – we'll wait until Wednesday. That gives us a chance to double-check. Right is better than fast in this case. Get quotes from everyone – and I mean *everyone*.'

'I hear you,' Harper said, heading back to her desk. 'I like not being sued, too.'

Outside, the storm had begun. The sky was an apocalyptic greenish black. Lightning crashed above the river. Water streamed down the window next to Harper's desk as she picked up the phone to call Jerrod Scott. He answered right away.

'Miss McClain. How can I help you?' His slow vocal cadence was becoming familiar to her.

Harper paused as thunder shook the building.

'I'm sorry to bother you again,' Harper said. 'I wanted to tell you about some court documents we found that Naomi filed six months ago. They're about Peyton Anderson.'

Sticking to the high points, she told him about the papers, and that other women had filed for injunctions as well.

When she finished, there was a long silence. All she could hear was the rain pounding against the glass like it wanted in.

'Well, she never told me she did that.' Scott's voice was uneven. 'Naomi was such a brave girl. Always did stand up for herself. But she didn't like to upset me. And she knew that would have scared me. Knowing she was having trouble. Knowing she did something like that against such a powerful family.' He drew a shaky breath. 'Does this mean the police believe that boy – Peyton – could be the murderer?'

Harper bit her lip. He'd been through so much. But he needed to know the truth.

'The police say he couldn't be the one who killed her,' she told him. 'They still think it's someone else.'

'Well, his daddy's got all the power, doesn't he?' Anger seemed to shake the sadness out of Scott. 'Giving up's always easier than fighting.'

'I'm trying to find out more about Naomi and Peyton Anderson,' Harper said. 'I want to know the story behind this document. But I gather she didn't tell you much?'

'No,' Scott conceded. 'The person she would have talked to about it was Wilson. I've been trying to get him to call you, like you asked. But he's too scared after all he's been through. You know how it is.'

By now, Harper was desperate to talk to Naomi's boyfriend. It seemed as if, one way or another, he held the keys to this case. But she was losing hope it would ever happen.

'If there's anything I can do to convince him,' Harper said. 'Just ask.'

There was another long silence as he thought it over. Lightning struck somewhere close, and the lights in the newsroom flickered ominously.

'Let me have another word with him,' he said, finally. 'Maybe I can change his mind. All he needs right now is someone who'll listen.'

'I promise I'll listen to him, Mr Scott,' Harper said. 'But I need to talk to him soon. Can you let him know that? It needs to be by tomorrow.'

'I'll do my best,' he said. 'And thank you, Miss McClain, for telling me about those court papers. I always believed Naomi would have been a wonderful lawyer. I think those papers prove that.'

There was one other call Harper needed to make. But she couldn't seem to do it.

She kept picking up her phone and putting it down again.

Her meeting with Luke at The Library had gone far better than she'd hoped but it had left her confused. Maybe she'd misinterpreted the attraction between them. *What if it was all her, and he wasn't interested at all?*

If he left those papers in her car, though . . . Was he sending her a message? And if so, what was he trying to say?

That he trusted her again? Or something else?

There was only one way to find out.

Taking a deep breath, she pressed dial.

It rang four times before he answered.

'Hang on,' Luke said, instead of hello. 'I'll step outside.'

She could hear voices in the background. He must be at work.

Then a door creaked open, and the background fell quiet.

'Harper.' She loved the way he said her name. A half-whisper – like they were alone somewhere in the dark. 'What's going on?'

'I'm sorry to interrupt you when you're working. I just wanted to ask you something.' She was talking too fast. Her voice was high and nervous.

'Sure,' he said. 'Shoot.'

'Today I found some very important court documents in my car,' she said. 'Did you by any chance put them there?'

'What are you talking about?' He sounded confused. 'What documents?'

She heard thunder crash, and didn't know if she was hearing it through the phone or the window.

'Documents related to the Naomi Scott case,' she said. 'Restraining orders filed against Peyton Anderson. It wasn't you?'

'It wasn't me.' His answer was definitive. No hesitation at all. 'You said they left them in your car?'

'Yes.'

Even as she spoke, Harper was trying to figure it out. *If it wasn't Luke, who was it?*

'You know, I was sure it was you because the car was locked and not everyone can get through that without leaving a scratch. But a detective could.'

'Harper, it wasn't me.' A new note of concern entered his voice. 'Do you have another detective contact it might be?'

'No. You're the only one I could think of. Daltrey wouldn't do it, would she?'

'Hell no. She'd saw off her right arm first.' Luke paused. 'Harper, was your car at the house or the office?'

Something in the way he said it made her stomach tighten.

'At the house.'

'I don't like the sound of this,' he said. 'Who knows where you live?'

Harper didn't like it much either. *If it wasn't him, who was it? What if it was the same person who tried to get into her apartment?*

'Luke,' she said hesitantly, 'there's something else. Someone tried to break into my place Saturday night. While I was with you. I'd just changed the code, and they set off the alarm when they punched in the wrong one. The locksmith said they had a key. Only, I know where all the keys are. And none of them are missing.'

'And now, all of a sudden, you find those documents in your locked car?' There was an edge to his voice. 'What the hell's going on?'

'I wish I knew.'

There was a long silence.

Then Luke said, 'I don't like what I'm hearing, Harper. This isn't right.'

Harper felt suddenly furious about all of it. The invasion. The intimidation. And the sheer distraction of it.

Nearly a week had passed since Naomi was murdered, and she felt she was nowhere nearer now than she'd been that night on River Street to understanding who had killed her.

When she spoke again, her jaw was tight.

'I don't know what's going on. But I've got a story to write. I'll talk to you later, Luke.'

Chapter Nineteen

After her conversation with Luke, Harper tried to focus on the Scott case. But her mind kept trying to piece everything together – the break-in. The documents. The sense she'd had for months now that she was being watched. There was more to this than she'd initially thought.

She just couldn't figure out what it all meant.

Opening her long narrow reporters' notebook to a clean page, she wrote down every occasion she could think of when her instincts had told her someone had been in her house, and she'd suppressed that voice, convinced she was paranoid.

A few days ago, she thought she'd smelled cigarette smoke, and had the distinct impression that someone had been inside her apartment.

Three weeks before that she'd been certain she left a glass on the kitchen table, but when she came home it was in the dish drainer. At the time, she thought she'd forgotten putting it there.

That day in April when she'd searched for a picture of her

with her mother, before deciding it must have fallen under something. She was sure it had been in a dresser drawer.

One after another, she traced a series of small, seemingly unconnected incidents when she'd thought she'd been scatter-brained or distracted, all the way back to last year. All the way back to the first break-in. When someone had trashed her apartment and painted the word 'RUN' on her wall in red paint.

When she finished, it was so obvious, she couldn't believe she'd missed it until now.

He'd been there all along.

There was no other answer.

Someone had keys. He knew her alarm code. And now he must know everything about her.

The place she'd thought was her sanctuary was never safe. Who knew what he'd done there while she was at work?

The realization made her stomach roil. She stood up so fast her chair skidded back.

DJ looked up at her curiously.

'I've got to go,' Harper said, grabbing her bag and scanner.

'See you . . .' he began, but she was already halfway across the room, '. . . later,' he finished, as she disappeared from view.

Harper ran down the stairs and burst out of the door into a full thunderstorm. Wind blew the rain sideways. Lightning crackled. Dark clouds roiled.

Harper didn't feel the rain. She was too angry.

When she reached the Camaro, she stopped and stood next to the car, letting the storm rage around her. Rain ran down her face, soaking her clothes.

People hurrying by, sheltered under umbrellas, stared at her curiously. But she didn't care.

She stood staring at the red sports car. Did he have keys to this, too? He'd put those documents on the seat of the car without leaving a scratch on the scarlet paint.

How could he do that without a key?

She knew the answer already.

He couldn't.

She opened the car door gingerly, and scanned the front and back seats – but there was nothing new. Just the usual clutter of used coffee cups and discarded notebooks.

No sign that anyone had been in the vehicle while she was working.

But she could no longer assume anything in her life was safe. Or private.

He'd touched everything. He'd gone through her life and explored it all.

She climbed into the car, dripping water on the seats and shut the door, sitting for a moment in silence.

Had he sat where she was right now, hands stroking the leather-wrapped steering wheel? Touching the dials and buttons? Rummaging through the glove box?

Gingerly, she turned the key to start the engine and began to drive home.

By the time she pulled up on Jones Street, she was so angry and frightened she could hardly breathe.

What was she going to do?

Thunder crashed with such force it shook the earth, waking her from her reverie. The winds were getting stronger. Tree branches rose and plunged, sending Spanish moss swinging wildly.

Climbing out, she ran across the street with her head down. The water in the gutters was already ankle deep as she splashed through it and up onto the sidewalk.

She was halfway up the front steps before she saw Luke.

He stood by her front door, his expression grave.

She hated how her heart leapt, seeing him there.

'Hey,' she said. 'You didn't have to come over.'

He moved back to make space for her on the sheltered top step.

'Sorry to show up like this,' he said. 'I thought you were here. Monday's your day off. I wanted to talk this through some more. I don't like what's going on.'

'It might be worse than I thought.' She cast a look down the darkening street, through the lashing rain. It appeared empty but she felt observed, and there was no way to know if it was all in her mind.

'You better come in.'

He stood behind her, waiting as she unlocked the three locks, one after another, and then read the code from her wrist and punched it in, quieting the alarm system.

She sensed him observing the steps she'd taken to make herself safe. Noting the baseball bat by the door. Missing nothing.

When she switched on the living room light, his expression was troubled.

The air-conditioning cooled the water on her clothes and skin, and Harper found she was shivering uncontrollably.

'I'm soaked – I need to change,' she said. 'Do you want a towel?'

Swiping the water from his face, he gave her a rueful look.

'Probably a good idea.'

'Two minutes,' she said, and ran down the hallway. As she did, she searched for signs that someone had been here while she'd been out. But, this time at least, everything felt normal.

Zuzu was curled up on one of the sofas. Harper had begun to realize the cat was never there on the days she now suspected an intrusion had occurred. She must run out through the cat door and stay out until she was sure Harper was back and everything was safe again.

Grabbing a towel in the bathroom, she stepped back into the hallway and tossed it to Luke, who still stood where she'd left him. He caught it easily.

'Thanks.'

In her bedroom, Harper ripped off her top, and found another towel to dry herself off. After changing out of her wet things, she raked a brush through her hair.

In the mirror, her color was high. Her hazel eyes looked confused. The dusting of freckles she'd never been able to fully cover stood out against her skin.

She looked younger than twenty-eight. She looked scared.

Taking a deep, slow breath, she walked back into the living room.

Luke was on the sofa next to Zuzu, who, in a rare gesture of conciliation, allowed him to stroke her fur.

Harper watched the two of them for a moment before breaking the silence.

'You want some coffee?' she asked. 'I could use the caffeine.'

'Yeah. That'd be great.'

After patting Zuzu one last time, he stood and followed her to the kitchen.

'The place looks good,' he said. 'I like the new sofas.'

'Thanks.' Harper turned on the kitchen light, and the spotless room, with its tall white cabinets and black-and-white-tiled floor, burst into view.

Luke leaned back against the counter as she picked up the canister of coffee.

She had to reach behind him for the coffeemaker. It seemed

too close – she could feel the warmth of his body against her skin.

He shifted out of the way.

The room seemed so small with him in it.

'Well,' he said, watching her scoop the coffee into the machine. 'Why is everything worse than we thought?'

Thunder rattled the windows as Harper told him what she suspected.

When she'd finished, she leaned back against the fridge and faced him.

'I still don't know if any of this is real or my imagination,' she said, when she'd told him everything. 'But if he took that picture of my mom . . .' She exhaled. 'Man. That pisses me off.'

'I don't blame you,' he said soberly. 'Harper, is there anyone you can think of who might be behind this?'

She shook her head. 'Nobody.'

'Have you dated anyone who seemed unusually attached in the last year? Someone who would know how to get in here? A cop?'

His voice was even but, still, heat rose to her face.

It was such a loaded question.

'No.'

'It could be anyone,' he prodded. 'Someone you only had one date with. Some random from a dating website. Maybe he didn't seem threatening at the time but . . .'

'There hasn't been anyone.' The words burst out louder than she'd intended. She lowered her voice. 'I haven't dated anyone. Not since you.'

A sudden silence followed, filled by the sound of summer rain falling hard, and the burble of the coffeemaker.

She couldn't look at him. Afraid of what she'd see in his eyes.

'I forgot the milk.' Harper hurriedly turned around to open the refrigerator.

With her back to him, she paused, letting the chilled air cool her skin.

When she spoke again, she thought she sounded fine.

'Do you want sugar? I know you usually don't, but . . .'

'No, thanks.' His tone was so bland, the previous conversation might not have happened at all.

She checked the milk to make sure it hadn't turned, and then made them each a cup.

Positioning herself with her back pressed against the countertop as far as she could get across the small room from him she nudged the conversation back to the break-in.

'What do you think? Could this be connected to the first break-in?'

'Maybe,' he conceded. 'But the MO is different. That time, the guy broke a window, right?'

'Yeah.'

'This guy has a key and your security code. And access to your car – possibly also with a key. On the surface, it seems like two very different styles. One's brute force, the other is finesse. I mean, how the hell could he get your keys?'

'Here's what I've been thinking.' Harper set her coffee down. 'What if the first break-in was when he got the keys?'

Luke's brow creased.

'Did your keys go missing?'

'I don't know,' she said. 'The whole place was trashed. Whoever it was dumped the fridge on the floor. Knifed every piece of furniture. Threw my clothes around, painted on the walls. It never occurred to me to check the keys.'

Turning to the cupboard behind her, she pulled out a ceramic jar marked TEA.

'I keep my spare keys in here,' she explained. 'I haven't even looked in here since the burglary. I mean, how often do you check your spare keys?'

Without waiting for an answer, she dumped the keys out onto the counter with a clatter. The two of them bent over the tangle of silver and brass. Her spare car keys were there, right where they should be, along with house keys, the keys to Bonnie's place, and a couple of random leftover keys, including one for a bike lock she'd long ago thrown away.

She looked up at Luke. He was standing too close. She could smell his familiar scent – cinnamon and sandalwood.

'It's all here,' she said. 'But that doesn't mean anything, does it?'

Luke shook his head. 'He could have had copies made and brought your originals back.'

Harper reached for the house keys.

'Don't touch anything,' he ordered.

She jerked her hand back as if it had been scalded.

Pulling a pen from his pocket, he used it to pick the keys up by the ring.

'Do you have a plastic bag?' he asked, glancing at her.

Harper got one out of the drawer and handed it to him.

'I'll get these checked for fingerprints,' he told her, dropping the keys inside. 'Just in case.'

Harper hated how well the scenario fit.

The entire break-in – all of the destruction – could have been a distraction to ensure she never thought to check her key jar. If that was the case, it worked. She'd fled her home to stay with Bonnie – leaving the clean-up to Billy and his crew.

A sudden thought made her breath catch.

'What about Bonnie?'

Luke gave her a puzzled look.

'Those are her keys,' she explained, pointing at the set still sitting on the counter. 'He could get in her house.'

He leaned over to study them.

'They're not marked. There's no way for him to know whose they are.' He glanced at her. 'I think the only keys he wanted were yours.'

Those last words hung there.

'Whoever this guy is, he's good, Luke.' Harper reached for her coffee to give her hands something to do.

'Yeah, he's good. But we're better.' He rubbed a hand across the edge of his jaw, staring at the keys as if they held answers only he could see.

'Let's assume he has keys to your car, too.'

She was already there.

'I'll have the car locks changed tomorrow,' she said. 'My mechanic will fit me in.'

'Good.' He paused to think. 'Get him to take a look at everything. Check for anything the guy might have left.'

It took her a second to figure out what he was saying.

She took a step back. 'Oh, hell, Luke. You think he put a tracker on my car.'

'I don't think anything,' he said. 'I want to be sure.'

'Who is this guy?' Anger made her voice rise. 'What does he *want*?'

'I intend to find out.' He held up the plastic bag of keys. 'We'll start with these and the car.' He hesitated before adding, 'You know, I still think you ought to move out for a while –'

'Not happening,' she cut him off, firmly.

A faint smile crossed his face.

'I figured that.'

He put the keys in his pocket.

'Well, if anything happens – anything at all – don't take any chances. Call me.'

'If anything happens,' she told him, 'I'll kick this guy's ass myself.'

He gave her a hard look.

'Call me.'

Harper didn't know what to make of this sudden protectiveness. Did it mean anything at all? Or was he just being a cop?

'I better go.' He glanced at his watch. 'I have to be somewhere.'

'Oh, sure.'

Turning quickly, she led him to the front door.

It was so weird the way he'd turned up, behaving like nothing ever happened. The hero again, coming to save her.

It left her disoriented.

Outside, the rain had almost stopped. The sun was already coaxing steam from the soaked sidewalks. In a few minutes, the city would be a sauna.

Harper leaned against the doorframe. 'Thanks for coming over.'

On the top step, Luke turned back, the light glinting off his hair. 'Take care, Harper.'

The moment felt haunted by different times. Times when they'd kissed on this very doorstep. When he'd talked about going but hadn't left. When they'd locked themselves inside and forgotten about murder for a while.

She wondered what he'd do if she reached for him, now. Pulled him close. Told him she was sorry.

But she didn't move.

'I will,' she said.

Then she shut the door so she didn't have to watch him walk away.

Chapter Twenty

Harper spent the night on the sofa with the baseball bat at her elbow, the scanner quietly humming. She slept shallowly – her fitful dreams filled with Luke, Naomi Scott, and danger.

She woke before the sun rose, but she didn't get up. Instead she lay in the dark thinking, with Zuzu at her side.

By the time dawn stretched long fingers of light across the polished oak floor, she'd made up her mind.

There was someone else she needed to talk to. Someone who might be able to help.

First though, she needed to take care of the car.

She left the house before eight, giving the Camaro a quick search in case anyone had left more packages inside.

Satisfied it was unmolested, she drove straight to Madsen's Motors on Veterans.

Howie Madsen had worked on her car since she bought it four years ago. He always cut her a good deal, and he knew Camaros.

This time, in addition to changing the locks, he also conducted a thorough search for tracking devices.

'Why're you worried about trackers, Harper?' he asked when he'd rolled himself out from under the Camaro on a wheeled backboard, looking up at her as he wiped oil from his hands with a stained red cloth. 'You pissed someone off?'

'That about sums it up.' She sat on a dirty plastic chair near the open garage door holding a large cup of coffee she'd acquired from the doughnut shop next door.

The warm air smelled powerfully of engine grease – a sugary scent she was surprised to find she sort of liked.

'Well there ain't nothin' there at the moment.' Howie stood up and kicked the board away. 'Keep an eye out, though. It's awful damn easy to fit one of them things without anyone noticing.'

A short while later, with the locks changed, she was driving west down Highway 280, with the sun at her back.

She'd been down this road four times over the last year – never once had she told a soul. This was her thing, and she intended to keep it that way.

It was an easy drive – the road was so straight and flat you could fire a bullet at one end of it and hit the markings right down the middle a hundred yards away. She drove fast through the lush Georgia countryside.

She used the time in the car to come up with all the questions she wanted to ask. She needed to focus the conversation from the start – there wasn't much time. She had to be at work by four o'clock.

She was still thinking it through when the cold white walls of Reidsville State Penitentiary rose up in the distance, surrounded by acres of glittering razor wire.

It was a chain-metal fortress, bristling with weaponry. Watchtowers marked each corner of the fence line. Sniper guns followed the car as it rolled up to the huge gate.

Harper stopped where the road markings told her to and waited as a guard approached her, a .45-caliber handgun on his hip.

When she lowered her window she saw herself reflected in his aviator sunglasses.

'Kill your engine,' he ordered, in a tone that managed to be bored and tense at the same time.

Harper turned the Camaro off and put her hands on the wheel, where he could see them.

'How can I help you today?' he asked, leaning in to see her scanner on its holder on the dash, and then turning to see the back seat, where Harper had thrown her laptop and notebook.

'I'm Harper McClain. I should be on your visitors' list for one o'clock,' she said.

Stepping back, the guard pulled a paper from his pocket and ran his finger down it – his expression told her instantly that she wasn't on it.

'I was a late addition,' she explained, before he could ask. 'They only added me this morning.'

His expression didn't change as he folded the paper away and clicked the button on the microphone at his shoulder.

'Got a McClain, Harper at gate four. Says she's on the list but she ain't on mine.'

He waited, head cocked expectantly, one hand hanging loose near his sidearm. A long minute passed as someone in an unseen office did some digging.

It was so quiet out here. A crow cawed in the distance, and Harper heard it like it was sitting on her car. Every sound seemed amplified in the stillness – the tick of the car's cooling engine, the long, low rustle of wind across grass.

She heard very clearly when a curt female voice responded

over his radio. 'McClain is approved for visit at thirteen hundred hours.'

The guard raised an arm at someone in the distance. A moment later, the massive metal gates behind him shuddered before rattling open, revealing the gray prison world on the other side.

'You have a good day, now.' The guard stepped back, mirrored sunglasses looking past her.

Driving into the prison grounds gave Harper instant claustrophobia.

She had to focus on not looking anywhere except straight ahead to steady her racing heart and calm her sudden, panicked desire to flee.

The visitors' lot was nearly full. The only space she could find required her to squeeze the Camaro in between an SUV and a mud-caked pickup truck with a confederate flag and an empty gun rack in the rear window.

A sign at the edge of the lot warned visitors to remove all valuable possessions from view.

Ironically, prison parking lots are not that safe.

She put her laptop, scanner, and phone in the trunk before heading across the sunbaked concrete to a thick metal door marked 'Visitors'.

Inside was a small dank room where the air-conditioning seemed to serve mostly to make the air so damp, drops of condensation formed on the concrete walls. At a table near the door, she put her keys in a plastic tray, which was shoved onto a shelf by a sullen guard who didn't look at her once.

From there, she lined up behind a raucous family who, apparently unconcerned by the setting, chattered with each other and the guards.

The two guards – a tall, emaciated young man and a woman

half his height, whose wiry dark hair was scraped back into the tightest of knots – let the kids play with their metal-detecting wands as they waited.

'And you're six now?' the female guard asked a small, round-faced boy, who nodded seriously while scanning the top of his own head.

'Six and *four weeks*,' he said, as if this were an incalculably large amount of time to be alive.

'Still obeying the law?' she asked.

The boy nodded hard.

A curly-haired baby smiled and waved a fat fist at Harper as his mother carried him through a metal detector, chiding and cajoling her other children out into the hallway.

After they'd gone, the room felt empty.

The two guards seemed to feel the same hollowness. They both stared silently at the top of the portal as she walked through until the light above her head turned green.

The thin man pointed down the corridor behind him, where Harper could see the noisy family making slow progress.

'Follow them,' he said. 'They'll get there sooner or later.'

She didn't tell him she already knew the way.

She could hear the visiting room long before she reached it – the tense, excitable rumble of conversation from people who had only an hour to get through a month's news and complaints.

The room was the size of a high-school dining room, with high ceilings. The few windows were covered with a web of metal. Most of the light came from fluorescent strips overhead.

'Name?' asked the guard by the door. He wore the same pale blue uniform of all the guards, mace and a high-caliber pistol hung at his hip.

'McClain,' she said.

He ran his finger down the M's, and made a mark when he found her.

'Table fifteen,' he said. 'We'll send him out.'

Harper walked to where he indicated, and sat on a bench that was bolted to the floor in front of a scarred wooden table with the number fifteen painted on top.

As she waited, she looked around at prisoners in their white jumpsuits with DEPARTMENT OF CORRECTIONS written on the back, and their families – some smiling, some somber.

The noisy family had settled at a table across the room. The woman held both the baby and the six-year-old on her lap somehow, with two other children perched on either side of her. They faced a man about the woman's age. He wore a white jumpsuit and had the same wide smile as the little boy.

The children, who had been so boisterous outside, were much quieter here.

It was impossible to know from looking at him what the man had done to get himself put in here. Reidsville was a maximum-security prison – it held a lot of murderers. This man didn't look like a killer.

But then, as she had learned, most killers don't.

The door at the end of the room opened, and Robert Smith shuffled in, with a guard at his elbow. Smith's hands were cuffed to chains in front of him, which were connected to chains around his ankles. Shackled in this way, every step jangled as he crossed the room toward her, a frown already clouding his face.

Watching him, Harper's heart twisted. Smith had been her mentor. She'd once loved him more than her own father. Then she'd learned the truth about him.

On so many levels he wasn't the man she'd thought he was. But she never stopped missing him.

He was a big man, with a craggy, lived-in face. His nose showed where it had been broken when he was young. He looked grayer every time she saw him, but also more muscular. There was nothing to do, he'd told her on a previous visit, except exercise and read.

The guard unlocked the cuffs from his wrists, leaving the ankle chains in place, and directed him to the chair across from Harper.

'No touching, no sharing of property,' the guard intoned. 'You have an hour. Enjoy your visit.'

When he'd gone, the two of them studied each other across the solid expanse of the table.

'How are you, Lieutenant?' Harper asked.

'Oh, I'm as well as I can be.' Smith's tone was steady but his piercing brown eyes were watchful. 'A little surprised to see you. Normally you let me know you're coming. What's happening? Pat and my boys OK?'

'They're fine,' she assured him. 'This isn't about them.'

Smith's record for cracking crimes was unbeaten. In fact, one of the few murders he'd failed to solve was the murder of Harper's mother. Which was how they'd first met, when she was twelve years old.

That day, she'd found her mother's body, cold, in a puddle of blood on her kitchen floor.

Smith and his wife had taken her under their wing. As the years passed, they'd continued to include her in their lives, even after she became a crime reporter.

Until last year. That was when Harper investigated a murder case that ultimately led to Smith. When the truth came out, he was sentenced to life in prison.

The case fractured her relationship with Smith's family, who she saw only occasionally now.

But Harper's mother's murder was still unsolved, and Smith knew more about that case than anyone. She needed him.

Every few months, she came out to the prison to talk the case through – to look for new leads. To go over old ideas. To try to figure out, once and for all, what happened that afternoon, sixteen years ago.

Today, though, she was here for something different.

'I wasn't planning on coming today, but something happened.'

Smith's expression didn't flicker.

'What exactly has happened that would make you drive all the way out here on a work day?'

Even in prison, he knew her schedule as well as she did.

'There was another break-in at my place,' she told him. 'I think it might be the same guy from last year. I need to know who it is. And what they want.'

He motioned with one hand. She'd seen him make that same gesture so many times, often with a cigar gripped, half-forgotten, between his fingers.

'Tell me everything,' he said in that familiar growl.

Talking fast, Harper told him about the suspected intrusions. The documents on her front seat. The keys in the kitchen.

Through it all, Smith listened carefully, rarely interrupting, and even then only to ask for more information.

When she finished, his expression was intense.

'The fact that he could get his hands on those documents,' he said. 'That he even knew they existed. You know what that means, don't you?'

'He's a cop,' Harper said.

'Or a prosecutor, a lawyer, a judge – someone in the court system,' he corrected her. 'Someone with access.'

'But who?' she asked. 'Is it someone I've written about? And why leave those documents? If it's the same guy who broke in last time . . .' She held up her hands. 'What does that mean? Is he connected to the Scott family?'

Smith gave her an impatient look.

'This is bigger than the case you're working on right now, Harper. This goes back much further.'

'How much further?'

'I need more information to answer that.' He shifted in his chair, his ankle chains jangling. 'Aside from the keys, did he take anything else? Anything at all?'

Harper didn't have to think about it. 'A picture went missing. It's a photograph of me and my mom. I thought it was lost but . . .'

His gaze sharpened.

'That's the only thing missing?'

'As far as I know.'

He leaned back in his chair, holding her gaze. In his eyes she saw what he was thinking.

'This is about my mom.' Her voice was quiet. 'Isn't it?'

He nodded. 'It makes sense.'

'But why?' Her stomach twisted. 'You don't think . . .?'

She didn't have to finish the question.

'I don't think so,' he said. 'Why would her killer leave you documents that help you with an unrelated case? No.' He shook his head. 'I don't think it's him. This is someone else.'

'But who?' Her voice betrayed her frustration. 'I don't understand why he's doing this. Watching me. *Studying* me.'

Smith gave her a stern look.

'Now, slow down, Harper. If you panic you can't see what's right in front of you. Let's break this down.' He ticked the items off on his fingers. 'We've got multiple entries at your house over many months. A photo was taken of you and your mother. We have a message written on your wall – a warning or threat. Later, he leaves you information that's valuable to you – an offering. There's no indication of sexual obsession. No attempt at violence.'

Smith stared past her, across the crowded, noisy room, with that inward look he got when he was working a case.

'What I see is a person keeping an eye on you. From what you say, these break-ins took place maybe every month. That sounds like a regular check-in to me. For what purpose? To help you or to hurt you?' He paused. 'I can't answer that. But he hasn't hurt you yet, and he's had opportunity. Why wouldn't he take it, if that's what he wanted? So it's got to be something else.

'Thing is, he's been communicating with you all along,' Smith continued. 'The message on the wall was his first try. That was a misfire – you didn't know what it meant and it scared the hell out of you. Taking a picture of you and your mother? That's him telling you what he's there about. The documents left in the car? He's telling you he wants to help. He's on your side.' He met her eyes directly. 'He knows you're on to him and you're nervous. And he's saying, "Trust me."'

Harper leaned forward intently. 'If he knows something about Mom's murder, I want to know what that is. Should I reach out to him? Find out what he has to say?'

'Seems to me you don't have any choice.'

Excitement unfurled in Harper's chest.

'Tell me about him.' Her voice was eager. 'Who am I dealing with?'

Their heads were tilted toward each other now, both of them lost in the details of the case.

'We only have so much to go on. He's obviously intelligent. Well trained, possibly ex-law enforcement. Maybe ex-military. But' – he held up one cautioning finger – 'we can't overlook that he is also obsessed with you. Obsessed with your mother's case. He's been systematic – exhibiting remarkable patience. Just because he's made this overture with the documents . . .' He shook his head. 'Don't give him what he wants. Don't trust him. But you can pretend to trust him. It's good enough.'

Across the room, one of the children at the table Harper had noticed earlier began to cry. Smith glanced over, before turning back to her.

'When you found the folder in your car, was there anything with it?'

Harper's brow furrowed. 'Like what?'

'Some other communication,' he said. 'Any attempt to connect with you personally. A note.'

'I didn't see anything like that,' she said. 'Only the papers I told you about. Why?'

'Well, the last time he communicated, he spoke to you directly. He warned you to run,' Smith explained. 'I'd have expected something like that. A direct message to you.'

'There was nothing,' Harper insisted.

The lines on Smith's forehead deepened.

'Leaving that file in your car? That was his big announcement. His coming out party. He knew you'd changed your alarm, figured you were on to him, and now . . . Ta-dah!'

He held up his hands.

'Here I am, Harper. You're on to me. Let's talk.' He dropped his hands back down. 'That's the moment when he would communicate with you again in some way. The fact that he didn't do that doesn't make sense.' He leaned back in his chair. 'Not for this guy.'

Harper tried to follow his thinking.

'What does that mean?'

Smith's worn face was alert and focused – he looked younger than he had when he walked in the door.

Crime was his comfort. It gave him purpose.

'I think you missed it. Did you search the car?' he asked. 'He could have left the note in the glove compartment or hidden beneath a visor. Maybe it fell behind the seat and got lost. It could be anywhere.'

Caught up in his theory, he leaned closer, hands reaching toward the middle of the table. A guard shouted a warning and he yanked them back, but his eyes didn't flicker.

'If it's the same person – and I think it is – there's a note somewhere. Find it.'

When Harper walked out into the bright sun she took a deep, cleansing breath. After an hour in the clammy prison, she thought she could feel it on her skin – coating her like oil.

The parking lot was still crowded, and her back pressed against an SUV as she opened the Camaro's door to let the volcanic heat pour out.

It was an extension of her office and it showed. Notebooks were stuffed into the side pockets. Disposable coffee cups nestled in the back floorboard.

What if there was a message and she'd simply overlooked it?

Smith was nearly always right. He'd always been the best detective the force had. He saw through people. Everyone but himself.

When she'd said goodbye, he'd said something she hadn't expected.

'If you get into trouble, call Blazer. He's a good cop. He knows how much you mean to me.'

But she wasn't about to go to Blazer for help. She was going to figure this out for herself. Starting now.

Climbing into the car, she checked behind the visors, in the glove compartment, between the seats. Finding nothing there, she pulled the driver's seat forward and rifled through the papers stuffed into the holder behind it. There were the receipts from the mechanic this morning, tire brochures, restaurant menus – but nothing useful.

Then she picked through the cups, making sure nothing was on the floor underneath them except the sturdy gray carpet.

From there, she felt under the front seats – but her fingers couldn't get far enough back.

Sweat ran down her face now, and strands of auburn hair stuck to her skin as she walked around the car and knelt on the pavement beside the passenger seat, leaning over until her cheek pressed against the carpet and she could see beneath it.

There was nothing under the seat. Nothing except a rumpled scrap of paper at the very back.

Harper reached for it, wincing as she squeezed her fingers into the narrow space and grabbed a corner of the paper.

She pulled it out and turned it over.

It was lined notepaper. Three words had been scrawled on it with a black pen.

YOU DIDN'T RUN.

Chapter Twenty-one

Just before five o'clock, Harper pulled up in front of the police headquarters and ran inside at such speed, Darlene gave her an alarmed look.

'Uh-oh,' she said. 'What's wrong?'

'Nothing,' Harper told her, grabbing the binder of police reports Darlene held out. 'I'm late.'

She didn't have time for chit-chat. The trip to Reidsville had taken too long, and she needed to get to the paper. Baxter was expecting her story on the restraining orders by six and she hadn't even started it yet. There'd hardly been time even to think about it.

Everything felt like it was happening at once. Weighing down on her. Naomi Scott. Wilson Shepherd. Smith. Luke. The note.

All the way back to Savannah she'd tried to figure out what the note meant. The main question – the one that she kept coming back to over and over – was: What did this guy *want*?

And for that one there were no answers. The note didn't bring any clarity.

She went through the stack of crime reports so quickly she barely saw the words on the pages. Then she shoved the stack back to a puzzled Darlene and headed for the door. Reaching it right as it opened and Luke walked in.

He stopped in his tracks. The stress must have showed on her face because, without a word, he turned around and followed her outside.

They stood to one side of the front door in the humid, afternoon air. Cicadas buzzed from the oak tree behind them.

'Everything OK?' he asked, searching her face. 'No problems last night?'

'Luke, I found something.' She took a step toward him, talking quietly. 'The guy who broke into my house last year – it's the same guy. I'm sure of it now. He left a note.'

'Wait, wait, wait.' Luke held up his hands. 'Start at the beginning. What note?'

'I kept thinking about that file,' she said, leaving Smith out of the story. Luke didn't know about the prison visits and she wasn't about to tell him. 'And it seemed to me, if it was the same guy who broke into my house, he'd want me to know. And I was right. I found a note in my car. It had fallen under the seat. I know it was him.'

'What does the note say?'

Harper gave him a look. '"You didn't run."'

Luke swore. 'Oh, come on. Who the hell is this guy? Why is he messing with you like this?'

She held up her hands. 'I wish I knew.'

'Can I see that note? Is it still in your car?'

They walked over to the Camaro. The note lay face down on the passenger seat.

Crouching down, Luke pulled a pen from his pocket and used it to flip the paper over.

'Do you mind if I take this? I want to run it for prints.' He glanced up at her. 'We didn't find anything useable on the keys, so this could be our only chance.'

'Take it.'

He took an evidence bag from his pocket and, pulling his shirt down over his fingers as a makeshift glove, picked the square of paper up gingerly.

'Is there any point in printing the whole car?' Harper asked, as he delicately maneuvered the small scrap of paper into the envelope.

'Did you get these locks changed?' he asked.

When she nodded, he grimaced doubtfully.

'He left that file a couple of days ago, and you and your mechanic have been all over the car since then. We could try, but the prints will be a mess.' He tapped the note. 'This is our main hope.'

'I wish I knew what to . . .' Harper began.

Behind them, the police station door opened and a traffic officer walked out, motorcycle helmet tucked under his arm.

Her voice trailed off.

Glancing at the two of them, he gave Luke a brief, sardonic salute and headed toward his motorcycle, which gleamed in the bright sun.

Harper waited until he was out of earshot before continuing.

'I wish I knew what to do,' she said. 'This guy knows where I live. Where I work. Who my friends are. He knows everything about me. How do I fight that?'

Luke met her eyes.

'We'll figure this out. Keep digging. At least we have this.'

He held up the note.

'If he left prints I'll find them.'

When Harper walked up to her desk fifteen minutes later, DJ spun his chair around and rolled closer to her.

'Heads up. Baxter's been sniffing around looking for your story on that River Street murder case,' he informed her. 'She asked me twice where you were. I told her I'm not your keeper.' He rubbed his chin. 'That went over well.'

Harper glanced across the room to where the editors' desks stood – but Baxter's seat was empty.

'Thanks,' she said, logging into her computer at record speed. 'I am so late and so screwed.'

He watched her with interest as she switched on her scanner with an unconscious flick of her wrist. Its low static filled the air as she looked through her notes.

'I take it the story isn't ready?' he guessed.

'I haven't even interviewed the suspects yet,' she said, typing grimly. 'This desk may be yours before the night is over.'

'Oh goody,' DJ said. 'I've always wanted two desks.'

Harper didn't smile. She barely even heard him.

Putting the note and Smith out of her mind, she read through the little information she had. There was no time for strategy at this point.

Her only option now was to shake all three suspects hard and hope something fell out of them.

Her first call was to Jim Fitzgerald. The phone rang once and went straight to voicemail.

'Hey there, this is Fitz,' the familiar, languid southern voice announced. 'Leave a message; I'll get back to you.'

After the beep, Harper talked quickly, using the kind of words that might get him to call her back.

'This is Bonnie's friend from the newspaper – Harper McClain,' she said. 'I know you don't want to talk to anybody right now, but things are happening. You *need* to talk to me. This situation isn't going to go away. Tell me your side of the story, Fitz. Let me see if I can help.'

After leaving her number she hung up and, without waiting to gather her thoughts, dialed a different number she'd found in her notes.

'Come on,' she muttered as the phone rang. 'Answer.'

But Jerrod Scott's phone, like Fitz's, went straight to voicemail.

'Dammit,' Harper muttered as his recorded voice played.

The story was slipping away from her.

'Mr Scott, it's Harper McClain,' she told the machine urgently. 'I hate to bother you but, to be honest, I'm desperate. If you're right, and Wilson didn't kill Naomi, he needs to call me soon and tell me his side of things. This story is about to blow up. Things are happening fast right now. We're running out of time.'

As she hung up, the first tendrils of panic uncurled in her chest. She'd never screwed up a story this big in her entire career.

It was all her fault. She'd wasted too much time chasing phantoms out at Reidsville, and now she really was in trouble.

There was only one suspect left to call. One more chance to fill the empty space in her article. And she didn't have his phone number.

Luckily, on the other side of the room, Baxter's desk was still empty.

Harper stood. If she craned her neck she could see the glass wall of Paul Dells's office. A small crowd had gathered inside. Baxter must be among them.

The fact that they were meeting for the second time in two days was not something she wanted to think about right now.

Typing so fast she had to redo it twice, she entered Peyton Anderson's name into the newspaper database. It brought back a few articles from his high school baseball years, and an article about a society party where he'd been present along with his parents.

Searching deeper in the resources section, she found extensive contact information for his father, Randall. Beneath that was a short entry for his son. It held only a phone number. There was no indication of how old it was. Or whether it still worked.

Murmuring a quiet prayer, she pulled a recorder from a drawer, plugged it into the telephone and dialed the number.

The phone rang five times. Six.

Harper closed her eyes.

Then: 'Hello? Who's this?'

She recognized his voice from Naomi Scott's memorial service. That distinctive Savannah upper-class accent. A private school crispness to the consonants.

She reminded herself that she'd gotten a good measure of him that night, and she thought she knew what approach to take.

'Hi, Peyton.' She smiled when she said it, forcing herself to talk slow and easy. Like they were old friends. 'This is Harper McClain from the *Savannah Daily News*. You might not remember me, but we met the other night. I wondered if you had a second to talk.'

There was a long pause.

'Of course I remember you.' A new note of caution entered his voice, but he remained at least superficially polite. 'The pretty redhead with all the questions. You know, I don't believe you mentioned you were a reporter at the time.'

'Didn't I?' she asked innocently. 'I thought I did.'

'No, you did not.' He sounded almost amused. 'What can I do for you, Harper?'

The way he said her name set her nerves on edge. She made herself smile so it wouldn't show in her voice.

'I wanted to ask you a few questions for a piece I'm writing about Naomi,' she said. 'You said some things at the wake that were so interesting to me. I'd like to talk to you on the record about how you knew her, and what she was like.'

'I'd be happy to help.' He sounded calm and unthreatened. Like this happened every day. 'I mean, I didn't know her that long, we met at law school. We had a couple of classes together. Hooked up a couple of times. The usual thing.'

'Didn't you tell me it was more than that?' Harper corrected him. 'I thought the two of you had a bit of a thing.'

He brushed that off. 'I wouldn't call it a thing. We were never serious. You know how it is. We went out for a while and moved on.'

'Oh, I remember those crazy college relationships.' Harper grinned. 'Everyone's always hooking up one day and then having to unhook the next. I imagine it was like that?'

'Exactly.' His tone brightened. 'I mean – I'm young. No one wants to be tied down when they're twenty-four. Actually, I was wondering if you're single?'

Harper gave her phone a disbelieving look.

'Not really,' she said. 'But let's talk about Naomi.'

'No wait.' He laughed. 'How can you be *not really* single? We need to talk about this, Harper.'

He was so cocky.

He must realize the police looked at him as a potential suspect – they must have spoken to him and verified his alibi. And yet, here he was, flirting with a reporter who could expose that.

'Oh, you don't want to hear about my boring private life,' she told him. 'Besides, I'm far too old for you. Now, I'd like to get back to Naomi. Were both of you cool with that? The whole hooking and unhooking thing?'

'Sure.' His tone was careless. 'Naomi had her own life. She was busy with work and school, anyway. There wasn't a big scene or anything.'

'I suppose you dated other people after you and Naomi unhooked?' Harper said. 'I mean, you're asking me out. I get the feeling you're a bit of a player.'

'That's harsh, Harper.' But his chuckle said he wasn't offended. 'I mean, I ask ladies out if I like them. If they like me they say yes. It's cool.'

His arrogance was grating. She decided it was time to turn the tables.

'What about Naomi?'

There was a pause. 'I'm sorry – I don't understand.'

'She dated other people, too. Were you fine with that?'

'Of course.'

'Even her relationship with Wilson Shepherd?' Harper pressed. 'From what I understand, the two of them were getting pretty serious. That didn't bother you at all?'

'No.' The lightness faded from his voice. 'If that was who she wanted to be with, if that's what she wanted to do with her life, it was none of my business.'

Tucking the phone beneath her chin, Harper scribbled notes. 'Peyton, I've got to say you don't sound very happy about it.'

'What does that mean?'

'I mean, you're telling me you were fine with Naomi dating Wilson, but you sound angry.'

'That's ridiculous.' His tone was cool now. 'Naomi was fine with me dating and I was fine with her dating. End of story.'

It was time to show her hand.

'Was everything really fine, though? Naomi filed a restraining order against you, didn't she? I've read it, and it doesn't sound to me like you were fine with her dating other people, Peyton. Quite the opposite, actually.'

Anderson fell silent.

Harper persisted. 'If you two were getting along so well, why would she tell the police you spied on her at home? That you followed her to work and to class. That you threatened her . . .'

'Oh come on, Harper.' Anderson had recovered from his surprise. He adopted a dismissive tone. 'I can't believe you're bringing this up. That was all right after we broke up. She was hurt and angry. She said things she didn't mean. We made up and we were fine after that.'

'Did she withdraw the injunction?' Harper asked.

'How would I know?' There was an edge to his voice now. 'We didn't talk about it. It was a dark stain on our friendship. I don't know if she did officially withdraw it. I hope so.'

'She didn't,' Harper informed him. 'It was still in place when someone murdered her.'

The silence after that was very long.

This time, Harper waited him out. She could feel that she was getting close now.

'Well,' Peyton said finally. 'I didn't know that. Look, Harper, I have to go. I'm supposed to be somewhere.'

'I've only got a couple more questions,' she assured him. 'I just need a few things for the record. I take it you deny the allegations contained in Naomi's restraining order?'

'Of course I do,' he said. 'Like I said, it was in the past.'

'It was six months ago,' she corrected him. 'She said you grabbed her shoulder so hard you left bruises on the skin. She submitted photographs to back that up. Did you grab her, Peyton?'

'No, I did not,' he said tightly. 'Do you have many more questions? Because –'

She didn't let him finish. 'Did you go to her house? Let yourself in? Sit on her sofa waiting for her to get out of the shower and find you there?'

'Not if she didn't want me to.' His voice was tense. 'I don't want to go through this line by line, if you don't mind.'

'Oh, that's fine,' Harper said. 'I'm through with that document. Now, I'd like to ask you about restraining orders filed against you by Cameron Johnson and Angela Martinez. I can't help but notice that their allegations are similar to those filed by Naomi.'

She could hear his ragged breathing through the receiver. She couldn't tell whether he was angry or frightened. But he must have figured out how much she knew.

'What is this?' he asked. 'What are you trying to do here?'

'I'm not trying to do anything,' she told him. 'I'm writing a story about Naomi Scott. And these restraining orders are part of it. I'm giving you the right to respond.'

There was another long pause. Across the room, she saw Baxter walk in from the back, and shoot her an urgent look. Silently, Harper waved her over, and hit the speaker button.

She had him where she wanted him. If he blew up at her now, every word he said would be on the record, and he was right on the edge. And Baxter would hear it all.

Peyton didn't speak for what felt like a full minute. When he did talk, he didn't blow up. Quite the opposite.

'Here's my statement on all of this.' His voice was even, now. He was back in control. 'The incidents with Cameron and Angela were regrettable misunderstandings, but I take full responsibility for them. I shouldn't have led them on. When you come from a family like mine, sometimes women get over-eager. They believe you're offering more than you are. And sometimes they want more than you can give. I believe their actions were vindictive and designed to punish me, but I never should have led them on in the first place.'

Baxter had reached her desk now, and stood silently next to her.

'In regards to Naomi Scott – she was a good friend,' he continued. 'I have wonderful memories of our time together. I would never hurt her. If you've investigated this properly, then you know many people have vouched for my where-abouts the night of her murder. Not only would I not have murdered her, I couldn't have. Physically, it was impossible.' He drew a breath. 'I can understand why you need to ask these questions. But please bear in mind that personal relationships are complicated. If Naomi misunderstood anything I said or did, that was between us. At the time of her death, we were still friends.'

'Such good friends,' Harper said, cutting him off, 'that she told the police, and this is a quote, "I think he's going to hurt me one day." With friends like that, she didn't need enemies, did she, Peyton?'

This time she got under his skin. When he spoke again the smooth voice was gone. He sounded furious.

'We are off the record from this point on. If you print these lies, my family will bring down your entire newspaper. And if you're any good at your job, you know we can do it.'

DJ turned around to listen.

'That sounds a lot like a threat, Mr Anderson,' Harper said.

'I'm telling you the facts,' he snapped. 'It's that simple. You print these lies, you're done. Believe me: *done*.'

The phone went dead.

'He sounds like a nice guy,' Baxter said, as Harper unplugged the recorder and set the phone down. 'Did you get anything out of him before he lost it?'

'Not much.' Harper flipped through her notes. 'He's careful.'

'Family of lawyers.' Baxter's tone left no doubt of what she thought of that. 'So, aside from the threats, what've we got?'

Harper tapped the folder on her desk. 'We have the restraining orders. The police acknowledge they're real. But they also insist they've verified his alibi. He could not be our killer, according to them.'

Baxter considered this. 'What other suspects are left? The boyfriend?'

'Yes. Wilson Shepherd is still on the list. I'm trying to get through to him but he's not talking. There's also Jim Fitzgerald, the bar owner.'

'What about him?' Baxter asked.

'Stalked a young female bartender a couple of years ago after his wife left him. Has no alibi for the night of the murder.'

Interest flared in Baxter's face.

'You talked to him?'

Harper shook her head. 'Can't reach him. He's been on a bender since the murder.' She hesitated. 'I know him. And I have to say I don't like him for it.'

Baxter made an impatient gesture.

'Put your own feelings aside on this. Go with what the cops tell you. He's a suspect.'

She tapped her fingers on the stack of injunctions. 'Right now, our story is in those documents. You lead with Anderson. You put in his denials, leave out his threats. Get in touch with the other two suspects. Hear them out. But emphasize his alibi.'

She glanced at the slim silver watch hanging loosely from her wrist.

'Get to work on it now. I'll warn Dells it's coming.'

It occurred to Harper that she'd said nothing at all about that serious-looking meeting in the chief editor's office. But there was no time to ask.

Pivoting, Baxter pointed at DJ, who had watched all of this with avid interest. 'You got plans?'

He nodded nervously.

'Cancel them.' She plucked the scanner from Harper's desk and held it out to him. 'You're on cop shop until she gets the story written.'

With that, the editor headed back across the room, her low-heeled shoes thumping against the hard floor. Her final words floated to them over her narrow shoulder.

'Type fast, McClain.'

Chapter Twenty-two

That night, Harper and Baxter worked on the news story for hours – going through it, word by word. Baxter was ferocious about the details, sending it back over and over for careful adjustments.

When she was satisfied with the article, Dells decided he needed to read it in person.

He strode into the newsroom just after eleven, looking even more expensive than he had during the day. His navy Brooks Brothers suit was unrumpled. His crisp, white shirt set off his tanned skin. He'd taken off his tie, and the faint hint of five o'clock shadow was annoyingly flattering on his clean jawline.

'What've we got?' he'd asked, heading to where Baxter and DJ were standing around Harper's desk.

'I think it's ready,' Baxter told him, moving to one side to make space.

'Let me take a look.' Dells leaned over Harper's shoulder, close enough that she could smell the cool, green scent of his cologne, and the faint, smoky tang of Scotch on his breath.

Harper tried to imagine where someone like Dells socialized. At swanky dinner parties in the suburbs, she supposed. Or in one of the pricey restaurants she'd never once visited.

'You didn't have to come in for this,' she told him. 'Baxter's all over it.'

He shot her a sideways look.

'I was on a blind date. Trust me, this is more fun.'

It was such an unexpectedly honest admission, Harper was disarmed. It had never, until that moment, occurred to her that he might be single. Much less exploring the dubious waters of Savannah's small dating pool.

In fact, she'd never really thought about him much at all, except as her boss – a distant figure she usually only encountered when she was in some sort of trouble.

She didn't dislike him – he hadn't fired her last year when the police tried to get rid of her. But there was no question Dells was a company guy – he'd laid off dozens of employees over the last five years.

And from the sounds of things, he was about to do it again.

He rested one ringless hand on her desktop as he scanned the article quickly.

They'd gone for a simple headline, and Harper had kept the opening paragraphs clean and succinct.

Murdered Girl Was Stalked by DA's Son

By Harper McClain

Murdered law student Naomi Scott was repeatedly threatened and harassed in the final months of her life by Peyton Anderson, a fellow law student and son of former District Attorney Randall Anderson.

According to a series of restraining orders filed in court by Scott, this pattern played out over more than a year. In those documents, she asserted that she feared for her life, and believed Anderson meant to do her harm.

When contacted by the newspaper, the younger Anderson rejected the allegations in the court documents, and denied any responsibility for Scott's death . . .

When he reached that point, Dells stopped.

'Change that,' he said, pointing at the screen. 'Make it, "denied any *involvement*".'

Harper, who had seen most of the words changed by Baxter already, objected.

'Everything in that sentence is true. You can't lose a libel lawsuit over truth.'

'I am aware of that,' he'd said evenly. 'But fighting a lawsuit is too expensive for us right now. We cannot give Anderson a single hook to hang a court case on. Responsibility is a more threatening word than involvement.'

Harper made the change.

It was like that all the way through the article. Dells made numerous cuts – all of them surgical.

Harper argued every point doggedly, until he finally lost his patience.

'Give the readers some credit, McClain,' he snapped wearily. 'Your writing is good. They'll get it.'

When he finished editing, Dells emailed the article to the newspaper's lawyer and asked him to read it over.

It was late by then. And there was nothing to do but wait. The rest of the paper was ready.

Baxter sent DJ home at midnight. After he'd gone, the three of them formed a small island of life in the sea of desks. Dells had draped his jacket over the back of an empty chair and was leaning against Harper's desk. Baxter, who had rolled a chair across, kept looking at her watch.

'We need to wrap this up,' she said, looking at Dells. 'The printers are on double-overtime.'

'I'm not going to rush this.' He straightened. 'Let's look at that layout one more time.'

He and Baxter crossed the room to her computer to look at the final design. Harper didn't follow – she'd seen enough of it. They'd run the story with two photos side by side – Naomi, eyes bright with youth and life. And a shot Miles had taken of Peyton Anderson the night of Naomi's wake at the Library Bar – looking confident and ambitious.

Harper knew this article would set off a firestorm. It was the kind of piece that could make or break a newspaper. The Anderson family didn't issue idle threats.

But this was the kind of article that got picked up by the wire service. That won awards.

Her phone rang, pulling her back to reality.

It was Jerrod Scott.

'Miss McClain, I got your message,' he said. 'I'm sorry to call you so late but I thought you'd want to know. Wilson says he'll talk to you. He wants you to come to his house tomorrow. Says he'll tell you everything he knows.'

Harper gave an air punch.

'Thank you, Mr Scott,' she said. 'I promise I'll treat him fairly.'

'I expect you to. I told him I trust you.'

They talked a while longer, arranging that Harper would go to Shepherd's home in Garden City at 10 a.m. He gave her the address and some basic directions.

When they finished, Scott said, 'He's a little shook up, Miss McClain. Don't be too hard on him.'

After they hung up, Harper raced over to Baxter's desk.

'I've got Wilson Shepherd,' she announced. 'He's going to sit down with me, tomorrow morning.'

'Nice job, McClain.' Dells turned to Baxter. 'Our follow-up could include the –'

He was interrupted by his phone buzzing.

Giving Baxter a look, he stepped into his office to take the call.

Harper and Baxter fell quiet, waiting. Harper strained her ears but he spoke so quietly she couldn't make out a word.

When Dells returned, his expression was grave.

'Tell them to print it,' he told Baxter, who picked up the phone.

Sweeping his jacket off the back of the chair, Dells pulled it on.

'Randall Anderson will not take this lying down. Expect blowback.' He turned to Harper. 'Can you come in early tomorrow?'

'You've got it.'

She had to admire his cool determination. He and Anderson traveled in the same circles. It would be Dells who caught most of the heat from this.

'It's good, McClain,' he told her, knocking his knuckles on the desk as he passed on his way to the door. 'Water-tight.'

'That's my job,' she replied, her tone so casual he might have thought his praise didn't matter.

But his approval had sent hope through her. If there were more layoffs coming, she didn't want to be one of those let go.

It was after one in the morning when she parked on East Jones Street. Before she even got out of the car, she saw Luke, standing on her front steps.

It took all her skill to keep her expression blank, hiding the whirlwind of emotions swirling through her. Confusion, excitement and, worst of all, happiness.

'What's going on?' she asked.

He must have come straight from work. He'd taken off his suit jacket and rolled up his shirt sleeves.

'Can we go inside?' he asked. 'We need to talk.'

The tension in his voice told her not to argue.

Without another word, she moved past him on the narrow landing to unlock the door.

As she punched in the alarm code still visible on her wrist, he kept his eyes on the street.

Even inside, he seemed twitchy – uncomfortable.

'Want something to drink?' Harper asked.

'Are you having something?' he asked. 'I will if you do.'

'All I've got is whiskey and coffee,' she said apologetically. 'I haven't been to the store.'

'Whiskey's fine.'

Harper, who'd never known him to drink anything stronger than a beer, said nothing as she headed for the kitchen.

Pulling the bottle of Jameson's from the cupboard, she grabbed two glasses and poured them each a generous measure.

When she walked back into the living room, he was standing in front of the fireplace, looking up at the blank stretch of white wall above the mantelpiece.

'You never put the painting back,' he said, as he accepted the glass she held out.

He didn't have to explain which one he'd meant. When her house was broken into a year ago, the intruder had slashed a portrait Bonnie had painted of Harper, putting a knife through her face.

'Bonnie tried to fix it,' Harper explained. 'But it was too damaged.' She gestured at the sofa. 'Tell me what's going on.'

She took a seat across from him, waiting as Luke took a sip and set the glass down on the coffee table and pulled the plastic bag containing the note from her car out of his pocket.

'We didn't get any prints off it,' he told her quietly. 'He must have worn gloves.'

'Dammit.' Harper sagged back.

She'd spent all night working on a story about a stalker. She wasn't missing the parallels in her own life right now. Was this how Naomi Scott felt? Trapped and helpless?

Luke set the note down next to his drink.

'What are you going to do, Harper?'

'Oh, hell, Luke, I don't know.' She rubbed her forehead, wearily. The day had been too long already. And the hits just kept on coming.

'I feel like I'm fighting a ghost.'

She finished her whiskey in one swallow, knowing it wouldn't help. Wishing it would.

Across from her, Luke did the same.

'The thing I can't figure out,' he said after a second's reflection, 'is what does he want from you?'

'I don't know, but that note didn't exactly make me feel like I've found my soul mate,' Harper told him caustically.

Luke gave her a look she couldn't read and then, grabbing their glasses, headed for the kitchen.

'Well, as long as we don't know who he is or what he wants, he's holding all the cards,' he said over his shoulder.

Harper thought of her conversation earlier that day with Smith. She didn't want to tell Luke what she'd learned, or try to explain how she'd come to those conclusions.

In fact, right now, she didn't want to talk about this at all. She was too tired to make good decisions.

A moment later, Luke returned, holding a glass out to her.

When she reached up, her fingers brushed against his.

Electricity crackled between them.

And then he ruined it.

'Well, I don't like you staying here alone until we know more.'

'That's too bad,' she said, shortly. 'Because I live here.'

'Stay at a hotel then. Anywhere but here.'

She almost laughed before she realized he was serious.

'Oh come on, Luke. I'm not walking away from home because of this.'

His face darkened. 'You've cut off his access, Harper. You didn't run when he told you to. If he's crazy enough and obsessed enough, he could come in here to do whatever he wants.'

'Let him,' she said, her voice heated. 'I can protect myself.'

'Yeah, I've seen your baseball bat.'

The way he said it made it clear he didn't think much of her self-defense plan.

'I'll be fine, Luke.'

'I know you will.' Finishing his drink, he set the glass down on the coffee table and stood up. 'Because I'm going to be standing right outside your door.'

Turning, he strode across the living room.

It took Harper a second to process what was happening. When she did, she jumped to her feet and hurried after him.

'Wait. What? What do you mean?'

She caught up with him in the entrance hall, where he was opening the front door.

'I'm going to stay out here,' he said, pointing at the front steps with a gesture that said this made perfect sense to him. 'And keep watch. Let him see me. Let him realize you've got people looking out for you.'

Before she could think of an appropriate response to this insane decision, he walked out and closed the door behind him.

Harper stood in the glare of the entrance hall light, staring at the closed door with frank astonishment.

What had gotten into him? He'd come back into her life after months, and all of a sudden he was an avenging angel, protecting her from unknown assailants.

She opened the door and stepped outside.

It was dark, and uncannily quiet. Harper couldn't even hear cars in the distance.

The night air was warm silk against her skin. Insects fluttered around the streetlight, dicing with death.

Standing a couple of steps down, Luke turned to look up at her.

'Come back inside, Luke,' she whispered.

'It's fine,' he assured her. 'I'll keep an eye out. Until the sun comes up.'

'This is ridiculous.' Harper let her voice rise just a little. 'Will you come inside? You can guard me there if you want.'

When he didn't react, she said, 'For God's sake, Luke. What if a patrol car comes by? Riley put the house on the patrol list. They'll see you. Word will get around. It'll be like last time.'

He stood unmoving for a long second as if thinking about arguing. Then, slowly, he mounted the steps.

'I hadn't thought about that.' He let the door shut behind him. 'Fine. I'll stay inside.'

They stood in the doorway, facing each other.

'You don't have to protect me,' she told him.

He held her eyes.

'I want to.'

The entrance hall was narrow, forcing them close together. She could smell the fresh air on him. Beneath that, the familiar, sandalwood scent of the soap he used.

It had been such a long, lonely year. She'd never stopped hoping that someday he would stand here again, looking at her the way he was looking at her right now.

Without even knowing she was going to do it, Harper reached out and touched his arm.

She felt the twitch of his muscles beneath her fingertips.

If she hadn't had that whiskey, if it hadn't been such a long day, if she hadn't gone out to Reidsville that morning – maybe she wouldn't have been brave enough to let her hand trace up the length of his arm to his shoulder, and from there to the fine edge of his jaw.

She'd forgotten how his skin felt. The warm life of him.

She kept thinking he'd pull away.

Instead, he leaned into her touch. His eyes fluttered shut, dark lashes soft against his tanned skin.

'Luke,' she whispered, moving close enough to feel his body against hers. 'I miss you so much.'

His eyes opened and looked down into hers.

'I miss you, too.'

It was the only thing she'd wanted to hear.

Reaching up, she pulled his head down, raising her lips to meet his.

Their kiss was tentative at first, and searching. But it grew in intensity almost instantly as they both accepted what was happening. His hands slid up her hips to her waist and pulled her hard against him as he kissed her hungrily.

Harper smiled against his lips, touching his teeth with her tongue. Giving in to the heat of him.

She'd waited so long for this.

'Harper,' he whispered, hands touching her everywhere. As if he, too, needed reassurance this moment was real. 'Harper.'

Each time he said her name she felt it inside her.

She'd never wanted anyone as much as she wanted him right now.

'Luke,' she whispered. 'Please stay.'

Breathing heavily, he tightened his grip on her, resting his forehead against hers and looking into her eyes.

'I'm not going anywhere.'

Chapter Twenty-three

'Why did we wait so long?' Harper murmured. 'We're so stupid.'

Her head was on Luke's chest, her fingers drawing loops against the smooth skin of his chest. She could feel his breath soft against her hair.

He'd been very quiet for a long time now, and she wondered if he'd fallen asleep. But she didn't look up at him. She didn't want to break the spell.

Sex had always been good with Luke. Tonight was no different. It was just as it had been before – they were perfectly in sync.

Everything between them had been fierce and hungry – as if they were starved for each other.

Now she felt like she'd ended up right where she belonged.

She was so happy. She wanted to stay happy.

'I don't know,' he said finally. 'It's been a hard year. For both of us.'

There was a curious note to his voice. A kind of distance. She could feel his chest rising and falling more rapidly beneath her cheek.

Reluctantly, Harper raised herself up on one arm to look at him. There was a new heaviness in the lines of his mouth. It hadn't been there earlier. He looked so . . . sad.

'Hey,' she said softly. 'What's the matter?'

He didn't reply. But she could feel his muscles tighten beneath her.

'Luke?' she said.

He drew in a long breath.

'It always feels so right with you, Harper.' He reached for her hand, holding it in both of his. 'That's why I don't understand.'

Swallowing the trepidation rising in her throat, Harper sat up. They were both naked. The sheets swirled around her waist, her hair lay tangled across her shoulders.

'What don't you understand?' she asked, weaving her fingers through his.

'Why we can't get it together.' The pain in his eyes sent shards of worry through her heart. 'There's always something stopping us from making this work. Something you do. Something I do. Our work. The timing. We never get it right. And yet, it feels right. Every time.'

Around them, the old house was so quiet it might have been holding its breath. No cars drove down the street. It was the still of the night.

'We couldn't before,' she said, watching him carefully. 'But we can now, right?'

Luke raised their joined hands to his mouth and kissed her fingers. Then he slipped his hand free of hers with clear reluctance and met her gaze.

'What just happened shouldn't have happened,' he said.

'Oh.' Reaching for the sheet, she pulled it up to cover herself.

She didn't ask for more information. She didn't want any. She knew all she needed to know from looking at his face.

Twisting her body until she could slide to the side of the bed and put her feet on the floor, she reached down, finding her top where they'd dropped it an hour earlier.

With her back to him, she pulled it on then, keeping the sheets tight around her waist felt the floor for her pants.

'Harper,' he said. 'Look at me.'

'I need my pants,' she said, refusing to turn around.

'Harper . . .'

'Let me get *dressed*.' Her voice shook.

She finally found them thrown across the footboard of the antique brass bed. Still not looking at him, she pulled them on and stood up.

Only then, did she turn to face him.

'Just say it.'

He sat up, the sheet loose beneath the smooth muscles of his chest. In the cool wash of moonlight filtering through the sheer curtains, he might have been carved from marble. He was so beautiful it killed her.

His throat worked as he searched for the right words to break her heart.

'I should have told you earlier. I just didn't know how. I didn't want to say anything. But I've . . . I've been seeing someone else, Harper.'

If he'd slapped her it wouldn't have hurt more. Harper felt almost breathless from it.

She stared at him in disbelief. Waiting for more. Waiting for the next blow.

But he just sat there. Watching her. Waiting for her to react.

I'm so stupid, she thought.

All this time – an entire *year* – she'd waited for him. She'd stayed alone in this house night after night thinking, somewhere in the back of her mind, that they would find a way. That the things they'd been through together mattered.

Surely, nobody could go through what they'd endured and then just walk away from it all.

She'd believed that so fundamentally it had never occurred to her to date someone else. Never occurred to her that whether or not they got back together might not be her decision.

And all that time he'd been seeing someone else. Getting over her. Moving on.

'Get out,' she said, the words low and venomous and filled with pain.

Then she turned on her heel and left the room.

The problem with small apartments is there's nowhere to hide. She wasn't about to lock herself in the bathroom. This was *her* home.

Instead, she went to the kitchen and began making coffee. Measuring the grounds, filling the jug with water. She didn't know why she was doing it – she didn't want coffee. She didn't want anything. But she kept going, her movements deliberate and careful, her hands steady.

She felt numb.

Not yet, her subconscious was telling her. *You'll feel it later. But not yet.*

When Luke walked in, he'd put on his jeans. His shirt hung loose, unbuttoned. He'd splashed water on his face. Some had gotten on his collar, and Harper found herself focusing on that detail – the circular spots of dampness.

It was easier than looking at his beautiful, lost face.

'How long?' she heard herself ask.

'A few months.'

He stayed by the door. His voice was steady but every muscle in his body was taut and tense.

A few months. Long enough.

'Why did you come here tonight?' Her voice was leaden. She didn't want to know. But she had to know.

'I was worried about you. And then . . .' He paused, a muscle in his jaw working. 'I wasn't lying. I do miss you.'

Harper ignored that completely.

'Does she know you're here?'

He gave her a tortured look.

'No,' he said. 'Look, I didn't come over here tonight expecting to do this.'

'Do what?' She met his gaze. 'Cheat?' He flinched, but she didn't back down. 'That wasn't what you wanted when you came here tonight? To have sex with me and see if you still had feelings for me? Just to check? "One last time with Harper in case there's something I missed?"'

'That's not it,' he insisted. 'It's not that simple.'

'Oh, it's very simple, Luke.' She shoved the coffeemaker away. 'You're with someone else now. I'm in your past. And then we ran into each other at that stupid crime scene and you thought, "Oh look. There's Harper. I've been ignoring her for a year but maybe I still care. Let's check."'

A tear ran down her cheek and she noted its presence with surprise because she couldn't fully feel the pain. But it was coming.

'So here you are, checking.' She took a step toward him. 'What did you feel, Luke? Do you care? Because, I'll share a little secret with you – I was *in love* with you.' She threw the words at him hard, watching them hit. 'I waited for you. And you did this.'

She drew a ragged breath, hands clenching.

'I didn't mean to hurt you . . .' he began.

'Well you did.' Her voice rose. 'You did.'

She almost couldn't speak now, her throat was closing on her words.

'A year ago you left me because you thought I betrayed you.' She made herself meet his eyes. 'Now we're even. And I want you out of my house.'

He stood in the kitchen doorway for a long time, looking at her, hands loose at his side. She couldn't bear to see him anymore. She spun around, turning her back to him.

'I do care, Harper,' he said quietly. 'That's the problem.'

'Please go.'

She wouldn't look up but she could sense him hesitating. Hear his breathing as he decided.

'I'm sorry,' he said, very softly. 'I truly am.'

She stood in the glow of her kitchen light, holding her breath, listening to his footsteps cross the living room.

In the deep quiet, she heard every movement. The clicking of the locks turning. The beep of the alarm. The faint creak as the front door opened.

The air moving as it closed with a final thud she felt in her heart.

Still she stood, unwavering, until the rumble of a car engine broke the quiet of the night.

Only then did she take a gasping breath and loosen her grip on the counter.

Slowly, silently, she slid down to the floor and buried her face against her knees.

Chapter Twenty-four

The next day, Harper thought about canceling her interview with Wilson Shepherd and staying home. She was in no fit state to work. She hadn't slept after Luke left. She was running on air.

In the end, though, she knew that wasn't possible.

Besides, she couldn't bear a day alone with her thoughts.

Her mind circled last night's activities like a predator around a fresh carcass.

She kept thinking how happy she'd been. And then hearing him say, 'I've been seeing someone else.' Imagining her own stricken expression.

Each time it was worse. More mortifying.

How could she have been so naive as to think he wouldn't be dating? He was good-looking, and a cop. He was only twenty-eight. There were so many women out there who would kill to have a hot young detective of their very own.

The more she thought about it, the more it all made sense. The way he'd looked at her when she told him there'd been no one since him – the surprise. And worse – the pity.

Of course he felt sorry for her. Who sits around for an entire year waiting for a man she'd dated for a few weeks to come back to her?

It was pitiful, actually. *She* was pitiful.

She hated being pitiful.

For hours, she'd sat in the kitchen, as Zuzu slept on the chair across from her, watching the sun rise over the old rooftops, nursing her wounds as the coffee she'd made when he was still there grew cold and stale.

Sometime around eight that morning, she realized that if she sat there long enough, she might actually go crazy. So, she got up and started moving.

She wasn't scheduled to interview Shepherd until ten o'clock. But, there were better things she could be doing than sitting in her house. God knew Luke wouldn't be sitting at home with a cat. He'd be with his new girlfriend, coming up with creative excuses about where he'd been the night before.

She dressed quickly, barely noticing what she put on. Then she grabbed her scanner and notebooks, and headed out.

The second she entered the newsroom, DJ waved her over urgently.

'What's up?' she asked.

'Anderson,' he hissed, jutting a finger toward the editor's office across the room. 'Just came in. He and Dells are throwing down.'

Only then did Harper hear the muffled shouting. Male voices, both talking at the same time.

Tilting her head to one side, she tried to make out what they were saying.

'Anderson father or son?' she asked.

The answer came from behind her. 'It's Daddy Anderson.'

Harper turned to find Ed Lasterson, the newspaper's court reporter, leaning forward as he, too, tried to listen.

He was in his forties, with straight black hair, and a tall, angular build that somehow made all his suits look like they were intended to fit someone else entirely. He was quiet and ordinarily kept to himself.

Harper rated him as a writer, although they didn't know each other well. He and his wife had young twins, and he was out of the office most days by five thirty on the dot.

'Did you hear what happened?' she asked, stepping closer to his desk.

'Everyone within five counties must have heard.' He pointed at the newsroom door. 'About five minutes ago, Anderson comes busting in here with the security guard on his heels, telling everyone he'll talk to Dells or sue this place to the ground. Dells comes out of his office and tries to calm him down but Anderson says, "You went after my son. I'll ruin you for this, you lying son of a bitch."'

Harper winced. 'Aren't the two of them supposed to be friends?'

Across the room, the voices from the glass office crescendoed.

'I don't have to listen to a goddamn thing you say!' a man shouted.

'That friendship appears to be getting shorter by the minute,' DJ observed.

They stood in a line, staring across the newsroom toward the editor's office.

Harper thought of Dells, leaning over her shoulder, carefully deleting anything Anderson might sue over.

'He didn't trust him,' she said, mostly to herself. 'I think he knew this would happen.'

Ed gave her a curious look but, before he could ask what she meant, the editor's office door flew open with such force it crashed into the wall behind it, sending a crack down the glass.

The newsroom fell silent.

A red-faced, stocky man with thick gray hair burst out, the jacket of his tailored suit swinging.

Dells was right behind him. His jaw was set, and his blue eyes were chips of ice. But he kept his voice under control.

'For God's sake, Randall,' he said reasonably. 'Calm down and talk this over.'

'I'll calm down when you're fired.' Anderson shoved his finger in his face. 'You retract that story or I'll bring you down myself.'

'If you had a case,' Dells told him, 'you'd have filed a lawsuit already.'

'You think so?' The other man glared. 'You always did underestimate me, Paul.'

With that, he stormed across the room, knocking papers off Baxter's desk as he passed.

Dells didn't follow him. He still stood in the entrance to his office – shoulders high and fists tight – as if he was preparing to protect it from invaders, as Anderson thundered down the steps.

For a moment, Dells stood where he was, looking at the newsroom door. Then he turned to scan the room.

Spotting Harper, he motioned for her to follow, and strode back into his office.

She could feel the other reporters watching as she hurried across the newsroom, which felt hushed in the aftermath of the argument.

As she passed Baxter's desk, Harper noticed it was empty; her computer screen was blank.

When she reached his office, Dells stood with his back to her, looking out the window at the blue ribbon of river, shining in the morning sun.

'Close the door, please.'

Harper did as he asked.

Crossing to the modern glass desk, he lowered himself into his chair.

Harper didn't wait for him to talk.

'How bad is it?' she asked, sitting across from him.

'Well, it's not *great*.' He took off his glasses and rubbed the bridge of his nose. 'You saw him. He wants my head on a plate.'

'Does he have a case?' she asked.

He glanced up at her. 'The story is solid. Don't worry about that.'

She leaned back against the leather and chrome of her chair. 'So we're safe.'

'I wouldn't say that.' He set the glasses down, and they clinked against the glass. 'Anderson thinks this is personal, so he'll have his staff going through all our articles, looking for anything he can use to get at us. Any mistake we've made in the last year, no matter how small, he'll find it.'

He shot her a rueful look. 'He's a vindictive son of a bitch. And he's a very good lawyer.'

'Why are you his friend?' she asked, wondering as she said it whether the lack of sleep was affecting her judgement.

His eyebrows rose, but he answered the question.

'He's useful,' he said simply. 'Sometimes it's valuable to have useful associates.'

He looked nearly as tired as she felt. Without glasses, his eyes were quite striking. Pale blue, and clear as lake water.

'You knew, didn't you?' she said. 'You knew he'd do something like this.'

'I had an idea he wouldn't be thrilled.'

A copy of the day's newspaper lay on his desk and he turned it over. Peyton Anderson's smooth face looked up at them beneath the damning headline they'd worked on so carefully last night.

'This is his son we're talking about. I guessed he'd come out swinging today.' He glanced at the damaged glass wall. 'I didn't think he'd do it in my office, though.'

Harper had worked with Dells since she started at the newspaper, and he'd never been as open as he'd been lately. There'd always been a bluntness to his approach to reporters, but he'd never been this forthcoming.

Seeing that he was in the mood for honesty, she decided to ask more.

'He can't really bring the paper down, can he?' she asked. 'We haven't done anything wrong.'

'We haven't. But he can make life very difficult for us,' he said. 'That's why I think we need to dig further into this story. Start with the other suspects. The boyfriend and the bar owner – let's find out more about them. We have to prove we're being fair.' He glanced at his watch. 'What about that interview – isn't it this morning?'

'I'm meeting him at ten,' Harper told him.

'Good. And the bar owner?'

She held up her hands. 'I'm trying. He's not answering his phone.'

'Track him down,' he ordered. 'This is a small town. Everyone can be found.'

'I'll get him.' She paused, before asking, 'What about the Anderson kid? Should we back off?'

Dells didn't answer right away. He picked up a heavy black pen from the top of his desk and studied it.

When he looked up, his expression was harder than she'd ever seen it.

'I want you to find out everything you can about Peyton Anderson. We know he has issues with women. Let's find the rest. Has he ever been arrested for hitting a woman? Or anything else? If he's had so much as a speeding ticket, I want to know about it.'

Harper couldn't believe it. He wasn't backing down. He was putting it all on the line.

'I'll find out all I can,' she told him. 'Also, we know of three women he's harassed – why don't I talk to the two who are still alive?'

He gave her an approving look.

'Do it. And remind me: Why don't the police consider him a suspect?'

'All anyone will say is that he has a good alibi,' she said.

'I want to know what that alibi is,' he told her firmly. 'Today.'

'I'll do my best.'

She wondered fleetingly what her editor would think if he knew she'd just had sex with, and been dumped for a second time by a detective working on this case. One who knew everything.

'Let me know if I can do anything to help,' he said. 'And I mean that. This is the biggest story you've ever worked on, as far as I'm concerned. I expect to be part of every step of it from here on out.'

Taking this as an indication the discussion was over, Harper stood and headed for the door.

Dells called her back.

'Harper.'

She turned to find him watching her with a look of ruthless determination.

'Let's do this right,' he said. 'The Anderson family is gunning for us. Don't give them an easy target.'

Chapter Twenty-five

Wilson Shepherd lived in Garden City – a workaday Savannah suburb filled with sprawling half-acre plots with small, weathered houses.

Shepherd's house was just as Jerrod Scott had described, a small blue one-story, with peeling paint and a crooked mailbox out front that looked like someone had backed into it.

When Harper parked at the curb, the late morning air was warm and thick as soup. Some kids were playing football down the road – shouting orders to each other and cheering. Otherwise, it was quiet.

The walkway to the house was cracked but the lawn was neatly trimmed.

When she rang the bell, the door opened so quickly she took a step back in surprise.

Shepherd was about five foot ten, with light-brown skin and a round face. He wore a blue Nike T-shirt with loose khaki shorts.

He looked so different from the man she'd seen arrested and released from jail last week, he might have been his brother.

His eyes were clear and focused. He looked drawn but not unstable as he studied her with some suspicion.

'Wilson, I'm Harper McClain,' she said, when he didn't speak. 'Jerrod Scott told me you were willing to talk.'

He didn't move or speak for so long she began to fear he might send her away.

Then, with clear reluctance that told her Scott had talked him into this moment against his will, he opened the door wider.

'I guess you better come in.'

Inside, the house was much like the outside – a bit shabby, in need of a lick of paint, but very clean. The faded linoleum floors shone in the entrance hall. Not a speck of dust besmirched the coffee table in the living room he led her into.

The OCD part of Harper recognized a fellow neat freak.

They sat across from each other on black, fake leather sofas.

Wilson seemed anxious, his hands knotted above his knees.

'Can I get you a drink?' he asked hopefully. 'Coffee?'

'I'm fine, thanks.' She wanted him looking at her, not doing something to distract himself. She needed to assess him. 'I appreciate you taking the time to meet with me. I know this must be difficult. I'm sure Mr Scott told you why I'm here. I need to talk to you about Naomi.'

His only reaction to his dead girlfriend's name was a kind of withdrawal – he seemed to curl up. Like someone who'd been punched so often he no longer really felt the blow.

'I'm sorry for your loss,' she added, belatedly.

There was a pause.

'You're the first person to say that to me.' He was soft-spoken, his voice deep but very quiet. 'Right now the only person who doesn't think I killed her is Jerrod Scott.'

'That's why I'm here.' She kept her expression open, approachable. 'I know you've answered a lot of questions for the police. I need to ask you a few more to make sure I understand.'

She pulled a digital recorder out of her bag. 'Would you mind if I recorded this?'

He leaned back on the sofa, studying her from beneath lowered brows.

'I have nothing to hide.'

Harper set the small silver recorder on the coffee table between them, its red light glowing. She didn't usually use one for face-to-face interviews, but she didn't want to spend this interview looking down at her notepad. She wanted to observe him.

'Tell me about you and Naomi. When did you get together?'

'At school.'

'She had a part-time job looking out for new students from difficult backgrounds,' Harper pressed. 'Is that how you met?'

'Yes. I'm the first person in my family to go to college. My father works in maintenance at an office building in Atlanta. My mother works at a hotel. They were so proud . . .'

His voice trembled and he looked away.

'They were so proud of me,' he said after a second, 'when I got into college, and then when I was accepted to law school. It was like they'd achieved something themselves, you know?'

His eyes searched her face for understanding. Harper's background wasn't the same as his, but she'd put herself through the first couple of years of college. She knew how hard it was. Filling out your own financial aid forms. Choosing your books, courses and dorm all alone.

'Naomi helped you.'

He nodded. 'She was one of the first people I met at school. She walked me through the first couple of weeks, making sure I got a good start. But it was more than that. We hung out after class, talking, for hours.' His face lightened at the memory. 'One day, I noticed how much I looked forward to seeing her. And I told her that. We became friends. It wasn't a job then for her – it was fun. I got into law school the same year she did.' He turned his hands over. 'After that, we started seeing each other more seriously.'

'Were you aware she'd had a relationship with a student named Peyton Anderson?' she asked.

His expression darkened.

'I read your article about the restraining orders in the paper this morning. You made it sound bad. But not nearly as bad as it was.'

'How bad was it?'

'I know how you're going to take this,' he said. 'But I believe he's insane. The things he did to her . . .'

'What did you mean when you said you knew how I would take this?' she asked.

He gave her a knowing look. 'I'm a law student. I know when a murder suspect tells you someone else is dangerous, you think he's trying to put the blame on that guy to save himself. But all I can tell you is – Peyton Anderson *is* dangerous.'

'Was Naomi afraid of him?' she asked.

'Hell yes, she was.' For the first time, he showed real animation, sitting forward on the sofa, talking fast. 'He showed up in her living room, uninvited, when she got out of the shower. He told her he'd kill one of us if she didn't break up with me. He threatened her openly.'

'Why didn't she tell her dad how bad it was?' Harper asked.

'She didn't want to upset him. She thought she could handle it.' His throat worked. 'Then she got shot and the police said it was me.'

So far, Harper was impressed. He seemed candid and sad. But she was also aware that he had legal training. It would be foolish to take him at face value. She needed to push him harder. See what happened.

'People who know you and Naomi say you were having trouble – maybe breaking up,' she said. 'That would be motive, as far as the police are concerned.'

A long moment passed before he replied.

'We were both law students – that's a lot of work all on its own. We both have jobs – I work afternoons until eight o'clock. Naomi's job kept her out most nights until nearly three in the morning. Sometimes days would go by when we only saw each other in class. It was hard, I'm not going to lie to you. But we weren't breaking up. We were trying to find a way. Naomi . . . she was looking for another job with better hours.' He blinked hard. 'I knew we were going to be fine. Because she was all that mattered to me.'

'Let's talk about the night of the murder,' she said. 'Walk me through it. Where were you? What did you do?'

He took a deep breath.

'I had a paper to write for one of my classes. I finished at about eleven, then I watched some television. I must have fallen asleep because the next thing I knew the phone was ringing.'

Up until this point, he talked quickly. Reciting facts he'd obviously been asked to explain many times. Now, his words came slower, getting harder to say.

'It was Naomi's dad. He said something happened to her. That was when I found out.'

'And nobody knew you were home?' Harper pushed back. 'You didn't talk to anyone?'

He gave a bitter laugh.

'You want to know something funny? The only person who can back up my alibi is Naomi. She knew where I was. I texted her.' Reaching into his pocket he pulled out his phone, touched the screen to open his texts, and held it out to her.

'See for yourself.'

Harper took the phone.

He'd opened it to a text conversation, dated the day of the murder. The name at the top said 'Naomi'.

At eleven twenty-six that night, Wilson had written:

> I'm done working. What time are you getting off?

Naomi had replied three minutes later:

> 2:30. It's quiet, though. Maybe I'll get out early. How'd it go?

> Meh.

> ☺ Meh for you is an A+ for anyone else. Are you at home?

> Yeah, gonna watch the news and crash.

> Jealous. Sleep tight. See you tomorrow.

It was the last thing Naomi had written.

After that there was nothing until a series of plaintive texts from Wilson written later that night, after her father called.

They were messages written by someone who desperately didn't want to believe.

4:12 a.m.: Nay, where are you? Your daddy says
something happened. Tell me he's wrong.

4:15 a.m.: Baby, please answer.

4:23 a.m.: I love you.

It was painful to read. When Harper handed the phone back,
he closed the screen without looking at it.

'I don't know how to make you understand.' His voice was
uneven. 'I didn't kill her. I wanted to *marry her*. I still want to
marry her. I don't understand how she's not . . . Excuse me.'

Standing abruptly, he left the room.

The house was small; Harper could hear Wilson in the next
room, blowing his nose.

When he returned, his eyes were red. He held a tissue in
one hand.

'You sure you don't want a cup of coffee?'

He needed something to do or he would fall apart in front of her.

'Sure,' she said. 'I like it black.'

Wilson Shepherd's kitchen was bigger than Harper expected,
given the modest size of the house. It had space for a table, which
he used as a work area. His laptop sat on one side, next to a
neat stack of papers.

She leaned against the counter, watching as he scooped coffee
into the coffeemaker. She'd carried the recorder with her, and set
it down just out of his view. It would be good if he could forget
it was there.

'This is a nice place,' she said, looking around. 'How long
have you lived here?'

'Six months.' He poured water into the reservoir and flipped the switch. The machine whirred into life, and the rich scent of coffee filled the air. Wilson's back was to Harper when he spoke again. 'Naomi was supposed to move in with me in a couple of months. When she stopped working nights.'

Pulling two clean white mugs from the cupboard, he arranged them on the counter with a sugar jar and creamer.

'Garden City might not be much, but you can rent a whole house for nothing out here. I thought we could live here until we graduated, and then find a place in town.'

As he told her of their now impossible plans, his expression was bleak.

'Wilson,' she said, 'you seem like a smart guy. A trustworthy guy. But the other night when you were arrested, you were waving a gun at the police. Why did you do that?'

He froze, hands hovering above the mugs.

'I hardly remember that whole day,' he said softly. 'I knew the police were looking for me, and I knew they wanted to blame me. But all I could think about was Naomi, and what happened. It tore me up, thinking about it. I knew they'd look at my back-ground – the things I did when I was a kid – and they'd blame it on me. If they did that, the killer would get away.' He met her eyes with sudden directness. 'If the police have someone to pin a murder on – especially a young black man – they wash their hands of the truth, you know that, right? I mean with your job. You have to know.'

Harper couldn't argue with him. After all, Daltrey and Blazer had made it clear they wanted it to be him.

It would make their lives so easy.

'So you ran,' she said, leading him back to the story. 'Where were you going? They caught you on the edge of town.'

'I don't know,' he said. 'I didn't have a plan. I was going crazy. And I know that makes no sense. But I was in pain. I lost it.'

'What about the gun?'

He gave a bitter smile.

'You'll never believe the truth.'

She didn't blink. 'Try me.'

'I bought that for Naomi. To protect herself. Because she was scared. But she wouldn't take it. Said guns didn't make anyone safer.' He gave her a tortured look. 'The police arrested me with the gun I wanted my dead girlfriend to use to stay safe.'

The coffeemaker had finished now, and Harper could hear herself breathe in the sudden silence.

'Wilson,' she said, 'who do you think killed Naomi?'

He didn't hesitate.

'I think Peyton Anderson killed her. I think his father is covering it up for him. And I don't believe the police will ever, in one hundred years, arrest him.'

In that instant, Harper decided that she agreed with him.

To disguise this, she reached for the carafe, pouring coffee into both their cups.

'The police say he has an alibi,' she told him. 'That he couldn't have done it.'

'Oh yeah?' He didn't sound convinced. 'That guy is made of money. He could pay people to say whatever he wants. Guys like him? They get away with murder.'

She couldn't blame him for sounding bitter. But she knew the police would never have accepted Anderson's word. They'd have wanted proof, regardless of who his dad was.

And if she was going to challenge that alibi, she was going to need proof of her own.

She turned to Wilson. 'If you really are telling the truth – if it wasn't you who killed Naomi – then help me prove it.'

His face lit up. 'What can I do to help?'

'I need you to tell me everything you can remember about Peyton and Naomi. And I need evidence. If you can find any emails she sent you about him, send those to me. Texts. Everything. I need it all.' She gave him a warning look. 'Don't alter anything. And no lies. I need complete truth or we'll both be in trouble.'

As he listened to her, a tear slipped down his cheek. He swiped it away.

'Please believe me, Miss McClain,' he pleaded. 'I'm no killer. And my family . . . They need to know it wasn't me.'

He drew a shaky breath.

'I'll get you everything I can.'

Chapter Twenty-six

After leaving Wilson's Garden City house, Harper headed straight back to the newspaper to transcribe the recording of the interview.

Her phone buzzed with sporadic demands from Bonnie, who wanted her to meet for coffee.

Harper's thumb hovered over the phone's tiny keyboard. She knew why Bonnie wanted to meet. And she just wasn't ready to talk about Luke yet. Not even with her.

'Can't,' she texted back. 'Working on a big story.'

The reply came instantly. 'Tomorrow then.'

Harper sighed. 'I'll try.'

Tossing the phone aside, she got back to work.

With her headphones on, lost in Wilson Shepherd's voice, she never heard Dells approaching until he tapped her on the shoulder.

She yanked the earphones from her ears.

'How'd it go with the boyfriend?' he asked. 'Any luck?'

'Pure gold.' She beamed at him. 'He let me see the text messages they sent to each other the night she died.'

As she spoke, Baxter walked up to join them.

'Are they useful?' Dells asked.

'She asked if he was at home, he said yes. Said he was going to bed early.'

'Be careful with that,' Baxter warned, glancing at Dells.

'Yes.' He leaned against the desk next to hers and crossed his ankles. His shiny black shoes looked like they might have cost more than Harper earned in a week. 'He could have been standing on River Street when he wrote that text, loading his pistol.'

'I know,' Harper said. 'But I've got to be honest. Having talked to him, I don't like him for it.'

'Why's that?' Baxter cocked her head, dark eyes watching her sharply.

'Instinct, I guess,' Harper said. Baxter made an impatient gesture but Harper kept going. 'He's fragile. He seems devastated in a way I would be if my girlfriend just got shot to death on her way home from work. Either he didn't do it or he deserves an Oscar for that performance.'

'Well, let's assume he's a gifted actor until we have more proof,' Dells said. 'In my experience, killers make great liars.'

'I'd lay money on it not being him,' Harper insisted.

'Then prove it's someone else,' Baxter told her shortly. 'What's next?'

Harper picked up the file of injunctions that lay on her desk. 'I'm going to talk to the other two women Anderson stalked. See what they have to say. I've tracked them both down, already. They're still in town. I've left messages for both of them.'

'Good,' Dells said. 'Keep it moving. We've got no more than three days left to pull this all together. Two would be better.'

When he'd walked back to his office, she turned to Baxter.

'What's happening in two days?'

The editor gave her a level look.

'There's a lot going on right now that you don't know about. Let's just say we all need to be very careful.'

Harper frowned. 'What does that mean?'

There was a pause.

'I know you've heard about the restructuring plans,' the city editor said. 'But remember, Dells can take the hits from the Anderson family. You can't. And, I've got to say, I'm not really happy that he's putting you in the middle of this.'

Before Harper could ask more questions, she reached into her pocket and pulled out a pack of Marlboro Golds.

'I'm going out for a smoke.'

It took several phone calls, and a lot of fast talking, but eventually Harper convinced Cameron Johnson and Angela Martinez to meet her the next afternoon when their classes ended for the day.

To set the women at ease, she'd chosen a public place for the meeting and so, at four o'clock, she set out for the Pangaea coffee shop.

It was, her own newspaper informed her, the hottest day of the year so far. The summer that would not end showed no sign of letting them out of its vice grip.

Harper was sweating before she reached the car.

With the air-conditioning cranked up high, she made her way across downtown. The scanner mounted in the dashboard holder crackled its litany of fender-benders and minor disasters, but Harper barely noticed.

Dells had said they had two days. Three max. This was the end of day one. And she didn't have much.

She had Wilson Shepherd's claims of innocence. She had the

two victims of Anderson's obsession waiting for her. But she'd been unable to get anyone on the police force to talk about his alibi.

Daltrey wasn't taking her calls, and Blazer just told her to back off and let the detectives work before hanging up on her.

Making things worse – Fitz was still off the radar. His voice-mail box was full now, so she couldn't even leave messages for him.

She had time, but it was ticking down.

Cars were parked bumper-to-bumper on Bull Street, and she drove halfway around Chippewa Square before an SUV pulled out of a space right in front of her. Harper raced into the spot, stopping in the shade of a sprawling oak tree so covered in Spanish moss, velvety gray fronds brushed the top of the Camaro like long, soft fingers.

She hadn't slept well the night before. The murder, Luke, Anderson – it all swirled in her head like shouting voices. She didn't fall asleep until nearly dawn.

But at least she did sleep. And she felt more like herself as she gathered her things in preparation for meeting the women. Checking her phone for messages, unplugging her scanner, and putting it in her bag. Making sure she had everything.

When she at last climbed out of the car, a man stood at the end of the block in the full glare of the sun, staring at her.

Normally she might not have noticed him at all, but she had the strangest sense that he'd been watching for some time. And more than that, she got the feeling she knew him from somewhere.

In the blinding white sunlight, she couldn't make out his features. He didn't leave when he realized he'd been seen. Instead, he stood there for a second, feet spread, arms crossed. As if he wanted her to notice him.

Something about this – his posture, a tension in his shoulders – made her uneasy. A warning prickle ran down her spine.

Shading her eyes with one hand, Harper peered at him.

'Hello?' she said, raising her voice, and taking a step toward him. 'Do I know you?'

Instead of replying, he walked away, moving fast.

Without knowing why, Harper found herself running after him.

But by the time she reached the corner, he was gone.

She turned a slow circle. The leafy square, with its statue of a sword-wielding city founder, held a handful of people – a cluster of tourists, a mother holding a toddler by the hand.

There was no sign of the man she'd seen. He'd vanished.

Bewildered, she made her way to the coffee shop, pausing, occasionally, to look over her shoulder.

Nobody was behind her.

Pangaea occupied a prime corner spot on the square. Most of the buildings around it were brick or gray stone. In that setting, the coffee shop's lemon yellow walls fairly glowed. Its swinging wooden sign showed a hand-painted globe with one sprawling continent.

Inside, the air was cool and fragrant with the spicy sweet scent of coffee. Harper spotted the two women almost instantly. They were both strikingly attractive. both had latte-colored skin; one had short black hair, the other had glossy dark hair falling in waves past her shoulders.

Peyton Anderson had a type.

They sat close together at a table against the back wall, talking in whispers, looking at the door with quiet apprehension.

Harper walked over to them, the sweat cooling on her skin with every step.

'Cameron? Angela?'

They nodded without speaking, their faces watchful.

'I'm Harper McClain. Thank you so much for agreeing to meet me.'

They shook hands. The woman with short hair identified herself as Cameron. She was the more outspoken of the two.

'We're still not sure this is a good idea,' she said, before Harper even sat down. 'We want to help. But we don't want the Anderson family coming after us.'

'I understand completely,' Harper said. 'You don't have to talk at all. Please, just let me explain what's happening first. And then you can make up your minds.'

They'd chosen a good spot – nobody was sitting near them. They could talk without being overheard.

After buying them both coffees, Harper sat down across from them.

Keeping her voice low and confiding she said, 'I know I told you both a little on the phone about what's happening. Let me explain the rest.'

She told them what she'd learned about Naomi's case, and her suspicions about Peyton Anderson.

'I've read your restraining orders. I know you're afraid to talk. I understand that. Why don't you tell me as much as you can off the record, and then we can discuss what, if anything, you want me to put in the newspaper. Maybe that'll be nothing. But it will help me understand what I'm dealing with here.'

The two women exchanged a loaded look. Neither of them seemed eager to be the first to speak.

'The thing you need to know,' Cameron said, after the silence had stretched on too long, 'is how vindictive the Anderson family can be.'

She was slim, with warm brown eyes. She wore snug-fitting white capri pants with a striped top. A delicate gold cross sparkled at her throat.

Angela was curvier, in a dark miniskirt and matching top. Her huge brown eyes were filled with suspicion.

'Maybe it won't surprise you to hear that we've both been threatened,' she said.

'Who threatened you?' Harper searched her face. 'Peyton? Or his father?'

Angela's mouth twisted in a bitter smile. 'Try both of them.'

'Yesterday, we each got a letter from the Anderson family lawyer outlining the libel laws,' Cameron explained in her soft Georgia accent. 'There was no explanation. Just a lesson in defamation. So . . .'

'You can imagine why we're not eager to talk to you right now,' Angela finished the thought for her.

Buying time, Harper sipped her coffee. She needed them to understand that she was on their side. She thought she knew how to do that.

'Peyton's dad came into the paper this week, threatening to shut it down over this story,' she revealed.

'So they're after you, too.' Angela shook her head. 'They think they own this town.'

'You should take him seriously,' Cameron advised. 'He doesn't make idle threats.'

'This is why I need your help,' Harper told them. 'I can't write this story without knowing everything. You're a key part in this.'

The two women glanced at each other.

'I'll tell you what I can,' Cameron said.

Angela dropped her gaze to her cup. Harper could tell she hadn't made her mind up yet.

Pulling her recorder from her bag, Harper set it on the table and switched it on.

The women gave it an alarmed look.

'This is only for my own use,' Harper said soothingly. 'I need to remember what you've said but I stick by my word. If you don't want me to put it in the paper, I won't.' She hurried on before they could think about it too much. 'Let's go over the basics. Cameron, can you describe in your own words how things first started with Peyton? How did he become obsessed with you?'

The woman picked up a teaspoon and stirred her coffee.

'It started in my last year of undergrad. I was doing pre-law. It's a small school, and Peyton transferred in from UGA to finish out his degree.' She gave Harper a look. 'I heard a rumor UGA threw him out. And that's why he ended up at Savannah State.'

Harper made a note of that. What had gotten Peyton tossed out of the University of Georgia? She had a feeling she knew.

'Were you friends with him?' Harper asked.

'Not really.' Cameron shrugged. 'I knew him in that way you know people in your classes. He was good-looking, so I noticed him. Then, one day, I arrived at the library to study, and he was sitting at my usual table. At the time, I thought it was a coincidence. Later, when I knew more, I started to believe it was intentional.'

She turned the teaspoon over in her hands.

'Anyway, we talked,' she continued. 'He was polite. Charming. Even funny at times. He asked me out, but I told him I was seeing someone else. He said something like, "What a lucky guy."' She set the spoon down. 'The next day when I walked out to go to class he was standing in front of my apartment.'

'Did he explain what he was doing there?' Harper asked.

Cameron smiled darkly. 'Oh, he always had reasonable explanations. Like, he was just passing by when I walked out. What a coincidence. Except I'd looked out the window ten minutes before I left the house and he was standing there. Staring at my door.'

'That's exactly what he did to me.' Finally emboldened to talk, Angela leaned in. 'I'd get out of class and he'd be standing outside the classroom, like it was hilarious to follow me around. I asked him to stop doing it and he'd say, "Doing what? I go to school here. What do you want me to do? Drop out?"'

'Was your experience the same as Cameron's?' Harper asked.

Angela's jaw was tight as she nodded, her dark hair swinging.

'I guess he noticed me after he gave up on you,' she told Cameron.

Turning to Harper she said, 'He was in my class at law school. He asked me out the second week of classes. I didn't know many people yet and he seemed so nice. Like Cameron says, he was good-looking. Always dressed well. I was actually excited before our first date. I spent hours deciding what to wear.' She gave an unhappy laugh. 'God, I was such an idiot.'

'What did he do to you?' It was Cameron who asked. She was watching Angela intently.

'We dated for a few weeks,' Angela's mouth turned down at the memory. 'The usual thing – we went to a mixer at school, and out to dinner on River Street. He seemed nice enough but I didn't feel it. We didn't click. He was very intense – always staring at me. Hanging on my every word. I found him creepy. When he wanted to take the relationship further, I decided to end it.'

'That's when it started,' Cameron guessed.

Angela nodded. 'Like with you, he seemed to take the news well. He said he appreciated my honesty.' She paused. 'The next day he was outside my apartment when I got home from class.'

Cameron turned to Harper – her eyes pleaded for understanding.

'It's so hard to explain how awful it is to be followed everywhere,' she said. 'It's this constant threat hanging over you. And no matter what I said to him to try and get him to stop, it only made it worse. He always pretended that I was the crazy one. He was like, "Why are you being so unreasonable? I was just walking home or to class . . ."' She glanced at Angela, whose hands were clenched in front of her. 'It was never a coincidence.'

'How long did this go on?' Harper asked.

The two exchanged a look. Cameron pointed at herself. 'In my case five months. How about you?'

'The same,' Angela said. 'Maybe a little longer. I lost track.'

'I've read your restraining orders. I know how bad it got,' Harper said. 'How did it end?'

'I told my dean what was happening,' Cameron said. 'She referred me to the Legal Aid Department, and they helped me file for a restraining order. This was after he broke in.'

'He broke into your apartment?'

Cameron nodded. 'I got up one morning, walked into the kitchen to find him sitting there, holding a cup of coffee.' She shivered. 'He said, "Good morning!" and I just . . . ran. I was in my pajamas, no shoes. But I ran downstairs and knocked on my neighbor's door. Luckily, she was home. She let me in and called the police.'

Harper wrote a hurried note, *Check police records for burglary charge*, and underlined it.

'What happened when the police got there?' she asked.

'They found him sitting on the front porch.' Cameron gave

her a bitter look. 'He told them who he was, who his father was. They treated him like a silly child who'd done something naughty. Instead of like the criminal he was. They told me I could file charges if I wanted to, but they made it sound like I was being unreasonable. It was only a prank.'

Harper could imagine this. The DA's kid committing a non-violent crime was their worst nightmare. He wasn't their boss – not really. But he was close enough.

'Did you file charges?'

'They charged him with disturbing the peace.' Cameron's lip curled. 'He pleaded guilty and the charge was expunged after six months of good behavior.'

'What happened after that?'

'He stopped following me,' she said. 'When I started at law school, I knew he'd be there, so I had a meeting with the dean before classes even began, and asked to be kept out of all of his classes. I showed her the restraining order, and she kept us apart.' She glanced at Angela. 'By then, he'd moved on.'

Angela grimaced. 'Lucky me.'

Harper turned to her. 'So what happened after you broke it off with him?'

'He started showing up at my work, my apartment, my classes. All of a sudden he was everywhere I was.' Angela's earlier reticence had faded. She seemed eager to tell Harper all she'd been through. 'It was creepy as hell. The thing is, I'm a law student. And I understand how things work. But how do you quantify *that* into a crime? He could always claim it was a coincidence. It wasn't, though. It was systematic. When I say he was everywhere – I mean it. I remember walking out of the girls' restroom at a bar one night and finding him standing in front of the door, smiling.' She folded her arms across her torso. 'He scared the shit out of me.'

'When did you file the restraining order?' Harper asked Angela.

Angela fell silent for so long, she thought she wasn't going to answer. She was about to give up and try a different question, when the woman finally spoke.

'One night,' she said, 'I was on a date. We had a great time – he was someone I could have imagined having a real relationship with.' She drew a breath. 'When he left in the morning, Peyton was waiting outside. He must have been there all night. He told him he just wanted to warn him, for his own good, that I was a slut. That I had slept with half the guys in my law school class. He showed him pictures on his phone that he said were me, doing things. Sex things. He kept saying, "I'm telling you this for your own good. I mean, she probably has diseases, at this stage."'

Her voice broke.

Cameron, who had been listening with horrified fascination, rested her hand on her arm.

Angela turned to her. 'I know you understand, even if no one else does. It shattered me. The guy – I don't know if he believed him completely, or he didn't want to get caught up in the mess but . . . I never went out with him again.' She swiped her cheek with one hand. 'The next time I saw Peyton, he told me if I ever went out with anyone else, he'd kill me.'

Harper's pen froze on the paper.

'He threatened your life?'

Angela nodded. 'And I believed him. I wasn't sure he was capable of actual murder, but in that moment, I believed he would at least give killing me a try. That was when I went to the cops.'

'Was he ever charged for stalking you or making threats?' Harper asked.

Angela's smile was thin.

'He pleaded guilty to misdemeanor drunken disorder,' she said. 'His lawyer said he'd been on an all-night bender and didn't know what he was saying. He got community service for six weeks, and was told to stay away from me. Which he did, thank God.'

Harper thought she could see the process of escalation right in front of her. There'd been no punishment for stalking Cameron, so he ratcheted things up with Angela. He threatened her and got away with it.

What if Naomi was his third try? And this time he took it all the way.

'Has either of you been interviewed by the police, since Naomi died?' she asked.

They both shook their heads.

'I knew Naomi,' Cameron said before Harper could answer. 'She was a sweet girl. Really smart. Just that bastard's type.' She fixed Harper with a piercing look. 'Do you think he did it?'

'I don't know,' Harper confessed. 'There are other suspects. Out of all of them, Peyton makes sense as the shooter. But the police say there's no way he did it.'

'Of course they do.' Angela's expression was dark. 'Daddy's going to protect his baby boy from all the mean women out there who say he hurt them.'

'My advice?' Cameron looked at Harper. 'Don't believe anything Peyton Anderson says. And don't count on the police to do anything about it.'

Chapter Twenty-seven

By the time Harper got back to the newsroom it was after five o'clock. Dells was usually there until six – tonight, though, his office was dark. But Baxter was at her desk as usual.

When Harper finished filling her in, the editor leaned back in her chair, tapping her silver pen against the black plastic arm.

'You're getting close. But you're still not there. We need more before we go out with this.'

Harper tried not to show her disappointment. She could sense how close she was to having the story Dells and Baxter wanted. But there was always something missing. One more interview. One more piece of evidence.

'If I could just get Anderson's alibi. I'm working on it as fast as I can. But the cops won't talk.'

'If they won't, they won't,' Baxter said. 'But I'll tell you something – I know cops pretty well, and I'm positive they won't be happy with how the investigation is going. If Randall Anderson is using them to protect his son, they'll want to tell you.'

She paused. The pen kept *tap-tap-tapping*.

'Work on Julie Daltrey,' she said, dropping the pen on her desk. 'I knew her back when she was a patrol cop. There's nothing about the Anderson kid Daltrey will like. Especially given what those women told you. You just need to catch her at the right time.'

'Sure,' Harper said, and headed back to her desk.

She didn't see the point in explaining that Daltrey had been one of the first to turn on her after the Smith case.

She'd have to find another way to get her hands on Anderson's alibi. And soon.

There was no time to work on it further that night, though, as first an armed robbery and later a shooting outside a bar kept Harper and Miles on the run.

Harper didn't mind. The work stopped her from thinking too much about last night.

But when her shift ended at midnight, and she parked in front of her house, she found herself staring at the empty front steps where Luke had waited for her.

It was hard to believe now that it had felt so much like the start of something.

When all along, it was the end.

Now she had to explain it all to Bonnie. Who still believed, in her optimistic way, that Harper and Luke were going to get married, buy a ranch-style house on the edge of town and adopt a pack of dogs.

With a sigh, Harper climbed out of the car and slammed the door harder than she needed to.

The Library was only a fifteen-minute walk away – one she'd made hundreds of times before. Tonight, though, it seemed longer and darker.

Everything that had happened in the last week had climbed inside her head and uncoiled.

She felt on edge. The skin at the top of her spine prickled.

When she heard the unmistakable sound of footsteps behind her, her heart began to race.

At first, she slowed her pace deliberately, pretending to check her phone.

The footsteps stopped when she did.

She knew she was tired. But she couldn't be imagining this.

She spun around to look behind her. The street light was shaded by the long oak branches that stretched out to touch each other, sending shadows skittering across the sidewalk. But she could see no one.

She forced herself to calm down. She'd told Luke she could protect herself. Now she had to prove it.

She began walking again, taking ten careful steps and then, bracing herself, she whirled again, ready for a fight.

There was no one behind her.

She felt bewildered. Betrayed by her own body. She'd been certain there was someone there.

She was nearly to the lights and traffic of Habersham Street. She was nearly to safety.

There was nothing else for it. She turned and ran.

When she reached the lights of Habersham, she didn't slow down.

She was out of breath and relieved when she turned in to College Row a few minutes later.

Nobody stood outside The Library, as they normally would on a Thursday night. Bruce Springsteen's melancholy voice poured through the bar's open door.

Junior held out his fist for her to bump as she opened the door.

'What's happening, Harper?' His gold teeth gleamed when he smiled.

Harper forced herself to give him a tense smile in return.

'The usual,' she said, and hurried by, in no mood for banter.

The bar was nearly as empty as it had been the night she came to meet Luke – a scattering of people occupied the tables. Nobody was on the dance floor.

The murder was killing business.

At the bar, Bonnie was waiting impatiently.

'Finally,' she said, one hand on her hip.

'I'm sorry I have a job that's eating my life.' Harper climbed onto a barstool. 'And other personal problems.'

She tried to keep her tone light, but Bonnie paused before replying.

'Well, at least you're here now.'

Without asking what she wanted, Bonnie flipped the cap off a bottle of Becks and pushed it across to her.

She'd dressed casually tonight, in denim shorts and ankle boots, her black Library T-shirt belted at the waist. Her blue-blond hair was loose over her shoulders. A dozen bracelets jangled when she moved.

'Add a Jameson's chaser to that, would you?' Harper said.

A surprised look flickered across Bonnie's fine-boned face. But 'Sure,' was all she said as she picked up a glass and lifted the slim, dark-green bottle from the rack behind her.

'Man, it's dead in here.' Harper turned to take in the room.

Setting the glass on a cardboard coaster in front of her, Bonnie gave her a significant look.

'It's not great. Fitz is losing his mind.'

'Has he been in?' Harper glanced at her. 'I keep trying to call him but it goes straight to voicemail.'

'He's hardly ever here,' Bonnie confided. 'When he does come in, he's wasted. The day manager and I, we're holding this place together. For now.'

She hesitated before asking, 'The cops don't still think it's him, do they?'

Harper didn't mince words. 'He's on their list because of what happened before, and because he hasn't got an alibi. But they want it to be Wilson Shepherd.'

Leaning her elbows on the bar, Bonnie looked at her.

'Was it Wilson, do you think? He always seemed like such a sweet guy.'

Harper thought of Wilson's earnest, heartbroken face. And her own lingering doubts about his honesty.

'I don't think so. But I don't know anything, anymore.'

She took a sip of whiskey, hoping it would burn some of the last twenty-four hours out of her. The heat of it made her shudder.

'Oh hell, I wish they'd solve this thing,' Bonnie said with unusual vehemence. 'Not knowing is tearing everything apart. It's breaking Fitz's heart and ruining his business. And mine – I'm not getting any tips. I don't know how long I can afford to keep working here.' She looked around the room, books gathering dust on the shelves. Music clicking to another song. 'I come in every night and think of Naomi. And what she must have gone through. I can't even imagine what her dad's dealing with.'

'He's trying to solve this murder,' Harper told her. 'Just like the rest of us.'

The thought was depressing. She'd done nothing but think about the murder all day. She hadn't come here to talk about it more.

'Enough sadness,' she said, changing the subject firmly. 'Tell me some happy news.'

Bonnie smiled broadly. 'Well, if it helps, I think I'm in love, with a capital L.'

'Again?' Harper picked up her beer.

'This time it's real,' Bonnie promised.

Harper gave her a dubious look. Bonnie went through boyfriends like Harper went through pens.

'OK.' She motioned for her to talk. 'Let's have it. Who is he?'

'His name is Charles Harrison,' Bonnie said. 'He owns a small gallery in Charleston. He saw some of my new paintings hanging at SCAD. He called and asked to see the rest of them, and then he offered to show them. Last night we went out to dinner and I swear to God I fell right in, head first. I'm telling you, he could be the one.'

She looked flushed and happy.

Harper, though, had seen it all before.

'Well that's wonderful,' she said, trying to sound enthusiastic. 'I'm happy for you. Tell me about him. Does he live up in Charleston?'

Missing the flatness in her voice, Bonnie nodded.

'I haven't been up to his place yet, but I'm going up there in a couple of weeks to see the gallery. Do you want to see a picture of him?'

Without waiting for Harper to respond, she picked up her phone and touched the screen, pulling up an image. She turned the phone around so Harper could see a smiling, well-dressed man with brown hair graying at his temples. He wore a white shirt, open at the neck.

'He's a little old for you, isn't he?'

'He's forty-three and he's perfect,' Bonnie said, defensive.

'Terrific.' Handing the phone back, Harper took a casual sip of her beer. 'Do you know much else about him? What part of town does he live in?'

A suspicious look crossed Bonnie's face. 'Why do you want to know?'

'Look.' Harper dropped the pretense. 'Don't argue. Give me the basics and I'll get someone to run a criminal background check on him.'

'Absolutely not.' Bonnie glared. 'You always do this, Harper.'

'Yes, I do. And that is how we found out the super-cute artist from Oklahoma who you wanted to marry had a wife and children in Tulsa,' Harper reminded her. 'You can't trust anyone, Bonnie. When are you going to learn that?'

Bonnie's chin rose.

'I will not have you invading his privacy.'

'Fine.' Harper shrugged. 'Date a pedophile, if that's what you want to do.'

'He is not a *pedophile*,' Bonnie's voice rose, attracting curious looks from the man at the end of the bar who'd been drinking so quietly they'd both forgotten he was there.

Bonnie gave him an apologetic glance.

'He's not a pedophile,' she assured him. 'He owns a gallery.'

'I don't see what the problem is,' Harper said, after the man had turned away. 'If you give me his address, I'll check him out. He never needs to know.'

Unexpectedly, Bonnie reached across the bar and squeezed her hand.

'You don't have to protect me, Harper. I'm a big girl. I can look out for myself.'

Harper was caught off guard. All her irritation faded.

'I've protected you since I was six,' she said. 'I always will.'

Bonnie smiled. 'I know.'

She began taking glasses out of the dishwasher and placing them on the shelves below the counter. She worked in silence for a few minutes before looking up at Harper.

'He lives on Belmont Street in Charleston. I don't have his exact address.'

Memorizing the information, Harper took a sip of beer.

Well, she had Bonnie's news. Might as well share her own.

'I suppose now would be a good time to tell you that I slept with Luke.'

Bonnie set a glass down with a crash.

'You *sneak*. How could you not tell me this before? You had sex news all along. How was it?' Her smile faded as her clear blue eyes searched Harper's face. 'Or do I want to know?'

Unexpectedly, tears burned the backs of her eyes.

She shook her head.

'Oh, hell.' Bonnie leaned across the counter, reaching out for her hands. 'What happened?'

Mortified, Harper ordered herself not to cry. She emptied her whiskey glass before she replied.

'He said he missed me. I believed him. We had sex and then he told me he was seeing someone else.' She drew a breath. 'And that was the end of our little reunion.'

'Oh, Harper. This is all my fault. I made you wear that hot outfit.'

She squeezed her hands.

'Dammit. I can't believe it. I never pegged Luke for a son of a bitch.'

Harper gave her a rueful smile. 'Me neither.'

'How could he do that to you? I could kill him for hurting you,' Bonnie fumed. 'I don't understand him.'

'Don't kill anyone.' Freeing one hand, Harper held up her empty glass. 'Just keep these coming.'

Bonnie reached for the bottle.

This time, though, after filling Harper's glass she poured one for herself.

'I think I need this, too.' She held her glass out to Harper. 'To better men.'

'I'll drink to that.'

They clinked their glasses.

Harper downed her whiskey in one.

Before Bonnie could ask all the questions Harper could see in her eyes, a woman came up to the bar to order, and she turned away to help her, leaving Harper time to think about her own questions.

She should have known something wasn't right the night Wilson was arrested. The way Luke had appeared, out of the blue. All friendly and understanding. Like nothing had ever happened to rip their lives apart.

It was so obvious in retrospect what was going on. It was laughable, really.

Here she was thinking Bonnie made bad decisions about men. It wasn't *Bonnie* who'd slept with her ex before finding out if he was already settling down with someone else.

That had been Harper's brilliant idea. And look where it got her. Crying in a bar with a bottle of whiskey. That's where.

After putting money in the register, Bonnie turned back to her.

'What about the break-in?' she asked, changing the subject. Probably – foolishly – hoping for some good news. 'They catch the guy?'

Shaking her head, Harper reached for her beer. 'Nope. And now we know he broke into my car, too.'

Bonnie's jaw dropped. 'When were you planning to tell me this?'

'Now,' Harper said. 'He left a note. Turns out it's the same guy who broke into my house last year. Or at least, it looks like him.'

'Are you *serious*?' Bonnie looked stunned. 'This is not OK. Are you safe there? What do the cops think?'

Harper didn't answer that question.

'I've done everything I can think of to make that place secure.' She sipped her beer, morosely. 'And he just walked right in.'

'That's it,' Bonnie told her firmly. 'You're not staying alone tonight. Either you come to my place or I'm coming to yours.'

Harper held up her empty bottle. 'First, get me another of these. Then we can move in together.'

While Bonnie pulled a fresh beer from the fridge. Harper turned around on her barstool, to check the room.

It was getting closer to closing time. The bar had emptied further while she'd been here. There was only the woman who'd come to the bar, and two men playing pool.

The music seemed too loud in such an empty room. She was thinking of asking Bonnie to turn it down when a door at the back of the main barroom opened, and Jim Fitzgerald shuffled in.

He moved slowly, bending over to close the door with effort.

Harper observed him with dismay.

The dapper bar owner seemed to have shrunk in a matter of days. His usually neat hair was unkempt. His clothes were rumpled. His face was blotchy and worn.

And he was very drunk.

He stumbled toward the bar.

'Bonnie,' he slurred, 'I'm going now.'

From the cash register, Bonnie gave him a worried look. 'OK, Fitz.'

But Harper, who had been calling him for days now, couldn't let this moment pass.

Jumping to her feet, she hurried over to him.

'Fitz, wait.'

He peered at her blankly before recognition dawned.

'Oh, it's you,' he said, without enthusiasm. 'The reporter.'

'Please talk to me,' she pleaded. 'I believe you're innocent.'

He reared back, as if she'd struck him.

'Well, I *am* innocent, goddammit. I've never hurt anyone.' He waved his arm, taking in the empty room. 'What've I done? I run a bar that people like. I mind my own business. I don't understand . . .' His voice trailed off, and he looked at her desperately, as if she might hold the answers. 'I don't understand.'

Harper knew she was on shaky moral ground, interviewing an intoxicated murder suspect. But she was desperate.

'Talk to me about the night Naomi died.' She guided him back to the facts, ignoring the way Bonnie was watching her with open concern. 'Where were you?'

He waved one hand in frustration.

'I was here. I left at midnight. Went home and ate a ham sandwich on my couch and watched replays of the Falcons game from Monday night. I gave up in the third quarter. Knew how it ended anyway. Must have been around two in the morning. Then I went to bed with a Lee Child novel I've been working my way through.' He rubbed a hand across his face. Talking seemed to be bringing him more focus. 'Next thing I know, the phone is ringing, and they're telling me Naomi's dead.' He raised his red-rimmed eyes to meet hers. 'Worst day of my life.'

People say drunk men tell no lies, and Harper knew full well that wasn't true. But drunk men find it difficult to lie smoothly about things that matter.

Fitz spoke passionately, without hesitating or stumbling over his words. He didn't fidget or avert his eyes. He didn't show any sign of deception.

He appeared baffled and lost.

Maybe he was a murderer. But she doubted it.

'You're going to be fine, Fitz,' she found herself telling him. 'They're going to catch this guy.'

'Well, they better catch him quick. Or it'll be too late to save this place.'

Turning, he shuffled toward the door, stopping after a few steps to look back at her.

'Naomi wouldn't want this,' he said. 'Whoever killed her – I feel like he's killing me, too.'

Chapter Twenty-eight

The next morning Harper steered into the crowded parking lot behind the newspaper building, black Ray-Bans protecting her eyes. A slight thudding behind her temples was the only remnant of the night before.

It was less than she deserved, as far as she was concerned.

After the bar closed for the night, Bonnie drove her home in Mavis, the pink pickup. Harper hadn't admitted to her that she didn't feel safe walking home. But Bonnie was now obsessed with the break-ins and insisted on accompanying her anyway, so no confessions were needed.

While Harper made up a bed for her on one of the gray sofas, Bonnie lectured her about security.

'Until the cops figure out who this guy is, you're not safe here,' she said. 'You shouldn't stay here by yourself at all.'

'I'm fine,' Harper had assured her. 'I have perfectly good security.'

'That's ridiculous. If this guy lets himself in while you're asleep, what will you do?'

It was late. Harper was tired. That was the only explanation she could come up with for what happened next.

Busy spreading the duvet, she talked without thinking. 'I don't know. Listen to him, maybe. Smith thinks there's something he wants to tell me. I need to stay here long enough to find out what that is.'

'Did you say Smith?'

Harper's breath caught.

'*Lieutenant* Smith?' Bonnie stared at her. 'You've seen him?'

Caught in the glare of her horrified gaze, Harper sat down on the bed she'd just made.

A long silence fell.

'I talk to him,' she confessed finally. 'Now and then.'

Bonnie searched her face as if she'd find clues there to her sudden insanity.

'You talk to Smith? Where? How?'

'I drive out to Reidsville Prison,' Harper told her. 'And we talk.'

Bonnie lowered herself onto the couch next to her. She looked stunned.

'How long has this been going on? How often do you see him?'

'Since the start.' Unable to bear the bewilderment in Bonnie's face, Harper looked down to where her hands worried the corner of the comforter. 'I go out there every few months.'

It took Bonnie a second to absorb that.

'What do you talk about?'

'My mom's case. The burglary. Smith thinks they might be connected, somehow. We're trying to figure out how.'

There was a long pause.

'How is he?' Bonnie asked.

Harper hadn't anticipated this question, but then, maybe she should have. After all, Smith had known Bonnie as long as he'd known her. He'd driven the two of them to roller-skating rinks when they were thirteen and picked them up after football games in high school.

Bonnie had always viewed him as sort of a kindly uncle who also happened to be a cop. Until he'd killed a woman.

After that, she had excised him from her vocabulary – rarely, if ever mentioning him. It was as if she'd removed him from her memory altogether.

Now, though, she sat looking at Harper with an expression of such deep sadness it tore Harper's heart.

'He's grayer. Older.' She thought about how the lieutenant had looked when he walked into the visiting room a few days ago. 'And he's harder. It's like prison's absorbing parts of him that we knew and turning him into an inmate.'

Bonnie's face closed. 'I think he did that to himself when he killed someone.'

'I do too.' Harper turned to Bonnie, appealing for her to understand. 'But, Bon, the Smith we knew – he's still in there. He still thinks like a cop when he talks to me.'

She waited for Bonnie to reply but she just sat there, her brow creased with thought.

'I'm sorry, Harper, I'm trying to process this,' she said at last. 'Why didn't you tell me all this before? Why hide it?'

Harper exhaled.

'I didn't tell anyone. I couldn't. I knew it would hurt you. But I've been thinking and I have to keep seeing him. If I'm ever going to solve my mom's murder, I need his help. Is that . . . Does that sound crazy?'

Bonnie's eyes searched her face. Then she let out a breath.

'No, it doesn't sound crazy.'

Putting her arm around Harper's shoulders, she pulled her closer and pressed her lips against her hair.

'I understand, Harper,' she said. 'I just worry about you.'

'I'm careful.' Harper leaned into her, breathing in her familiar scent of lemony perfume, and the faint but not unpleasant hint of oil paint that always clung to her hair and skin.

'Be *more* careful,' Bonnie said.

Harper smiled. 'I have three locks.'

They both laughed, and the tension was broken.

That night, to her own surprise, Harper slept dreamlessly for the first time in days.

And as she parked in the lot behind the paper she felt calmer – more focused. As if telling Bonnie the truth had lifted some of the load she'd been carrying lately.

She was determined not to get sidetracked now. She was so close to knowing the truth about what had happened to Naomi Scott. She owed it to the dead girl not to get distracted.

When she reached the newsroom, Baxter wasn't at her desk. The door to Dells's office was closed. Through the glass wall, scarred by the long crack Randall Anderson had made, she saw that he was on the phone.

She started to back away but, spotting her, he motioned for her to come in.

Harper slipped inside, seating herself in one of the sleek leather-and-chrome chairs facing his desk.

'I know what you're saying,' Dells said into the phone, 'but that's the last thing I want to hear. Let's look at cheaper suppliers first. We're bleeding paper at this point.'

Glancing down, Harper noticed that the files open on his desk showed charts and spreadsheets, filled with incomprehensible numbers. Some he'd circled with looping swooshes of his pen. They were pretty big figures.

'Take a look,' he told whoever he was talking to, 'and get back to me. Thanks, Tom.'

Squinting, Harper tried to get a better look at the numbers but Dells closed the folder.

'Quit peeking.' He shook his finger at her.

'You know what I do for a living, right?' she asked.

'I pay you to investigate other people, McClain.' But he sounded amused. 'Let's keep it that way. Speaking of which . . .'

He motioned for her to speak.

'A lot has happened.' Harper leaned forward eagerly. 'First, I interviewed the two women Anderson stalked and they told me everything.'

Talking too fast in her adrenaline rush, she told him what she'd learned.

When she finished, he shook his head in disbelief.

'Dammit, what is wrong with the cops? This can't be a co-incidence. Stalkers kill. He's made threats. How can they say this is unrelated?'

'It all comes back to his alibi,' Harper said.

'Good point.' Dells leaned forward, resting his elbows on his desk. 'Where are we at with the alibi? What's your detective got to say?'

'That's what I'm doing today,' she said, with confidence she didn't feel. 'It's just taking a little time to get the cops to talk.'

In truth, she didn't know where that information would come from. Nobody on the police force was talking.

Dells gave her a warning look.

'Get on that,' he said. 'We can't do much else until we know what he's told them, and why they believe him. This is the biggest missing piece of the puzzle.'

'I promise I'll have it today.'

'You better.' His face darkened. 'Everyone's breathing down our necks on this one.'

Harper hesitated before broaching the subject.

'Has Anderson done anything, yet? Filed a lawsuit?'

'As far as I know, he hasn't taken legal action.' Dells gave her a dark smile. 'But I'm told he had lunch with MaryAnne Charlton yesterday.'

'Shit,' Harper breathed.

'Exactly,' Dells said.

MaryAnne Charlton was the head of the paper's board of directors – and the heir of the family that had owned the newspaper company for more than sixty years.

Harper had seen her now and then when she'd made state visits to the newsroom – she was an old school southern belle, with a penchant for Chanel suits and oversized necklaces.

If she was meeting with Anderson, then he'd gone straight to the top.

It was impossible to tell if this situation made Dells anxious. He affected a permanent air of calm distance. Some of that had broken down as they worked on the story together but not enough that she really had any clue what he was thinking.

Still, one thing she knew for certain was that Charlton could fire both of them in an instant.

'Has she called you?' Harper asked. 'Said anything?'

'Not yet.' His response was succinct. And his expression indicated that he'd said all he intended to.

An awkward silence fell.

'Oh, I almost forgot,' Harper said after a moment. 'I finally got hold of Jim Fitzgerald.'

'Good,' Dells said. 'What'd you learn?'

'He's a broken man whose business is going under because the cops won't take him off the suspect list,' Harper said. 'If he killed anyone, I'll eat my computer.'

Dells slapped a hand on his desk so hard his pen jumped.

'There's a story. That's what you take to your detective. That's how you get her to talk. While she's failing to solve this crime, there are real-life ramifications happening for all the people they haven't cleared. Their mistakes have a cost.'

When he talked about the police, his expression grew predatory.

'Don't hold your punches. Tell her all we know. Make her defend her case to you. Tell her we're gunning for them.' He rocked forward in his chair. 'When can you get me a first draft?'

'Tomorrow, maybe?' Harper suggested cautiously.

'Tomorrow, definitely,' Dells corrected her. 'We need to get something together no later than tomorrow's deadline. Something publishable and legal and devastating and *right*.'

He looked at her with those ice-blue eyes.

'If that doesn't happen, we're going to be in trouble, you and me. And I don't like the look of the jury.'

Chapter Twenty-nine

When Harper walked up to the police headquarters that afternoon, she was determined to stay there until she had what she needed.

As she walked into the icy wave of industrial air-conditioning, Darlene waved her over to the front desk.

'There she is.' Her voice boomed in the empty lobby. 'Miss Freedom of the Press, herself.'

The few people waiting on plastic chairs turned to look at her.

'You're a bit early today.' The receptionist slid the folder of crime reports over to her, and leaned one elbow on the desk. 'Something happening?'

'Nah,' Harper said. 'Just busy.'

'Busy!' Darlene scoffed. 'You ask me, it's too quiet. Everyone's saying there's nothing to do. Couple of traffic accidents. One shooting in three days.' She leaned her elbows on the tall desk. 'Too hot out there for crime, I guess.'

'That's good news, though, right?' Harper said.

'I guess.' Darlene sniffed, unconvinced.

Opening the folder, Harper hurried through the stack of overnight crime reports – it was, as the desk officer had said, much smaller than usual.

Usually, summer months were the busiest. The heat brought the worst out in people. Arguments that might have ended with fists made it all the way to guns much faster in August than they did in November.

Her eyes slid across the incident descriptions one after another. *Burglary. Burglary. Burglary. Fall. Affray. Affray. Burglary. Shoplifting.*

Reaching the end of the stack, she slid it back across.

Glancing around to make sure no one in the waiting room could overhear, she lowered her voice.

'Any gossip about the Scott case? They still trying to pin it on the boyfriend?'

Her face brightening, Darlene leaned closer.

'I think they don't know *who* to pin it on,' she confided. 'Now the mayor's backed off a little, because she's got her safety commission promising to keep all the tourists wrapped up and protected, so she doesn't care anymore. The chief's hoping everyone forgets that girl ever existed.'

'Daltrey's not going to forget, though,' Harper said. 'You know she wants to get the guy who did it.'

Darlene's eyebrows arched to her hairline. 'Julie Daltrey wants to get herself promoted, is what I think.'

'Well, let me see what I can find out,' Harper said. 'Is she in right now? I need to ask her a few questions.'

'She's in the back,' Darlene said, her voice returning to its normal volume. 'You want me to buzz you through?'

'Yes, please.'

The buzzer broke the quiet as she pressed the button on her desk and released the lock on the security door.

The shadowy corridor was quiet. Harper turned right, then made a sharp left into a wide staircase. She climbed to the second floor, barely noticing the scuffed walls in need of paint, or the ageing posters reminding the cops to 'Be Safe. Be Aware'.

The hallway upstairs smelled of pine disinfectant and stale air. Harper didn't hesitate as she turned right out of the stairs and made her way past a number of small offices.

She'd been up here many times in the past.

The homicide detectives shared a sprawling office at the end of the hallway. The door was closed. As she approached, Harper could hear voices from inside.

Steeling herself, she tapped confidently, and pushed the door open.

Inside, eight desks were arranged along the walls, a battered office chair in front of each. Five were occupied. And five startled faces turned to look at her as she entered.

No matter how many times you do it, it is always daunting walking into a room full of detectives. They do not take intrusion lightly.

'What the hell?' A tall, rangy man in his late twenties leaned back in his chair, endless legs sprawling out as if he didn't know where they'd come from or what to do with them, and stared at her.

Harper recognized him as Detective Davenport. Also in the room were Detectives Ledbetter, Shumaker, Daltrey . . . and Luke, who glanced up at her with something like alarm.

It struck her with sudden horror that he might think she was here to see him.

'I'm uh . . .' She turned to Daltrey. 'Detective Daltrey – I'm here to see you. Didn't Darlene call?'

Daltrey, whose small features were set in an expression of bemusement, shook her head.

'Darlene likes to surprise us now and then,' she said, glancing at the others for agreement.

'Keeps us on our toes,' Detective Shumaker drawled. He'd draped his jacket across the back of his chair, so there was nothing to hide the way his shirt stretched tight across his beer belly, as he watched her with open suspicion.

'She can be tricky,' Davenport agreed, good-naturedly.

Having them arrayed in a semi-circle around her, all talking to one another while looking at her was unnerving.

Harper kept her focus on Daltrey.

'Do you have five minutes? It's about the Scott case.'

'What about it?' Crossing her legs, Daltrey studied her with little interest. She wore a navy suit with a masculine cut.

'It's about Peyton Anderson . . .' Harper began.

'Uh-oh.' Ledbetter turned to look at Daltrey, whose calm instantly eroded.

'Oh hell, McClain,' Daltrey snapped. 'Are you still obsessed with the Anderson boy?'

Anger flared, hot and unexpected, in Harper's chest.

'Maybe. Are you still failing to solve that murder?' she shot back.

'Ooh . . .' The other detectives hooted, looking back and forth between the two women as if they were facing each other across a net.

'Oh, *grow up*,' Harper told them. She turned back to Daltrey. 'Can we go somewhere else to talk? Please?'

The detective stood so abruptly her chair skidded back.

'Come with me.'

Daltrey was small, but she moved fast, sweeping past Harper to the door.

As Harper turned to follow her, her eyes met Luke's for a split second. There was so much in that look – worry, confusion, doubt.

With effort, she tore her gaze away and followed Daltrey into the hallway.

The detective stopped halfway down the corridor outside an open door.

'This better be good,' she said, switching on the light and stepping inside.

It was a small office – there were files stacked on the desk. A charger cable for someone's phone trailed across the fake wood. A window above the desk let in faint, grimy daylight through half-closed blinds.

Harper closed the door. The two women faced each other across the limited expanse of cheap carpet.

Daltrey made an impatient gesture with one hand.

'Get to it, McClain.'

'I'm working on a story about Anderson,' Harper told her, forcing calm into her voice. 'A follow-up to the piece that ran the day before yesterday. I've met with the two women who claim he stalked them the way he stalked Scott.'

'Johnson and Martinez?'

Harper nodded. 'Detective, if what they say is true, Anderson's obsession and violence grew with each victim. You know he stalked Scott. How does this not look like a pathway to murder?'

'I don't care what it looks like.' Daltrey sounded exasperated. 'McClain, I've told you why we're not investigating Anderson. I don't know why you won't let go of this.'

Mindful of what Dells had said about hitting Daltrey with police failures, Harper launched into her planned attack.

'I won't let go of this because nothing else makes sense. More than a week has passed since Naomi Scott was murdered and what have you got? You've got nothing, as far as I can see. Jim Fitzgerald is a broken man whose business is being destroyed by an open-ended investigation with no evidence against him aside from the fact that he stayed home to watch TV that night. Wilson Shepherd is a heartbroken boyfriend who waited all night for the girlfriend who was never coming home. Naomi Scott spent her time volunteering, working, and studying. She had no money to steal. No drug problem. What she *did* have was a rich guy with a powerful family stalking her for four months.' She drew a breath. 'I want to do right by this girl, Detective. Don't you? Doesn't her family deserve that?'

Daltrey, eyes flashing, appeared poised to take up the argument. But then, abruptly, she stopped herself.

'Listen, McClain,' she said after a long pause, 'I can see what you see. I have no doubt that Peyton Anderson is a piece of crap posing as a human being. Between you and me, I believe those women, too.'

'Then why won't you investigate him?' Harper's voice rose.

'Would you stop assuming I haven't?' Daltrey snapped. 'I *have* investigated him. The simple truth is, I want Peyton Anderson to be our guy. But he can't be. Because on the night Naomi Scott was murdered, Anderson was assaulted on the street. He was found by a member of the public, bleeding from a stab wound to his arm. Transported to Savannah Memorial Hospital by ambulance. And treated in the emergency room where he was interviewed by Savannah Police officers.' She drew a breath, before adding, 'We have nurses, doctors, and cops who all say he was there. We have CCTV footage of him arriving on a stretcher.'

Seeing the surprise on Harper's face, she gave a thin smile.

'You've been looking for Anderson in the wrong files, McClain. You should have looked for him under "victim".'

'So his alibi . . .' Harper began, still trying to process it.

'. . . is the police,' Daltrey finished her thought for her. 'Yes, it is. We are his alibi. When someone was shooting Naomi Scott to death, Peyton Anderson was lying in a bed at Savannah Memorial Hospital.'

Harper studied Daltrey's face for any sign of deception and found none.

'I can't believe it.' She sagged back against the wall. 'Who attacked him? How did it happen?'

'The crime occurred between eleven o'clock and midnight,' Daltrey said. 'It appeared to be a random mugging.'

'Arrests?'

The detective shook her head. 'He gave us a description but we haven't found the guy.'

'Anything taken?'

'Wallet and phone.'

Harper went through it in her mind, imagining Anderson walking down the street, someone jumping out to attack him – at eleven o'clock, though? The streets would be crowded at that hour.

She glanced at Daltrey. 'Where did this happen?'

'Near City Market.' Daltrey spoke without hesitation. 'Two patrol officers responded. I'm surprised you didn't show up at the scene.'

City Market was a trendy downtown development with restaurants and bars. It made perfect sense that someone like Peyton Anderson might be there.

Harper stopped to think about that night over a week ago,

and what had happened before she'd ended up at The Library at one in the morning.

'There was a shooting that night,' she said slowly. 'Just after ten thirty. Looked like it was going to be a homicide. I must have been at that. I wouldn't leave an attempted homicide for a robbery.'

'It was busy that night,' Daltrey agreed. 'We were stretched thin. And you're right – the assault wasn't a big deal. Anderson's wounds weren't severe. They kept him overnight as a precaution.'

Harper hated that it all fit. Anderson's alibi – the reasons why the cops believed it so completely.

'Damn,' she said as it all sank in. 'I really wanted it to be him.'

'You want to know a secret?' Daltrey met her gaze. 'I did, too. But it can't be. And that leaves us nowhere. And it's *killing me*. That's why we had to keep Fitzgerald as a maybe. Because I'm not convinced the Shepherd kid has it in him. And without him, we're screwed.'

She leaned back against the desk, her shoulders slumping.

'There's no one else. The victim's dad's a goddamn saint. She never dated anyone else. Like you say, she was a good person. And. . . . Yeah. We're letting her down.'

In the sudden quiet that followed, Harper could hear voices from down the hall. The ringing of a phone. The hiss of air conditioning coming from the vents above their heads.

The room seemed weighted down by their combined inability to solve this.

'Are you looking at anyone else?' she asked. 'Off the record?'

'We're looking at several people. Scott met a lot of people at that bar,' Daltrey said. 'Quite a few of them have interesting criminal histories.'

'Anything solid?'

A smile flickered across Daltrey's face. 'If I had anything solid, the newspaper is the last place I'd go to talk about it.' She straightened. 'But let's say, there's nothing obvious so far, and everyone in that room has been working their asses off on it.' She glanced at her watch. 'I've got to get back.'

Harper followed the detective out into the corridor.

She kept thinking about those restraining orders. How could it not be Anderson?

'Maybe there's some way he could have done it,' she suggested. 'Something we haven't thought of.'

Daltrey cast her a sideways glance.

'If you think you can find it, knock yourself out, McClain. I've never had more witnesses for an alibi in my entire career.'

Just before they reached the door of the homicide squad's office, Daltrey turned to face her.

'You want some advice? Be careful with this one. The family's lawyer is so far up our asses right now he could shine a flashlight out of our mouths. If they know you're looking into his alibi, they'll turn that attention on you. And, trust me, you don't want that.'

Coming from Daltrey, this was akin to an act of solidarity. Harper was touched by it.

'Thanks,' she said.

Daltrey held her eyes for a second, then, giving a crisp nod, she opened the door and stormed back into the room full of men.

'Are you just sitting around holding your dicks or are you working?' Harper heard her ask.

She had a brief view of the detectives turning to look at her before the door closed and she was alone.

Chapter Thirty

All the way back to the newspaper, Harper was piecing through what she'd learned and trying to figure out what they were all missing. It had to be there.

It was getting too late for the meter maids, so she parked on Bay Street in front of the newspaper offices and climbed out without paying. The edge was just coming off the heat.

A breeze blew her hair into her eyes as she slammed the car door. It smelled of car exhaust and river mud.

Her phone rang as she hit the button on the remote to lock the doors. The number on the screen was unrecognized.

'McClain,' she said, raising her voice to be heard above the traffic.

'We need to talk.'

The voice was male, familiar. For a split second she thought it might be Luke. Her heart kicked.

But almost instantly she realized that it wasn't him. This voice was younger. The accent was all wrong.

Then her mind found a name to go with that soft, patrician voice.

Peyton Anderson.

It was Friday afternoon – the sidewalks were packed. Beneath the palm trees and live oaks tourists in shorts mingled with workers in suits.

Jostled, Harper moved out of the way.

'Sure. What do you want to talk about?' She tried to keep the surprise out of her voice.

'Why did you write that article about me?' he asked. 'I had nothing to do with what happened to Naomi, and you know it. You've been talking to the cops and I know they've told you it couldn't be me. Why are you writing lies?'

He sounded aggrieved, but there was an odd undertone to his voice. He almost sounded . . . amused.

Warning signals went off in Harper's mind. Something wasn't right here.

'I never said you were involved in her murder,' she pointed out.

'Don't treat me like a child. You *implied* it. You told me you were writing about Naomi's life. But all you wrote about was me and those women.' He paused. 'I don't like being tricked.'

There was something ominous about that last line. Harper reached in her pocket and pulled out her notebook. He knew she was a journalist and he hadn't said he wanted this to be off the record.

If he didn't know the rules, he ought to learn them.

'Did you stalk Naomi, Peyton?' she asked. 'She told a judge you showed up at her house, her work, her classes, constantly harassing her. That you threatened her when she started dating Wilson Shepherd. Was she telling the truth?'

'What do you think? I mean, you put my picture on the front page, Harper. You must have opinions.'

'It doesn't matter what I think,' she said. 'What really happened?'

'Here's what I think,' he said, ignoring her question. 'I think you're so desperate for a front-page headline, you'd write anything. You'd sell your soul for attention. I think that story made Paul Dells all hot and excited. And now you're his favorite pretty little reporter. Who knows what he'll do for you in return?'

This was dangerously close to what was actually happening at the paper. How did he know?

'Was anything I wrote untrue?' she asked, trying to draw him back to the subject. 'I am very willing to talk to you again if you want to give me your side of the story.'

'I don't want to talk about me,' he said. 'I want to talk about you. You intrigue me, Harper. You take risks you shouldn't take. You put yourself in danger. Why is that? Does it have to do with your mother?'

Harper froze.

'What about my mother?' It came out ice cold.

He chuckled. 'Didn't you think I'd look you up? Someone murdered your mother when you were a child. You found her body. That kind of experience changes you. It makes you dangerous. I'll bet you're an animal in bed, Harper. I'd love to find out.'

Her stomach curdled.

This must be what Naomi went through day after day. This oily voice picking at her, objectifying her, filled with hate and longing in equal measures. Making her feel violated and afraid.

There was no way to win. He liked women to be scared. He liked them to get angry. She'd read those injunctions. She knew what turned him on.

She wouldn't give him what he wanted.

'I hear you were attacked the same night Naomi was

killed,' she said briskly, as if he hadn't spoken. 'Can you tell me about it?'

'Oh, you are as cool as I thought.' He sounded gleeful. 'Yes, I was violently attacked. Why do you ask about that now? Did you just find out? Did I ruin your plans? Your great idea to blame everything on Randall Anderson's son? You must have thought you'd win a Pulitzer, huh, Harper? Is that what you thought? I'm sorry to spoil it for you.'

'All I'm trying to do is cover a murder,' she said. 'I don't have a problem with you, as long as you're not the man who shot Naomi Scott to death on River Street. This isn't personal.'

There was a pause.

'You're wrong there, Harper. This is very personal.' She could hear him smiling. 'By the way, what did Angela and Cameron tell you? Man, they are looking hot these days.'

Harper suppressed a gasp. How could he know that she'd met them? She hadn't written the story yet.

'You talked to those two jealous bitches and then you ran straight to talk to the police,' he continued. 'I guess they set you straight. Because you sure don't look too happy right now. But I like the way you look in that black top. And even when you're not smiling, you're kind of sexy. That red hair . . .' He let out a long, hissing breath. 'Does the carpet match the curtains, I wonder? I might have to find out.'

Harper's blood chilled.

He was watching her.

Leaving the car behind, she ran into the middle of the sidewalk, the phone still pressed to her ear, scanning the crowded street.

There were too many people. He could have been anywhere. In one of the brick buildings across the street. In the hotel nearby, on an upper floor. In a car, parked at the curb.

But he was somewhere close. And he'd been watching her since yesterday.

'Careful there, hon,' an older woman said, as she swerved to avoid Harper, who was blocking the sidewalk.

'Now you get it.' Anderson gave a pleased chuckle. 'I know everything you do. So, run inside your little newspaper office and tell Dells that my father is going to bring him down.'

The phone went dead.

Standing on her toes, Harper scoured the people in the distance.

For a second, she thought she saw a tall, slim figure in the shade of an oak tree on the far side of the street.

But when she leaned out to get a better look, there was nobody there.

When Harper walked into the newspaper building a few minutes later, she felt shaken.

She should have seen this coming, she supposed. Three women had been stalked by Peyton Anderson, and three times the police had failed to protect them.

If she was right and somehow he'd killed Naomi Scott and gotten away with it all with a slap on the wrist . . .

He must feel superhuman by now.

Why wouldn't he turn that power on the reporter who embarrassed him on the front page of his hometown paper?

For a moment out there, that sensation of being observed had felt so familiar, she realized she'd been feeling that way all year. In her apartment. In her car.

That creeping, preternatural awareness of observation had become part of her life.

And now there were two people watching her. One she knew. And one she didn't.

Baxter was hanging up the phone as Harper walked up to her desk.

Her anxiety must have shown on her face because the city editor gave her a puzzled look.

'Something wrong?'

'Can we talk?' Harper asked.

Baxter stood and, motioning for her to follow, led her into Dells's empty office, closing the door behind her.

'What's the matter?'

'I just got off the phone with Peyton Anderson,' Harper said. 'He's been following me.'

'What?' Baxter asked, incredulous. 'Following you where?'

'Everywhere.'

Harper filled her in on what had happened.

'And you didn't see him?' Baxter asked when she finished.

'I thought I might have seen him in the distance, but when I got a good look he was gone. But he knew everything I've been doing for the last couple of days. He knew I'd seen those women who filed restraining orders against him.' Harper stopped, covering her mouth with her fingertips. 'I better warn them. He might try to hurt them if he thinks they're helping me.'

Baxter held up one hand. 'Slow down. Let's work this through. And the police say he couldn't have killed Naomi because he was attacked that same night?'

Harper nodded. 'The cops questioned him at the hospital at eleven o'clock.'

Baxter eyed her doubtfully. 'And you still like him for it?'

'After that phone call?' Harper's voice was tight. 'I think he's our guy.'

'What does Daltrey think?'

Harper waved the question away. 'She says no one else makes

282

sense. He's the obvious suspect. Except for the alibi. Which she says is solid.'

Baxter's gaze narrowed.

'So your story's dead. Unless you're going to write that the killer is definitely him, except that there's no way it could be him, because he was absolutely positively somewhere else at the time Naomi Scott was killed?'

Harper couldn't believe how obtuse she was being.

'I just told you the little psychopath has been following me for two days,' she said, sharply. 'Doesn't that tell you anything?'

'It tells me he's a stalker,' Baxter said. 'Which is the one thing we already knew about him. What it does not tell me is that he bought a gun, tracked down a bartender and shot her on River Street ten days ago. I still don't know who did that.'

'He did it.' Harper's voice sharpened. 'I know he did. I can *feel* it.'

'I don't deal in feelings,' Baxter retorted. 'I deal in facts. The facts say we need to give his picture to the guard at the front desk so he knows to call the cops if he ever tries to get in this building. The facts do not tell me he is a murderer.'

Harper started to argue but Baxter stopped her.

'Don't bring me feelings, McClain,' she said, her voice rising. 'When you figure out how this guy could be in two places at once, we can talk. Until then, as far as I'm concerned, you've got no story. And don't let Dells put ideas in your head. I will quit before I let this paper run an article that could end your career, you hear me? If you're not careful you'll find yourself in the middle of his private war. And if that happens, MaryAnne Charlton will eat you alive.'

They glared at each other across the glossy, modern office.

'I don't even know what that means,' Harper said.

'You're a reporter. Figure it out.'

Harper stormed to the door.

'Fine,' she said, yanking it open. 'I'll get you more. Because I'm telling you right now – Peyton Anderson killed Naomi Scott. I know he did.

'And I'm going to prove it.'

Chapter Thirty-one

The argument with Baxter was infuriating. And the worst part was, the city editor wasn't wrong. If Anderson's alibi held up, Harper didn't have a story at all.

What she didn't understand, though, was what Baxter had said about Charlton. What had she meant about a 'private war' between the owner and Dells?

She wasn't about to ask. Not until they'd both calmed down.

Baxter had disappeared, anyway. Probably outside for a smoke.

Harper still had the day's crime to cover but, first, she made a call to Savannah Memorial Hospital. If Anderson had been taken there the night of the stabbing, there should be a record of it.

When she got the hospital press officer on the phone, however, the woman was far from helpful.

'All information related to patients is private,' she said.

'I'm not asking for any information about him,' Harper pointed out. 'I'm asking if he was in your hospital last Tuesday night.'

'All patient information,' the woman repeated evenly, 'is private.'

'Can't you give me a yes or no?'

'All information . . .' the woman began.

Harper hung up.

The hospital wasn't going to help.

She'd have to find another way.

A few hours later, Harper drove back to police headquarters for the second time that day.

The lobby was much emptier now than it had been earlier.

Alone at the front desk, night desk officer Dwayne Josephs was watching a baseball game on a small television.

'Hey, Harper.' He glanced at his watch. 'Things must be quiet out there if you're hanging around here.'

'It's dead,' Harper said. 'If someone doesn't get shot soon the front page will be blank.'

'That would be a pity,' he commiserated.

She leaned against his desk.

'Dwayne.'

He looked at her, his brow furrowing.

'I need a favor.'

A hint of caution entered his expression. Doing favors for Harper had nearly cost him his job the summer before.

But all he said was, 'OK . . .?'

'Could you pull me a crime report from last week?' she asked, adding hastily, 'It's nothing big. Just a stabbing last Tuesday at around eleven o'clock, near City Market. I missed it the night it happened or I'd already know everything about it.'

His wide smile reappeared.

'Oh sure. That's an easy one. I thought you were going to ask for something hard.'

Dwayne turned to his computer. He typed for a couple of minutes, searching through last week's forms.

'I think I got it.' He glanced at her. 'Victim name of Anderson?'

Harper nodded. 'That's it. Can you print me a copy?'

A few minutes later, Harper sat in her car at the edge of the police parking lot, reading the report of Anderson's mugging.

As Daltrey told her, it took place shortly after eleven, around the corner from the busy City Market area. The description of the crime was straightforward.

Victim was walking on Congress Street when two black males approached him, demanding money. Victim produced wallet and phone. One suspect yelled, 'Too slow, bitch' and stabbed him with a bladed object. The two suspects fled the scene on foot. Victim was transported to Savannah Memorial Hospital by EMS.

In the space for the victim name, the officer had written 'Peyton Anderson'. Clear as day.

It fit Daltrey's description of the events perfectly.

And Harper didn't buy it.

She'd covered a lot of muggings over the years. Hundreds of them. Knives were almost never involved.

Why would any self-respecting mugger use a knife that could so easily be turned against him? Guns were a dime a dozen on Savannah's rougher streets. And much more reliable if a victim decided to fight.

Also, 'Too slow, bitch'?

That sounded like something from a TV show.

And yet, if Anderson was taken to the hospital then someone must have stabbed him.

But who? And why was he lying about it?

She was stuck. Anderson had his alibi. And with the hospital refusing to cooperate, there was no way to disprove it.

She needed advice. And there was one person she'd trust to give it.

Grabbing her phone, she scrolled until she found the name she wanted.

'Tell me there's a murder somewhere,' Miles said, by way of hello.

'Nope,' Harper said. 'All of Savannah's criminals have expired from the heat.'

'I guess it's the unemployment line for you then,' he replied.

It wasn't a good joke, given what was going on at the paper. Harper let it pass.

'Hey, I need some advice,' she said. 'You busy?'

Fifteen minutes later, Harper pulled into the sheltered parking lot behind a bank on Congress Street.

They often met here, late at night, when things got quiet. It was shielded on all sides by a high hedge, which blocked them from prying eyes. But it was right in the middle of downtown, very handy if trouble kicked off.

Miles drove in about two minutes later, pulling up so his car was next to hers, parked toe-to-tail, so the driver-side windows faced each other.

Harper rolled her window down. Warm night air flooded in, chasing the air-conditioning to the corners.

'Hey,' she said. 'Thanks for doing this.'

'I'm thrilled by the distraction,' he told her, his smile a flash of white in the shadows. 'What's happening?'

'It's the Peyton Anderson story,' she told him.

'Ah.' He didn't look surprised.

Talking slowly at first, but then faster, she told him where her investigation had reached. When she got to the part about Dells's involvement, and Baxter's warnings that she should be careful, Miles blew out a breath between pursed lips.

'Ah dammit,' he said. 'This is not good.'

'I don't understand,' she said. 'What did Baxter mean about me getting caught in Dells's war?'

'It sounds to me like Dells is taking on MaryAnne Charlton and the board, and he's using your story to do it,' he said. 'Peyton Anderson's father has been on the newspaper board of directors for years, so I can almost see his logic. *Almost.*'

'What does that have to do with me?'

He gave a bitter smile. 'You're the one writing the story.'

'Writing the story is my *job*.'

'Be that as it may, a fight's brewing and you are smack dab in the middle of it,' he said. 'Charlton wants layoffs and Dells doesn't. Your article could bring down one of Charlton's buddies on the board of directors. Getting rid of Anderson would leave Charlton weaker, and Dells might be able to work some sort of a deal with the other board members to get what he wants.'

The pieces fell into place.

Now Harper understood why Baxter had been so angry.

'And Charlton could stop all this by getting rid of Dells. Or getting rid of me.'

'You've got it,' Miles said.

'Well, Charlton might as well save her energy. At the moment, I can't break Peyton Anderson's alibi.'

'If he was really in the hospital when Scott got herself shot?' Miles shook his head. 'It's hard to argue with that.'

'I know,' she said. 'But I've read the report and it doesn't jell for me. Feels off.'

'Feels off how?'

She described the stabbing. What Anderson told the police his attacker had said.

Miles made a face.

'Well, I'll admit it sounds a little unlikely.'

'How do I prove it?' she asked. 'The hospital spokesperson won't even confirm that Savannah Memorial Hospital exists.'

He snorted a laugh.

'Yeah. Hospitals aren't big talkers.' He thought for a second. 'Have you talked to Toby? He might know someone with access.'

At the mention of the paramedic, Harper sat up straighter. 'Why didn't I think of Toby? His wife works there one day a week. She might know someone who could help.'

'There you go. Hospitals won't talk.' He reached for his thermos of coffee. 'But doctors gossip like teenagers.'

From somewhere in the distance she heard raised voices. The sound of someone honking angrily. Leaning on the horn.

It was a hot night. Tempers were rising.

'What do you think I should do about Dells?' She turned back to Miles. 'I don't want to get dragged into anything.'

'You need to mind your ps and qs,' he told her. 'Keep Baxter involved – sounds like she wants to protect you if she can.'

All signs of humor were gone now from his long, lean face. He looked deadly serious.

'Dells is playing a dangerous game right now. If he's not careful, he'll run out of road. Charlton is not someone you want to mess with. My advice? Do what you would do if you were writing about anyone else. Work through that alibi. If the Anderson kid lied, write it the way you see it. Don't worry about the games the bosses are playing. But be *right*.

'Or they will hang you out to dry.'

Chapter Thirty-two

The next morning, Harper stood on her front steps, looking up and down East Jones Street.

The tree-lined street with its sturdy nineteenth-century houses was quiet. In the bright sun, oak branches sent skeletal shadows stretching out across the lane.

There was no sign of Peyton Anderson, or anyone else for that matter. But he could be there, she knew, watching her. He could be anywhere.

After talking to Miles last night, she'd given Toby a call. He'd been working a late shift and couldn't talk but he'd made a promising suggestion.

'Let's meet at the hospital tomorrow. See what we can dig up.'

She walked to the Camaro, feeling unseen eyes on her and knowing it was probably her imagination. Nevertheless, her skin felt raw from it.

The car started with a powerful, low rumble, and Harper glanced back at the tall house.

She was less worried about leaving the apartment empty than she might have been, though. Late last night, she'd heard Mia come home. As she climbed the side stairs, it became clear she wasn't alone. In the rumble of conversation, Harper recognized Riley's distinctive baritone. She'd never heard him leave, so he was probably still upstairs.

There's no better security than a cop in your house.

Now, she just had to worry about herself.

She pulled out from the curb, keeping her eyes on the rearview mirror.

No one pulled out behind her.

She took a long, circuitous route through the city, heading first to the dark green edges of the marshes, where there was no traffic at all, before turning back.

A Volkswagen stayed behind her for about five minutes, setting her nerves on edge until it turned off as she approached the graceful fountains at Forsythe Park.

By the time she pulled into the visitor lot at Savannah Memorial Hospital, she was convinced she wasn't being followed.

Leaving her scanner in the car, she hurried through the midday heat to the main entrance.

The automatic double doors swung open as she approached, sending a wave of cool air with a slight antiseptic edge into the summer heat.

Following the directions Toby had given her the night before, she made her way down a wide corridor to a row of elevators marked 'B', and got on with an elderly man with a cane who positioned himself by the floor buttons.

'Where're you headed?' he asked, glancing at her from beneath silver eyebrows as thick as bird wings.

'Fifth floor, please,' she said.

His hand hovered above the numbers.

'You sure? No one's up there. It's Saturday.' He peered at her, owlishly. 'It's dental surgery on five. They're too rich to work on weekends. Who're you seeing?'

Harper was thrown. He was like some sort of ancient hospital savant. She scrambled to think of a good explanation.

'I . . . I'm visiting a friend who works here,' she explained, after a beat.

'Oh.' He punched the button, his expression condemning. 'Personal visit.'

They rode the rest of the way in silence. The old man got off on the third floor without saying goodbye, grumbling to himself as he limped out into the hallway.

On the fifth floor, she stepped out into a quiet corridor. The old man was right – it was empty. To one side was a silent waiting room, where rows of empty chairs sat in front of a darkened television.

She could hear voices from down the corridor, and the sound of doors opening and closing. But nobody was in view.

Following Toby's directions, she turned into the first hallway she passed and knocked on a door marked number 572.

It was flung open by Toby, in rumpled green scrubs that looked like he'd slept in them.

'Harper!' He grinned at her from beneath a disheveled thatch of blond hair. 'You found us.' Stepping back, he held the door open. 'Welcome to our hiding place.'

Harper stepped into a small examining room. Painted the same white as a doctor's coat, it held little furniture – an examining bed, a small desk, and two chairs. In one of the chairs sat Toby's wife, Dr Elaine O'Neil.

She was tiny, her neat figure dressed in dark slacks and a

turquoise sweater. A laptop was open in front of her, and an overstuffed, burgundy briefcase lay at her feet.

'Hi, Harper,' she said, smiling as if they were meeting for drinks and dinner instead of illicitly sharing information on a closed floor of a hospital.

Harper had known the two of them for years – since Toby was a rookie paramedic, and Elaine was an intern in the emergency room.

'Are you sure we're OK to be up here? I don't want to get you guys in any trouble.'

Elaine's shrug was serene.

'Toby sleeps up here when he pulls overnight shifts – everyone's used to seeing us skulking around. Now have a seat, and tell us what's going on.'

Toby had taken the chair next to his wife, so Harper perched on the edge of the examining table, her feet dangling. She felt like a patient.

'I hate to drag you into this,' she told them. 'But I'm stuck. And you're the only people I can think of who might be able to help.'

She'd given Toby the barest details the night before. Now she filled them in on Peyton Anderson.

'All my instincts tell me it was him,' she said, at the end. 'But the police say he was here. What I want to know is, are they missing something? Maybe he was released earlier than they thought. Or maybe there's something in the hospital records that could explain what happened.'

She'd expected a discussion – even an argument – about hospital rules. But to her surprise, Elaine gave a crisp nod.

'Give me a second.' She swung around to the desk and opened

the laptop. As soon as the screen lit up, she began typing. 'Peyton is spelled P-E-Y-T-O-N, right?'

Jumping to her feet, Harper moved closer.

'Yes,' Harper said, eagerly. 'What do you see?'

'The system's slow,' Elaine warned her, 'this'll take a second.'

Sitting backward on the chair with his elbows on the back plastic chairback, Toby glanced at Harper.

'You're really going after Randall Anderson's kid? His daddy's not going to like that.'

'Yeah,' she said dryly. 'He's already made his feelings pretty clear.'

'Here we go.' Elaine pointed at the laptop screen. 'I hate to tell you this but hospital records back Anderson's story. He was treated here that night.' She pointed at a code. 'This says he was kept overnight for monitoring, although it doesn't look to me like his wound was that severe. He had ten stitches, lost a bit of blood. Went home first thing in the morning.'

This was as expected.

Harper leaned over the computer. 'Now what I want to know is, was he here the whole time? And is it possible his wound was self-inflicted?'

The two of them stared at her.

'You're kidding,' Elaine said, not typing.

'You think he stabbed *himself* to give himself an alibi?' Toby let out a puff of air. 'Man, that would be a special kind of crazy.'

'That's what I'm wondering.' Harper looked from him to Elaine. 'Is that even possible? His story about the mugging doesn't wash with me. Would a doctor notice if he cut his own arm? Are there signs?'

Toby and Elaine exchanged a look.

'Not if the cut was clean,' Elaine said.

Seeing Harper's blank expression, Toby explained.

'Usually if someone tries to stab himself, there are telltale signs. Hesitation wounds, we call them. Little shallow marks where they tried to cut but chickened out. If we see those, we call the psych ward.'

'But if it was a clean cut?' Harper asked.

'If it was a clean cut and he came here in an ambulance, we wouldn't even think about it,' Elaine told her. 'We'd stitch him up and send him home.'

'Is it possible to cut yourself clean like that?' Harper asked.

'I've seen it a few times,' Toby said, 'with mental illness cases. Some of them are so far gone they don't even seem to feel the pain.'

'I don't see how that matters,' Elaine interjected, pointing at the laptop screen. 'The records say he was here all night. Even if he did cut himself, he was in this building when that girl was shot.'

'As far as we know,' Toby corrected her.

Elaine made an impatient sound.

'There are bed checks all night for in-patients. Nothing in his record says the nurses checked on him and found him gone.' She glanced at Harper. 'I'm afraid your theory's a little far-fetched.'

'Wait a minute. I still think it could be done,' Toby argued. 'It wouldn't be easy. He'd have to know the hospital well. But if he did, he could swing it.'

'Oh, come on,' Elaine wasn't convinced. 'There are too many chances to get caught. Patients are checked every two hours. That's not enough time for him to get out, kill someone, and come back again.'

'Really?' Toby cocked his head. 'I can get to downtown from here at one in the morning in about twelve minutes.'

Elaine opened her mouth to argue, but then closed it again.

'Dammit,' she muttered, turning to the computer and typing something. 'Now you've got me thinking he could do it.'

'It would be risky.' Toby turned back to Harper. 'He'd need to have a handle on the nurses' schedule. If one thing went wrong he'd be busted.'

Her hands on the keys, Elaine glanced up at them.

'What time did the murder happen, Harper?'

'Around two in the morning.'

Elaine typed something. A grid appeared on the screen. She traced it with her finger, staring at the numbers. Muttering something to herself, she typed some more. The grid changed again.

'See?' she pointed. 'There's just . . .'

Her voice trailed off. She leaned forward, peering at the screen.

'What?' Harper stared at the yellow and white squares.

'Hold on.' Turning to her husband, Elaine pointed at the screen. 'Tell me I'm not crazy. Do you see what I see?'

Looking where Elaine indicated, Toby gave a low whistle.

'You're not crazy.'

'What is it?' Harper asked, crowding in next to them to see.

'It's probably nothing,' Elaine cautioned. 'It's just – there's a gap in the schedule. All the nurses take their dinner breaks between one a.m. and three a.m.'

'I don't understand,' Harper said, looking from her to Toby. 'What does that mean?'

'For those two hours, one nurse handles an entire floor,' Toby explained. 'That means no bed checks. They only check on patients during that time if an alarm goes off.'

Harper took a step back as what he was saying sank in.

'You're telling me that from one a.m. to three a.m. on the night Naomi Scott was murdered, nobody checked on Peyton Anderson?'

Elaine nodded.

'That's what the chart shows.'

Harper turned to Toby. 'That gives him plenty of time to get to River Street, kill her, and get back here without being seen.'

'He could have killed her twice in that time,' he agreed.

Harper was so excited she had to force herself to take the time to think it through.

The hospital was big but, at that hour, it would have been very quiet. Even on a busy day, she'd worried about being noticed and asked what she was doing here.

A patient walking the floors in the middle of the night would be easy to spot.

'How did he get out without being noticed?' she asked.

'That's the million-dollar question,' Elaine said. 'Security is very good here. Especially at night. There are security guards and CCTV cameras at every main entrance.'

'Yeah, but there are ways.' Toby looked over Elaine's shoulder at Anderson's record. 'What room was he in?'

His wife tapped a square on the grid.

'Two nineteen?' He glanced at her. 'Where is that? The Wilson wing?'

Elaine nodded. 'They brought him up from Emergency, so that makes sense.'

For a second, he stood next to her, deep in thought. Then, he moved toward the door, motioning for them to follow.

'Come on, y'all. Let's go take a look at that room.'

Harper jumped up to follow him, but Elaine glanced at her watch. 'You two go, I've got to check in with work.'

Folding the laptop, she slipped it into the briefcase at her feet, and got up.

At the door, she paused.

'I hope you get your guy.' She gave Harper a critical look. 'You should come to dinner soon. You look hungry.'

'You got it,' Harper promised.

Kissing her husband lightly, Elaine turned right, and disappeared between a set of double doors marked 'Staff only'.

Toby pointed in the opposite direction. 'This way.'

Harper followed him through a maze of hospital corridors until he turned into a bright, empty stairwell.

'Nobody ever takes the stairs,' Toby told her as he bounded down, his voice echoing loudly. 'They're crazy. That elevator takes forever. And it's full of sick people.'

They spiraled down three floors before emerging into another quiet corridor. They'd only walked for a few seconds when they reached the nurses' station – a long, curved desk with five chairs, set directly in front of the elevator doors.

Two nurses in green scrubs stood at one end, looking at something on a computer screen.

Toby waved at one of them. Who smiled at him.

'Hi, Toby. What are you up to?'

'Oh, you know.' He flashed his amiable grin. 'Passing through.'

She returned to her work as they moved down the hallway.

When they were out of earshot, Toby told Harper, 'I don't know how Anderson got out, but no way did he take that elevator without being noticed. Even at one in the morning.'

'They can see everyone coming up the stairs, too,' she pointed out. 'Damn.'

'Don't give up yet.' Toby looked at the long row of doors ahead. 'What was his room number again?'

'Two nineteen.'

They paused to check the next room they passed. Two sixty-seven.

'Must be further down,' Toby said, striding off.

When they found it, room two nineteen was at the opposite end of the ward from the nursing station. Its broad, faux wood door was half-open.

Cautiously, they stepped inside. The private room held a bed with a bare mattress. Next to the bed stood an IV machine, unplugged, cables wound behind it.

On the far wall was a window, which did not appear to have a handle.

'Is that sealed shut?' Harper asked, pointing.

Toby nodded.

'So he didn't get out on the elevator, and he didn't get out by climbing out that window.' He glanced at her quizzically. 'Can this guy fly?'

'Not as far as I know.'

Harper didn't want to admit it, but her faith in her own theory was fading fast. There was no way to walk around this place freely. Patients couldn't leave and come back at will.

The police were right. Anderson couldn't be her killer.

Which left her with what?

Absolutely nothing.

They walked out to the corridor in silence.

'Stay here a second,' Toby told her. 'I want to check something.'

Leaving her there, he walked further down the corridor, looking at doors. First he went right. And then, passing her, he walked the other way, checking each door he went by.

After a minute, he paused, then turned and motioned for her.

When she reached him, he pointed at the door. 'What do you think?'

A green sign on an otherwise unmarked door read, 'Fire Escape'.

She looked from him to the door. 'Is it alarmed?'

Toby grabbed the door handle. 'Let's find out.'

Startled, Harper reached for his arm.

'Toby, don't,' she hissed.

With a defiant look, he turned the handle.

The door opened without a sound, revealing a staircase.

'Oh man,' Toby said, grinning. 'That was a buzz. You looked scared shitless.'

She didn't laugh.

'How did you know there wasn't an alarm?'

'That's not how hospitals work,' he told her, stepping through the door. 'This place is all about getting from A to B as fast as possible and not waking people up. Most staircases double as fire escapes.'

His voice echoed as the door closed behind them.

'Now, come on. Let's see if there's any way your guy did this thing.'

This staircase was narrower and more utilitarian than the one they'd used earlier.

They walked down one floor. The stairs ended in front of a set of unmarked double doors.

'I'll bet you all kinds of money those lead straight to the parking lot,' Toby told her.

He pushed the bar on the door. It swung open, letting in a wave of hot, humid air.

Outside, rows of cars stretched in all directions, gleaming in the sunlight.

'Bingo,' Harper said.

Once outside, the two of them looked around.

Beyond the parking lot, Harper could see the busy road in the distance, hear cars heading to and from downtown.

Suddenly, she could see it all. She could see Anderson, getting out of bed, throwing on his clothes, coming down those stairs. Pushing open the door. She could see him walking out into the dark night, and everything that happened next.

She could see his alibi falling apart.

Toby examined the door. 'There's no handle. If he got out this way, how'd he get back in?'

In response, Harper began searching the ground. Almost immediately, she found what she was looking for. Bending, she picked up a broken brick.

'Did you ever sneak out of school?' she asked, holding it up. 'This is how Bonnie and I used to do it.'

She set the brick down between the door and the doorjamb. Then, she let go of the door. It went as far as the brick and stopped, leaving a small crack. To any passerby, it would look closed.

But you could get in and out with ease.

'I'll be damned,' Toby said.

He was smiling but his eyes were hard.

'He's your murderer, isn't he? That rich kid killed that girl.'

'I think so.' Harper swung the door open again and let it close with a thud. 'All he had to do was come down the stairs, leave that door propped open, go kill Naomi Scott, slip back in, kick the brick away, let the door close, and go back to bed. It wouldn't have taken him forty minutes if he timed it right.'

'Works for me,' Toby said.

'Yeah,' Harper murmured, looking up the dark staircase. 'Now all I have to do is prove it.'

Chapter Thirty-three

Harper raced back from the hospital to tell Dells and Baxter what she'd learned. But when she got to the newsroom a short time later, Baxter was not at her desk, and Dells's office was dark.

The usual Saturday crew was in – a few writers from the 'Living' section, and the woman who covered government stuff. But the room felt oddly hushed.

As she plugged in her scanner, a cluster of men in dark gray suits with visitor passes hanging around their necks passed through the newsroom talking to each other and looking at no one else, heading into the stairwell that led to upper floors, where the advertising and management offices were. They seemed to know the building well.

Harper watched them, puzzled.

Still, she didn't give it much thought. With Baxter away, she had the chance to put all the pieces of her theory together before she presented it. She needed it to be convincing.

Setting her scanner on her desk with the sound turned low, she started writing up what she had.

Police Fail to Investigate Prominent Savannah
Man for Murder

By Harper McClain

The evidence police have against Peyton Anderson, the law student son of former District Attorney Randall Anderson, would be enough to bring any less connected suspect in for questioning in the murder of Naomi Scott.

And yet police do not, at this time, consider him a suspect.

According to court documents, and Anderson himself, Anderson and Scott were former friends, who briefly dated. Six months ago, Scott filed for a restraining order, accusing him of stalking and threatening her. That order was granted by a district judge.

Anderson was ordered to stay a minimum of a hundred yards away from Scott at all times. He was told not to contact her.

Twelve days ago, Naomi Scott was shot to death on River Street. The crime remains unsolved.

Police refuse to comment on whether they have any suspects at this time.

The *Daily News* has learned that court documents show Anderson has a history of stalking and threatening multiple women. Over the last two years, he's been accused on three occasions of stalking female students at the law school.

He followed the women relentlessly, breaking into their homes, pursuing them during the day and late into the night.

Scott's own injunction, filed months before she died, portrayed the same ruthless approach. Naomi Scott told a judge she was 'constantly afraid' and that she feared Anderson would kill her boyfriend, Wilson Shepherd, out of jealousy.

In the end, it wasn't Shepherd who died but Scott herself.

On the night of the murder, shortly after eleven p.m., police were called to a street outside City Market, where they found Peyton Anderson bleeding from a stab wound. He said his wallet and phone had been stolen in a violent mugging.

Stabbed in the left arm, he was taken to Savannah Memorial Hospital, where he was treated, and kept overnight for observation.

Therefore, police believe he couldn't possibly have committed the murder. At the time Naomi Scott was gunned down on River Street, Anderson was in his hospital bed.

But hospital records seen by this reporter show nobody checked on Anderson between 1 a.m. and 3 a.m.

The murder was called in to police at 2:08 a.m. Anderson's whereabouts at that time cannot be independently verified.

The hospital refused to comment for this story.

Harper was so engrossed in her work she didn't hear DJ walk up to his desk until he rolled his chair around to face her.

'Hey,' he said, whispering, 'did you hear about Dells?'

Harper stopped typing. His face was serious, but with that excited lift that comes with bad news.

A sudden tightness gripped her chest.

'What about him?'

DJ propelled himself closer.

'Charlton suspended him,' he said. 'For insubordination.'

Harper stared.

'Are you serious?' She searched DJ's face for any sign that this was an elaborate joke.

'I am coronary levels of seriousness,' he assured her. 'It happened an hour ago. I only came in to get my gym bag. I wasn't going to stay. But then MaryAnne Charlton marched in here with a bunch of men I've never seen before. They had a big argument. Dells stormed out. They locked themselves in his office for half an hour, going through his stuff. Then they all left. Dells never came back.'

'Gray suits?' Harper said, remembering the men she'd seen earlier.

He nodded.

Harper dropped her head to her hands.

They'd run out of time. The chief editor's gambit had failed.

'This is all my fault.'

She sensed rather than saw DJ's look of surprise.

'Why would it be your fault?'

'The Anderson story.' She raised her head, peering at him miserably. 'The one about the restraining orders. Randall Anderson's on the newspaper board. He and Charlton are buddies. Dells told me he thought we had three days to get evidence against the Anderson kid and prove we were right. I didn't know it was because he thought he was going to get fired. I thought he just wanted the story fast.' She looked at her watch. 'He was wrong. We had two and a half.'

'Have you got it now?' he asked, pointing at her computer.

'If you've got enough to prove you were right, you can take it to Baxter . . .'

She shook her head. 'I'm close but not close enough. I was going to ask him for more time . . .'

Her voice trailed off.

What was she going to do? Without Dells, the story was dead in the water. And without the story, Anderson would never be charged.

He would get away with murder.

'Dammit.' She kicked the leg of her desk. 'I blew it.'

She looked at the story that would never run, and glanced back at the front of the room, where Baxter had now walked in and was sitting at her computer, staring into the distance, her face drawn.

She was heartsick at the thought of what Anderson might do now. If he got away with murder, he would stalk more women. Maybe kill them.

And his father would protect him.

She didn't know how she was going to tell Jerrod Scott his daughter's killer was going to get away with it. She didn't know where she'd find the words.

But there was nothing she could do. Charlton had outplayed them all.

With slow reluctance, she saved the article as 'draft' and sent a copy to herself, just in case. Then she closed the file.

For now, the Anderson story was dead.

Whatever had been keeping Savannah's criminals quiet all week ended that night.

Harper's scanner started humming at sunset and did not stop. There were three shootings and a stabbing all within a few hours of each other.

She sped from one crime scene to another, running fast to try to keep up. There was no time to think and, maybe that wasn't such a bad thing.

When she pulled up on Waters Street to the third shooting, it was a few minutes after eleven o'clock.

She hadn't been back to the newsroom in hours. Mostly because she was busy. But also because she couldn't face it right now.

The cops were no longer bothering with niceties like crime tape. They, too, had become a flying squad, rushing from crime to crime. Harper left her car two blocks away from the blue lights, and walked straight up to the ambulance.

The air was hot and heavy with the grainy-sweet smell of exhaust. Beneath that high note, was a low note – something metallic and dangerous that set her nerves on edge.

The flickering lights illuminated a young black man on a stretcher, his eyes closed, skinny arms limp. He was lean and tall – his long legs sprawled from baggy shorts. He didn't look out of his teens.

The EMTs had already cut his T-shirt open, and Harper could see the wound high on his ribs on the right side. Blood poured dark red onto the blue stretcher cover.

Harper didn't like his chances.

Paramedics clustered around him, giving quick clear orders to each other. One was dressing the wound, as another attached an IV. A third was checking vitals and calling it in to the emergency room.

Spotting Miles, crouched down near the curb, shooting the dangling IV bags, against the backdrop of the ambulances glaring lights, Harper ran over to him.

'What've we got?' she asked, watching the EMTs work. 'Or do I need to ask?'

'It's exactly what it looks like.' He spoke as he took the shot.

'Kid was selling crack on the corner. Two guys walk up, one has a gun. Bang bang.'

Harper pulled a battered notebook from her pocket.

'They did this in front of witnesses?'

Miles stood. 'What I heard was, half the block was out on the street.'

'Jesus, what a night,' she muttered, scribbling notes.

He tilted the camera to check his shots.

'Been hot too long. Things boil over.' He glanced at her. 'How's Baxter taking the news about Dells?'

'She hasn't said a word. I think she's furious.'

'Don't blame her.' Miles hung his camera from his shoulder. 'Charlton's crazy to let him go. There's nobody else on staff who knows how to do that job. It throws Baxter in it, waist deep.'

'Guess you were right about Dells pushing his luck,' she said.

He gave her a look. 'Least it was him and not you.'

'This time,' she said.

She glanced at her watch. 'I've got to go talk to some witnesses or I won't make deadline. See you at the next shooting?'

'I'll be there,' he said.

Harper made her way to the curb to talk to neighbors, who were not very interested in sharing their thoughts with a journalist.

In the darkness, she passed Josh Leonard from Channel 5, lugging his own camera. As soon as he saw her, he stopped.

'Heard about Dells.' He gave her a look. 'Charlton's lost her tiny mind if she thinks she can run that paper without him.'

'That's what everyone says.' Harper shoved her notebook in her pocket. 'You guys hiring? I might be looking.'

To her surprise, he didn't smile.

'You ever come looking for a job, Channel 5 would hire you without even thinking twice.'

'Shut up,' she said.

His expression was serious.

'I'm not joking. Do it. Get me off the murder beat. Come join the dark side.'

He glanced over to where the ambulance workers were treating the victim.

'I've got to go get some more shots. Good luck with all that. Let me know if you decide you want to be me for a while. I'll hook you up.'

With that, he walked away, leaving Harper staring after him in astonishment.

There was no time to think about their discussion, though, it was a crowded and chaotic scene. The patrol cops were in a bad mood, shouting 'Get back!' at the residents, who were restive and unwilling to be corralled.

Trying to avoid getting caught up in that growing tension, Harper took a step backward, running into a police officer behind her.

He had his Kevlar vest on – it felt like running into a rock.

'Sorry,' she began, turning around, and then she recognized Riley's familiar face.

He looked out of breath. In his tired brown eyes she detected the same bewilderment she felt.

'What the hell is going on?' she asked. 'Has everyone in Savannah gone crazy?'

'I wish I knew. I just got through chasing some teenage gangster half a mile through the city. Lost him.' Running a hand across his forehead, he wiped the sweat from his face. 'I'm getting too old for this shit.'

She pointed at the ambulance next to them. 'Any idea who shot this guy?'

Riley shook his head. 'All I know is we're looking for two possible shooters, who fled on foot.'

Harper flipped through her notebook, struggling to find a clean page.

'Any other description?' she asked.

Riley's weary shrug spoke volumes. 'Young men. Ought to be at home.'

A voice spoke on his radio, and he cocked his head to listen. In the quiet, Harper heard it as clearly as he did.

'All units on Waters – caller reports seeing two armed suspects in the 400 block of Liberty.'

He sighed and pulled his keys out of his pocket with a jangle of heavy gear.

'I've got to go.' He took a step away before pausing. 'You had any more problems since the break-in?'

She shook her head. 'Nothing at all.'

'Good,' he said. 'Your place is on our watch list. I've been driving by to keep an eye on it.'

Her eyebrows rose.

'Oh, it's my *apartment* you're keeping an eye on? I thought you might have your eye on my neighbor.'

A wicked smile lit up his face. His dimples were ridiculous.

'Don't worry,' he told her. 'I'm keeping an eye on Mia, too. Got to make sure she stays safe. This town keeps getting more dangerous.'

'Be nice to her,' Harper ordered. 'She'll blame me if it all goes wrong.'

'Oh, come on.' He held out his arms, still backing toward his car. 'I'm always nice.'

After he drove away, Harper made her way down the street past the ambulance. If she could talk to the detective on the scene, she'd be done here.

When she saw a cluster of officers gathered at the side of the road, she knew she was in the right place. Her phone buzzed in her pocket, but she didn't look at it – Baxter had been calling her all night, asking for updates.

As she approached, the group parted, and she saw the detective who'd pulled the case.

Her heart sank.

Why did it have to be Luke?

Stopping mid-stride, she thought about turning around then changed her mind, nearly tripping in her indecision. The sudden motion caught Luke's attention and he looked up.

Their eyes met.

The hurt Harper had been suppressing for days tightened its grip on her heart.

Desperately she looked around for another detective to interview, but with so many violent crimes in one night, they were stretched thin. He was alone.

This was why she never should have dated him in the first place, she told herself. It interfered with her work. Made it impossible to focus on what she needed to pay attention to – the bleeding man on the stretcher.

When she looked up again, the uniformed cops had fanned out across the block, and Luke was striding toward her.

'Harper.' He glanced around to see if anyone was looking at them. 'Can we talk?'

The way he said her name killed her, every single time.

She swallowed hard.

'Now isn't a great time,' she said.

'Later then.' He stepped closer. 'We can't leave it like this. I need to explain.'

'What's the point?' Her voice was cold. 'You're seeing someone else. I get it. That's all you ever had to say.'

'I'm not –'

He stopped, lips tightening as two uniformed cops brushed past them, glancing at Harper curiously.

'We can't do this now, Luke,' she told him when they were gone.

She pulled a pen from her pocket.

'Have you got a quote for me? I understand you're looking for two suspects. Is this a gang thing?'

He held her eyes. For a second she thought he might refuse to answer. But then he gave in with obvious impatience.

'Probably. Witnesses say the three people involved knew each other. They had an argument over territory. Everyone had a gun. Our victim drew the short straw. We're searching for suspects now.'

Harper wrote it all down, glad to have something to look at that wasn't him. When she finished, though, he was still standing there, surveying the scene with something like despair.

He raked his fingers through his hair.

'This fucking night,' he said. 'Some eighteen-year-old kid shot twice over nothing. EMTs don't know if he'll make it. And I can't . . .'

His gaze swept across the scene, which flickered in blue lights. When he turned back to her his eyes were anguished.

'Harper, I'm so sorry,' he said. 'I screwed up.'

Her throat was tight.

'Don't.' It was the only thing she could say.

'I didn't mean to hurt you,' he said. 'I shouldn't have come to you until I sorted out my own situation. But I didn't want to lie to you.'

Harper blinked hard. She wanted to tell him that he'd broken her heart twice now. And that was enough. That there had to be someone else out there for her. Someone who wouldn't do this.

But she couldn't find the words.

Someone down the street called his name. Luke raised his hand to acknowledge him but stayed where he was.

'I'm going to fix this,' he said. 'I know I don't deserve it. But please have some faith in me.'

Then, before she could ask what he meant, he turned and walked away.

Harper stood and watched him go – that long, cowboy stride of his, steady and unhurried.

She hated that he could still do this to her after everything. The way he'd looked at her – no one had ever looked at her like that before. She felt that look on her skin.

The night seemed colder the second he turned away.

But she couldn't keep doing this. Telling herself each time it would be different.

She couldn't take it if he hurt her again. And he would.

That's what guys like him do.

It took all her willpower to walk back to her car. Every step heavier than the one before. Yet she kept moving, down the dark street, away from the flashing blue lights. Away from Luke.

Putting one foot in front of the other, as she had all her life, she kept walking.

Chapter Thirty-four

'Where have you been?' Baxter glared from behind her computer as Harper walked into the empty newsroom, her scanner buzzing in her hand. 'I've been calling you for half an hour.'

In no mood to engage in their usual debate about her reachability, Harper headed straight to her desk.

'It's crazy out there,' she said. 'People won't stop killing each other.'

'You should thank them. They're your job security.' Baxter followed her through the rows of vacant desks. 'What've we got?'

'One dead.' Dropping her scanner on the desk, Harper turned to her. 'Six injured in three separate incidents.'

'This is out of control. Call the mayor,' Baxter said, drumming her fingers on her desk. 'Wake her up. Ask her how it feels to be in charge of a goddamn shooting gallery.'

Harper blinked.

'I don't have her home number.'

'I've got it,' Baxter said. 'Tell her the headline's going to be

"City Reels from Night of Violence". And we're not pulling any punches this time.'

She was talking fast and angry, a hail of words.

Harper felt suddenly sorry for her.

As if she knew what Harper was thinking, the editor changed the subject abruptly.

'Fucking MaryAnne Charlton. Firing Dells and leaving us with this mess to handle alone.'

'Is he really fired?' Harper asked. 'I thought he was suspended.'

'She'll never let him back in here,' Baxter fumed. 'Jesus, what are they thinking? Dells isn't perfect but Charlton's out of her gourd if she thinks she can run this place without him. That woman knows about as much about running a newspaper as I know about building an atomic weapon. Which, come to think of it, is a skill I wish I had right now.'

Cutting herself off, she raked her fingers through her hair. 'God, I need a cigarette.'

Harper wasn't sure how to take this sudden onslaught of honesty. Baxter had always been a company girl. 'Abide by the rules and this is a great place to work', she'd said more than once, even though that had become transparently untrue over the last few years. She'd personally laid off many of her own friends.

Each round took something out of her – another piece of her soul. But Harper got the feeling she'd genuinely believed it was for the greater good.

It was as if all of a sudden she no longer believed the myth.

'What about the story I've been working on?' Harper asked hesitantly. 'The Anderson story. Is it dead?'

Baxter gave her a level look.

'MaryAnne Charlton will not run that story without Dells to make her do it. And I simply don't have the power he did.'

Harper wanted to argue but Baxter looked so angry and defeated, she decided now wasn't the time.

'Are there going to be more layoffs?' she asked. 'Everyone's saying.'

'Count on it.' Baxter's voice was grim. 'As long as there are people breathing in this building, MaryAnne Charlton will want them off her payroll. Besides, I hear she just bought a villa in the Caribbean. Those things cost money.'

'We're already down to the bare bones here,' Harper said. 'How will we keep putting the paper out if even more people go?'

Baxter stared out the window into the darkness – as if she could see something there Harper couldn't. Without answering, she turned and headed back to her desk.

'You better get to work. I'll get you that number.'

By the time Harper left the office that night, she needed a drink.

She stood on the sidewalk at the edge of Bay Street, trying to decide where to go.

It was after midnight, and the heat was easing. A breeze blew off the river, ruffling her hair, and bringing its cool, green, water scent.

Leaning her head back, she breathed in – as if the air could somehow purge her of this entire day.

She felt beaten. They'd got all the stories in – some were shorter than others. But Miles had brought in some brilliant photos and the front page wouldn't look like it came from a newsroom in meltdown.

Her car was parked in the lot behind the building, but she didn't head in that direction. She didn't want to go home to a lonely apartment, and she didn't feel like The Library. Bonnie would see right through her and, tonight, she didn't feel like being seen.

She just wanted a quiet drink with other miserable people.

Turning left, she headed toward the trendier bars and restaurants of downtown. She walked slowly, trying to think of the right place.

She knew if she went to Rosie Malone's, she'd find other people from the newspaper to gossip with about Charlton and Dells, but she didn't want that, either.

Shoulders hunched, she walked past Reynolds Square, where the snake-like oak branches writhed overhead, Spanish moss trailing. Medusa's hair against the street lights.

She saw a sign for the Pink House, which had a great bar, but she wasn't in the mood for the touristy thing.

A block away, though, a new hotel had opened in a modern building. It was one of those expensive international chains with an instantly forgettable name.

Through the windows, she saw a quiet lobby with a bar beyond it. Everything was lit in cold blue light. It looked empty. Anonymous.

Aware that her clothes were rumpled and that she probably looked like hell, Harper squared her shoulders and pushed open the door.

One staff member was working at the reception desk; she gave her a bland smile as she crossed the spacious lobby – where minimalist chairs in a smooth dark fabric gathered around glass coffee tables under chandeliers as big as her apartment – toward the blue-lit bar she'd seen from the street.

Hidden speakers played jazz classics at a volume low enough to avoid becoming annoying. A long bar, illuminated from beneath, stretched along the back wall. Rows of bottles glittered on mirrored shelves behind it.

The room was wide, with well-spaced clusters of tables. Most were unoccupied.

Only one person sat at the bar – a man in a suit, hunched over his glass.

Harper headed up to order a drink from the lone bartender. She didn't look at the customer. People drinking alone usually like to be left alone.

'Whiskey, please,' she said. 'Neat.'

'Irish or Scottish?' a voice at her elbow enquired.

Harper turned to see Paul Dells watching her with an amused expression, as if all of this was perfectly normal.

'Irish,' Harper said, staring at him.

'Good choice.' Catching the bartender's eye, Dells pointed at a bottle with a green label. 'Jameson's. Make it two. Put it on my tab.'

Raising his glass, he finished his drink, pushing the glass across to the bartender, before turning to Harper.

'How's your night going?' he asked. 'Mine gets better with every glass.'

Harper was momentarily speechless.

He looked fine – his face was smooth, his suit unwrinkled. He didn't look like a man who'd been fired earlier that day.

'What the hell happened?' she said, when she found her voice.

His expression spoke volumes. 'I warned you we didn't have much time.'

The bartender set their drinks down on thick napkins with the hotel's monogram stamped in gold.

Picking his glass up, Dells stood and motioned for her to follow.

'Let's find a corner.'

Harper followed him across the bar to a quiet table. A candle glittered at the center of it. Frank Sinatra crooned from the speakers.

It felt like an awkward date.

'Are you fired?' Harper asked, when they were both seated.

He gave her an approving look.

'Straight to the point, McClain. See, now that's what I like about you. No bullshit. You call it like you see it.'

'Were you?' she pressed. 'I can't get a straight answer out of anyone.'

'Not yet. Technically speaking, I have been suspended.' He tilted his glass at her with a cynical smile.

'Suspended for what?' Harper didn't hide her frustration. 'And for how long? What happens now?'

He ticked the answers off on his fingers. 'For not doing what I was told. Indefinitely. Who knows?'

She opened her mouth to ask another question but he pointed at her glass.

'Drink. You'll hurt the bartender's feelings.'

Picking up her glass, Harper took a quick swallow. It burned through her body, taking some of her tension with it.

She gave an unconscious sigh of relief.

Dells nodded and clinked her glass with his.

'Doctor's orders,' he said.

Harper studied him curiously. He hadn't shaved since this morning. The five o'clock shadow suited him. It made him look less perfect. More human.

He'd obviously had enough to drink so that the rules of boss and subordinate had been lifted between them.

'Aren't you upset?' she asked, taking another sip. 'Baxter's furious at Charlton.'

His face softened.

'Emma's a rock,' he said. 'And Charlton better not even think about taking her on. She'll burn the whole place down.'

'Was it over layoffs?' Harper said. 'Or was it our story? Is it my fault?'

'A bit of both.' He paused, meeting her gaze. 'And thanks for the "our". It's *your* story. But working on it with you reminded me why I got into this business in the first place. Maybe that's where I went wrong.'

He drained his glass, and stood, pointing at hers. 'Take your vitamins. Don't want you getting scurvy.'

Harper drank the rest of her whiskey obediently, and handed him her glass.

'Oh great,' Dells grumbled. '*Now*, you decide to do as you're told.'

'Only because I like what you're telling me to do.'

She heard him laughing as he walked to the bar.

She watched as he ordered fresh drinks, bantering with the bartender, who seemed to know him – or, if nothing else, to have seen all of this before.

When he returned, he set the glasses down carefully.

She wondered how much he'd drunk before she arrived.

'In answer to your questions,' he said, as if there'd been no pause in the conversation. 'Charlton is in need of an infusion of cash. Her favorite method for acquiring cash is to lay off staff. Thus cutting back on salaries, and pocketing the difference. She's been doing this for years. I have gone along with it, every time, like a good little boy. This time I refused.' His voice was emotionless. 'We quarreled over her judgement and morality, and what her parents, who used to run the newspaper, would think of her actions if they were here to see them. She took umbrage at my tone – which I admit was aggressive – and suggested the newspaper might be better run if I were not involved in the process. I told her to enjoy finding out.'

He held her gaze steadily. 'If she tells anyone this is about the Anderson story, you need to know she's full of shit. Anderson is the excuse. Greed is the real reason.'

Harper stared at him as he took a drink.

If what he was saying was true, then Charlton would surely fire him. He'd never get away with talking like that to the owner. To save face, she'd let him go.

And she'd hire someone more likely to do as they were told.

'Oh hell,' she said, emptying her glass.

'My thoughts exactly,' he agreed.

Raising his hand, he got the bartender's attention – swirling his index finger in silent communication. The bartender nodded and immediately set to work.

It was like an alcohol conveyor belt. Harper was going to have to pace herself.

A minute later the new drinks arrived at their table. The bartender's impassive face showed nothing of what he thought of the speed with which they were consuming the drinks.

'Enough about me,' Dells said, when he'd gone. 'How are things going with the Anderson story, anyway?'

Harper told him about Anderson's alibi. She told him her theory that he'd stabbed himself. She described her trip to the hospital, and what she'd learned about the understaffed floor, the easy access to the parking lot.

'But I don't know how he would have known things like the nurses' schedule, or where those stairs even were,' she confided. 'You'd have to have some connection to the hospital to know about that.'

A knowing look crossed his face.

'If they hadn't fired me, I could have answered that for you,' he said. 'Mrs Randall Anderson has been on the board of directors at Savannah Memorial for fifteen years. She is very involved in hospital activities. I'd say it's more than likely Peyton Anderson was a volunteer at the hospital when he was in high school.' He waved a finger at her. 'Got to get those volunteer credits if you want to get into a good college.'

Harper stared at him. 'Is that true?'

He tilted his glass at her. 'Check it yourself. She'll be on the hospital website.'

For some reason, this wasn't good news. Harper took it like a gut punch.

'He really did it. Peyton Anderson killed Naomi Scott, didn't he?'

Dells held up a cautioning hand. 'Hold on, now. There are still holes in your theory big enough to drive a truck through. For one thing, even if he did stab himself, how did he get from the hospital to downtown? Did someone help him?'

'That's the part I'm stuck on, too,' she conceded. 'Now I guess I'll never know.'

He looked at her as if she'd disappointed him.

'You can't let this go just because I'm out, McClain. You know it's a good story. You're really onto something here.'

'Yes, I am.' She took a long drink. 'And Charlton will never run it.'

'No, no, no.' Dells leaned across the table toward her, his voice passionate. 'Come on. He can't get away with this. That girl – she deserves better.'

That girl.

Harper thought of Naomi working at the bar. Her beautiful face. A smile that could light up a room. She thought of Wilson Shepherd's lonely Garden City house. And Jerrod Scott's blood-shot eyes.

'Naomi,' she said. 'Her name was Naomi Scott.'

'And what are you going to do for her?' Dells challenged her.

'I can't help her. I can't help anyone, now.' Harper slid down in her seat. 'Charlton's going to reassign me to quilting bees or debutante balls.'

'And you're going to take that? That doesn't sound like the Harper McClain I know.'

Maybe it was the whiskey, but suddenly Harper *wanted* to fight Charlton.

'I don't know what to do,' she admitted. 'How do I make her run this?'

'You have to find another way to get the word out.' He said it flatly.

'How?'

'That Josh Leonard at Channel 5, he's always looking for a good story.' He swung his glass gently, sending the amber liquid inside in a slow circle. 'Does he know what you've learned?

'Maybe it's time to share.'

Chapter Thirty-five

It was after three when they left the bar. The street outside had that deep, late-night hush.

Harper had lost count of how many drinks she'd had. She welcomed the numbness it brought – she was no longer anxious about her future at the paper, sad about Luke, or worried about what would happen if Dells was permanently out.

In fact, she wasn't worried about a thing, except falling down.

When she walked through the door, the sidewalk swayed beneath her feet, as if blown by a light breeze, and she stumbled against Dells, who grabbed her before she could fall.

'Whoopsy daisy,' he said. 'Beware of the sidewalk. It's meaner than it looks.'

'I like whiskey,' Harper informed him solemnly. 'But not this much whiskey.'

'Tsk,' he chided. 'Don't be small-minded.'

He appeared to have a limitless ability to drink alcohol. Each drink just seemed to make him more charming.

He made a sweeping gesture at the empty street as if it held a coach and horses only he could see.

'Now. Where would you like to go?'

'Home,' Harper said, without hesitation.

The thought of her soft bed with its cool sheets seemed almost desperately attractive.

Then a problem occurred to her. 'Oh wait. My car's at the newspaper.'

Frowning at the unfamiliar buildings in front of her, she tried and failed to turn a circle before giving up, and looking at Dells, who still held on to her firmly.

'Where's the newspaper?'

'Oh no you don't.' He shook his finger at her. 'You can't drive. Look at the state of you.'

He waved his hand up and down in front of her.

Confused, Harper looked down at her black pants and simple top.

'What's wrong with me?'

'I've called a taxi,' he announced, not answering the question. 'It will take you home. I think the driver will be sober.'

Dells was still holding her up. She was too drunk to think about whether this was appropriate. All she knew was that his arm was warm across the small of her back, and his shoulder was sturdy against hers. She let herself lean against him.

'Where is it?' she asked.

'Where's what?'

She yawned. 'The taxi.'

'Right in front of you.' He held out one hand just as a yellow cab pulled up.

'That's magic,' Harper whispered.

Dells walked her to the car, opening the back door.

'In you go.'

She climbed in more easily than she'd expected – sitting down, it seemed, was simpler at this point than standing up.

'Where we going?' The driver glanced over his shoulder at them, experienced eyes assessing the intoxicated pair with clear caution.

'I don't know. Where do you live?' Dells asked, turning to Harper.

'East Jones Street.' She hiccupped unexpectedly, and clapped a hand over her mouth. 'Excuse me.'

For some reason, Dells found this funny.

'Jones Street first,' he told the driver. 'Then East Gaston after that.'

'East Gaston.' Harper tried to picture it. She'd never covered a crime there, but she knew it. 'Isn't that over by Forsyth Park – with all the big houses?'

'Something like that,' he said.

At some point his arm had ended up around her again, and she didn't mind. She rested her head against his shoulder, and looked up at him.

He did have a nice face – a straight nose, strong jaw (but not too strong). Absurd cheekbones. And he smelled so pleasant – that cool, green cologne he wore. He wasn't so bad, for an older guy.

'Don't throw up on me,' he ordered, looking down at her.

'I never throw up,' she assured him, outraged.

'Let's not make this the first time.'

'That's a terrible thing to say,' she muttered, straightening.

Chuckling, he pulled her back against his shoulder. She let herself be pulled.

It was a short ride to Jones Street. When they arrived, Harper leaned out the window to help the driver find her house, although he kept telling her he was capable of locating it himself.

'Right there!' she announced excitedly, when it came into view.

Giving them both a weary look, the driver stopped in front of it.

Dells opened the door and climbed out, leaning over to help Harper. Her feet kept getting tangled up as she slid across the back seat. In the end, he lifted her by the shoulders, and then half-carried her to the front steps.

'Wait here,' he told the cab driver over his shoulder.

'I'm fine,' Harper insisted, although she was secretly glad he held her up.

She couldn't remember the last time she'd been so drunk. She was too drunk to be ashamed of it, but sober enough to worry about the shame that would follow.

When they reached the door, she dug in her bag for the keys, finding them after some searching, and holding the keyring up triumphantly.

'Women,' Dells informed her, 'need smaller bags.'

'Men need to keep their opinions to themselves,' Harper replied.

Leaning over, she stabbed at the top lock with the key, but for some reason it wouldn't go in.

'I think the lock's broken,' she told him.

After a second of this, Dells took the key from her and turned the lock with infuriating ease.

Harper glared at him as he figured her multiple locks out, one after another.

Finally, the door swung open. The alarm beeped.

Dells bowed politely. 'Fort Knox awaits you.'

Harper stumbled to the alarm, and held up her wrist to

read the number, but her eyes wouldn't focus on what she'd written there.

The alarm's warning beeps were coming faster now.

Panicking, she waved her arm at Dells. 'What does this say?'

'What does what say?' he asked, bewildered.

'My *arm*.'

He grabbed her hand, holding her arm still, as she pointed at the code she'd written on her wrist that morning.

He gave her a disbelieving look. 'You write it on your arm?'

The beeping was getting louder.

'Type in the number, quick,' she urged, shoving him at the machine. 'It's about to blow.'

Grumbling about security and insanity, he punched in the four digits.

The beeping stopped.

'I don't think that's the perfect system.' Dells turned to face her, right as she reached over his shoulder for the light switch.

Their faces were so close she could smell the whiskey on his breath – sweet and intoxicating.

His eyes searched her face, sweeping from her eyes to her lips and back again.

'Oh, no,' he said softly, as if reminding himself of something he already knew. 'This would be a terrible idea.'

His words, for some reason, made Harper think of Luke.

Have faith in me.

How could she, though? Why should she? He was the one who dumped her. He was the one who was seeing someone else.

She needed to stop thinking about him. Wanting him. For a while the whiskey had done the trick. But when Dells left it would come back. She knew it would.

Reaching up, she touched his face, her fingertips grazing his cheek – the rough velvet brush of stubble.

'I like terrible ideas,' she whispered.

And then they were kissing. She didn't know who'd moved first – her or him – but it didn't matter. His lips were gentle, and unexpectedly soft.

His arms tightened around her, pulling her against the hard flatness of his chest. His suit was silky beneath her fingers as she slid her hands up his back, fingers cautious on the unfamiliar fabric.

She'd never kissed anyone in a suit before. It felt weird – like kissing her accountant.

And yet, she liked the way he touched her – with a firm politeness that was pure Dells. Almost like he was still trying to be businesslike and appropriate while they made out in her hallway.

His tongue touched her lips and they parted for him automatically, she felt his breath catch.

Some part of her wanted to keep kissing him. And to do whatever followed the kissing.

But a nagging voice in her head kept telling her to stop.

Even through the haze of alcohol, she knew Dells was handsome and funny and rich. But he was, at least for now, her boss.

And he wasn't the one she wanted.

'Hey, wait.'

Carefully, she extricated herself from his hands.

Stepping back, he gave her a questioning look.

'I'm sorry,' she said. 'I can't do this. I thought I could, but it turns out I can't.'

'Is this the instant sobriety of kissing your boss?' His tone was light, but she saw something more complicated in his eyes.

'Something like that.' Harper leaned against the wall, and looked up at him. 'And there's someone else. Or there was. It didn't work out. But I'm still . . .'

Unexpectedly, he smiled at her.

'Don't worry. You don't owe me an apology or even an explanation. I'm the one who should know better.'

But there were things she wanted to say.

'I think you're great,' Harper told him. 'You're a good person. And I liked drinking with you. I liked working for you, too. You're fair. And you're good at it. I hope you're not fired. Because it won't be the same without you.'

He studied her, his blue eyes suddenly serious.

'There's something I want you to know, too. Just in case I am fired. You're the best reporter I've ever worked with, Harper, and this isn't the alcohol talking.' His voice was clear and focused, each word steady as a stone. 'You are brilliant at what you do, and don't you ever doubt it. You're a natural.' He took a step toward her. 'I was lucky to get to work with you.'

He reached forward, brushing her cheek with a touch so light Harper could have almost believed she imagined it. She might also have imagined the regret in his eyes.

'Well,' he said, after a second. 'I'd better go. The cab driver's waiting.'

They exchanged a smile.

'Goodnight, Harper.' He turned to the door.

'Goodnight . . .' She'd been kissing him for five minutes. She couldn't call him Dells. '. . . Paul.'

OK. So that felt weird.

Outside, he turned on the top step to look back at her with sudden insistence.

'Don't let the Anderson story die,' he told her. 'Somehow, you have to get the word out about what happened. Use your police contacts – get them involved. If nothing else, give it all to Josh.' His eyes were dark. 'If you don't, you won't be able to live with yourself.'

'I will,' she promised.

He nodded, as if her words were enough to satisfy him.

'And that other guy,' he said. 'The one you mentioned?' He held her eyes. 'Don't wait too long for him. If he doesn't appreciate you, he doesn't deserve you.'

Then he gave her a jaunty salute and headed down the stairs, whistling the Sinatra tune that had been playing when she walked into the bar – 'One More for My Baby'.

Seconds later, the taxi disappeared into the darkness.

Chapter Thirty-six

Harper woke late the next morning.

For one brief, blessed moment, she wasn't sure why her head hurt so much or how she'd come to be sleeping fully clothed on top of the bed sheets.

But as her sun-filled bedroom swam into view, it all came back to her.

'Oh, *fuck*,' she breathed.

She sat up slowly, hands on her head, which felt like someone was wrenching it in two with cold metal tools.

'Oh hell's bells. Harper, you imbecile.'

Zuzu, who was draped across the foot of the bed, glanced up at her with cool green eyes.

'I kissed my boss,' Harper informed her, as she swung her feet to the floor. 'Top that one, cat.'

The room felt unstable around her, and she had to find her balance before making her way down the hall to the bathroom for Ibuprofen.

There, she reached for the medicine cabinet door but her reflection arrested her hand.

Her russet hair kinked and coiled around her. The long day of work and night of booze had left her hazel eyes bloodshot and her skin blotchy.

'You look like an idiot,' she told herself.

She swung open the medicine cabinet door and her face disappeared.

I hope he's fired, she thought, uncharitably, as she downed the pills with water she cupped in her hands. *Oh God. What if he's not fired?*

It wasn't all on her, of course. They'd both been involved in that kiss. But that didn't make it any better.

At least it was Sunday – she didn't have to be back in the office until Tuesday. She had two days to recover. Two days to figure out how to handle things if he and Charlton worked out their differences. Or if they didn't.

While she waited for the shower to warm up, she leaned against the wall and tormented herself by remembering the last minutes of the night – the way his lips had felt unfamiliar and curious against hers.

And that it had been quite a memorable kiss.

She was climbing into the shower when it struck her that he'd never once pulled back. If she hadn't stopped things there was no indication that he wouldn't have been happy to go to bed with her.

She wondered if he was waking up somewhere now, swearing. Maybe he was hoping he was fired, too. But she doubted it. He didn't seem the type to feel bad about kissing her.

After a shower, Harper brewed a pot of strong coffee, and sat at the table with her laptop and phone, forcing down a piece of toast her stomach didn't want, and coming up with a plan.

Dells was right – she had to get the Anderson story out there.

She could take it to the cops or to Josh at Channel 5. But first she needed to answer those last unanswered questions.

Before Harper could go to Daltrey or Josh with her theory about how Peyton had done it, she needed one person – just one – who'd seen him that night, out of the hospital.

She wasn't at all sure this was possible. But she had an idea. Steeling herself, she picked up her phone.

Jerrod Scott answered on the first ring.

'Mr Scott,' she said. 'This is Harper McClain.'

'Oh, hello, Miss McClain. What can I do for you?'

His voice was so distinctive – formal but warm – as if they'd known each other for years.

'I've been looking deeper at your daughter's case,' Harper said. 'I think you might have a point about Peyton Anderson. But I need your help to prove it.'

'Well, thank the Lord.' She heard him take a deep breath. 'Tell me what you need.'

Harper explained the very basics.

The missing piece was all about travel. How had Anderson got from the hospital to the murder scene and back again, without a car, and without anyone knowing he'd done it?

There were several possibilities. Maybe Anderson had planted his car at the hospital before stabbing himself. If that was the case, she might never be able to prove a thing. But she didn't think he'd take that risk.

Someone could have driven him – a friend. But he didn't seem the type to leave himself open like that. People talk.

She'd come up with an answer last night on the way home from the bar. But the idea hadn't crystalized until she sobered up.

A taxi.

It was so obvious, she wasn't sure at first. But the more she thought about it, the more likely it seemed.

The way the driver's eyes had assessed and dismissed the drunken pair of them – the way his look said he'd seen it all before and wasn't interested now. That was when she began to think it through. Cab drivers pick up dozens of passengers a day. They pick up many people at hospitals – it was so normal. So forgettable.

And before she'd fallen asleep last night, it had occurred to her that Jerrod Scott had driven a taxi in Savannah for more than thirty years.

'I want you to see if you can track down a taxi driver who picked up Peyton Anderson at Savannah Memorial at around one-thirty a.m. that night,' she told him. 'His left arm would have been heavily bandaged. If you can find that driver, bring him to me.'

Scott, who had listened as she explained her theory, didn't say anything for so long, she wondered if he was still there.

'Mr Scott?' she asked hesitantly.

'I'm here.' He paused. 'Miss McClain, even if we find this cab driver, will anyone believe us?'

'Look,' she said, 'I can't promise we'll convince them. But I believe if we don't find out how he got from the hospital to downtown, Peyton Anderson will walk free from this. Eventually, he'll kill someone else. I don't want that to happen.'

A long silence followed. When Scott spoke again, his voice was gruff.

'Well, I'm grateful to you for trying. Tell you what – I reckon I know every cab driver in this town,' he said. 'Let me see what I can find out.'

'Mr Scott,' Harper said. 'I need this fast. Tomorrow might be too late.'

*

Harper spent the day sitting at her kitchen table, writing up everything she'd learned on the Anderson story. She wrote fast, not taking time to make it pretty. She just needed all the information in one place.

When she finished writing that night, she knew she'd made a devastating case. With one missing piece.

But Scott still hadn't called.

When her phone rang at eleven, she pounced on it, her heart sinking when she saw Bonnie's name on the screen.

She forced her tone to stay neutral.

'Hey, Bonnie.'

'I'm checking in,' Bonnie told her. 'I haven't heard from you and I was starting to get worried.'

'You shouldn't worry,' Harper said. 'I'm fine.'

Bonnie wasn't convinced. 'You want me to come over? I'm off tonight.'

'Bonnie, I love you but I do not need a babysitter.' Harper pulled her feet up onto the sofa. 'There's been no sign of the weirdo in days. Also, Mia's now sleeping with a cop so I'm protected.'

'I don't like you being there at night alone,' Bonnie told her. 'You should come over here and drink my wine.'

Harper shuddered.

'No wine. Ever again. I'm on the wagon.'

'Coffee then,' Bonnie said. 'Chamomile tea. I don't care. I want to watch you being safe.'

'You are kind and wonderful. But I have important plans to stay on my sofa. Also, I'm waiting on a phone call so I have to go.'

'If this is a pretend phone call and you're trying to get rid of me, God will know,' Bonnie warned her. 'Also, since you won't come over, I'll tell you now – I think I'm breaking up with the pedophile gallery owner. He turned out to be totally flakey.'

'I'm going to need some time to recover from the shock,' Harper said. 'I'll call you tomorrow.'

'Sarcasm isn't pretty, Harper,' Bonnie said. 'Love you. Call if you get scared.'

After she hung up, Harper checked her voicemail in case Scott had called while she was on the phone.

But there were no messages.

That night, she sat up for hours, listening to her scanner and waiting for the call that didn't come.

Chapter Thirty-seven

Monday morning, Harper was still willing Scott to call, but when her phone beeped the message was from DJ.

> Dells remains AWOL. Charlton's hanging around like a fart in the room. Rumors are flying. It's a bad scene – don't come back.

The newspaper's chaos was a welcome distraction. She and DJ exchanged a series of profane and apocalyptic texts about their chances of survival. He ended it with:

> Everyone loves crime. No one gives a shit about schools. I'm toast.

There was no small amount of truth in that. But, Harper wasn't about to say so.

> Don't worry. I'm looking for an assistant.

His reply was instant:

> Fuck you, McClain. I'm going to work at Starbucks.
> At least there I'll get free coffee.

After that, though, her phone fell silent again.

The day seemed endless. She edited her story, cleaned the house, went out for groceries and came back again, her phone always at her side. It didn't ring.

By eleven that night, she was on the sofa, staring blankly at the television, as her mind went through all the possibilities.

She'd picked up her phone and put it down a hundred times. She should just call him. But she was too afraid he'd tell her he hadn't found anything.

Zuzu jumped on to the sofa and curled up beside her, a whorl of striped gray fur. Harper stroked her gently.

She could almost hear Baxter's voice in her head: *You can't win 'em all, McClain.*

She could still take what she had to Daltrey, or to Josh, as Dells suggested. It laid everything out. But she felt the missing piece like a lost tooth. It was so obvious.

The thing that drove her in this job – the thing that kept her coming back night after night – was seeing crimes solved. Justice served. It fed something hungry inside her. That part of her that was never satisfied until it knew who did it and saw them arrested – it wouldn't let her sleep if she walked away from this case.

She knew how it felt to be the one left behind. To be the one left wondering forever why.

She couldn't bear for Jerrod Scott to go through that. Or anyone else.

When her phone rang and Scott's name flashed on the screen, she snatched the device off the coffee table.

'McClain,' she said.

'Ms McClain, this is Jerrod Scott,' he said, talking more urgently than she'd ever heard him. 'I know it's late, but I need you to come meet me.

'I think I found the person you're looking for.'

It was midnight when Harper pulled off of Congress Street into the parking lot behind a modern office building. Eight floors of dark windows looked down on her blankly.

It was the same lot where she'd met Miles a few nights ago. When she'd described it to Scott, he'd known instantly where she meant – if anyone knows a city as well as a reporter, it's a cab driver.

The unlit parking lot was empty, save for two taxis parked in the center, side by side. One was a white and black Savannah Taxi, the other was yellow, with LIBERTY CABS emblazoned on the side.

Harper drove towards them. In the stillness, the Camaro's engine seemed too loud.

Her headlights illuminated two men standing between the two cars. One was Jerrod Scott, the other was a short, bald man in jeans and checkered shirt.

She pulled up beside the yellow cab, and cut the engine.

When she climbed out, a warm breeze swept her hair back. It was almost oppressively silent. The only sound was a freight train passing through, its horn mournful in the distance.

'Miss McClain,' Jerrod said as she walked up. 'Thank you for meeting me.'

'Thanks for calling me,' she said, holding out her hand. 'Please, Mr Scott, call me Harper.'

'Harper.' Scott had a firm, enveloping grip – his hand was warm and dry.

Turning, he motioned to the shorter man, who stepped forward hesitantly. He had a smooth head, and a chubby, amiable face. Harper pegged him at about forty-five years old.

'This is Elton Richards,' Scott said. 'I think he can help us.'

Harper studied Richards. He didn't appear nervous – his arms hung loose at his sides. Mostly he seemed a little puzzled, watching the two of them with a worried frown.

She held out her hand. 'I'm Harper McClain, Mr Richards. Thank you for coming out.'

He shook her hand with quick efficiency.

'I don't know why I'm here, to be honest,' he told her. 'Jerrod put the word out he was looking for anyone who picked up a man with an injured arm at Savannah Memorial on the night his daughter was killed.'

Harper held his eyes. 'Did you pick up a man fitting that description?'

'Yes, I did. Took him to the Hyatt on Bay Street. Said he was a tourist, got himself mugged. I told him I was sorry to hear it – that's not the kind of thing we ever like to see here in Savannah.'

Harper's heart quickened.

The Hyatt hotel on Bay Street was steps from River Street, and only a few blocks from where the murder took place.

Pulling her phone out of her pocket, she opened a picture of Peyton Anderson and turned the device around, holding it out to Richards.

'Is this the man you picked up?'

He leaned forward, cupping his hand around the phone and squinting at the image. The light of the screen illuminated his face with a pale blue glow.

'That's him,' he said.

'You're sure?' she pressed him. 'It was late. Maybe you didn't get a good look at him.'

'Oh, I did,' he assured her. 'He was standing under a streetlight on the road outside the hospital when I drove up. I remember his left hand was bandaged up to here.' He pointed at his elbow. 'He looked sick – he was pale, sweating. And I mean sweat was running down his face. I told him I didn't think he should be released looking like that, but he told me it was fine. He said he wanted to get back with his family, and I could understand that.'

Frowning, he looked from Harper to Scott.

'What's this about? Jerrod? This got something to do with what happened to Naomi?'

Scott met Harper's gaze. The hope she saw in the deep brown depths of his eyes was hard to look at.

'It might,' she said, turning back to Richards. 'We don't think that man was a tourist. We think he might know more than he's saying about the killing. He told the police he didn't leave the hospital that night. You're the only person who can prove he did.'

Richards wasn't stupid. He could hear all the words she wasn't saying. Blanching, he turned to Scott.

'Oh, Jesus. Tell me I didn't drive your girl's murderer straight to her.'

'We aren't sure yet.' Scott rested his hand on his arm. 'Even if you did drive him, it's not your fault. There was no way for you to know.'

Harper was impressed by Scott's calm. This was his only daughter they were talking about. But he was steady as a rock.

Richards, though, looked sickened. He'd taken this news like a body blow.

Harper needed him not to panic. She had to know more if she was going to take this to the police.

Stepping closer to the two of them, she adopted her most soothing tone.

'Mr Richards, it might not be the man who killed her. This is what we're trying to figure out,' she said. 'I need to ask you a few more questions.'

He nodded hard, anxiety still simmering beneath the surface. 'Anything.'

'What time did you pick him up?'

'One twenty-three a.m.' He said it without hesitation. Seeing the look on her face, he explained, 'I checked my records when Jerrod called. I keep a very precise log of my fares. Write down every one. Just in case the IRS ever comes knocking. I got my proof.'

'Did he pay by card?' she asked hopefully.

He shook his head. 'Log says he paid cash. Tipped me four dollars on top of the twelve-dollar fare.'

'You say you took him to the Hyatt on Bay,' she said. 'When you dropped him off – did you see him go inside?'

He stopped to think, his brow creasing.

'No,' he said after a second. 'When I drove away, he was standing in front of the door. Looked like he was messing with his phone.'

Harper nodded, but something about this answer nagged at her. Something wasn't right. But she couldn't put her finger on it.

It sounded reasonable. She imagined Anderson, standing outside the hotel's big, glass doors. Looking down at his phone, avoiding the cab driver's eyes . . .

His phone.

'Wait,' she said, and this time she didn't keep the urgency out of her voice. Richards's head snapped up. 'You said he was looking at his phone. Are you sure about that?'

Richards nodded, shooting her a puzzled look.

'I'm sure. I remember because he was having trouble holding it with his bad hand. He nearly dropped it. It looked like it hurt. And I thought he should wait until he went inside and his family could help him. But I didn't say nothing, because . . .' He shrugged. 'Wasn't none of my business. You know?'

Harper could have hugged him.

'Would you be willing to talk to a detective about this?' she asked.

'You bet. Whatever you need.' He turned to Scott. 'If I somehow helped the monster who hurt your little girl . . . I'll do anything to make this right.'

Scott put his hand on his shoulder.

'It isn't your fault. We never know who's in our cab.' Despite his words, Harper saw the pain in his eyes. She knew how much this night must be costing him emotionally.

'I can't thank you both enough –' she began, but she didn't finish the sentence.

A tremendous *bang* shook the night.

Harper was conscious of multiple things happening at once. A bird flapped its wings in panic and broke away from a nearby roof – a dark shadow against the night sky.

Richards made a strange sound and fell hard. She heard the awful thud of his head hitting the tarmac.

Scott, his face covered in blood, stared at the entrance to the parking lot.

Following his gaze, Harper saw the shadow of a man, a gun in his hand, backlit by the streetlight.

Then he shifted and, for an instant, the light caught his face.

It was Peyton Anderson. His gun was pointed at Scott. He was smiling.

'Get down!' Harper grabbed Scott and threw him to the ground, just as the gun went off again.

Chapter Thirty-eight

The quiet following the gunfire had weight to it. Harper could feel it pressing down on her as she lay flat on the ground, one arm flung across Scott's back, as if that narrow length of flesh and bone could somehow protect him.

Her ears were ringing. The harsh rasp of her own breathing seemed too loud.

With her face pressed to the rough tarmac, she could smell dirt and oil, and the sweat of her own fear.

Cautiously she raised her head to see Richards. He'd fallen a few feet away, and now lay on his back, hands clutching his chest. His breathing made a sickening gurgling sound that made her stomach churn.

Scott turned his head to look at her – his eyes gleamed in the dark through the blood on his skin.

'Are you hurt?' she asked, searching his face for wounds.

'Not my blood.' He was breathing hard.

In shock, she thought.

'Was that *Anderson*?' he asked. 'He tried to kill us.'

'Shh,' Harper hissed.

She cocked her head, trying to locate the shooter. But she could hear nothing.

They stayed still for a minute, listening to the terrible sound Richards was making. Then Scott had had enough.

'I've got to get to him,' he told her.

Harper didn't want him to move – if Anderson was out there, any motion could give him a target – but Richards sounded bad.

'Stay low,' she told him. 'I'll get help.'

Raising himself on his elbows, Scott crept toward the wounded cab driver. Harper pulled her phone from her pocket, shielding the screen light with one hand as she dialed 911. She slid on her belly over toward Richards as the call went through.

'It's bad,' Scott said.

Richards was struggling to breathe. The bullet had hit him in the ribs. His neat, plaid shirt was soaked in blood.

Harper didn't know much, but she knew the chest was a bad place to get shot.

'Put both hands on the wound,' she instructed Scott. 'Press firmly. I'm calling an ambulance.'

Raising herself up, she peered to where Anderson had stood earlier. The parking lot entrance was empty now. But those high hedges would make a great hiding place. He could be watching them and she'd never know.

When a crisp female voice spoke in her ear, she flinched.

'911. What's your emergency?'

'This is Harper McClain,' she whispered urgently. 'I need police and an ambulance in the parking lot behind 369 Congress. A man's been shot. Warn responding officers: the shooter may still be in the area. We are hunkered down.'

The dispatcher's tone changed instantly. 'I'm sending them now. You OK, Harper?'

In the background, Harper could hear her typing. Her voice was familiar. Was it Sharon? Or Dorothy?

'I'm not hit.' Harper was whispering, although surely if Anderson were nearby he'd have made himself known by now. 'But the victim – he's in bad shape. It's a nine millimeter to the chest. Looks like hollowpoint.'

'Is he breathing?' the dispatcher asked.

'Yes.' Harper looked to where Scott was bent over Richards's body, hands glossy with blood as he pressed against the wound. 'But it doesn't sound right.'

'Apply pressure to the wound. Keep him flat. Ambulance is en route.'

Harper could hear sirens in the distance.

'Find Detective Daltrey,' she said. 'Tell her the shooter was Peyton Anderson.'

'Help me, Harper,' Scott pleaded, his face contorting. 'I think he's dying.'

'I've got to go.' Dropping the phone, Harper crawled back to him. Richards's eyes were half-closed. His breathing had weakened.

'We've got to do something to stop the bleeding. Do you have anything we can use?' she asked Scott, urgently. 'A towel? A T-shirt?'

'Hang on,' he said.

Jumping to his feet, he ran to his cab, heedless of his own safety. She heard him yank open a door as she pressed her hands against the wound where Scott had been trying to hold back the flow. Richards's blood was hot against her skin. It seemed impossible to stop – an irresistible, tidal flow.

Scott dropped to his knees across from her, a towel in his hand.

'It's not very clean,' he told her, apologetically.

'It will have to do.' Moving fast, she rolled up the cloth into a tight ball, and pressed it against the hole in Scott's chest, as the first police car roared into the parking lot, its siren screaming.

Squinting into the blinding lights, Harper held up a bloody hand.

'Over here!'

She heard the thud of boots against the pavement as the two officers ran towards her.

The following minutes were a blur of paramedics and police taking over the crime scene. Police questioned her and Scott. They explained what had happened but the whole time they were watching as EMTs swarmed around the wounded man.

Harper saw Toby among them, but there was no chance to speak to him as he attached Richards to machines, pumping fresh oxygen into him and, finally, lifting him onto an ambulance and spiriting him away.

Then Daltrey appeared, climbing out of a dark, four-door sedan in her neat, black pant suit, eyes sweeping the scene.

'McClain,' she barked as she walked up to them. 'You better be sure about this.'

Harper held out her bloodied hands. 'I can only tell you what I saw.'

The detective turned to Scott. 'Mr Scott, did you see the same thing as McClain, here.'

He nodded fervently. 'The Anderson boy – he shot Elton Richards right in the chest. He was turning the gun on me when Miss McClain knocked me down so hard I nearly lost my teeth.' He looked at McClain. 'I forgot to thank you for that. I think I'd be dead if it wasn't for you.'

Harper didn't want his thanks. She wanted Anderson in jail.

'I'm sorry you had to go through this,' she said, giving Daltrey a hard look.

As the shock dissipated, the realization that a man who had suffered so much already had just watched a friend nearly die for no reason at all, filled her with a sudden righteous fury.

Her tone accusing, she asked the detective, 'Have you located him? Are you going to arrest him?'

'We're doing our best, McClain. But we need to talk to both of you.' Gesturing for a nearby uniformed cop to come over, she pointed at Harper and Scott. 'Bag both their hands. Get them to the station.'

Glancing back at the two of them she said, 'I'll meet you as soon as I can. The officers will take care of you.'

When the patrol car pulled up at police headquarters a few minutes later, Harper waited impatiently to be let out.

The back seat was hard, and smelled of old urine and sweat. Her hands, still covered in blood, had begun to perspire inside their plastic cases, and she clenched and opened them repeatedly.

Over her objection, she and Jerrod had been placed in separate cars. This, she knew, was so they couldn't compare details on the way to the station. They'd be kept in separate rooms until they could be interviewed.

She hoped he wasn't too shaken up.

The cop driving took his time getting out, putting his equipment in place, and then finally rising from his seat. He was a big guy – the car rose with him.

He shuffled in her direction, utility belt jangling. It seemed to take a year for him to open the door.

Harper swung her feet out, breathing in the fresh air, gratefully.

When they walked into police headquarters, Dwayne's head snapped up.

'Harper!' He ran out from behind the desk. 'I heard about the shooting. All the dispatchers are talking about it. Are you hurt?'

'I'm doing better than the guy who got hit,' she told him. Her voice was gruff, but she gave him a grateful look.

'You've got blood all over you.' He swung a fierce look at the silent mountain of a cop escorting her. 'You take care of her, you hear me, Carl?'

'I'm going to do a GSR, and then she can get cleaned up,' Carl replied, sounding offended. 'I'm not *abusing* her, Dwayne.'

He and Dwayne kept sniping at each other, but Harper tuned out.

A GSR – a gunshot residue test.

Those tests were done to prove if someone had recently fired a gun. Normally, they were done on suspects.

'Why?' she asked abruptly, interrupting Carl's unconvincing defense.

They both turned to look at her.

'Why do you need to do a gunshot residue test?'

A brief silence fell.

'Daltrey asked for it,' Carl told her, as if that explained everything.

'She probably wants to exclude you from the suspect list.' Dwayne's tone was soothing. 'It's normal for witnesses.'

It made sense. But it still felt like an accusation.

And as Carl led her across the lobby through the security door, she began to shiver.

*

An hour later, Harper sat alone in a windowless room, staring at herself in a two-way mirror and clutching a cardboard cup of terrible coffee.

The test had been quick and painless and, after that, she'd finally been allowed to wash off the blood. In the bathroom, she'd discovered Richards's blood wasn't only on her hands, but on her clothes and face, even in her hair.

She'd done the best she could with scalding hot water, government-issued soap and cheap paper towels.

Since then, she'd been sitting here, alone with her thoughts in a room like a cell. She'd had plenty of time to figure out how it all went down. How Anderson happened to be in that parking lot, with a gun in his hand.

Plenty of time to blame herself.

When the door swung open without warning, she twitched.

Daltrey bustled in, holding a notepad and a bottle of water, which she set on the table at Harper's elbow.

'Thought you might be thirsty. The coffee's undrinkable. You ready to get started?'

She pulled out the chair across the table and sat down, flipping open her notebook.

The flurry of activity after the long minutes of quiet was discombobulating. It took Harper a second to find her voice.

'Any word on Richards?'

'Last time I checked, he was still alive,' Daltrey said curtly. 'Just.'

Pulling a remote control out of her pocket, she turned on a video camera mounted to the ceiling in the corner, its lens directed at the two of them.

'OK. Detective Julie Daltrey interviewing Harper McClain.' She rattled this off, looking at her notebook the whole time. 'Let's start at the beginning. What were you doing in the parking lot off Congress Street at midnight, tonight?'

Too tired for long explanations, Harper kept it short.

'I went to meet Jerrod Scott.'

'Why did you meet him in a parking lot in the middle of the night?' Daltrey studied her, a fine line between her eyebrows. 'Would it have killed you to meet in a bar?'

'It wasn't a date,' Harper's tone was dry.

'What was it then?' Daltrey challenged her. 'Why did Scott want to meet you in a parking lot at midnight? And why is a man lying half-dead on an operating table now, McClain?'

It was time to tell her everything. Harper knew this. The police had been her next stop, anyway. She just hoped Daltrey was ready to listen.

'He said he had information for me,' Harper said. 'About the murder of his daughter.'

Daltrey's eyebrows rose. 'Why did he come to you? Last time I checked, I'm the one investigating that murder.'

Harper didn't take the bait. Two people were dead. There was no time left for games.

'He knows I've been working on a story about the murder. He thinks police are on the wrong track. He told me he had some information I needed to know.'

'So, you went to the parking lot at 369 Congress Street to meet Jerrod Scott to investigate *my* case.'

'Detective,' she said, meeting her eyes, 'I didn't think you'd believe a word either of us had to say until we could answer every question you might have. Now, I think I have all the answers you need.'

She waited for Daltrey to make a sarcastic remark.

Instead, the detective opened her notebook.

'I'll hear your story in a minute. First, walk me through the shooting. Start from your arrival at the parking lot. What happened?'

Aware that her story would be compared to Scott's line by line, Harper told her about pulling into the quiet lot. Seeing Richards and Scott standing next to their cars, waiting.

'Richards drives a Liberty cab. He told me he picked up a man at Savannah Memorial the night of Naomi's murder,' she said. 'He described him as tall and slim, with straight brown hair. He said his left arm was wrapped in bandages from his elbow to his fingers. I showed him a picture of Peyton Anderson and he positively identified him.' She paused. 'And then Anderson shot him.'

'We'll get back to what Richards told you in a second.' Daltrey's voice was steady, as if there was nothing new or surprising in what Harper had to say. 'Describe the shooting to me.'

Harper thought of the moment the quiet was shattered with a sound like a bomb.

'We were finished,' she said slowly. 'We were ready to say goodbye. Richards had agreed to come talk to you. I was going to call you when I got home to arrange for him to tell you his story. That was when it happened.' She kept her eyes on Daltrey, who never changed expression. 'None of us saw him coming. We just heard the shot.'

She paused, remembering the confusion, and the sudden realization of what had happened. But all she said was, 'Richards went down fast.'

'You didn't see Anderson fire?' Daltrey asked.

Harper shook her head. 'I looked up, and he was standing in the entranceway, pointing a gun at Scott. I grabbed Scott, and we got down before he fired again.'

'How many times did he fire?' Daltrey asked.

'Two,' Harper said. 'The first shot hit Richards. The second missed.'

'And you're certain the shooter was Peyton Anderson?'

'I'm positive.' She shuddered at the memory. 'He smiled at me.'

Daltrey's brow creased. 'He smiled . . .?'

Before she could finish the question, someone knocked on the door to the interview room.

The door opened, and Luke looked in at them. His eyes met Harper's and her stomach tightened. Some part of her – which would not learn – longed to throw itself into his arms. But then his attention shifted to Daltrey.

'Can I talk to you a second?' he asked the detective.

'Yep.' Turning off the recorder, Daltrey walked out of the room, carrying her notebook and the remote. Before they closed the door, Harper heard Luke say, 'I thought you'd want to know . . .'

As she waited, she stared down into her coffee, as if it held the answers she sought. Daltrey had given her so little information – she had no idea whether the detective believed her or not.

She'd been in this room too long. Her mind kept whirling from Anderson to Scott to Richards to Luke and back to the beginning in an obsessive loop.

Glancing up, she caught a sudden glimpse of her own reflection in the mirror. Her hair was out of control, and her top was bloodstained. Her forehead was creased in a frown she didn't know she was making.

With no windows, no clocks, and no phone, she didn't know how much time passed before the door opened and Daltrey bustled back in.

'OK, then. Where were we?' the detective asked, setting the

notebook back down on the table, and seating herself in the metal chair.

But by then, Harper had had enough of this.

'What's going on?' she asked sharply. 'Have you located Anderson? Why are we sitting in here when we could be out looking for him?'

Daltrey looked at her, her expression shadowed.

'Elton Richards died on the operating table ten minutes ago.' Her voice was flat.

Harper dropped her head. She thought of the kindly bear of a man in a checked shirt, so worried he might have been an inadvertent player in Scott's tragedy.

'Oh hell,' she whispered.

'This is now a murder investigation,' Daltrey's voice was measured. 'And if your identification of the killer is solid, then it's a double-murder. So we have to follow the rules here, McClain. We put one step wrong in this thing, you know what his daddy will do with us.'

There was no way for Harper to argue with that.

'We're going to have to go over this again and again, until I am convinced that I know everything you know,' Daltrey said. 'It's time to tell me everything.'

Harper raised her eyes to Daltrey's.

'Anderson threatened me,' she said. 'Two days ago. I think he's been following me. That must be how he knew where I was tonight – who I was meeting. He followed me there. He's probably been following me for days. Maybe ever since I wrote that story about him.'

Daltrey's breath hissed between her teeth.

'Ah damn it, Harper,' she said reproachfully. 'Why didn't you tell me sooner?'

'I didn't think it mattered.' Unable to take that piercing look any longer, Harper dropped her gaze. 'I never thought he'd target anyone but me.'

There was a pause.

'You know, Harper,' Daltrey said with unexpected gentleness, 'at some point you're going to realize you're not responsible for every person who gets hurt in this town.'

Harper didn't know what to say to that.

After a second, the detective picked up the remote and turned the recorder back on.

'Detective Julie Daltrey is back in the room,' she told the device. 'Let's resume.'

Then, in that methodical voice she saved for anything that might be used in court as evidence, she said, 'Tell me about Peyton Anderson.'

Chapter Thirty-nine

By the time Harper stumbled out of the police station that morning, the sun was up and the day had begun to broil.

All her muscles were stiff from sitting in that chair, hour after hour. Daltrey, in her determination to get everything right, had been relentless. By the end, she wasn't sure she was making any sense.

She needed to call Baxter. Make sure she had the story for the website. First, though, she needed to go home and take a shower. And change. There was blood on her clothes.

Shielding her eyes from the sun, she stumbled toward the parking lot where she usually parked the Camaro, before realizing the car was still parked in the lot off Congress Street.

'Crap.' Raking her fingers through her tangled hair, she turned toward Habersham Street, wondering if she might be able to find a taxi.

She was so tired – it was hard to think.

'Harper.'

The voice came from her left.

Turning, she saw Luke, standing next to his car. He was in the same clothes he'd worn last night, although he'd ditched the suit jacket and tie. Dark sunglasses hid his eyes.

She was too worn out to be hurt and angry right now. She just missed him.

'Hey,' she said.

He was watching her in that way he had – unnervingly observant.

'Thought you might need a lift.'

Maybe another time, she would have refused. Right now, though, all she wanted was to get into that car with him. And go home.

She walked over to where he stood, under the sprawling branches of an oak. The Spanish moss hung so low, she had to push it aside to reach him – it felt like feathers against her fingers.

He held the passenger door open for her, and she got in without saying a word.

The leather seats were smooth and warm. She clipped the seatbelt in place as he started the engine, and the a/c came on, blowing hot air that gradually cooled.

He pulled away into traffic, hands steady and assured on the wheel.

Harper tried to think of something to say to break the silence between them, but the night had drained her of small talk. Luke seemed to know this. He let her be.

After a while, she leaned back in her seat and closed her eyes. The darkness behind her lids was filled with violence, though. She saw Richards, reaching out to Scott. Heard the shot.

Saw Anderson's cold smile as he raised the gun again . . .

Blinking hard, she jerked upright, gripping the armrest.

From the corner of her eye she saw Luke glance at her, but he said nothing.

The journey to her house took about ten minutes. Luke pulled up to the curb, leaving the engine running.

There was so much Harper wanted to say to him. But she didn't know where to start. It was a library of unspoken words.

'Are you OK?' he asked, when she thought the silence might crush them both. 'It was a tough night.'

Harper looked down at her hands, knotted in her lap. There were dark stains at the edges of her nails.

'I couldn't get all the blood off,' she said, as if that explained everything. 'I tried for so long . . .'

She looked away, biting her lip.

It was just that she was so tired. Normally she'd be handling this better.

'You need to know it's not your fault.' Luke turned to look at her, taking the sunglasses off so she could see those night-sky eyes, shadowed by lack of sleep. 'What happened to Richards – that's not on you.'

Harper didn't believe him.

'Anderson must have followed me. I led him straight to the one man who knew for certain that he was lying about where he was that night. I helped him kill the witness who could have sent him down. *How* is that not my fault?'

'Because it isn't,' he said. 'That's not how this works. You were not responsible for a killer's actions.'

'But he'll get away with it now, Luke,' she said miserably. 'And that's my fault.'

He shook his head.

'We have Richards's log, Harper. It was in his cab, and it lists the pickup at the hospital that night, exactly like you said.

Daltrey got the CCTV footage from the hospital and the hotel. He's on there. Clear as day. We've subpoenaed his phone records. If he was communicating with Naomi Scott, and we believe he was . . .' He reached across, putting his hand on hers. 'He's going down.'

Not trusting herself to speak, Harper looked at their entangled hands.

'The person responsible is Peyton Anderson, and you will help us put him away.' His thumb stroked the side of her hand. 'We're looking for him now. We've got a warrant to search his apartment. His father is cooperating.'

Letting go of her hands, he touched her chin, tilting her face up, making her look at him.

'That's what you did, Harper. You caught a killer. You did right by Naomi Scott. Keep that in your mind.'

As she listened, something that had held tight in Harper's chest since that first shot last night, loosened, just a little.

She blew out a shaky breath and nodded.

'OK,' she said, as much to herself as to him. 'OK.'

'Get some sleep,' he said. 'When you wake up, this will all be over.'

Nodding, Harper reached for the door handle. But at the last minute she turned back.

'Luke,' she said, 'when this is all over . . . let's talk.'

His eyes held hers. 'I'd like that.'

She got out of the car feeling the weight of her own exhaustion so heavily, she barely noticed as Luke drove away.

She trudged up the front steps, wondering how much time she had before she needed to go into the office. It was not yet eight o'clock. If she could sleep for three hours, she was sure she'd be fine.

She was putting the key in the third lock when she heard her phone ringing inside.

Hastily, she shoved the door open, typed the code into the beeping alarm, and ran into the living room, dropping her bag on the couch, and grabbing the phone off its stand on the sixth ring.

'Hello?'

'Finally,' an unfamiliar voice said. 'This has been a long time coming.'

The voice sounded older. Male. Harper frowned.

'Who is this?'

'Someone who has secrets to tell.'

'Look,' Harper said wearily, 'I've had a long night. If this is about a story, call me at the newspaper this afternoon. Right now, I . . .'

The chuckle in her ear made her voice trail off.

'Come on, Harper. You're a reporter. You must be more curious than this. You figured out how I was getting in, and you cut off all my access routes. So now I have to call you. It's a hell of a thing.'

Harper's blood turned to ice.

'Who is this?'

'I think you know who this is.'

For one second, she stood frozen, the phone in a vice-like grip. Then she grabbed her bag and rifled through it, pulling out a notebook and pen. Flipping furiously to a clean page, she wrote: *Over 45 years old. No southern accent.*

'You must have questions for me,' he said, almost kindly, as if he knew she was tired.

'Why did you break into my house?' Harper's voice was airless. 'What do you want?'

'I have some information for you. But before I gave it to you, I wanted to know who you were.'

Harper frowned. 'What do you mean?'

'We met, long ago,' he said, not answering her question. 'When you were young. I knew your parents. How *is* your father, anyway?'

Harper's pen slid across the page, scratching a thick black line.

'You know my dad?'

'I knew him back then.'

His voice was steady, unafraid. Almost helpful.

Whatever she'd thought she'd do in this moment left her mind now. She had to force herself to *think*.

'Were you a friend of my parents?'

'Of a sort.'

'You said you wanted to know who I am,' she said. 'Why?'

There was a pause. Harper thought she heard a car through the phone, driving by him. Was he on a street?

'At first,' he said, 'I wanted to warn you that you were in danger. I told you to run. But you didn't. That surprised me. You're not much like your father. And, I suppose, in the end, that's what I wanted to know, when I first checked in on you. I wanted to see if you were more like your mother.'

Harper's knees gave. She found herself sitting on the sofa with no memory of lowering herself there.

'You knew my mom.' The words came out as a whisper.

'Yes. I knew Alicia,' he said, and she thought – although this must have been wrong – that she heard emotion in his voice.

Harper didn't want the man who broke into her house and invaded her life to talk about her dead mother with such longing and loss.

'I don't understand what you *want*.' Her voice hardened. 'Why are you telling me this? Who are you?'

'I'm telling you,' he said, 'because I want you to know I'm for real. And because you're in danger. The person who killed your mother is looking for you. He's been in prison for a long time and he's about to get out. And he's going to come for you.'

The phone nearly slipped from her nerveless hand.

'Who killed my mother?' she demanded, no longer interested in being toyed with. 'If you know so much, tell me. If this is some sort of joke, I swear to God, I will find you and –'

'I don't joke.' His voice was steady and insistent. 'If you are as smart as I think you are, you'll know that. I'm telling you to find a safe place and go there until I can sort this out. The person we're talking about is very good at what he does. He considers his job unfinished.'

'Who is he?' Harper demanded. 'Who killed my mother?'

'I can't tell you,' he said. 'Over the last year, I've learned what kind of person you are. And I know what would happen if you knew. You'd go look for him. That cannot happen. Because that is a fight you will not win, Harper McClain. For once, I need you to do the smart thing, not the brave thing. Get out of my way, and let me take care of this. I've waited a long time for this moment. I owe your mother this much. It's not enough. But it's something.'

Harper stared across the room, trying to absorb this. She had no idea who she was talking to, but all her instincts told her to believe him, which was insane. He'd broken into her house. He'd broken into her car. He'd invaded her life. She had no idea who he was.

And yet.

Still, she wasn't naive. She knew better than to believe.

'Why should I trust you? You broke every law to get to me. And now, all of a sudden, you're full of advice I'm supposed to take. How do you think that plays?'

'Badly, I'd imagine,' he said. 'But I think you know I'm telling the truth. You're a good reporter, Harper. Listen to those instincts.'

She heard what sounded like a bus rumble by him, and his voice faded for a moment.

'Hold on,' he said, his tone changing to something like alarm. 'What's this?'

'Just tell me who you are,' she said. 'I won't tell anyone . . .'

'Harper, listen.' His voice had changed completely. He sounded urgent and tense. 'There's a man walking up to your house. He's got a gun. Don't open your door.'

Harper stood up. Was he outside her house right now?

'I don't understand . . .'

'You don't *need to understand*.' His voice sharpened. 'Call the police. Do it now. Tell them Peyton Anderson is outside your door. Do it, Harper. Trust me.'

'Wait . . .' she said.

The phone in her hand went dead, just as someone pounded his fist against her door.

Chapter Forty

Harper's ribs felt too tight around her lungs – she couldn't get a breath. She stared at the windows across the room, her hand still clinging to the dead phone.

Someone pounded on the door again. Three heavy bangs. She felt each one in her chest.

'Come out, Harper. Come out and play.'

It was Peyton Anderson's voice.

The voice on the phone had been telling the truth. He was watching her. And she was in trouble.

There was only one reason for Anderson to be here now.

She dialed 911 so quickly her fingers slipped on the phone. As it began to ring, she jumped to her feet, heading for the door.

'911 what's your . . .' a voice began.

'This is Harper McClain. Peyton Anderson is outside my house right now. He's got a gun. I need help.' The words came out fast but clear. '317 East Jones Street. Call Daltrey.'

She drew a quick breath before adding, 'Send an ambulance.'

Before the operator could respond, she hung up. She didn't

want to get into a conversation with Anderson standing on her front porch.

Avoiding windows, she crossed the living room to the entrance hall and stared at the front door. The peephole was a sinister black eye, looking back at her.

No way was she putting her face up against that right now.

She turned herself sideways, pressing her back against the wall. If he fired through the door, she wanted him to miss.

'What do you want, Peyton?' She raised her voice, trying to sound authoritative but not shrill. Like a cop.

'I only want to talk,' he insisted. 'Come outside. I'm not going to hurt you.'

'Sure you're not,' she said. 'I saw how you talked to that cab driver last night. You can talk through the door.'

He laughed then, a gasping, angry sound.

'You're such a coward,' he said. 'All of you. You write lies in your newspaper, but you won't say it to my face. You've got no soul.'

'What did I lie about, Peyton?' she asked. 'Didn't you kill Naomi? Didn't you kill that man last night? I saw you do it, Peyton. I was *there*.'

'So what?' He was angry now, his voice rising. 'He was going to lie, too. You all lie.'

There was something in his voice – an unevenness she recognized.

Is he drunk?

It wasn't a good thought.

'I've called the police,' she told him. 'They're on their way.'

'I knew you would. They were going to find me eventually anyway. My dad told me to turn myself in.' He gave an angry laugh. 'My own *dad*. He believes you, do you know that? I thought getting rid of that cab driver would put an end to this.

But then you messed it all up, you stupid little bitch.' He drew a breath. 'Now I've come to thank you. Come *out*.'

There was a pause. Harper could hear sirens in the distance. Anderson must have heard it, too.

'I don't have time for this,' he said, with sudden clarity. 'Open the door, or I start shooting your neighbors.'

Harper stopped breathing.

He'd already shot one innocent person today. And if she'd learned anything from seven years on this job it was that the first kill made all the other kills easier.

When she didn't reply, he grew impatient.

'You like that old lady, don't you? The one with the ugly little dog? Never shot a dog before. But there's a first time for . . .'

'*Stop*.' Harper turned to face the door. 'I'll come out.'

Her eyes fell on the baseball bat leaning against the wall.

He couldn't kill anyone else. She wouldn't let him.

There was no time to plan. All she had was the element of surprise. And she was going to take it.

She picked up the bat and, moving fast – her hands surprisingly steady – she unlocked the door.

Hoisting the bat in her hands, she turned her body sideways and burst out onto the porch holding it like a hitter at home plate.

She had time to clock Anderson's pale sweaty face. To see his eyes widen, and the gun in his hand start to rise.

She swung.

She put all her strength into it – swinging that bat with her whole body. It connected with his shoulder with a sickening crunch. The gun flew from his hand.

Anderson screamed and grabbed his arm.

With grim determination, Harper swung the bat back, and hit

369

him again as the first police cars pulled up on the street outside, sirens blaring. This time the bat connected with his chest.

Anderson collapsed to the ground.

He was sobbing, one hand held up as if it could stop the next blow.

Uniformed officers jumped out of the cars and ran toward her, guns drawn. She stood over Anderson's huddled form with the bat raised, breathing heavily, her heart hammering against her ribs.

He wasn't going to hurt her. He wasn't going to hurt anyone.

Voices shouted at her: 'Stand back!'

She could barely hear them through the roar of blood in her ears.

A crowd of officers rushed up the narrow steps, shoving her aside and surrounding Anderson, who lay groaning on the floor.

'We need an ambulance,' someone said.

'There's a gun somewhere on the ground,' she heard herself tell them.

Someone took the bat from her.

More police cars were pulling up on the street below. Blue lights flashed in all directions as her neighbors emerged from their houses to see what was going on.

Between the cars, Harper caught sight of a man. He stood back from the fray. She wouldn't have noticed him were he not watching her so steadily.

He was tall and slim, with steel gray hair. His upright stance betrayed military training. His eyes had the sharp intensity of a police officer. He wasn't a neighbor. She'd never seen him before.

Harper took a step forward, trying to get a better look. Their eyes met.

'Is it you?' she whispered, unaware that she'd spoken aloud.

An ambulance rolled down the street, blocking him from view. When it passed, he was gone.

One Week Later

Harper stood in her bedroom, a suitcase open in front of her. Zuzu watched her balefully from atop the dresser. She'd gone up there as soon as she'd seen the first box, and refused to come down since.

Harper took the last items of clothing from the dresser and put them on top of the rest of the clothes, then looked around the room for anything she'd forgotten.

But she'd been pretty thorough.

Peyton Anderson was in jail, awaiting trial. His father had hired him an excellent defense lawyer, naturally, but the police case was solid.

The dramatic news of Anderson's arrest on two counts of murder had filled the paper for days.

All the tiny missing pieces had fallen into place. Police believed Anderson had texted Naomi Scott on the night of her murder, demanding she meet him. He'd threatened to kill Wilson Shepherd if she didn't.

She'd insisted on meeting in a crowded place – River Street.

When she'd shown up, though, the street wasn't crowded. And Anderson hadn't wanted to talk. He'd had other plans.

He'd killed her and thrown her phone in the river to destroy the evidence of their conversation. He'd told police his own phone had been stolen on the same night.

Harper had to admire the plan. He was smart.

He would have made a great lawyer.

The article she'd sat at her kitchen table writing the day Richards was killed had at last been published. Charlton hadn't said a word when Baxter told her she was doing a front-page splash.

There were rumors that Dells might come back – that his suspension might not turn into a full firing. But, so far, his office had stayed dark.

Baxter grumbled mutinously about the idiocy of newspaper owners, but the other rumor circulating was that she was in line for a promotion.

Amidst all of this furor, at least so far, the planned round of layoffs had not occurred.

When she wasn't working, Harper had been searching every spare minute for the man she'd seen that day, standing on her street. He hadn't been in touch since.

She believed him when he told her she was in danger. And, for once, she decided to listen to advice.

She'd gone to Blazer. And told him about the phone call, the break-ins. What the man had said.

He'd been skeptical, at first, just like her. But in the end, he'd told her she should consider moving. At least for a while.

'He can find you at the paper, but there's an armed guard at the front door there. If you move, leave no forwarding address.'

He'd also offered to look through her mother's case for anything that might have been missed sixteen years ago.

Harper was grateful to him. But she didn't think he'd find anything she and Smith had overlooked.

The only person who knew who killed her mother had called her from a burner phone and then disappeared.

She needed to talk to that man again. Somehow, she needed him to find her.

It was time to find out the truth about her mother's murder. If she was going to do that, she was going to need his help.

When she walked out of the house with a suitcase in one hand and Zuzu's carry box in the other, her landlord, Billy Dupre, was pulling up to the curb in his battered blue pickup.

He put the suitcase into her trunk with the others and slammed it shut. Zuzu yowled from the cat box as if Harper were strangling her instead of setting her gently on the back seat.

She closed the door, shutting off the ruckus.

After that, she and Billy stood for a moment, staring back at the Victorian house with its tiny porch and stained glass window.

Harper had lived there for seven years. It was the closest thing to home she could think of.

'It ain't gonna be the same,' Billy told her, sadly. 'Doesn't feel right renting your place out to some stranger.'

Harper tore her eyes away from the building. It was only boards and paint anyway. A house is a house.

But even as she told herself that, she knew it wasn't true.

'I'm going to come back,' she promised him. 'Whatever it takes. I'm going to work this out. And then I'll come back.'

He put a hand on her shoulders.

'You have to,' he said. 'You got six months left on your lease.'

Both of them smiled. She hadn't had a paper lease with him in more than five years. They'd had what he called 'a handshake lease' all that time.

He'd been a rock through all of this. When she told him what was going on, he hadn't hesitated.

He'd put her in touch with a friend who owned beach rental houses on Tybee Island. Her timing was good – it was late August and beach season was wrapping up. That woman had a vacancy, and Harper took it, sight unseen.

She figured she'd live out there for a few months until she sorted this all out.

'Well. You stay safe,' Billy told her. 'Anyone tries to hurt you, you've got my number. I'll make 'em think twice.'

Without warning, Harper flung herself at him – hugging him tightly.

'You've been the best landlord, and the best friend,' she told him. 'Thank you.'

He patted her shoulder fondly. 'You know you're like a kid to me. Always will be.'

Harper handed him the keys and turned away quickly.

'I've got to go,' she said, dashing a hand across her cheek. 'I'll see you.'

'You better.'

She climbed into the Camaro and started the engine.

Zuzu stopped complaining and fell into ominous silence as she pulled away from the curb and headed to the edge of town.

The sky on the horizon was bruise-colored; the winds were picking up.

The long, hot summer was ending at last. Autumn was coming.

With every mile, Harper sent a silent call to the man who held the answers she'd been searching for.

Come find me. Come find me . . .

Acknowledgements

Huge thanks to my wonderful editor at Harper Collins, Sarah Hodgson, for your patience, laughter and thoughtful edits. Also to everyone on the HarperCollins team, especially Kathryn Cheshire, Felicity Denham, Emilie Chambeyron, Anne O'Brien, and Julia Wisdom – I'm very lucky to have such a fantastic group of people to work with.

More thanks go to my amazing agent, Madeleine Milburn, who makes all things possible. Where would I be without you? And to her extraordinary team – Hayley Steed, Alice Sutherland-Hawes, and Giles Milburn – I'm in awe of all you do!

Big love to my author/editor posse: Holly Bourne, Melinda Salisbury, Ruth Ware, Sam Smith, Alexia Casale. Thank you for keeping me sane.

To Jack, who listens to all my wildest ideas with endless patience and laughs at the funny lines – I'm so lucky to have you.

Finally, I wrote in the book that for women, being killed by someone who claims to love them is the most ordinary murder of all, and it's true. My mother was a victim of domestic abuse, so I feel this cause very deeply. She survived her marriage. Too many women aren't that lucky. If you are in a relationship that frightens you, or if someone is stalking you, please don't hesitate to seek help. Police, churches, and non-profit organizations can help you find refuge and safety. Call the National Stalking Helpline (0808 802 0300) StalkingHelpline.org. Or visit ScaredOfSomeone.org. You can also find resources at PaladinNSAS (0203 866 4107) PaladinService.co.uk. I say this as a former reporter who has covered many murders of women who didn't get out in time – if you're scared: run.